PRAISE FOR ROBERT BAILEY

"*The Professor* is that rare combination of thrills, chills, and heart. Gripping from the first page to the last."

—Winston Groom, author of *Forrest Gump*

"Legal thrillers shouldn't be this much fun and a new writer shouldn't be this good at crafting a great twisty story. If you enjoy Grisham as much as I do, you're going to love Bob Bailey."

—Brian Haig, author of *The Night Crew* and the Sean Drummond series

"Robert Bailey is a thriller writer to reckon with. His debut novel has a tight and twisty plot, vivid characters, and a pleasantly down-home sensibility that will remind some readers of adventures in Grisham-land. Luckily, Robert Bailey is an original, and his skill as a writer makes the Alabama setting all his own. *The Professor* marks the beginning of a very promising career."

—Mark Childress, author of *Georgia Bottoms* and *Crazy in Alabama*

"Taut, page turning, and smart, *The Professor* is a legal thriller that will keep readers up late as the twists and turns keep coming. Set in Alabama, it also includes that state's greatest icon, one Coach Bear Bryant. In fact, the Bear gets things going with the energy of an Alabama kickoff to Auburn. Robert Bailey knows his state and he knows his law. He also knows how to write characters that are real, sympathetic, and surprising. If he keeps writing novels this good, he's got quite a literary career before him."

—Homer Hickam, author of *Rocket Boys/October Sky*, #1 *New York Times* bestselling author

"Robert Bailey is a Southern writer in the great Southern tradition, with a vivid sense of his environment, and characters that pop and crackle on the page. This book kept me hooked all the way through."
—William Bernhardt, author of the Ben Kincaid series

"Bailey's solid second McMurtrie and Drake legal thriller (after 2014's *The Professor*) . . . provides enough twists and surprises to keep readers turning the pages."
—*Publishers Weekly*

"A gripping legal suspense thriller of the first order, *Between Black and White* clearly displays author Robert Bailey's impressive talents as a novelist. An absorbing and riveting read from beginning to end."
—*Midwest Book Reviews*

THE
LAST TRIAL

ALSO BY ROBERT BAILEY

McMurtrie and Drake Legal Thrillers
Between Black and White
The Professor

THE
LAST TRIAL

ROBERT BAILEY

THOMAS & MERCER

Published by Thomas & Mercer, Seattle

www.apub.com

Amazon, the Amazon logo, and Thomas & Mercer are trademarks of Amazon.com, Inc., or its affiliates.

ISBN-13: 9781503953147
ISBN-10: 1503953149

Cover design by Brian Zimmerman

Printed in the United States of America

For my wife, Dixie Davis Bailey

PROLOGUE

Boone's Hill, Tennessee, June 2010

Wilma got home about 8:00 p.m. All she wanted to do was kiss her girls on the forehead and go to bed, but when she pulled in the gravel driveway she was met by a surprise. Ms. Yost's car was not there, and the house was pitch dark. Even the fluorescent bulb in the carport, which the old woman always left on at night so she could see when she went out for a smoke, was off. For several seconds, Wilma kept her headlights aimed at the clapboard siding of the tiny dwelling where her children and babysitter should be but which appeared, for all intents and purposes, abandoned. *What's going on?*

Heart pounding, she parked in the driveway and quickly walked to the front door, fumbling in her purse for the keys. She finally got the door open and turned the light on. There on the coffee table was a note. She ran to it, a sense of dread coming over her. When she picked up the paper, she held it for a split second. *Please, God. Don't let anything have happened to my babies. Please . . .*

She began to read.

Dear Wilma,

I have tried for some time now to find justification for your actions. But I can no longer stand by and watch you do this to your children. I knew you were a stripper. People talk, you know. I didn't approve, but I wasn't going to cast stones. A couple of weeks ago a lady from church said she'd heard you were a prostitute. I didn't want to believe. Then I heard that message on your answering machine. I left it for you to hear.

With a heavy heart I have reported you to DHR. Your kids are now in the custody of the county. Jackie doesn't know. She thinks she's on a field trip. But Laurie Ann is devastated. I'm sorry, but I had to tell her. I hope that you will change your ways.

I know it doesn't seem so, but I'm your friend, Wilma. I'm doing this for your children. I hope that one day you can be with them again.

With love,
Carla Yost

Wilma was numb. *No. It was all for them. Everything. All of it. For them. Not me. Them.* She walked back to her bedroom and saw the blinking light on the answering machine. *No.*

She pushed it. "You have one saved message," the monotone voice said. "Received 10:30 p.m. Monday."

"Monday? What was I doing . . . ?" Wilma closed her eyes, thinking of all the roofies he had forced her to take. The long blackouts. *No.*

The message began with static. Then his voice.

"Ah, God, Wilma this is so good. You. You are so good."

It was JimBone. She could hear panting in the background. Then a low moan. She recognized the sounds as her own. But she couldn't remember. *No. God . . . no.*

The entire message lasted forty-five seconds, and Wilma hung her head in shame as the monster's sick voice filled the bedroom. When it was over, she lay on her bed for two hours without moving, crumpled in the fetal position, slowly whispering, "No. No. No. Nothing for me. Everything for them. Nothing for me. Everything for them." At some point, she lost control and started sobbing, crying so hard she thought her heart would stop. She had been raped. The bastard had *raped* her. Repeatedly. But that was not how the message on the tape sounded. She couldn't blame Ms. Yost for doing what she did.

Wilma gazed across the bedroom to the closet in the corner. Through the open crack in the door, she could barely see the handle on top of the briefcase peeking out from under a pile of dirty clothes. Inside the case was the remainder of the $100,000 down payment they'd given her the night she made the deal. She was due another hundred grand after committing perjury at the trial in Henshaw, but JimBone said it might be a month before she'd get it.

Wilma choked out another sob, feeling hollow. *The money was for the girls. For Laurie Ann. For Jackie.* She ground her teeth together. *Nothing for me. Everything for them.*

Now they were gone. And deep down, Wilma knew they were better off without her. Glaring at the closet, she felt hate for herself burning inside her like an inferno.

Everything is my fault. She let her eyes drift to the open bedroom door and out to the empty hallway. The house was normally bustling with the sounds of her girls. Laurie Ann, a teenager talking about boys and cheerleading, and Jackie, still in the "boys have cooties" stage of elementary school. She smiled at the memories, but her eyes clouded with tears. The house was silent as a morgue now.

They're gone, she knew. *And I have nothing. Nothing . . .*

She wiped her eyes with the back of her hand, got up, and walked over to her dresser. She pulled the pistol out of the top drawer and slowly loaded it.

What comes around goes around.

She took off all her clothes and turned on the overhead light in the bedroom. Then she looked in the mirror and pointed the pistol at her head.

You deserve this.

Then she closed her eyes.

And pulled the trigger.

PART ONE

PART ONE

1

Tuscaloosa, Alabama, May 8, 2012

Raina Farrell probably wouldn't have heard the gunshots if she hadn't been so hyperaware of her surroundings. Even after the beers she'd had at Buffalo Phil's and despite it being a Tuesday night and neither she nor Dr. Newell having seen anyone else on the Riverwalk, Raina was still on edge. As they sat next to each other on a wrought-iron bench at the Park at Manderson Landing and gazed out at the dark waters of the Black Warrior River, Raina whipped her head around to look behind her, to the side, and then back to the water. For early May, there was a slight chill in the air, but the cold had nothing to do with why she was shivering.

"Relax," Dr. Newell said, whispering in her ear as he moved his hand under her skirt. "Lift up a little."

Raina smelled beer mingled with the faint undertone of nicotine on his breath. She had never been with a smoker before, and the scent didn't bother her as much as she thought it would. If anything, it added to the overall feeling of naughtiness, of crossing an ethical line, that made what they were doing so damn hot. Trying to calm herself, she took in a gulp of air and swallowed, tasting the afterburn of the shot of Fireball they'd done before leaving the restaurant. When she was nervous on the golf course, she had taught herself to concentrate on her breathing. She would also focus on objects in the distance as she waited to hit a shot. The green. The fairway. A clump of trees. Anything that took her mind off her score or how she was playing and let her engage in the moment. Trying this now, she drew in another deep breath and slowly exhaled. Then she looked across the river and trained her sight on a dock on the far shore about three hundred yards away. *Inhale* . . . The structure jutted out into the dark water at least fifty feet and was illuminated by a fog light shining down from an adjacent boathouse. *Exhale* . . . Keeping her eyes on the dock and feeling Dr. Newell's breath again in her ear, she raised her hips, and her heart thudded as he slid off her underwear. The bench felt icy cold on her bare buttocks, and she giggled.

"What?" he asked as he unclipped the belt buckle on his pants.

"Nothing. Just thinking how crazy this is. What if we get caught?"

"The risk is half the fun," Dr. Newell said, and slid his hand up her thigh. Raina gasped, and she forgot about the cold as her body began to throb with the warmth of his touch. She gazed back across the river to the dock. Blinking her eyes, she noticed that a man was now standing at the edge of it.

"Sean, there's a guy on the dock across the river." She pointed and then moaned with pleasure. "Do you think he can see what we're doing?"

"Sure," he said, and he removed his hand and tapped the telescope stand that he had mounted by the railing. "Just an astronomy professor and his bright and inquisitive student out looking at the stars on a clear night." Then he lowered his pants and lifted her into his lap, and she had the odd, perverse thought that she was about to tell a mall Santa Claus what she wanted for Christmas. He carefully raised her skirt and placed himself inside her, and Raina closed her eyes, all visions of St. Nicholas gone. She soaked up the sensation of the act with all her senses, the smell of his beer- and cigarette-laced breath on her face mingling with the intoxicating scents of sex and the river. The feel of the breeze coming off the water coupled with his hands moving under her blouse and caressing her breasts. And the sound of the waves breaking on the shore below.

When she heard the first gunshot, her eyes flew open. The man on the dock was now on his knees and a figure was hovering above him, pointing something at him. This time she saw the fire from the barrel of the gun as it went off and heard the crackle of the weapon, which sounded like a truck backfiring. "No!" Raina raised off her lover and reached for a railing just as a third shot was fired. The man on the dock fell over on his back and then the shooter knelt beside him.

"Raina, what are you . . . ?" Dr. Newell's frustrated voice broke through her focus and she wheeled on him.

"Did you see that?" she asked, hearing the excitement and panic in her voice as she pointed across the river to the dock. "That man was just shot. I think he's dead."

Dr. Newell was pulling his pants up, his eyes darting back and forth across the park. "I didn't see anything." Then, cursing under his breath, he added, "I should've known this was going to be a cluster. Let's get out of here."

Raina turned to watch the scene unfolding across the river. The shooter appeared to be looking under the dock for something. "Do you have a camera?"

"A *what*? Have you lost your mind? Let's get the hell out of here. If someone catches me with you, I can kiss my life goodbye. My job. My marriage. Everything." He paused. "And you can forget about your golf scholarship."

Ignoring him, Raina dug through her purse and pulled out her phone, clicking on the camera function. Then she turned and focused on the dock. She started to enlarge the image when Dr. Newell snatched the phone away from her.

"Are you crazy?" he said, spittle flying from his mouth. "You can't take a picture. It'll prove you were here."

"I'll say I was alone."

"The whole class knows I run here every night, and you weren't all that stealthy about flirting with me at Phil's. Someone will put two and two together. *You were never here.*"

"Then why did we bring the telescope?"

"So if some random person did catch us out here, we'd have an excuse." He sighed. "We need to go. *Now.*"

Raina shot a glance across the Black Warrior. The figure was still on the dock. "Give me my phone back! I just witnessed a murder for Christ's sake." She pointed toward the dock, but the doctor didn't move his eyes off her. Nor did he release the phone. Instead he picked Raina's lace panties off the ground with his other hand and flung them at her.

"Put these back on and let's go."

She swatted the underwear away and ripped off her blouse. "Give me my phone or I scream bloody murder."

"Raina, are you—?"

"Help!" she screamed. "Please, someone help me!" Then she squealed as loud as she could, and Dr. Newell dropped the phone and began to run.

Ignoring him and her clothes, Raina lunged for the phone. She clicked it on, but nothing happened. The screen was cracked. *Son of a bitch broke it.* "Damnit," she said. Then, turning back to the railing, she saw that the shooter was now standing on the edge of the dock and . . .

. . . *looking right at me.* Raina hesitated for only a second. Then she pressed her right eye into the viewer of the telescope and adjusted the lens down until . . .

"I see you," she said. For a split second, she saw the killer in profile. Then the figure was running away from her, down the dock and up some steps leading to a house. *"She's gone,"* Raina whispered.

Raina Farrell backed away from the tripod. Her legs were trembling with fear, and she took no notice that she was naked from the waist up as she sat down and wrapped her arms around her knees.

"I just witnessed a murder."

2

At three o'clock in the morning, the silver Yukon pulled to a stop amid a sea of blue and red flashing lights. At least ten Sheriff's cruisers were parked at the curb nearest the water's edge. Wade Richey stepped out of the SUV and trudged toward the group of officers, his path lit by the beams coming off the headlights of the police vehicles.

Wade wore black jeans and a black T-shirt and, with his thick salt-and-pepper hair and similarly colored mustache, he brought to mind comparisons to Sam Elliott in *Road House*. As he pressed his way through the hodgepodge of deputies, he came face-to-face with a man holding a clipboard in one hand and a megaphone in the other. From his uniform lapel, Wade saw the name "Lusk."

"Detective Richey."

Wade nodded. "One and the same. Is it him?"

Lusk was a muscular man whom Wade estimated to be in his late thirties or early forties. He had a clean-shaven face, dark hair cut high and tight, and piercing blue eyes. "We think so, but it is hard to be sure." The deputy's voice was clipped and had a nasal tone to it, which

Wade figured intensified when he was under pressure. "The body is filthy from the river. If it is him, he's lost a lot of weight and grown a beard since his mug shot."

That fits, Wade knew. "What's the status?"

Lusk angled his head toward the shore, where, fifteen feet away, Wade saw a tall, slender black woman shining a flashlight on what must be the corpse and speaking into a Dictaphone. "Ingrid's been here about fifteen minutes."

"And?"

"Nothing so far," Lusk said, shaking his head. "She shooed us away so she could do her thing."

Without waiting for any further details, Wade walked toward the shore. When he was a few feet behind the woman, who continued to talk into the recording device, he spoke in a wan voice. "Of all the crime scenes in all the world, you had to wander into mine."

"I would know that baritone voice anywhere." Ingrid Barnett, the chief medical examiner for Tuscaloosa County, took a step back so that Wade could have a clear view.

"Jesus . . . H. . . . Christ," Wade whispered, feeling his breath catch in his throat. The dead man was even skinnier than he had been the previous summer. Scruffier, too, with a thick gray beard. But there was no doubt in Wade Richey's mind as to the identity of the deceased.

"You OK, Detective?" Ingrid asked.

Wade blinked his eyes, trying to regain his focus. "I'm fine, Ingrid." He squatted for a better look. There was a bullet hole just above the dead man's right temple. It was small, and Wade knew it had to have come from a handgun.

"Pistol?" Wade asked.

"Yep," Ingrid said. "I'm not a ballistics expert, but that would be my guess. Probably a nine-millimeter."

"Any ideas on time of death?"

"I'll need to do some more testing, but based on the condition of the body, he hasn't been dead long. My preliminary opinion would be somewhere between 10:00 p.m. and midnight."

Wade gazed at the corpse and tried to take a mental inventory of everything about the dead man. His hair, still damp from the river, was mostly gray, with a few dark specks and a bald spot in back. His clothes, also soaked, consisted of blue jeans with some type of light button-down collar shirt. The sleeves were rolled up, and Wade noticed a tattoo under his right forearm with the letters "TCB" in black ink above a similarly colored lightning bolt. "Taking care of business," Wade said out loud.

"Elvis fan, huh?" Ingrid asked.

Wade smiled, keeping his eyes on the body. "You manage to impress me every time I see you, Ms. Ingrid." A scar ran along the side of the dead man's nose, but it looked old. The scratch marks on his neck, however, appeared to be fresh.

As if reading Wade's mind, Ingrid spoke from behind his shoulder. "You see the ligature markings on his Adam's apple?"

Wade nodded and cocked his head. "Does he have any skin or blood under his fingernails?"

"Nothing at first blush. They look clean to me. Some dirt from the lake and sand are all I can discern, but I'll test further in the lab."

"The river is nasty, so maybe you'll find something. If there is skin, blood, hair . . . hell, any kind of DNA in his fingernails, that could point to some logical conclusions."

"He got into an argument with the perp . . . which led to a physical altercation . . . which led to . . ." Ingrid trailed off as Wade stood up and looked at her.

"We won't know where any of it leads until you complete your testing. When do you think you'll have a report ready?" He was already walking back toward the uniforms.

"Not sure," Ingrid yelled after him. "I'm going to need at least another hour here at the scene to gather evidence, and you know the crime lab in Birmingham."

Wade stopped walking and turned toward her. "A week?"

She snorted. "Wade, you know that a full report with toxicology and DNA testing usually takes a minimum of two weeks, and sometimes over a month."

Wade stepped closer to her and lowered his voice, choosing his words carefully. "Ingrid, I have a feeling that the press is going to be on this case like bees to honey. We need to expedite everything."

Blinking her eyes, she glanced down at the corpse and squinted back at Wade. "You knew him, didn't you?"

Wade nodded and spoke under his breath. "Unfortunately."

The location of the body was less than a half mile west of the Cypress Inn Restaurant, off of Rice Mine Road. Two brothers from the Phi Delta Theta fraternity at the University of Alabama discovered the corpse while attempting to hit a golf ball over the Black Warrior River.

"I thought the kids tried to hit the ball over the Black Warrior in front of the restaurant," Wade said after hearing Deputy Lusk recount the frat boys' story.

Lusk scoffed. "Most do. It's almost exactly three hundred yards from the Cypress Inn side of the shore to the bank on the far side. But these two guys can't hit that far, so they went seeking a shorter distance." He paused, shaking his head. "I haven't measured it or anything, but looks like the distance across down there"—Lusk stopped and pointed across the river to the opposing shore—"is maybe two hundred seventy or two hundred eighty."

"So, their story makes sense," Wade said, pulling on his chin.

"They each have a Callaway Big Bertha driver in the vehicle they were in." Lusk nodded in the direction of a Chevy Silverado truck. He paused. "Course we also found a bong hidden underneath the passenger seat. Didn't find any weed, but there was a half- drunk sixer of Monkeynaut beer in the floorboard."

"Monkey what?" Wade asked.

Lusk laughed. "Monkeynaut. It's an IPA made by a brewery in Huntsville. Good stuff."

Wade nodded. He was a Miller High Life man himself but was aware of the craft beer craze that had engulfed Alabama. "So, two frat boys out getting drunk and high and trying to hit a golf ball over the river."

"That's about it," Lusk said, shrugging. "Nothing suspicious that I saw, but you'll probably want to interview them yourself."

Wade would, but he doubted his conclusions would be any different than Lusk's. Hitting a golf ball over the river below the Cypress Inn was a rite of passage for students at Alabama, and getting drunk and high on a Saturday night couldn't be considered suspicious when hundreds of other coeds and young adults were doing the same thing on the Strip just a few miles away. Walking down the river a ways to get a better shot at clearing the water was a bit different, but Wade didn't see anything overly odd about that either.

Wade turned his head so that he could examine their location in all directions. He saw that Lusk had already dispatched officers and dogs to search the area.

"Have they turned anything up yet?"

"Nothing so far, but we haven't been here long."

Wade rubbed his chin and looked back toward the river, where Ingrid continued to talk into her Dictaphone. "Since the body was found in the water and the time of death was sometime between three and five hours ago, we probably need to expand out the search to a couple miles in both directions, focusing most of the team west." Wade pointed in that direction. "If the corpse was dumped in the river, then it drifted with the current, which flows west to east along this stretch."

"Ten-four," Lusk said, waving a hand at the two fraternity brothers sitting on the tailgate of the Silverado. "You gonna talk to 'em now?"

"Yeah," Wade said, taking out his cell phone. "But first I have to make a call."

"I've already notified the sheriff," Lusk said. "He's the one who told me to call you."

"I know," Wade said, clicking through his contacts until he found the name. He wasn't calling the sheriff. "Why don't you get those two"—Wade motioned with his head toward the two Phi Delts, both gazing aimlessly at the ground—"a cup of coffee or a Coke or something? They look like they could use it."

Lusk brought his right hand up in a salute and trudged away as Wade pressed send on his phone. Eight seconds and three rings later, he heard the familiar voice on the other end of the line.

"Whatcha got?" The voice was groggy, half-asleep.

"A cold one. On the banks of the Black Warrior a little ways west of the Cypress Inn. The victim has a bullet hole in his head." Wade paused. "Thought you'd want to take a look."

A pause on the line followed by a grunt. "I'll be there in ten. Has the body been identified yet?"

Wade could hear rustling in the background and figured the man on the other end of the line was putting on a pair of pants. "Yes, it has." He rubbed his eyes and sighed, still not quite believing what he had just seen on the shore. Then, clearing his throat, he added, "I . . . identified the body."

"*What?*" The grogginess was now gone, replaced by hyperalertness. The rustling had stopped. "You recognize the victim?"

"Yeah," Wade said, glancing over his shoulder and looking past Ingrid to the waters of the Black Warrior. "So will you. The *deceased* . . . is Jack Willistone."

3

Nine minutes after they'd hung up, Wade smiled when he saw the black Dodge Charger pull to a stop. The lights were cut, and a sandy-haired heavyset man stepped out of the car wearing khaki pants, a white button-down, and a fire-engine-red jacket.

Ambrose Powell Conrad, the newly appointed district attorney for Tuscaloosa County, Alabama, shut the door to the Charger and ambled toward Wade, sipping from a steaming cup of coffee. As he did, Wade noticed that the other officers had straightened up and a few pointed. At first, the detective thought the men were surprised to see the head prosecutor at a crime scene. The prior DA hadn't liked getting his hands dirty.

But as his friend came closer, Wade knew his initial feeling was wrong. It wasn't surprise that he saw in the deputies' eyes. It was awe. *Pulaski,* he thought. Nothing had been the same since Pulaski.

"Let's see it," Powell said, not bothering with pleasantries, his voice so tense and loud that a couple officers standing nearby almost jumped out of their skin.

Wade nodded and the two men walked shoulder to shoulder back down to the shore.

As Ingrid rehashed what she'd already told Wade, Powell listened and sipped his coffee, occasionally grunting. When she was finished, he swished the remaining liquid around in his cup and squinted at the coroner. "What about prints? Hair follicles? Any other DNA?"

"The shirt collar appears to be dry, so that is our best chance," Ingrid said. "The rest of the clothes are soaked to the bone. There was also a cap that was found on the dock, and we'll test it too." She glanced at Wade. "As I told Detective Richey, if I'm able to collect any DNA, I'll have to send it to the crime lab in Birmingham, and it may take a couple of weeks to obtain the results."

"What about the area?" Powell waved his arm in the direction of the woods surrounding them.

"We've got officers and dogs on the ground looking for anything within a four-mile radius," Wade said.

"Good deal," Powell said. "Well, let's get out of Ms. Ingrid's way."

As they started to walk away, Ingrid yelled after them. "Hey, Conrad."

Powell looked over his shoulder. "Yeah."

"Nice jacket."

The two men leaned against Powell's Charger and split a Kit Kat bar. A deputy had gone to a twenty-four-hour gas station, bringing back a gallon of coffee, and Powell and Wade both sipped from steaming hot Styrofoam cups. Wade licked his fingers and smiled at his friend. "I think Ingrid may be sweet on you."

Powell grunted, ignoring the comment. "When did that SOB get out of jail? Yesterday?"

Wade shook his head. "Not quite. It was two days ago. I got a call from the warden of the St. Clair Correctional Facility, in Springville, Monday morning saying he'd been paroled."

Powell sipped his coffee. "So, he's out thirty-six hours and somebody puts a cap in him."

Wade nodded. "Willistone had enemies. You know that better than I do."

Powell nodded and sucked melted chocolate off his thumb. Then he threw out the remains of his coffee. "Have you interviewed Frick and Frack over there?" He pointed at the two fraternity boys, still sitting on the tailgate of the Silverado.

Wade shook his head and gave a wry smile. "I wanted you here for that."

"Sissy," Powell said.

"No," Wade said, beginning to walk toward the truck. "I just don't want your ultra-intense ass questioning my report later."

Todd Shuman was a short, skinny kid with wild curly brown hair. Something was vaguely familiar about him, but Powell couldn't quite place it. Both of Shuman's hands shook, and the ice cubes in the plastic cup of Coke that he was holding rattled as he talked. "I . . . I don't know nothing. We were just trying to clear the river with a drive and Happy saw the body."

"Did either of you knock it over?" Powell asked.

Shuman managed a smile. "I did."

"Bullshit," the other fraternity brother chimed in. Powell shifted his glance to the larger man sitting to Shuman's right. William Henry "Happy" Caldwell was just a shade under six feet tall but had to weigh at least two hundred pounds. He was built like a bowling ball, with his shaved head adding to the effect.

"No?" Powell asked.

"Not a snowball's chance in hell. Screech hadn't hit one over a hundred yards in an hour." Caldwell smiled, and when he did his eyes squinted into small slits. The kid oozed confidence and self-assurance.

"Screech?"

"Shuman's pledge name," Caldwell said, chuckling. "You know, from *Saved—*"

"*By the Bell,*" Powell interrupted, snapping his fingers. That's why the kid looked familiar. He was a dead ringer for the character from the old '90s sitcom.

"The dispatcher said that one of you two guys recognized the victim. Would that be you?" Wade nodded at Caldwell, who returned the gesture.

"Yeah, I'd seen that guy in a couple of online videos earlier this week. Jack Willistone. He was released from prison on Monday, and it was all over Twitter. One clip showed him walking out the front door of the correctional facility in Springville and into a waiting car." Caldwell crossed his arms. "Willistone owned one of the biggest trucking companies in the world and was a huge player in Alabama business until he went to prison after that trial over in Henshaw County. You guys remember that one, right? It was all over the news."

Powell glanced at Wade and then cocked his head at Caldwell. "No offense, kid, but how do you know all this about Willistone? I mean, I get that you saw these videos on Twitter and all, but—"

"I'm prelaw at Alabama," Caldwell said. "During my freshman year, me and a couple classmates went to the trial in Henshaw. There was a lot of press about it because of Professor McMurtrie." He paused and gave his head a jerk. "Do you know him?"

Powell smiled. "Maybe a little."

Caldwell whistled and folded his arms, gazing down at the gravel. "I'll never forget it. The place was packed. Seeing McMurtrie cross-examine Willistone's accident expert clinched it for me." He looked up at Powell. "I knew I was going to be a trial lawyer after that."

Powell nodded. He, too, had been in Henshaw that week. And right after the trial, he had put Jack Willistone in handcuffs. He glanced over his shoulder at Ingrid Barnett, who was now squatting over the ornery bastard's corpse. *And now he's dead. Thirty-six hours out of prison . . . .*

Wade conducted the rest of the interview. Caldwell and Shuman started the night at Innisfree Irish Pub, on the Strip, around 8:00 p.m. After wolfing down a couple of cheeseburgers and three pitchers of Sweetwater 420, Caldwell wanted to meet several other Phi Delts at Gallettes bar, so there they went. On the way, Shuman bet Caldwell a hundred bucks that he could hit a ball over the Black Warrior. At Gallettes, they each had a couple more beers, listened to the band, and unsuccessfully attempted to get several different coeds to agree to come to the river with them to watch the contest. At 1:30 a.m., they left the bar. They stopped at Shuman's apartment in Northport and grabbed a six-pack of Monkeynaut, a shag bag of golf balls, and two drivers. Both clubs belonged to Shuman, who was a self-professed eight handicapper.

The duo pulled into the Cypress Inn parking lot at approximately 2:00 a.m. Their car was the only one in the lot, and they didn't see or hear anything suspicious as they walked around the restaurant and down to the shoreline. After thirty minutes of hacking balls, none of which came close to making it over, Shuman suggested that they walk down the river a ways. By this point, both candidly admitted that they were drunk. Neither could remember how many shots they had tried at the new location before Caldwell stumbled over the body.

Wade wrapped up the interview by handing each kid his card and requesting a call if they remembered anything else. Then he told the two to hold tight and that a deputy would come by in a little while to drive them home.

"Dead end," Wade said as he and Powell walked back toward the Charger.

"Maybe not," the prosecutor said. "Should probably bring them in for another go at it in a couple of days after the shock wears off and they realize that they aren't being charged with anything."

"I guess, but even if they remember something new, they both have admitted to being hammered during the operative period."

Powell grunted, which Wade knew was his begrudging agreement. As they approached the Charger, Wade saw Lusk jogging toward them, his face flushed red with either excitement or anger. "We got an iPhone. It was found about a half mile west of here on the edge of a dock." He paused, catching his breath. "It's Willistone's."

"Have the last few texts and calls been reviewed?" Powell asked, his voice so loud that Lusk jumped back.

Blinking his eyes, the deputy recovered and nodded his head. "There aren't many of either." He paused. "But the last three texts are all from the same number."

"Did he have it saved as a contact?"

"No, but we ran the number through our cellular database and got a match." He paused, catching his breath and taking a folded sheet of notebook paper out of his pocket. "The number is registered to a Wilma Christine Newton."

Lusk glanced up at Wade, but the detective wasn't looking at him. Wade Richey was watching Powell, whose face had turned ashen. "You alright, brother?"

Powell gazed down at the trampled grass that led down to the shore of the Black Warrior River. "What's that name again, Officer?"

"Wilma Christine Newton," Lusk repeated, moving his beady eyes back and forth between the detective and the district attorney.

Powell grunted and gave a jerk of his head. *Wilma . . . Newton.* He thought about the trial in Henshaw and all that had happened since. Then he raised his eyes to meet Lusk's. "What do the texts say?"

Lusk lowered his eyes back to the page he held in his hand. "Newton says that she's reconsidered his proposition and wants to see him, and Willistone tells her to meet him at his attorney's house on the Black Warrior at ten fifteen. He gives the address and says it's in the Bent Creek subdivision and the house is at the bottom of the hill closest to the water."

"Who owns the dock where the phone was found?" Wade asked, his voice rising with excitement.

"Zorn," Powell whispered, his tone oddly detached. "Greg Zorn."

Lusk lowered the page to his side and cocked his head at Powell. "How did you know that?"

Powell squatted to the ground. He snapped off a weed and placed it in his mouth, sucking on the wire grass.

"How did he know that?" Lusk turned to Wade, who waved him off. "Never mind him. Tell me."

Lusk shook his head with exasperation and spoke in a high-pitched nasal whine. "The district attorney is correct. Gregory Zorn owns the property. I just got off the phone with him. He's in the middle of a two-week trial in Birmingham. He confirmed that he was Jack Willistone's attorney and that Willistone called yesterday evening and asked if he could stay at the house for a couple of nights. Since Zorn was out of town and was about to sell the house anyway, he agreed. Zorn refused to provide any other information, based on attorney-client privilege."

"His client is dead," Wade said.

"I advised him of that fact, but he wouldn't budge," Lusk fired back.

"He will," Wade said. "Was anyone else living in the house?"

Lusk shook his head. "No. Zorn is divorced, and the kids live with their mother in Orange Beach."

Wade took several seconds to think it through and then jammed his right fist into the palm of his other hand. "Ten fifteen is consistent with Ingrid's time of death. I think we may have just identified our primary lead. Good work, Lusk." Wade clapped the deputy on the back. "Tell the search crew to double down by that dock. Let's focus everything we've got within a quarter mile of that spot."

"You gonna tell Ingrid, or you want me? I'm sure she'll want to do a comb-through after she finishes here."

Wade glanced at Powell, who was walking slowly back to the Charger. "You do it," he said. "I'll be right down."

Lusk remained in place, but his eyes were watching Powell. "He OK?"

"He's fine. You go on and I'm right behind you." Wade placed a firm hand on Lusk's shoulder and gave him a nudge toward the river. The deputy began to trot toward Ingrid.

Wade strode toward the Charger, where he found Powell leaning against the driver's side and looking down at the gravel. His hands were stuck deep in the front pockets of his khakis. "You see a ghost?"

Powell raised his head. "Not yet."

"You know the lady he was meeting? Wilma"—Wade glanced at his own pocket notebook—"Newton?"

Powell's face was blank and even paler in the moonlight. "Not really. But I know who she is . . . or was. And . . . it makes sense." He paused, and his eyes narrowed. "I think we could have more than a lead. We may have a prime suspect."

4

In the dream she woke to every morning, the broken glass sliced her arms, legs, and face like jagged rocks. And there was blood. On her hands. In her eyes. Everywhere. And each step she took was laced with the pain of glass digging into the heels and toes of her feet. When the blood and pain were so thick that she couldn't see and she felt the scream beginning in her chest and working its way up her throat, she would open her eyes. In the first few days after her children were taken away, the scream made its way out of her mouth at full volume.

Now, the only noise was a low gasp, followed by a whispered, "Damnit."

Wilma Newton gazed across the tiny bedroom, her mind still stuck in the dream. In reality, when she had pointed the pistol at her reflection in the mirror almost two years ago and pulled the trigger, the shattered glass had mostly fallen in her hair, with a few tiny shards catching on the back of her neck. There had been no blood and no screams. But there had been pain. Unspeakable . . . unfathomable . . . pain.

She had wanted to "off herself," as she'd heard some of the guards in jail describe suicide. Why else had she stripped down? That was what you did, right? You made a production of it. If you were an officer, you put your uniform on, faced a mirror, and stuck a gun in your mouth.

Wilma wasn't an officer. She was a stripper. She had also been a prostitute. When she stood naked before the mirror at her rental home in Boone's Hill, she was wearing her "uniform."

Then why hadn't she just done it? *Why*?

"Nothing for me. Everything for them," Wilma whispered as she rolled out of bed. Those six words had become her mantra for life, and all of her actions could be summed up by them. Including what she had done last night . . .

Wilma hung her head in shame, not wanting to look at the mess. Finally, after a few seconds, she forced her eyes open. Her clothes from the previous evening—jeans and a black blouse—lay at the foot of the bed in a pile. She sighed, knowing that the garments prob-ably reeked of smoke. *And of him,* she thought, remembering the mingled scent of bourbon and A.1. Steak Sauce that she had smelled on his breath. There had also been the stale scent of incarceration that, regardless of how many times a person washed after getting out, never seemed to dissipate. Wilma knew that odor all too well. She could still smell the Giles County Jail in her pores even now, three months after being released herself.

She slipped on a pair of sweats and a long-sleeve T-shirt and traipsed down the short hallway toward the living area of her one-bedroom apartment. She leaned against the threshold and noticed the white to-go sacks adorned with the familiar green cactus and yellow and red letters of Taco Casa littered on the kitchen table to the right. She winced when she saw the half-eaten burrito lying open next to a plastic container of dried cheese dip and an empty pint of vodka. *Hell of a life I've carved out for myself,* she thought, rubbing her temples and realizing that she would start this day, as she had begun almost every one since getting out of jail, hungover. She looked away from the wasted food before the nausea set in and began to rub her sleep-deprived eyes. For a few seconds, she wondered what time it was and where she would go searching for work today. In the three months since her release from jail and her less-than-triumphant return to Tuscaloosa, she had been unsuccessful in obtaining a job. For some reason, employers weren't chomping at the bit to hire a convicted prostitute whose last gainful employment was dancing the pole at the Sundowners Club in Pulaski, Tennessee.

But without a job, she had no chance to regain custody of her girls. So she would try again . . .

As she stepped fully into the living room, Wilma almost chuckled as the bitter thoughts began their daily invasion, but her breath caught in her throat when she saw the figure kneeling by the window adjacent to the front door and peeking out through the blinds.

"This place is a pigsty."

Wilma stood stock still and gazed at her eldest daughter, the experience like looking into a mirror. Laurie Ann had Wilma's dirty-blond locks, thin, sinewy frame and, when she stood, was five feet, six inches tall—the same height as her mother. The only sign of Dewey was the color of her eyes, dark brown like her father's as opposed to Wilma's green. Now fourteen years old, Laurie Ann could easily have passed for seventeen but for the gray Tuscaloosa Middle School sweatshirt she was wearing.

"Thanks," Wilma finally managed, crossing her arms. Shock had turned to curiosity. Laurie Ann was in the eighth grade. Since the sentencing hearing, she and Jackie had been living with Wilma's cousin Tawny and her husband, Sam, in Tuscaloosa. "What time is it?"

"Eight thirty," Laurie Ann said, still gazing through the blinds.

"Shouldn't you be at—?"

"School? Yeah, normally I would be. But the Tuscaloosa City School system set aside some 'snow days'"—she made the quotation symbol with the index and middle fingers of both hands and rolled her eyes—"and it didn't even sleet this winter. So, voilà, school's out today. You would know this kind of information if you hadn't been in jail when the schedule came out." Laurie Ann spoke in the same sharp, bitter tone that had inundated all their conversations since Carla Yost turned the girls over to the Lincoln County Department of Human Resources twenty-three months earlier. She glared at Wilma, brown eyes blazing with fury. "And don't ever tell me what I should or shouldn't be doing."

Wilma sighed but didn't respond. She didn't have the energy for another fight with her daughter. Truth be known, she was just grateful that Laurie Ann had come to see her. For the past month, her visits had become more frequent, and she had even spent the night a couple of times. *Progress,* Wilma thought, knowing that regaining her daughters' trust would be a long and arduous process. She had yet to make any headway at all with her youngest, Jackie, who shied away every time Wilma came by to visit, barely saying a word.

"So what brings me the pleasure?" she asked, plopping down on the dark-khaki couch that she had bought from the Northport Salvation Army for seventy-five dollars. The sofa carried the permanent smell of cat urine, but it was comfortable, and Wilma's shoulders sank into the cushions.

Laurie Ann's gaze softened, but when she spoke again, her voice remained bitter. "Jackie had a friend over to spend the night, and I wanted to give them some space."

Wilma nodded. "When did Tawny drop you off?"

Laurie Ann rolled her eyes. "She didn't."

"That high school boy?" Wilma tried to keep her tone neutral, but it was no use. She could hear the disapproval in her own voice.

"His *name* is Brewer." Laurie Ann peered back through the blinds. "And yes, he drove me here last night, and he was supposed to pick me up thirty minutes ago."

Wilma bit her lip, trying to choose her words carefully. "So what are y'all going to do today?"

Laurie Ann shrugged. "I don't know. We might go to Moundville with some of his friends."

"And do what?"

"Oh, you know, the usual. Throw the Frisbee around. Drink some beer. Sneak off behind one of the Indian mounds and make out."

"Laurie Ann, you are too young—"

"Life lessons from my mother, the convicted prostitute," Laurie Ann interrupted. Then she turned from the window and stomped over to the kitchen table. She snatched the empty pint of Smirnoff and glared at Wilma. "I don't think this is the drink that comes with the burrito meal."

When Wilma didn't say anything, Laurie Ann pursed her lips and slammed the bottle down on the table. "What did you do last night, Mom?"

For several seconds, silence engulfed the apartment. The disappointment evident in her daughter's eyes burned Wilma's conscience like a hot iron. Finally, she sighed and looked away. She started to say something but was cut off by the wail of a siren. The sound was close and getting closer.

"What did you do last night?" Laurie Ann repeated. The slightest hint of desperation had now leaked into her tone. "Did you go see him? Did you talk with Mr. Willistone?"

Wilma ignored the questions and, with as much calm as she could muster, walked to the window and grabbed the string to pull the blinds open. Her heart sank when she saw the red and blue flashing lights in the parking lot below. Two SUVs with the blue and gold crest of the Tuscaloosa County Sheriff's Office blazoned across the side had pulled to a stop right outside the building.

Wilma trudged back toward the couch. She could feel her daughter's eyes on her, but she could not bring herself to look. Outside the window, she heard the clang of doors slamming shut, followed by the clicking of shoes on the steps. Wilma slumped down on the couch and waited, hoping that the sinking feeling in her gut was wrong.

"Mom—"

Four loud knocks cut off Laurie Ann's voice. Wilma saw at least three uniformed officers through the open blinds.

"Open the door, baby," Wilma said.

"Mom—"

"Do it."

Laurie Ann grabbed the knob but looked at her mother with pleading eyes before turning it. "You're going to need a lawyer."

"I know," Wilma said, trying to sound strong as the door swung open.

PART TWO

PART TWO

5

Mayfair Park is a Little League baseball complex in Huntsville, Alabama. It is located in the southeast portion of the city in a neighborhood commonly referred to as the Medical District due to its close proximity to the hospital. Just beyond the centerfield fence of the Majors' field, where the twelve and under boys play their games, is a concession stand with several picnic tables.

Thomas Jackson McMurtrie stood next to the table closest to the fence, his arms folded, watching the action. At six feet, three inches tall and a shade over two hundred pounds, Tom found the bleachers behind home plate to be a little tight for his large frame. Besides, he felt that standing behind centerfield gave him a better view of the entire field.

His grandson, Jackson, had pitched the first four innings of the game and had reached his pitch limit, so he would be taking a new position to start the top of the fifth. Tom watched the home dugout and saw Jackson emerge, glove in hand, and begin running toward the outfield. When he saw his grandfather, the boy smiled, and Tom approached the fence, waving him over.

At twelve years old, Jackson was a barrel-chested, stocky kid with light-brown hair. "Hey, Papa. Did you see me pitch?"

"Not bad, Forty-Nine," Tom said, referring to Jackson's jersey number, which the boy had worn every year since he'd started Little League. This choice was a special source of pride for Tom, as he'd worn the same number for Coach Paul "Bear" Bryant's 1961 national championship football team. "Seven strikeouts, three walks, and only two hits. Hard to beat that."

"Well, one of the hits did bounce off the concession stand," Jackson said, giving a sheepish grin.

"Got to keep the ball low and away to that Gentry kid or he'll hit it to Birmingham," Tom said, grabbing his back as a stab of pain shot down his side.

"You OK, Papa?"

"Yeah, son," Tom said, wincing and trying to shake it off. "Just old. You remember what I said about the outfield."

"First step back, find the ball, and then go to it."

"Bingo," Tom said, and winked as the boy strode to his position in centerfield. While the outfielders warmed up by throwing a ball back and forth, Tom yawned and looked around the park, which had T-ball, girls' softball, and coach pitch contests happening under the lights at four different fields. Every so often, Tom would hear a roar from one of the other games, indicating that a big hit or nice play had been made. He smiled, enjoying the unseasonably cool breeze that gusted toward him. With the wind blowing out, it was a good night for a home run, Tom thought, knowing that "hitting a dinger," as Jackson called it, was his grandson's number one goal for the season. He leaned against the fence and breathed in the scent of hot dogs and popcorn, trying to stretch his back. It had started hurting during a walk last week with Lee Roy. The damn dog had lunged at a squirrel that had scurried past, and Tom felt a twinge when he had grabbed the leash. *Getting old is no bowl of cherries,* he thought as he felt a hand tugging on his arm. He looked down and saw his grand-daughter, Jenny, smiling up at him, her lips and teeth tinged in purple.

"Papa, will you buy me a slow cone?" At five years old, Jenny hadn't quite grasped all the sounds of the alphabet. She had even lighter brown hair than Jackson, but her eyes were what always made Tom's heart catch. They were the same crystal blue of her grand-mother, and, even at the age of five, Jenny had mastered that pleading look that Tom had always been incapable of refusing.

"Looks like you've already had a snow cone, sweetie," Tom said, pinching Jenny lightly on the nose, which made her laugh.

"That was a grape one," she said. "I want a strawberry one now."

"Ah," Tom said, feeling his cell phone vibrate twice in his pocket.

"Please, Papa,"

"OK, Jenny girl," he said, walking with her toward the concession window. Tom got himself a popcorn and Diet Coke and sat down next to his granddaughter, who had already stuck her entire face into the snow cone, as strawberry red began to mix with the purple on her lips. As she started to chew the ice up, she wiped her mouth and squinted up at Tom. "Did Nana ever watch one of Brother's baseball games?"

Jenny had called Jackson "Brother" from the time she could talk, and it appeared that the nickname, at least for her, was going to stick. Tom smiled. He'd had a teammate at Alabama that everyone called "Brother," and he had always thought it was cool. Then as he remem-bered the question his granddaughter had asked, the smile faded.

"Yes. When y'all were still living in Nashville, me and Nana came up one weekend and watched Brother's T-ball game."

"Was that the only time?"

Tom felt an ache in his chest as he looked into the child's eyes. He nodded. "Yeah, that was the only time."

"Did she go up to heaven after that?"

Tom blinked his eyes, feeling the heat behind them, and he forced himself to look back at the ball field, seeing Jackson bend his knees as the pitcher threw the opening pitch of the inning. When he and Julie had made the trek to Nashville, she had been going through treatment for breast cancer. It was March of 2007. She would die a month later.

"It wasn't much longer," he said.

Tom felt the little girl's tiny hand touch his own, and he squeezed her sticky fingers as he looked at her. "I'm sorry I made you sad, Papa."

He pinched her nose again, relishing the sound of her laughter. "You could never make me sad, honey," he said, feeling the vibration of his cell phone again. As he watched her bounce back toward the bleachers, Tom threw the remains of his drink and popcorn in the trash and reluctantly pulled out the mobile. He started to enter his security code—1961—but as he clicked the last digit he heard the crack of the bat from home plate. His eyes shot up and he saw the ball traveling toward centerfield. Tom's body tensed as he watched Jackson. The boy's first instinct was to step back with his right foot. Then, after a half second's hesitation, he sprinted in and caught the ball on the run, flipping it to the second baseman before returning to his position. He looked at his grandfather for approval, and Tom gave him a fist pump. "That a boy, Forty-Nine!" he yelled, feeling his chest swell with pride.

By the time his eyes returned to the phone, the screen had turned dark and he had to reenter his code. When he did, he saw that the text was from Powell Conrad, his former student and the district attorney for Tuscaloosa County. Tom opened the message and read it.

Professor, you may have already heard, but if not, I thought you should know. Jack Willistone was murdered last night. I'm sorry to bother you, but I need to talk with you about the suspect we have in custody. I'll be working for several more hours, so feel free to call me any time tonight. Otherwise, let's talk tomorrow.

"*Jack Willistone.*" Tom whispered the name out loud, feeling his breath catch in his throat.

"What did you say, Papa?"

Tom glanced down and saw that Jenny had returned from the bleachers and was again standing right below him. Her lips curled into a strawberry-tinged smile. "Who is Jack Willy . . . stone?" She cocked her head up at him, and Tom realized that his entire body had tensed. The girl's eyes widened and she looked scared. "Is he bad?" she whispered.

Tom kneeled and looked his granddaughter in her crystal blues. "Yes, he was a bad man, but . . ." Tom paused, not wanting to upset the child with talk of death but still coming to grips with the news himself. "He can't hurt anyone anymore."

"Why not?"

Despite the goose flesh he felt on his forearms, Tom managed a smile. Five years old and she already took a better deposition than him. "He's gone away," Tom said, standing up and turning his attention back to the field. "Far away."

After the game, Tom took Jackson and Jenny to the Mellow Mushroom for a Mighty Meaty pizza. Then he brought them to their home in Jones Valley, a series of neighborhoods and streets bustling with young families and older couples that all buttressed the Jones Farm, a beautiful thousand-acre spread cut right in the middle of Huntsville. As he pulled into the driveway, he saw his daughter-in-law, Nancy, walking out of the garage. Once he cut the ignition, Jackson and Jenny ran to their mother, and Tom followed behind. As the kids huddled below her, each trying to get her attention, Tom leaned over them and gave Nancy a peck on the cheek. Then he glanced down at her growing abdomen. "You look great, girl. Remind me again when there's gonna be another McMurtrie running around here."

"December 1 is the due date," Nancy said, placing her hands over her stomach and looking down at Jackson and Jenny. "But since these two both came early, I bet we have a baby by Thanksgiving."

Tom smiled, but it was hard not to feel a twinge of sadness that Julie would never see this grandchild. But sadness, as Tom well knew, was a part of life. He had been reminded of this truth all too well during the first few months of the year.

"When are you heading back to Tuscaloosa?" Nancy asked after she and the kids had walked with Tom back to his car.

He glanced up at the moon through the ever-increasing clouds in the sky. "I have a hearing tomorrow morning, so . . ." He trailed off, and he could hear the reluctance in his voice. It was getting harder and harder to go back. "I'll sleep at the farm tonight and get a fresh start at first light."

Nancy took a step closer and spoke in a low voice. "How is your partner doing? Is he back yet?"

Tom shook his head and gazed down at the cobblestone driveway. He had called Rick several times during the week, but there had been no answer. "Not yet."

"I can't imagine what he's going through," Nancy said, frowning. "Is his girlfriend still working for the firm?"

"No," Tom said. "And Dawn's not his girlfriend anymore. They broke things off about a week before the accident. It's . . . a complicated situation." Tom swept his foot over loose gravel, not knowing what else to say. That had been a common theme this year. Even for someone like him, who'd made his living with words as both a lawyer and teacher, there were times when nothing could be said that would help or explain a situation.

Nancy touched his arm. "Tom, you can't be running that firm by yourself. Didn't Dr. Davis tell you that you needed to retire from trial work after Pulaski?"

Tom smiled. Bill Davis was Tom's urologist, his pseudo–family doctor, and most importantly, one of his oldest friends. Twenty-eight months ago, Bill had diagnosed Tom with bladder cancer after he had noticed blood in his urine. Two surgeries and six rounds of chemotherapy later, Tom was deemed to be in remission, but he would need to be scoped every six months to make sure no masses had come back. Tom's last bladder cystoscopy was three weeks ago, and it was clean as a whistle. During the office visit afterwards, Bill had instructed Tom in no uncertain terms that he had to walk away from the courtroom. Bill himself had semiretired from private practice, telling Tom that he was only working on call at the hospital once a month and only treating patients in the office who had been with him since Lyndon Baines Johnson was president. Tom had laughed, since he knew that the only patient Bill had who was still alive and had been seeing him since LBJ roamed the White House was himself. *"Tom, it's time for us to dust off our golf clubs and leave the jury trials and gall bladder surgeries to the youngsters."* Tom had laughed again, but Bill's face had turned grave. *"Seriously, old man. That ruckus in Pulaski nearly killed you. I'm afraid that the next trial will."*

"Tom." Nancy's voice broke through his reflections and he looked down into her concerned eyes. "Didn't Dr.—?"

"Yes," Tom interrupted. "He did. Look, Rick will be back soon. He just needs some time, and I can handle things while he's gone."

Nancy started to say something else, but Jackson's excited voice mercifully interrupted her.

"Hey, Papa. I have another game next Friday night. It's against Bankowski. They have the best record in the league."

Tom ruffled the boy's thick brown hair. "Unless I'm in court late that day, I'll be there, Forty-Nine."

Jackson smiled, showing off a small gap in his front teeth. The boy would probably have braces soon.

"Thanks for my slow cones, Papa." Jenny had grabbed his hand with both of hers, which weren't sticky anymore after she washed them at the restaurant. He picked the child up and kissed both cheeks. "Anytime, Jenny girl." As he placed her down on the cobblestone driveway, he winced as another shot of pain ran down his back.

Glancing at Nancy, he saw her smile change to admonishment. "Did you not get it x-rayed?"

Tom didn't immediately answer. He was growing frustrated at the motherly way in which his daughter-in-law was treating him but didn't want to end the night in a bad way. Finally, he sighed and smiled down at her. "Tell Tommy I'm sorry I missed him and that I'll come by for an X-ray next trip or I'll get Bill to do it. With the funeral and all, I just couldn't fit it in this time."

She started to protest but then leaned in and pecked his cheek. "Tommy hated that he was swamped with procedures this week. But with his partners both out—"

"He's an orthopedic surgeon," Tom said, feeling his chest swell. "He was doing his job, and I'm proud of him for it." Then he moved his eyes from Nancy down to Jackson and, finally, little Jenny. "Love y'all."

The harmonious "Love you, Papa" was drowned out by the door to the Explorer slamming shut as Tom climbed in and turned the ignition.

As he backed out, he waved at the three and watched as Jackson ran down the driveway to check the mailbox, giving Tom one last gap-toothed smile before he opened the slot. Tom smiled back and waited until the boy had disappeared into the garage before he put the car in gear.

By the time he reached the end of the street, the sadness had set back in.

6

At 9:55 a.m. the next morning, Tom rode the elevator to the second floor of the Tuscaloosa County Courthouse with a bustle of other attorneys all going to the same place: Judge Poe's status docket. He had heard these hearings referred to as "cattle calls," and the name fit. As he and the other suited-up warriors poured into the courtroom, it was hard for a farmer's son like Tom not to think of cattle being herded into a pen.

Tom sidestepped and elbowed his way toward the front, nodding and exchanging pleasantries with numerous former students along the way. "Mornin', Professor." "How you doing, Professor?" "Whatcha got today, Professor?" Tom replied to every inquiry, proud to see faces that he'd once instructed in class now engaged in real-life litigation.

He took a seat in the second row of the gallery next to one of the only lawyers in the courtroom older than he was. "Well, look what the cat dragged in," the other man said, standing and extending his hand.

Tom smiled and shook hands. "Rufus, what brings you to Tuscaloosa?"

William Rufus Cole was the oldest board member of the University of Alabama School of Law and the founding partner of Cole & Cole, a family-run law firm in Choctaw County, a good two hours away. Rufus liked to brag that there had been a Cole practicing law in Alabama since the turn of the century. He and Tom had been friends and colleagues for over four decades, and when Tom was a professor at the law school, he considered Rufus his strongest ally on the board. Rufus grimaced and nodded toward the bench. "I sent my son to cover the last docket with this ornery son of a bitch, and little Rufus got dressed down and lost a motion we should have won. This is our only case in Tuscaloosa County, and it's a big one. A father and son from Butler were coming back from the Arkansas game last year and got T-boned at the intersection of Skyland and McFarland. Dad dead and son paralyzed for life. So from here on out, Poe gets to see my ugly mug." Rufus paused and smacked his lips. As the bailiff entered the courtroom with the judge right on his heels, Tom and Rufus remained standing as the familiar words rang out over the courtroom: "ALL RISE."

Tom took his seat and heard hot breath whispering in his ear. *"You know, I used to think that son of a bitch just had it in for young lawyers,"* Rufus said.

"And now?" Tom raised his eyebrows at his old friend, and Rufus gazed up at the bench.

"Now, I just think he hates everyone."

The Honorable Braxton Winfield Poe was a short, round man of sixty, who for as long as Tom had known him, which was over thirty years, had had a full head of silver hair cut in a military-style crew cut. Even when Poe was one of Tom's first Evidence students in the early '70s, his hair was already prematurely gray and always trimmed like a Marine's. He wore bifocals that rested on the tip of his nose, and his raspy, cigarette-scarred voice was a consistent mixture of irritation and impatience that bordered on contempt. He had the habit of calling all attorneys under forty "young lawyer," and it wasn't a term of endearment. Being older than the man, Tom himself had never endured one of Poe's "young lawyer" tantrums, but he'd heard former students tell war stories about being dressed down in much the same way Rufus's son had been.

The judge peered over the bench with cold, dead eyes. "I'm going to call your case, and if it is ready for trial, you say 'Trial.' If it's not ready, say 'Pass.' If you have a motion you want me to rule on, then ask to approach and I'll consider it, but let me warn you that I don't like having the court's time wasted with pissant discovery disputes that you should be able to work out on your own." He paused and cleared his throat. "If you say the case is ready for trial, then I'm going to set a trial date, but I'm also going to enter an order for mediation. I don't want to hear your whining about how your case has no chance to settle. All civil suits filed in this courtroom go to mediation. Now . . ." He snatched a stapled stack of paper, which Tom knew was the docket showing the list of cases, and peered down at it through his spectacles. "*Atkins v. Brewer.*"

A female attorney in the row in front of Tom stood up. "P-pass, Judge."

"Speak up, young lawyer. I can't hear you."

"Pass, Judge."

"*Beech v. Reynolds.*"

A high-pitched male voice in the back rang out. "Pass, Judge."

Tom wondered how many clients from all over the state would be paying thousands of dollars in billable hours for their lawyer or, God forbid, lawyers to drive to Tuscaloosa and say two words. He forced back a smirk as he eyed Braxton Poe. This was the part of the practice of law that Tom could do without, and, unfortunately, he was seeing more and more of it with his partner out of the office.

For the next forty-five minutes, over a hundred cases were called, with the majority response being "Pass" and only a handful of attorneys saying "Trial."

Tom didn't want his matter to be the first one up for motion, but alas, as he heard Poe's raspy voice call out "*Simpson v. JPS Van Lines,*" Tom winced and stood from his seat. When he did, a shot of pain ran down his back all the way to his leg, which he realized was half-asleep. "Judge, we're ready for trial, but we also have a pending motion. May we approach?"

Poe glared at Tom from his perch on the bench and sighed loud enough for everyone in the courtroom to hear. "Alright then," he said, motioning with a quick flick of his right index finger for the attorneys to come forward.

Tom walked toward the front of the courtroom and placed his briefcase on one of the counsel tables. By this point in the docket, the tables were vacant, as the previously packed courtroom was now less than a quarter full. Before addressing the court, he waited for opposing counsel.

Jameson Tyler, attorney for JPS Van Lines, strode toward the front with two young associates flanking him. At almost fifty years old, Jameson was the managing partner of Jones & Butler, the largest law firm in the state of Alabama. He wore a charcoal-gray suit, white shirt, and red power tie and broke into a toothy grin as he extended his hand. "Professor, how are you doing?"

"Jameson," Tom said, nodding at the man and grasping his hand in a firm grip. "Did you bring some reinforcements today?" Tom smiled at the two lawyers behind Jameson. Annie Gipson had been on one of Tom's last trial teams at Alabama, and Coulter Bowman had been in two of his Evidence classes. They both offered their hands and gave him a nervous smile.

"I always like to have some muscle with me when I'm dealing with you," Jameson said, slapping Tom on the back as he brushed past him toward the bench.

Tom gasped as a shot of pain radiated down his shoulder.

"Are you OK, Professor?" Annie asked, touching his arm. Her ebony face softened and her brown eyes registered concern.

"I'm fine, Annie," he managed, gritting his teeth. "Just old." Tom forced a smile and then took a position to the left of Tyler in front of the pulpit. He gazed up at the judge as Jameson asked, "Your Honor, how are you?"

Poe grunted. "I'd be better if your opponent would save evidentiary issues for the pretrial hearing." He squinted down at Tom. "McMurtrie, why are you filing a motion to exclude at this point? If we weren't already having a status conference today, I would have denied your motion without oral argument." Of all the judges and lawyers in the state of Alabama, Poe was the only one who routinely addressed Tom as "McMurtrie." His old friends like Rufus called him "Tom," and the others typically deferred to Tom's years of service to the university by calling him either "Professor" or "Professor McMurtrie."

But not Braxton Poe. The slight bothered Tom more than it probably should have. Despite his admonition to his trial team members over the years to "never let them see you sweat," he had difficulty following this rule with Poe, who, as Rufus had so eloquently stated, was an "ornery son of a bitch." But Tom knew that Poe's feelings toward him went deeper than simple ill temper. Poe was carrying around a thirty-year grudge.

"Well . . ." Tom said, forcing himself to keep his cool, though he could feel his adrenaline charging up. "Timing is everything, right?"

"So let me see if I understand," Poe said, ignoring the rhetorical question and smiling without humor. "This is a car wreck case. Your client, McMurtrie, was driving to soccer practice and hit the driver working for Mr. Tyler's client at the intersection of Hackberry and Paul Bryant Drive. She was high on marijuana at the time of the collision, and you want me to exclude the evidence of the pot. That about cover it?"

"Not exactly, Judge," Tom said, keeping his tone measured. "My client is Grace Simpson, a seventeen-year-old senior at Tuscaloosa High, who had a lacrosse scholarship to the university. She was traveling on Hackberry and entered the intersection on a green light. The driver for JPS was going fifty-five in a forty and plowed through the red light, hitting Grace's Honda Civic on the driver's side. Grace was rushed by ambulance to Druid City Hospital, where doctors fought to save her. They succeeded, but she will be paralyzed for the rest of her life. During the first night of her hospitalization, a urine sample was taken, which indicated a minuscule amount of cannabis in her system. During her deposition, Grace testified that she had tried a synthetic marijuana cigarette for the first time in her life a week prior to the accident while pulling an all-nighter to study for two final exams. My expert toxicologist, Dr. Patricia Walsh, was deposed last month, and she testified that the amount of cannabis found in Grace's system was nominal and would in no way have impaired her ability to drive her vehicle on the day of the accident. Dr. Walsh also testified that a blood sample is the preferred test to determined cannabis toxicity and that a urine test was untrustworthy. Mr. Tyler's retained expert, Dr. Wendell Brooks, is a pharmacist, who is not qualified to give an opinion on toxicity, and, even if he was qualified, Dr. Brooks only testified *it was possible*, not probable, that the marijuana present in Grace's urine could have impaired her driving. As set out in our brief, pursuant to Rule 702 of the Alabama Rules of Evidence and the

Daubert standard, Dr. Brooks's expert testimony should be excluded, as it would not aid the jury in any way. Also, any relevance attached to these urine results would be greatly outweighed by the prejudice to Grace." Tom paused. "The motion is due to be granted, Judge, and there is no rule of civil procedure that precludes an exclusionary motion at this juncture."

Poe turned his head to Jameson. "Response?"

"Yes, Your Honor," Jameson said, again flashing his patented toothy grin. "Any issues that Tom has with Dr. Brooks's qualifications and opinions should go to the weight of the testimony, not its admissibility. Further, I agree with Your Honor that this issue would be better reserved for the pretrial hearing after discovery has been completed."

"Anything else?" Poe asked, looking back at Tom.

"No, Your Honor."

"Good. Then I'm going to deny the motion at this time." He paused and looked at a laptop computer to his left. "My first available civil trial docket is January 28, 2013, so I'll set this case for trial then. The pretrial hearing will be January 21, and mediation is to be attempted on or before December 31, 2012." He paused and looked at Tom. "If you want to refile your motion prior to the pretrial, I'll be glad to reconsider it, but I doubt my ruling will be any different." Looking down at his docket sheet, he added, "You should find an order in your email inbox this afternoon setting out these rulings, Counselors. I would urge both parties to try to settle this matter at mediation. A case like this should be resolved without wasting the court's resources."

Poe leaned toward the microphone. *"Grissom v. Savona."*

From behind him, Tom heard a woman's voice say, "Pass, Judge." He glared at Poe, trying to comprehend what the man, a former student of Tom's, had just said. Finally, he asked him. "Judge Poe, did you just say you didn't want to waste the court's resources by *trying a case?*"

Braxton Poe returned Tom's glare with one of his own. He placed both hands on the bench and leaned over it. "That's *exactly* what I just said."

"I thought so," Tom said, holding the man's gaze until Poe finally broke away. Tom gathered up his briefcase and walked slowly down the middle of the courtroom. Behind him, Poe's voice rang out even louder and raspier. *"Helstowski v. Birmingham Steel."*

"Pass, Judge," Tom whispered the refrain he knew was coming as he stepped through the double doors.

7

As Tom came off the elevator on the lobby level of the courthouse, he found an unwelcome visitor waiting for him. "Stick around to rub it in," Tom said, walking past Jameson toward the exit sign.

Without missing a beat, Jameson caught up and walked in stride with Tom out of the courthouse and into the midmorning sun. "Win some, lose some, Professor. You know that." He chuckled. "I do seem to be winning more of these skirmishes in front of Poe than in other courtrooms."

At the bottom of the steps, Tom stopped. He was tired from the two-and-a-half-hour drive that morning and his back still ached from Jameson's pat in the courtroom. He turned to face his former student. "Is there something on your mind?"

Jameson Tyler had been one of his favorite pupils, and for many years Tom considered him to be a good friend. But that all changed two years ago when Jameson became chief counsel to the university and assisted the law school in removing Tom as professor. Though Tom was eventually offered his job back and Jameson apologized for his role in the coup, the sting of the betrayal remained. Subconsciously,

Tom knew it was one of the reasons why he had rejected the school's offer to return. That and his desire to try cases again.

"Did you hear about Jack Willistone?"

Tom blinked as he remembered the text he received from Powell the night before at the ball game. He still owed the district attorney a call. "Yeah, I did hear. Are you speaking at the funeral?" Jameson had represented Jack Willistone in Tom's first trial back as an attorney two years earlier.

Jameson laughed. "Not hardly, Professor. That old cowboy deserved whatever came to him. If he hadn't tampered with the witnesses in Henshaw and just let me do my thing, we would have won."

Tom smiled. "You keep thinking that, Jameson."

As he started to walk away, he heard Jameson's voice behind him. "Poe's ruling on the marijuana changes things, Professor, and you know it. I have authority of a hundred fifty thousand dollars to settle the case today and we can avoid mediation and trial. What do you say?"

Tom looked over his shoulder but didn't stop walking. "We'll take the policy limits or let a jury decide. We both know I'll get any adverse verdict overturned on appeal if the marijuana comes in."

"Rolling the dice on appeal is a fool's errand, Professor."

Tom stopped and placed his hands on his hips. He gazed back at Jameson and shook his head, pointing an index finger at the court-house. "Maybe so. But I'll be damned if I'm going to let that SOB dictate how I litigate a case. Regardless of the poison that spews out of Braxton's mouth, the purpose of the courtroom is to try cases, not to force settlements. What's the matter with you, Jameson? I thought you liked to tee it up."

Before the other lawyer could respond, a baby-blue convertible BMW pulled to the curb beside him. Coulter jumped out of the back seat and grabbed Jameson's briefcase. Behind the wheel, Annie gave Tom a tentative wave. He nodded at her but was perturbed by the scene. Three lawyers attending a status conference, and some crazy insurance company was paying for it. Jameson walked around the rear of the BMW and gave the license tag a love tap with the palm of his hand. Tom glanced down and saw the personalized inscription "BIG CAT."

"I didn't get that nickname settling cases, Professor," Jameson said, chuckling. "I love to tee it up, but I'm not a dinosaur. The courthouses in this state are overflowing, and judges are pushing lawyers to settle." He shrugged. "Clients are too. I'll deny this if you repeat it, but my company would be just as happy to settle for one-fifty now as they would to pay me and my team the same or more to get a defense verdict in a few months. What does Coach Saban say? It is what it is."

Tom gritted his teeth as another stab of pain went down his back. "Maybe so, but unless your client pays the limits, we're going to verdict on this one."

Jameson flashed his teeth one last time with a grin that had seduced over a hundred juries. "I'll look forward to it." He opened the door, but before climbing in, the grin faded and he gazed at Tom with what appeared to be sincerity. "If you're gonna keep doing this, Professor, you have to roll with the times. You remember what happened to the dinosaurs, don't you?"

Before Tom could say anything in response, Jameson slid into the car, and the convertible slithered forward. For a few seconds, Tom watched it, wondering if his evidence courses and trial team instruction had been worth anything to a generation of lawyers that would hardly, if ever, see a jury foreman stand up to render a verdict. Had he accomplished anything in all those years?

As he trudged toward his Explorer, he had the awful feeling that Jameson might be right. Maybe the profession had passed him by, and before long he, too, would be extinct. He flung his briefcase in the back seat and thought about the mountain of paper that awaited him at the office and the phone call he owed Powell.

Thomas Jackson McMurtrie yawned as he turned the key and the vehicle roared to life. Closing his eyes, he gripped the wheel and resolved that the office and telephone would have to wait. *This dinosaur needs a nap . . .*

8

Tom awoke to hot, foul breath on his face and a damp coarseness on his cheek. Opening his eyes, he gazed into the wrinkled face and flat nose of his only housemate.

Lee Roy Jordan McMurtrie was a two-year-old white-and-brown English bulldog that weighed close to sixty pounds. Tom tried to push him away, to no avail. The dog was too heavy and persistent. Lee Roy leaned in, sniffing Tom's face, neck, and arms before planting his tongue against Tom's cheek for another kiss.

Tom looked at the clock on the bedside table. 8:17 p.m. He had slept a full eight hours when he had only intended to have a catnap. He sighed and propped himself on his elbows, trying to wake up. As the last vestiges of a dreamless sleep left him, he rolled to one side and swung his legs to the floor. When he did, Lee Roy put both paws in his lap and licked his face again. Tom grabbed the dog around the neck and gave a squeeze. "Alright, you win. I'm up."

While Lee Roy waited impatiently by the bed, Tom used the bathroom and washed his hands and face. As he grabbed a towel to dry off, he gazed at the mirror above the sink and ran his index finger along a faint quarter-inch scar on his right cheek—the last remnant from the attack in Pulaski. Though he was able to shave now, which was a relief, as he never liked wearing a beard, the scar still occasionally stung if the wind hit it just right or if he began to sweat on a hot day or during a workout. *Could've been worse,* he knew, squinting at the mark on his face as his mind drifted back to Pulaski. *Much worse . . .*

Tom took a step back from the mirror and straightened his pants and shirt, which he'd been too tired to take off when he'd gotten home. Then, knowing that more sleep would be impossible after such a long nap, he walked back into the bedroom and grabbed his keys off the top of the dresser. As he strode down the hallway with Lee Roy tight on his heels, he looked down at the dog and smiled. "You want to take a ride, boy?"

The law firm was located on a side street off of Greensboro Avenue, a couple blocks from the Tuscaloosa County Courthouse. Tom parked the Explorer in the lot in front of the office and grabbed a sack of food he'd picked up at a drive-through. Keeping Lee Roy away from the grub had been a chore for the remainder of the trip, but it was worth the fight. Tom was famished and looked forward to getting his fix when he got inside. He stepped out of the vehicle and waited as Lee Roy scurried from the passenger's side over the driver's seat and down to the ground. Per his routine when Tom took him to the office, the dog peed on the fire hydrant adjacent to the lone light pole. Tom couldn't help but chuckle as he followed behind. Piss on this, Tom often thought to himself. Then he imagined Lee Roy relieving himself on the Honorable Braxton Poe's leg, and his chuckle turned to a full-fledged laugh.

Tom stopped before entering the breezeway and gazed up at the black letters that adorned the second floor of the two-story brick building: "McMurtrie & Drake, LLC."

The office wasn't flashy by any stretch. In fact, some clients had a hard time finding it. But Tom thought the obscure location added to the office's charm and, despite the success the firm had achieved in the last twenty-four months, Tom did not want to move. He enjoyed thinking of his partnership with Rick Drake as a hidden treasure similar to Archibald's Barbecue, in Northport, which Tom still had a difficult time finding even though he'd been there hundreds of times. If you wanted the best pork sandwich in town, you were willing to dig around for it. Tom hoped the same held true for legal advice.

The ground floor of the building was occupied by Larry and Barry's Interior Design, a successful company formed by two gay lovers from Missouri, Larry Horowitz and Barry Bostheimer. When Rick had initially leased the space, which was before forming the partnership with Tom, he had gotten his first few referrals from Larry and Barry, who had both been very supportive and continued to be so.

At this time of night, Larry and Barry had long since closed shop, and Tom knew his secretary and receptionist, Frankie Callahan, would be gone too. The space should be quiet, which was exactly what he wanted.

When he reached the stairwell—there was still no elevator, but the owner would be installing one soon—he flipped on the light and began to trudge up the steps. As he felt the first twinge of pain in his back since waking up, his thoughts returned to the status conference that morning. The sting of losing the motion and Judge Poe's indignance toward him was still fresh, and sleep had done nothing to ease his worry that maybe Jameson was right. Maybe the legal profession was starting to pass him by.

Tom's thoughts were mercifully interrupted when he almost tripped over Lee Roy, who had stopped dead still halfway up the stairs. Catching his balance, Tom groaned as another pang knifed into his right side. He started to scold the dog, but Lee Roy's growl drowned him out.

"Aren't there leash laws in this town?"

Tom's eyes darted up the stairs toward the voice as Lee Roy again growled below him. A girl was sitting on the top step. She wore a houndstooth cap with a red *A*, so it was hard to see her face.

"Yes, I suppose there are. But at this time of night I didn't expect to have any visitors, and it is hard walking up these stairs with Lee Roy here." He paused and took another step up so that he was even with his dog. "What can I do for you, young lady?"

"Where have you been all day? I waited inside for three hours, and your secretary said she expected you in this afternoon."

"I was unavoidably detained," Tom said, smiling and continuing up the steps, with Lee Roy walking in tow. The dog wasn't growling anymore, but his body shook with adrenaline. As he approached, the girl stood and crossed her arms over her chest. When she did, Tom noticed that she was carrying a backpack over her shoulders. *Teenager,* he thought.

"Does he bite?" the girl asked, glancing down at Lee Roy.

Tom chortled and dug his keys out of his pocket. He petted Lee Roy behind the ears and looked up at her. "He shouldn't, but . . . all the same, I'd probably leave him alone if I were you, and I would advise against any quick, jerky motions."

She smiled and Tom could tell that, under the cap, there was an attractive young lady. "You never answered my question," Tom said, putting the key in the lock and turning. "What can I do for you?"

As the door swung open, the girl took her hat off, and her dirty-blond hair fell over her shoulders. She looked at him with brown eyes that had squinted into slits.

Sixteen, Tom guessed. *Maybe younger.*

"My momma needs a lawyer, and I want you to represent her."

Now it was Tom's eyes that wrinkled as he stood in the doorway. "Pardon me for asking, but how old are you, Ms. . . . ?"

"Newton," the girl said. "My name is Laurie Ann Newton, and I'm fourteen years old. It is nice to finally meet you, Professor McMurtrie." She extended her hand.

Tom felt a tickle run down the hair of his arms as he shook the girl's hand and considered her brown eyes. *Newton . . .*

"Are you—?"

"I'm Dewey Newton's daughter." A trace of defiance had snuck into her tone. "The truck driver that was killed in the wreck in Henshaw three years ago. You and your partner were the lawyers for the family that was killed. You sued Daddy's company, Willistone Trucking, and got ninety million dollars. It was all over the internet and TV." Her voice had turned bitter. "Big hero. *The Professor* rides into court again and saves the day."

Tom blinked down at the girl. "Then that makes your mother . . . Wilma Newton." Tom would never forget that name.

"Yes, sir, it does. I bet you remember her well."

Tom nodded.

"I've read the transcript of the whole trial. Your cross-examination of Momma was the first time you'd said anything in the case. The transcript doesn't mention why you were late getting there."

"It's a long story," Tom said.

"Whatever," she said, rolling her eyes. "Anyway, you tore Momma a new one. Exposed her as Willistone's whore, which turned the tide of the case. Am I right? Have I gotten anything wrong yet, Professor?"

Tom blinked his eyes and rubbed the back of his neck. He had forgotten about the sack of food he held in his left hand. Glancing down, he saw that Lee Roy was looking at him, as if he, too, were waiting on Tom's response.

"I don't remember anything about your mother being a . . ." He paused, trying to think of a kinder word. "Prostitute."

"Oh come off it, old man. I've read the transcript. Hell, I've memorized the damn thing." She placed her hands on her hips and looked at the side wall of the stairwell. "'Ms. Newton, didn't you spend several hours in the VIP room at the Sundowners Club two weeks ago with Jack Willistone and the man sitting behind him in the courtroom?'" She turned her eyes back to Tom. "Remember asking Momma that question? Did I get that about right?"

She had, Tom knew. The impression was spot-on. Then he wondered how a fourteen-year-old girl had managed to obtain the transcript to a two-year-old trial. Of course, the better question was why.

"I was only trying to insinuate to the jury that your mother had been given a financial benefit to change her story. She had originally told my partner that your father's driving schedules were crazy and forced him to speed. Then, at trial, she changed her tune. I was showing her potential bias."

"Whatever," Laurie Ann said. "Sounded to me like you were calling her a whore." She paused. "And hey, it worked, right? Ninety million dollars. Woo-hoo." She let her eyes dart around the stairwell. "Seems like you guys could tidy up your digs a little with all that money. Maybe get an elevator, you think?" Without hesitation, she leaned down and petted Lee Roy behind his neck. Tom bent to stop her, but then the dog began wagging his tail.

For a few seconds there was silence in the dimly lit stairwell as Tom watched the girl pet his dog. "What happened to your mother after the trial?" he finally asked.

Laurie Ann snorted. "Her life went to hell in a handbasket. We were living in Tuscaloosa when Daddy died. After the accident, we moved to Boone's Hill, Tennessee, and rented a house from Ms. Yost, one of my grandmother's old friends. Momma had grown up in Boone's Hill when she was a kid." Laurie Ann sighed and took a seat on the top step, continuing to pet Lee Roy under his ears. "It wasn't so bad at first. Momma took a waitressing gig at the Sands and Jackie and me . . ." She paused. "My sister's name is Jackie. We started going to school at Ralph Askins Elementary, in Fayetteville, and we were doing OK. It was tough. We missed Daddy a lot. But we were making it. Then . . ." She stopped and looked up at him. "You know the rest, don't you?"

Tom shook his head. He didn't. Once he had cross-examined Wilma Newton, he had barely thought of her again. Gazing down at the broken girl below him, he felt guilt wash over him.

"Anyway, she started working at the Sundowners Club, that strip joint you crossed her about at trial. She was a dancer and began to do a few other things for money." Her voice cracked. "She left us with Ms. Yost for almost a week when the case in Henshaw was tried. During that time, Ms. Yost turned us in to DHR." She glared down at the wooden steps. "That woman told me that Momma was a prostitute and that we would be better off under the state's protection. For the next five months, we lived at the Lincoln County child protective services facility, with its spotty air-conditioning, moldy floors, and bland, tasteless food. Finally, around Thanksgiving of 2010, Momma's cousin Tawny said she'd take us in, and so we moved back with her to Tuscaloosa to live with her and her husband, Sam, in their double-wide trailer." She looked up at Tom. "And Momma went to jail."

"Where was she incarcerated?" Tom asked. As pain again rippled down his back, Tom almost started to invite her in the office, but his instincts told him not to interrupt the flow of the conversation. Instead, he squatted and sat next to Laurie Ann on the steps. Lee Roy had placed his chin in the girl's lap and she continued to rub his ears.

"The Giles County Jail in Pulaski."

Tom thought about it. Since the Sundowners Club was in Giles County, that made sense. "Was there a trial?"

Laurie Ann shook her head. "No, Momma just pled guilty. She didn't even put up a fight. She said she couldn't. She said that me and Jackie might be hurt if she tried to defend herself."

"Did she have a lawyer?"

"No. She said she didn't want one." She paused and looked at Tom. "She said that lawyers had never done anything for her and that she would just take her medicine."

Tom gazed back at Laurie Ann Newton. He thought about the cattle call docket he'd attended in front of Judge Poe that morning. So many lawyers, most of whom had been taught by him, wearing their suits and carrying their briefcases and announcing to the court that their case wasn't ready to be tried. All of them standing before a judge, also a student of Tom's, who seemed intent on forcing litigants into unwanted settlements instead of doing his job. And here was this girl, all of fourteen years old, who, along with her mother and sister, could have desperately used some sound legal assistance during the nightmare they had endured the last two years, but the mother was so distrustful of lawyers and the system that she chose to go it alone. *Do I blame her?* Tom thought, feeling sick to his stomach. "I'm sorry," he finally said. Then he added in a soft voice, "Why does your mother need an attorney now?"

Laurie Ann smiled, but her eyes were sad. "You haven't figured it out yet?"

Tom cocked his head at her, not understanding. "No."

She sighed and rose to her feet, looking down at him. The smile was gone. "Jack Willistone was murdered two nights ago. The online article I read said his body was found on the banks of the Black Warrior."

Tom felt a cold chill run down his spine as he remembered the text he had received from Powell at Jackson's ball game.

I really need to talk with you about the suspect we have in custody.

"*Wilma . . . Newton* is the suspect," he said, almost to himself, as he glanced down at the steps, still not quite believing it.

For several seconds, the only sound in the stairwell was Lee Roy's panting. Then Laurie Ann cleared her throat and asked the question that Tom knew was coming.

"Professor McMurtrie, will you please be Momma's lawyer?"

9

The gun that killed Jack Willistone was a nine-millimeter Smith & Wesson. It was more than twenty years old and, based on an investigation of the serial number, had last been purchased in a pawn shop in Fayetteville, Tennessee.

The registered owner of the weapon was Wilma Christine Newton.

The medical examiner had stated that the bullets found in the victim's sternum were the type utilized by a Smith & Wesson nine-millimeter, as were the shell casings found on Greg Zorn's dock. She was still waiting on the ballistics report, but Ingrid had no doubts on what the conclusion would be. "This is the murder weapon," she'd said, pointing at the gun through the clear plastic covering. "I'd stake my reputation on it."

Fingerprint analysis showed that the gun had three prints on the handle, all matching samples taken from Wilma Newton. There were no other prints on the weapon.

Powell Conrad gazed down at the pistol held in an evidence bag at the end of the conference room table. Then he raised his head and looked through the plexiglass window at the suspect.

Wilma Newton's clothes had been taken for testing, so she now wore the orange jumpsuit of a Tuscaloosa County Jail inmate. She sat in a plastic chair and leaned her elbows on a small rectangular table made of faux wood. Two empty chairs sat across from her, which Powell and Wade had just abandoned after Wilma again said she wouldn't talk with them. They were now standing side by side in the adjoining room, watching her through the glass partition.

Finally, Wade cleared his throat and took a sip of black coffee from a tall Styrofoam cup. He spoke in a low drawl. "It's almost been forty-eight hours, hoss. We need to fish or cut bait. We can't hold her here forever."

Powell grunted, still gazing through the plexiglass. He had wanted to talk with the Professor before making the arrest, but despite several texts, his mentor had not called him back. *He must have a good reason,* Powell knew. Still, this would be his first high-profile case as district attorney and he wanted the benefit of the Professor's advice.

"Can you think of any reason not to charge her?" Powell asked, as much to himself as Wade.

"No," Wade said without hesitation. "I can't. The murder weapon was registered to her, only has her prints, and was found underneath the dock where Willistone was murdered."

Powell turned from the window and began to walk alongside the table, where photographs of the weapon had been organized side by side. He shook his head and grunted.

"Based on my investigation, no witness can provide her with an alibi for the time of the murder," Wade continued. "And Willistone's cell phone records show she was the last person to communicate with him."

"What about motive?" Powell asked.

Wade turned from the window. "Revenge. Her husband was killed driving a Willistone truck. After his death, she moved to Boone's Hill, Tennessee, became a stripper, and was convicted of prostitution. She lost custody of her girls and had moved back to Tuscaloosa after being released to be closer to them." He paused. "Add it all up and she blamed Willistone for ruining her life."

"That's weak," Powell said, continuing to look at the photographs, thinking it through. "She testified for Willistone in the trial. She was on his side. She said that Willistone treated his drivers well."

"I thought you said that was all a lie." Wade pulled on his mustache. "Your first reaction at the river when hearing her name was that she fit for the crime, because you think Willistone either bought her off or blackmailed her during that trial."

"I know, and I do think that. But I can't prove any of it in court. It's too messy. Do we have anything else?"

Wade shook his head. "Not right now, but I'm still digging."

"I want more." Powell paused and then he snapped his fingers, remembering something else he'd wanted to ask. "Have there been any breaks at the Riverwalk?" As part of the investigation, Wade had sent a team of deputies to comb the four-mile walking trail that ran parallel to the Black Warrior, focusing special attention on the Park at Manderson Landing, which was directly across the water from Greg Zorn's dock. Flyers had been strategically placed on trees and at the gazebo where the bathrooms were located asking for any information that anyone had about the murder.

"We found a pair of panties."

Powell raised his eyebrows. "What?"

"Women's underwear," Wade said. "Pink lace. Nice. We found them lying by one of the benches closest to the railing."

Powell couldn't help but smile. "Now how do you figure that, Detective?"

"Well . . ." He held out his arms. "Being the hardened crime solver I am, I'd say that a couple of coeds were likely engaged in sexual activity on one of these benches and maybe had to leave sooner than they wanted to leave. One of them forgot her underwear."

"You're good, Richey. Someday you're gonna make captain."

"Bite me," Wade said, smoothing out his mustache and squinting at his friend from across the room. "Look, I'll get more on motive and we'll keep pressing the Riverwalk, but what's the deal? I've seen you charge on a lot less than this and win. Outside of a signed confession, what more do we need, brother?"

Powell grunted and watched Wilma, who had begun to rub her temples with her thumbs. "Jack Willistone had a lot of enemies. You said it at the river, and it's true. You remember how we nabbed JimBone Wheeler, don't you?" Powell glanced at Wade, who nodded.

"Willistone," Powell continued, gazing down at his shoes. "When me and the Professor interviewed Willistone at the St. Clair Correctional Facility, we obtained information that led us right to Wheeler."

"Correct me if I'm wrong, but JimBone Wheeler is sitting on death row in Nashville. There's no way on earth that he could've killed Jack Willistone on the Black Warrior River three nights ago."

Powell nodded. "Still, Jack had enemies, and JimBone was pretty resourceful. And what about Willistone's family?"

"What about them?"

"Is his wife clean?"

"As a whistle. Kathryn Willistone has an airtight alibi. Was out at Pepito's with a couple of her girlfriends. Probably on her third margarita when Jack bought the farm."

"How much does she stand to gain from his death in life insurance?"

"Three million dollars."

Powell whistled. "Then I'd say she has motive out the yin yang."

"She has an alibi and her fingerprints aren't all over the murder weapon that's registered to that lady in there, whose prints *are* on it." Wade pointed at the window, his frustration palpable.

"If she's got an alibi, then what about her father?" Powell crossed his arms and glared at Wade. "What about Bully Calhoun, brother? Does he have an alibi? I'm sure you know who that is."

Wade crossed his arms as well, holding Powell's eye. "I know Bully, and he's as dirty as a pig in a pen. I don't know whether Bully has an alibi or not. He wasn't at the Willistone house when I interviewed Kathryn. He had already gone back to Jasper."

"But he had been up here, right? Wasn't he the one who picked Jack up at the prison?"

Wade held out his palms and finally smiled. "Look, I get it. Whoever represents Newton will have some avenues to explore, but the bottom line is that the gun that killed Jack Willistone belonged to that lady in there. Her prints are the only ones on it and she was the last person to talk with Jack. She's guilty of his murder, and it's time to charge."

With his arms still folded, Powell began to pace back and forth along the side of the table. After four trips, he stopped and put both hands on the plexiglass, looking again at Wilma Newton. "Alright," Powell said. "Let's charge her."

Wade gave a quick nod and headed for the door. "I'll start drafting up the paperwork." When he grabbed the knob, he looked over his shoulder. "According to his wife, Jack was supposed to have at least three hundred dollars in his wallet, and it was empty except for his license. His vehicle, which was parked in Zorn's garage, was looted of everything in the glove compartment, and a briefcase that should have been in the back seat or the trunk has not been located. With robbery as a clear aggravator, are we going to—?"

"Yes," Powell interrupted, sighing and still gazing at the soon-to-be defendant. "We'll have to seek the death penalty."

10

Tom parked in the visitor's section of the Tuscaloosa County Jail at ten o'clock in the morning. His eyes burned from lack of sleep and his back ached from working through most of the night, but he was alert and on edge. He had promised Laurie Ann Newton that he would talk to her mother. That was all he had promised, and he was going to follow through before he talked himself out of it.

After Laurie Ann left the office—Tom offered her a lift home, but she said she already had a ride—he'd made a pot of coffee and tried to eat his drive-through meal. But the fix he was hoping for didn't come; his talk with the young girl had caused him to lose his appetite. He fired up the computer and dug around on the internet for any articles on Wilma, but thus far the only news he'd found was that a suspect was in custody. The name had not been released. Tom then read over the stories regarding the death of Jack Willistone. His body was found on the banks of the Black Warrior River, and the presumed cause of death was a gunshot wound. Most of the articles dealt with Willistone's rise to stardom as the largest trucking magnate in the Southeast and then his downfall after the trial in Henshaw two years earlier. Tom saw his own name mentioned several times as the lawyer who exposed Willistone's crimes. There were also several references to the county's new district attorney, Powell Conrad, who had made the arrest in Henshaw.

As Tom trudged toward the entrance to the jail, a sense of guilt crept into his veins. He had not called Powell about the "suspect" the state had in custody, despite his former student's multiple texts. And Powell was more than just a former student. He was Tom's partner's best friend. *He's my friend too.*

Since his return to the practice of law, Tom had yet to oppose someone close to him. Conflict was bound to happen; friends litigated against each other in conference rooms and courtrooms all over the state. *But this is different,* Tom knew. It felt like a betrayal. *Why in the hell am I doing this?* Tom asked himself as he grabbed the door handle and pulled it open.

The answer lay in the broken eyes and voice of a fourteen-year-old girl who up until twelve hours ago Tom hadn't known existed.

Tom sighed and approached a reception window with steel bars. *All I'm going to do is talk with her,* he told himself as he noticed a plump woman speaking on a telephone. She held up a finger for him to wait, and Tom glanced around, realizing that in over forty years as a lawyer and law professor he had only been to the Tuscaloosa County Jail a handful of times, the most recent visit over ten years ago during a workshop for the law school. The place hadn't changed much, offering up a burgundy leather bench with a tear in the middle and several plastic chairs. The floor was a dusty white and black tile. Suffice it to say, the layout and furniture wouldn't be making any editions of *Southern Living.*

"Can I help you?" The woman's voice was raspy, reminding Tom of Judge Braxton Poe.

"Yes, ma'am. I'm here to see a suspect you have in custody. Wilma Newton."

The woman looked Tom up and down. He was glad that he had taken the time to drive Lee Roy home this morning and clean himself up. "I recognize you," she finally said. "The professor from the law school, right? McMurray?"

"McMurtrie," Tom said, smiling at her and extending his hand through one of the openings in the steel bars. "Tom McMurtrie."

Her grip was firm and Tom could feel the callouses of a hard life. "Willie Burgess," she said. "Are you Newton's attorney?"

Tom knew the question was coming, but it still caused his stomach to roll.

"If you aren't her lawyer, Professor, then I can't let you back there. No visitors allowed for a murder suspect."

Tom blinked and cleared his throat. "I'm her lawyer."

11

Tom heard a click and the steel door adjacent to the reception window opened. A uniformed officer with the name "Dep. Lusk" embroidered over his shirt pocket ushered him through. "Follow me," he said in a clipped, almost nasal tone. Tom was led down a short hallway with two rooms. Above one of the doors appeared a black sign with the stenciled words "Holding Cell." Lusk knocked on the adjacent door and waited. Two seconds later, it opened and Tom saw a familiar face.

"What is it, Lusk? We're in the middle of drafting the . . ." The man stopped when he noticed Tom standing behind the deputy. "Well I'll be dipped in horseshit."

"Nice to see you too, Wade," Tom said, cracking a smile.

Wade Richey returned the gesture and pushed past Lusk, slapping Tom hard on the back. Tom winced as a lightning bolt of pain hurtled down his shoulder blades and legs all the way to his feet.

"Well, I'm mighty damn glad to see you," Wade said, shaking his head and keeping his arm around Tom's shoulder. He leaned close and whispered in Tom's ear, *"I think we've got an open-and-shut murder case, but I know Powell wanted to talk with you before making the charge."*

Tom's eyes had watered from the pain of Wade's back slap and he was still gathering himself when he heard Lusk's voice from behind him.

"Detective?"

"What is it, Lusk?" Wade turned, glancing at the deputy and then back at Tom. "Have you two been introduced?"

When neither man answered, Wade gestured at Tom. "Lusk, this is Professor Tom McMurtrie."

The deputy nodded but didn't make any move to shake Tom's hand. He blinked his eyes, moving them from Wade to Tom and back to Wade.

"Is something wrong, Deputy?" Wade finally asked.

Before Lusk could answer, the door that Wade had come out of opened again, and the district attorney of Tuscaloosa County stepped out. Powell Conrad wore khaki pants and a white shirt; his red tie was loosened at the neck. His sandy-blond hair lay like a mop on his head, and Tom probably would have chuckled a bit if the circumstances of his visit had been different. Powell always had a bit of a disheveled look about him that Tom found endearing, and he knew juries did as well. The smile of relief that spread across Powell's face felt like a hot poker on Tom's chest. "Professor, I was just hoping for a phone call. You didn't have to come over in person."

Tom couldn't find the words as he gazed at his former student. Mercifully, Lusk broke the awkward silence.

"He says he's Newton's attorney."

"What?" Powell asked, looking at Tom and not believing his ears. "Is that true, Professor?"

"Powell, I intended to return your text messages, but before I could a member of Ms. Newton's family asked me to talk to her."

"So, it is true then." Powell's voice, which was normally loud and boisterous, was so low that Tom could barely hear it.

Tom glanced at Wade, whose face had grown pale, before returning his eyes to Powell. "I'm her attorney for the limited purpose of talking with her right now, OK? I promised her daughter that I would do that and . . ." He held out his palms. "Here I am."

"You need to run for the hills, son," Wade said, his voice a low drawl. "Like I just told you, this is an open and shut—"

"*Enough!*" Powell cut him off, his tone sharp and the volume turned up full throttle. He glared at Wade and gave Tom the same look.

Tom kept his face neutral and nodded at the holding cell. "Can I see her now?"

For several seconds, Powell just looked at Tom. The glare had softened into a glazed expression of confusion and disappointment. Finally, he grunted and gave a quick jerk of his head. "Lusk," he said, his eyes now focused on the tile floor. "Show Ms. Newton's lawyer to the attorney room."

12

The "attorney room" was a drab five-foot-by-eight-foot enclosure with cinder-block walls and a fluorescent overhead light that flickered every few seconds. There were no air vents in the room and no fan, and Tom suspected that these omissions were intentional. By the time Lusk returned ten minutes later with the suspect, Tom had removed his jacket and rolled up his sleeves, still sweating. He was also thirsty but doubted anyone would be offering him a drink.

He stood when Wilma Newton entered the room. As Lusk removed the cuffs, the suspect gazed across the small space at Tom. She opened her mouth, but no words came out. Once the deputy had closed the door and they were alone, Wilma took a step closer and squinted at her visitor, cocking her head. Finally, she spoke. "Professor McMurtrie?"

Tom nodded. The only pieces of furniture in the room were a square folding table and two plastic chairs, and Tom sat in one of the chairs and gestured for Wilma to sit in the other. But the suspect remained standing.

"Why . . . ? How? I didn't call you. I called Morris Claiborne and Larry Reed. I left messages with their receptionists. I just thought . . ."

Tom had taught Larry Reed two decades ago, and he knew of Claiborne. Both made their bread and butter working criminal defense cases. He wasn't surprised that she would call them. "Larry and Morris are both excellent lawyers."

Before Wilma could say anything else, Tom added, "Your daughter asked me to talk with you."

Wilma wrinkled her eyebrows. "Laurie Ann?"

"Yes. She came to my office yesterday and requested that I take your case. I . . . promised her that I would talk with you."

"Why?"

Tom blinked and looked down at the table. *Why?* He repeated the question in his own thoughts, remembering the look of betrayal he received just moments ago from Powell Conrad. *Why are you here, old man?* The truth was that he really didn't know. For the first time since being forced into retirement by the law school and simultaneously learning he had bladder cancer over two years ago, he felt unstable and a bit unsure.

"McMurtrie?" Wilma had taken a step closer, but she still remained standing.

Finally, Tom sighed. "Ms. Newton, would you please sit down?"

Wilma crossed her arms but didn't move. She glared at Tom. "Not until you tell me why you came down here. I don't remember us being friends, and last time I saw you, you were busy ruining my life." She took another step closer and leaned over the desk. "Now, I'm going to ask you again, and if you don't answer, I'm knocking on the door for the deputy to come get me. *Why* are you here?"

"I don't know," Tom said, figuring the truth was his best option. "Your daughter asked me to come, and she was very persuasive and persistent. She filled me in on some of the things that have happened to you since the trial and . . ." He trailed off.

"So you feel sorry for me. Is that it? Poor old Wilma." She scoffed. "I guess a rich, famous attorney like yourself can indulge in pity meetings at the jail with clients he's never going to actually represent."

Tom had heard enough. "No, Wilma. That's not it. I don't feel sorry for you. You are an adult woman, and your choices have put you where you are." He paused and stood from his chair. "But I felt very bad for your daughter. She's an innocent victim of your actions and . . . to a much lesser extent, mine. If I hadn't come to the courtroom that day and cross-examined you—"

"Willistone wins the case, I get my money, and Laurie Ann is a cheerleader at Lincoln County Middle."

Tom squinted at her. "Money? What money?"

Wilma sighed and her lip began to tremble. *"Damnit,"* she whispered under her breath, covering her face with both hands. "Just . . . go, Professor. You can't help me. Ain't nobody can help me."

Tom felt a prickle of pain vibrate along his shoulder blade and he lowered himself to his seat. Rubbing his back with the palm of his right hand, he looked up at her. "Did you kill Jack Willistone?" Tom knew he had just broken the cardinal rule of criminal defense attorneys. *Never ask your client if he or she did the deed.* But he didn't care. He was old. His back hurt. And he was too tired to hold on to the unwritten commandments of a profession that he was beginning to lose faith in. He wanted to see her reaction.

Wilma removed her hands from her face and met Tom's eye. "I wish that I had. I wish . . ." Her lower lip began to shake again. "I wish I would've had the guts to kill that bastard."

"Did you kill Jack Willistone?" Tom repeated the question.

Wilma wiped her tear-streaked eyes and shook her head. "No."

For several seconds they looked at each other across the small, stuffy space. Finally, Tom once again gestured to the chair. "Then sit down, and let's talk this out."

13

An hour later, Tom trudged out the exit to the jail, weighed down by his briefcase, fatigue, and the story he had just heard. It was impossible to know if Wilma had held anything back, but he believed the parts that she had revealed. At the end of the day, crazy as it all sounded, she sounded sincere and . . .

. . . I believe her.

Thinking about his next move, Tom placed his briefcase in the back seat and felt a hand squeeze his shoulder. He flinched and looked behind him.

Wade Richey held up his hands. "Sorry about that. Is something up with your back?"

Tom shook his head. "You come out here to fuss some more?"

Wade smiled and rubbed his mustache. "How long we been friends?"

Tom shut the door and leaned his back against it. "Since Nixon was president."

"A long time, right?"

Tom nodded.

"I meant what I said in there, Tom. You need to run for the hills."
Then, looking left and right to make sure no one was in earshot, Wade
took a step closer to Tom and spoke under his breath. "The murder weapon was registered in Wilma Newton's name and was found
with only her prints on it underneath the dock where Willistone was
killed." He paused. "You want me to tell you how many cases I've
lost in thirty years in the Sheriff's Office when we have the murder
weapon and it belongs to the defendant?" He made a zero symbol
with the thumb and index finger of his right hand.

"Does Powell know you're telling me this?" Tom asked, also
shooting a quick glance around the lot before looking into Wade's
blue eyes.

"Who do you think asked me to come out here?"

Tom wiped sweat from his forehead. At almost noon, the
Tuscaloosa heat had announced its presence with authority. "Tell him
I appreciate the heads-up." Tom knew that most prosecutors wouldn't
share evidence—especially of the magnitude of what Wade just told
him—absent a request from the defense attorney and would hold out
as long as ethically possible before turning it over.

"Will do." Wade took a couple steps back. "You're not seriously
thinking about taking this case, are you?"

Tom opened the driver's-side door to the Explorer, stalling for
time.

"Well?"

Tom finally looked at him. "Since she's only a suspect, there isn't
a case to take. When are you going to charge her?"

"This afternoon," Wade said. "Like I told you in there, the reason she hasn't already been charged is that the district attorney had
wanted to talk with his mentor about the case. But the funniest thing
happened. His old law professor blew him off and lo and behold
showed up at the jail today and said he's Newton's lawyer." Wade

leaned in closer and spoke through clenched teeth as he pointed at the brick facade of the Sheriff's Office. "My guy in there has been loyal to the bone to you, Tom. He helped you in Henshaw two years ago, and him and I both came to your aid last year in Pulaski."

"I know that, Wade, but—"

"I'm not finished," Wade said, his voice rising. "This is Powell's first big murder case since being appointed DA. You know the deal. Griffith stepped down last October to care for his wife, who has Alzheimer's, and the governor had to appoint a replacement. Well, guess what had just happened?"

Tom gazed down at the pavement.

"Powell and I had just arrested JimBone Wheeler on the square in Pulaski. You've seen the video, haven't you?"

Tom nodded.

"Powell tackled Wheeler before he could kill anyone else on the square and took his gun away from him. *Took a psychopathic killer's gun away from him.* They don't teach that kind of bravery in law school, Tom." Wade paused to catch his breath. "Powell was appointed DA because arresting Wheeler made him a rock star. It was the popular move and the governor seized on it, and you and I both know that Powell was already the most talented prosecutor in the office."

"He's a natural," Tom agreed, gazing up at his old friend. "What are you trying to say, Wade?"

"What I'm trying to say, old friend"—Wade stuck a finger in Tom's sternum—"is that because Jack Willistone is the victim, the press is going to be all over this case. Hell, they've been crawling the halls of the office since the body was found. Right or wrong, the success of Powell's term and his chance for election may hinge on what happens here." Wade looked Tom right in the eye. "That's why he wanted your counsel. But instead of advice and support, he gets . . ."

Wade cocked his head to the side and smirked. "Whatever the hell you're doing."

Tom shook his head. "Look, tell Powell I'm sorry. When I got his text, I was at my grandson's baseball game. I had been in Huntsville for Billy Neighbors's funeral and, with everything going on with Rick, I'm having a hard time keeping track of who I've called back and who I haven't. Ms. Newton's daughter showed up last night at my office and begged me to talk with her mother, and I just couldn't say no."

For a few seconds, neither spoke. Wade broke the silence. "I'm sorry about Billy. I know how close everyone on that team is."

Tom nodded and gazed at the ring on the third finger of his right hand. Around the edge and stenciled in gold were the words "National Champions." In the middle were the numerals "1961." His throat had become dry and he blinked down at the asphalt to gather himself.

"You didn't answer my question. Are you going to take the case?"

Tom wiped sweat from his forehead and continued to gaze down at the ground. "I don't know what I'm going to do yet. I . . . need to talk with my partner."

Now it was Wade who blinked, and the detective also looked down at the pavement. "Well, tell the kid I've been praying for him." He shook his head and started to walk away.

"Hey, Wade."

The detective stopped and turned his head as Tom climbed into the SUV. Squinting at his old friend, Tom managed a tired smile. "Have you talked with Bully Calhoun yet?"

The detective's face hardened and his voice was even harsher. "Don't do this, Tom. You know I love you, and Powell worships the ground you walk on." He paused. "But if you take this case, you won't get any more freebies from us. We'll play for blood."

The smile faded from Tom's face. "I would expect nothing different." He put the car in gear and eased it forward, pausing next to the detective as he walked back toward the entrance.

"Hey, son," Tom said.

Wade looked at him.

"You didn't answer my question." Before Wade could respond, Tom pressed the accelerator. In his rearview mirror, he noticed that the detective had stopped walking and was watching him leave with his hands on his hips.

14

Henshaw, Alabama, is a small farming community halfway between Tuscaloosa and Montgomery. For as long as anyone in town can remember, there's been a gas station and convenience store at the intersection of Limestone Bottom Road and Highway 82. Originally, it was known as Sloan's Bait and Beer, but in 1990 old Tom Sloan sold out to Texaco and retired to the sandy white beaches of Gulf Shores.

The intersection also has a stoplight, where, in the midmorning hours of September 2, 2009, an eighteen-wheeler owned by Willistone Trucking Company and driven by Harold "Dewey" Newton collided with a Honda Accord operated by Bob Bradshaw. Newton had massive head injuries and died at the hospital. Bradshaw, a thirty-year-old tax attorney from Huntsville, and his two-year-old daughter, Nicole, burned to death when the Accord exploded after flipping several times. Jeannie Bradshaw, Nicole's mother and Bob's wife, was thrown from the car and died from massive internal injuries, but not before trying to pull her daughter from the wreckage.

Tom sat on the bench outside the Texaco and gazed past the four pumps to the traffic light, thinking of the carnage the accident had wrought and the lives affected, including those who had perished and those left behind. Ruth Ann Wilcox—Jeannie Bradshaw's mother and Tom's college sweetheart. Wilma Newton and her two daughters. Jack Willistone.

Me . . .

Tom knew the accident had changed his life forever, putting together a chain of events that eventually led to him returning to the courtroom after forty years as a professor and winning the largest jury verdict in west Alabama history. But as he saw the rusty Saturn approach on Highway 82 and flick its blinker on, Tom knew that his own redemption couldn't have happened without a certain young lawyer who called this town his home.

The Saturn took a left on Limestone Bottom and an immediate right into the station, parking in one of the places that ran along the side of the building. Tom stood as Rick Drake opened the door and slid out of the car.

As his partner approached, Tom couldn't help but think that the "kid," as Wade Richey had called him, who wasn't yet thirty, looked as if he had aged a decade in the last few months. He wore a pair of faded blue jeans, a sweat-stained gray T-shirt, and boots caked with dried mud. His normally clean-shaven face now carried at least a week's worth of brown stubble, and his hair, which was typically trimmed short for court, was over his ears and longer in the back than Tom had ever seen it. His head was covered by a blue cap pulled low over his eyes with the words "Drake Farms" embroidered in gold on the front.

Tom shook Rick's hand and held it for a second. "How you doing?"

Rick shrugged. "Making it." Then he gestured with his right arm, and Tom noticed another man emerge from the Saturn. He had fuzzy brown hair and a scruffy beard and reminded Tom of Mr. Edwards from *Little House on the Prairie.* The man wore blue-jean overalls with no shirt underneath and had a toothpick stuck in his mouth. If he was an inch under six feet six, Tom wasn't buying.

"Professor, this is Keewin Brown. He was Dad's right-hand man, and he's been mine these last few months."

Tom nodded and shook hands with Keewin, whose grip was as strong as an oak tree and caused Tom to grimace.

"Pleasure, sir," Keewin said. Then he headed for the front door. "Want your usual, Ricky?"

"Yeah, that'll be good," Rick said. "I'm going to need a few minutes."

"I know. I'm going to eat mine inside and pester Ms. Rose."

Rick took a seat next to Tom on the bench. "I'm sorry that I look like a wreck. But I'm going to get filthy again this afternoon, so—"

"No need for an apology, son. You forget. I grew up on a farm myself."

Rick smiled, but the sadness behind his eyes was palpable.

"How's your mom?"

He shrugged. "Same. Still blames herself. Still not sleeping much." He paused. "Her whole life was him, you know? Sweethearts since they were twelve years old . . ."

"Any news about the other driver?"

"Nope. Sheriff Ballard says the investigation is ongoing, but they'll never find him. It was a hit-and-run at nine thirty at night in Henshaw County. No witnesses because most folks around here are in bed by then."

"What was he going to get?"

"A carton of milk. How ironic is that? A farmer who's herded cattle his whole life gets killed in a hit-and-run accident on the way back from the store to get milk."

Tom shook his head, not knowing what to say. Billy Drake was killed on Highway 82 just a few miles from the turnoff to his farm. *Probably less than two miles from where we're sitting,* Tom thought.

He was run off the road and his truck collided with a tree. When he hadn't returned home by ten thirty and didn't answer his cell phone, Allie Drake had called the sheriff. The truck was discovered an hour later, but Billy was long since dead by then. He was fifty-six years old.

"I'm sorry, son." Tom finally broke the silence.

Rick gazed at the highway. "You know what's also ironic?"

Tom didn't say anything. He knew his partner needed to get some things off his chest and he was happy to be the sounding board.

"This stretch of highway gave me my biggest case. Hell, it made my career as a lawyer." He shook his head. "But it also took my father." He stood and walked a few steps away from the bench, stuffing his hands in the front pockets of his jeans. "I hate this road."

"I understand," Tom said. "Before you got here, I was thinking about all the lives changed by the accident between Dewey Newton and Bob Bradshaw." He paused. "I met another one last night."

"What?" Rick turned his head and squinted at Tom. "Who?"

Tom gazed over the gasoline pumps and upward toward the setting sun. He crossed his arms. "Laurie Ann Newton. Daughter of Dewey Newton. She showed up at our office at nine o'clock last night and asked us to represent her mother."

Rick wrinkled his brow. "Wilma . . . Newton?"

"The one and only."

Rick gazed down at the pavement. "Based on what that bartender in Pulaski told me last year, I thought she might be dead."

"She's alive and she needs a lawyer."

"Why?"

"Because she's about to be charged with the murder of Jack Willistone."

They looked at each other, and Tom immediately could tell by Rick's open mouth that he didn't know.

"He was shot and killed three nights ago and his body washed up along the banks of the Black Warrior."

"I thought he was in prison in Springville."

Tom nodded. "He was released on Monday." He paused. "Found dead early Wednesday morning."

Rick let out a low whistle and shook his head. "I can't believe Powell didn't call me."

Tom stood from the bench and stretched his legs. His back was hurting and he was already dreading the forty-five-minute drive back to Tuscaloosa. "I'm sure he didn't want to bother you with it." He kicked a loose piece of gravel. "He texted me Wednesday night with the news and said he wanted to talk with me about the suspect they had in custody. Before I could call him back, Laurie Ann Newton showed up on the steps to our office." He paused. "I met with Wilma this morning."

Rick's eyes widened. "And?"

"And it's quite a story," Tom said, gesturing at the bench. "Sit down and let me fill you in."

"Wilma Newton was offered two hundred thousand dollars by Jack Willistone to lie on the stand in Henshaw during the trial. She was paid half before trial and was supposed to get the other half after she followed through on the stand. If you will remember, Wilma did a complete one eighty at trial and, after telling you and Dawn that Dewey's driving schedules were crazy and forced him to speed, she testified that his schedules were fine."

"I'll never forget that as long as I live."

"In the lead-up to trial, Willistone sent his henchman to Pulaski to keep tabs on Wilma and make sure she showed up when it was time."

"JimBone Wheeler I presume?"

"Exactly. Wheeler met with Wilma once a week prior to trial and then drove her to Henshaw and stayed with her at a hotel in

Tuscaloosa during the week of trial. According to Wilma, she spent the hours of that week that she wasn't on the witness stand in a roofie-induced haze." He paused. "Wheeler raped her repeatedly while she was drugged up."

"Jesus," Rick said.

"It gets worse. After the trial, Wilma returned home, and her two daughters were gone. They had been staying with an old friend of Wilma's mother named Carla Yost, who lived close by. Yost owned the house in Boone's Hill that Wilma was renting and typically kept the girls there. When Wilma came home, Laurie Ann and her sister, Jackie, were nowhere to be seen. Yost left a note on the table that she had turned the girls over to DHR because of an answering machine message on Wilma's phone." Tom kicked at a loose rock. "Wheeler had left the message during one of his sessions with her and it gave the impression that she was a prostitute."

Rick crossed his arms and shook his head. "Unbelievable."

"DHR sent the girls to live with Wilma's cousin in Tuscaloosa and turned the case over to the Giles County district attorney's office."

"Uh-oh," Rick said, smirking. "The General?"

Tom nodded. "General Helen Lewis charged Wilma with prostitution and she pled guilty. She served twelve months in the Giles County Jail. Got out last February and moved to Tuscaloosa to be closer to her girls. She was put on two years' supervised probation."

"Why didn't she fight the prostitution charge?"

"JimBone said that he'd kill her children if she ever said anything. At the time she pled guilty, he was still on the loose. Powell and Wade didn't apprehend him until October of last year."

Rick nodded to himself, thinking it through. "Well, that explains why she changed her story at our trial and what's happened to her since." He paused. "It doesn't explain whether she killed Jack or not, but it would sure give her a lot of motive. Does she have an alibi for the time of the murder?"

"I don't know. I don't know the time of death yet so I didn't ask her. But she said she didn't kill him."

"Do you believe her?"

Tom took his time as he considered the question and Wilma Newton's demeanor in the consultation room a few hours earlier. "She was convincing," he finally said.

"Does Powell know you met with her?"

Tom nodded. "Yes, and he and Wade were not happy campers."

Rick whistled. "I bet not."

"Before I left the jail, Wade told me that the murder weapon is a pistol registered in Wilma's name with only her prints on it."

For several seconds, neither man spoke. Inside the store, Tom could hear the voices of Keewin and the manager of the Texaco, Rose Batson, whom Tom had met during the Willistone trial two years earlier. Above the stoplight on Highway 82, the sun had almost made its final descent. Darkness was about to come to Henshaw County.

"So are you really considering representing Wilma Newton?" Rick asked, standing from the bench. "The same Wilma Newton who almost sabotaged our case?"

"You remember the phone call we received the night she testified?" Tom asked. "Warning us about Dawn."

Rick nodded. "Wilma."

"It had to be, right? I mean, who else could that have been?" He paused. "But she confirmed it today. She crawled across her hotel room and made that call, which probably saved our friend and associate's life." Tom knew that Dawn had once been more than just a friend to Rick but didn't want to go there.

"OK . . ." Rick started. "I'll give you that. Still, though. Why defend her on this charge?"

Tom rose from the bench and rested his right foot on it, leaning forward and stretching his aching back muscles. "The girl."

"What about her?"

"She impressed me. Fourteen years old, coming to our office in person and having the courage and street smarts to ask for legal representation for her momma."

"Why did she come to you?"

Tom smiled. "In the years since the accident and trial, Laurie Ann has become obsessed with it. She's read the transcript. Knew all the players. Could even recite my cross-examination of her mother." Tom paused. "I don't know. Her anguish was so pure and raw. It made me realize that Wilma Newton and her daughters were also victims of that accident, and they're still paying the consequences."

"Professor, Dewey Newton was speeding, and he killed an innocent family. He was going too fast because of Jack Willistone's scheme to make more deliveries than his competitors. The jury returned its verdict, and it was just."

"I know that, Rick, but it doesn't change the fact that Wilma and her daughters were also victims. But instead of closure, they got caught up in the legal machine and can't seem to get out." He sighed. "I'd like to help them if I can."

"Is Wilma gonna pay?"

"We didn't discuss that, but if I take the case, I was going to offer to do it pro bono."

"Professor, are you out of your mind?" Rick asked. "You're gonna try a murder case for free?"

Tom took a couple steps toward the gas pumps and stuffed his hands in his pockets. He spoke without looking at his partner. "Rick, I'm seventy-one years old. I've spent my career trying cases and teaching students how to try cases. I didn't come back to the practice of law two years ago so I could sit in on cattle calls in front of Braxton Poe, and I'd rather shovel dirt than negotiate settlements at mediations." He paused. "I'm not sure how many more trials I've got left. The case in Pulaski last year nearly killed me." He turned and looked at Rick, whose face was illuminated by the neon Natural Light sign behind him. "But I know I've got one more and . . . this feels right."

"What about Powell? He's my best friend. He's your friend too. This will be a huge case for him, his first big one as district attorney. Have you thought about that?"

Tom nodded. "I have, and I'm dreading that aspect of the proceedings. Today at the jail was awkward, and I'm sure it'll only get worse. Powell and Wade are both very good friends of mine. It would be much easier if the head prosecutor was a turd like Jameson Tyler."

"Then why take the case?"

Tom approached his young partner, stopping when he was just a foot away. "Because it's the right thing to do."

The door to the store jangled open and Keewin stepped out. He held a twenty-ounce Coke in one hand and two Little Debbie Oatmeal Creme Pies. He flipped one of the snack cakes to Rick, who caught it with both hands. Then he handed him the drink. "I had mine in there with Ms. Rose."

Before Rick could answer, a plump woman came tottering out with a wide smile on her face. "Ricky Drake, come here and give me a hug." He did as he was told, and the woman picked him up off the ground, almost causing him to drop his Coke. "Hey, Ms. Rose. You doing alright?"

"If I was any better, there'd be two of me." Then the smile waned. "How's your momma?"

"Doing OK."

She put an arm on his shoulder. "I'm bringing a roast, mashed potatoes, and a pecan pie for supper tomorrow night. You tell her not to cook anything, you hear?"

Rick nodded. "Yes, ma'am."

Then she looked past him to Tom. "Well, I'll be a monkey's plaything. I remember this handsome man." She stepped forward, and Tom braced himself for a hug that he knew would hurt worse than anything Wade Richey had given him earlier that day, but she surprised him by pulling up and grabbing his right hand with both of hers instead. "Good to see you, Professor." Then, leaning in close, she whispered, "Been real worried about Ricky. His daddy was his hero. I'm glad he has you."

Tom nodded and squeezed her hands. "It's good to see you too, Ms. Batson."

She left in the same whirlwind that she had arrived in, slapping Rick on the back and telling Keewin to come back tomorrow because she'd have boiled peanuts. As his huge friend trudged back toward the Saturn, Rick turned to Tom. "Professor, I'm sorry. I wish I could come back to the office, but my mom—"

"It's OK," Tom said, putting a hand on his shoulder. "You're doing exactly what you should be doing."

They shook hands, and Rick began to walk away. When he reached the door to his vehicle, he looked at Tom, who had sat back down on the bench. "Powell is my best friend, Professor. But you're my partner. If you want this case, I'm fine with it."

Tom gazed past the stoplight on Highway 82 and then beyond it to the stars in the cloudless sky. *Do I want this case?* Finally, he cleared his throat and spoke through the near darkness. "Thank you."

Rick opened the door and held it there for several seconds.

"Something else on your mind?" Tom asked.

"Yeah," he said, looking at the steering wheel. "Powell."

"What about him?"

Rick raised his head and his eyes met Tom's. "He's good, Professor. He's . . . really good."

Tom watched as his partner shut the door. As the Saturn pulled onto Highway 82, Tom whispered his response to the shadows above. *"I know."*

15

Powell Conrad sat on the plush leather couch and drank from a glass of iced tea a little too sweet for his liking. For that matter, the sofa was too soft and he felt like he was going to sink through the cushions at any moment. Next to him, Wade fidgeted and gazed down at the shag carpet. Powell set the glass down on the coffee table in front of him and scooted to the edge of the couch. "Mrs. Willistone, thank you for having us on such short notice, and we apologize for interrupting your evening."

Sitting across from the duo in a satin lounge chair, Kathryn Calhoun Willistone wore a black tank top and gray Under Armour athletic shorts, her face and arms gleaming with sweat. "No problem, Mr. Conrad. And please call me Kat. I'm sorry that I'm such a mess. Running takes my mind off what's happened." She gestured at her toned body, which looked anything but a mess. Then she looked around the room with sad eyes. "Jack called this his Elvis room."

Powell, who went to Rhodes College, in Memphis, for undergrad before heading to Tuscaloosa for law school, nodded. He had been to Graceland several times, and the green shag carpet and leopard-skin rug were right on, as was the grand piano in the corner. He pointed at it. "I wasn't aware that Jack could play."

Kat laughed. "He couldn't play a lick. He bought that for me."

Powell smiled. You would expect that the second wife of a tycoon like Jack Willistone would be arm candy, a trophy wife. But Kat wasn't the big-bosomed bleached blond that Powell had always imagined. Instead, she wore her brown hair in a ponytail and, though certainly attractive, came across as understated and even younger than her thirty-seven years. She reached into her purse, which she had placed at her feet, and dug around before emerging with a small tube of Tylenol. She opened the top and popped two capsules in her mouth.

"Headache?" Powell asked, feeling stupid and awkward.

"Every day since the murder. Can't seem to kick it. Exercise helps, but . . ." Her voice faded away. "So why are you guys here?"

Powell nodded at Wade, who cleared his throat. "Ma'am, earlier this morning we charged a woman named Wilma Christine Newton with the murder of your husband. Do you know Ms. Newton?"

Kat wrinkled her brow. "Not personally, but the last name sounds familiar. Wasn't she the wife of the trucker killed in that wreck in Henshaw a few years ago?"

Wade nodded. "Yes, ma'am. We're still nailing down all the details, but your husband was shot with a nine-millimeter pistol registered in Wilma Newton's name with only her prints on it." He paused. "Cell phone records also confirm that Ms. Newton was the last person to call or text Jack."

Kat folded her arms tight across her chest and shook her head slowly back and forth. "That accident is the gift that keeps on giving, isn't it?" She chuckled bitterly.

"Ms. Willistone . . . er, Kat," Powell began, thinking his words through. "Jack got out of prison on Monday, correct?"

She nodded. "Daddy picked him up in Springville around nine. They were in Tuscaloosa by one o'clock."

"I know you've already covered this once with Detective Richey, but can you run me through everything that happened from the time Jack got out of prison to the time you got the visit from the Tuscaloosa Sheriff's Office early Wednesday morning?"

She took a sip of her tea and sighed. "Nothing real glamorous. I think they ate at the Cracker Barrel in Bessemer on the way home from the prison. Got here around one. We had dinner out on the back deck around six thirty that night."

"Did Jack leave the house Monday night?"

"No. We went to bed around ten."

"I hate to pry, Ms. Willistone, but did you sleep—?"

"The name is Kat, Mr. Conrad. And yes, we slept together Monday night."

"Tell me about Tuesday."

"Jack woke up late, which for him was past nine o'clock. He said he wanted a dozen glazed from Krispy Kreme, so I went and picked that up for him. We ate a few doughnuts and then he said he needed to get a new cell phone. He took the 4Runner and called me about an hour later from the Verizon store with his new phone. Said he was going to run a few more errands and then hit the Oasis in Cottondale for a late lunch—Jack thought they made the best cheeseburgers in the world—and asked if I wanted to join him. I wasn't up for a greasy spoon just after having doughnuts, so I passed and told him to have fun." She paused and looked down at the floor. "I never heard his voice again. When he didn't call before dinner, I decided to meet some friends at Pepito's. They have half-price margaritas on Tuesday nights, and a group of us from the gym went every week."

"Were you worried that Jack hadn't called?" Wade chimed in.

She gazed down at her purse. "I guess maybe I should've been, but you have to know Jack. Before all the trouble in Henshaw and his arrest, he rarely came home at night before ten o'clock. That man worked from the time the sun rose until long past dark. He always told me that trucking was a 24/7 gig and that was who I married." She chuckled. "I was raised by a man who worked similar hours, so it never bothered me."

Powell nodded along, but he felt the first tingle in his gut that something was off. Kat's answer sounded too good, as if rehearsed. "When *did* you get worried?" he asked. He saw her jump back a bit at the volume of his voice, but Powell didn't apologize. He knew he talked loud by most standards, but by this point in his life, Powell Conrad had resolved to just roll with it. He thought the high volume came from being a union worker's kid from Decatur "By God" Alabama. When Powell was a boy, his daddy let him tag along to work, and he had to scream over the whir of the machines to be heard. Or, hell, maybe God just put extra woofers in his pipes because the Big Man upstairs makes us all a little different. Powell didn't know, but he'd found that his voice carried weight in a courtroom, especially in the cross-examination of witnesses and when emphasizing key points during closing arguments. He'd grown to like and embrace this quirk about himself during his second year of law school, when he had made Professor Tom McMurtrie's trial team. The Professor preached that juries see right through lawyers who are faking it. "*Real* is what wins over the people in that box," the big man would say, pointing at the area where the jury sat. "Own who you are, and let the jury hear from that person. Anything less and you're cheating them . . . and you're cheating yourself."

Powell blinked the thoughts away and refocused on Kat Willistone, who had yet to answer the question on the table. "You called 911 around one o'clock Wednesday morning," Powell said. "Stands to reason that you were worried by that point."

She nodded. "When I still hadn't heard from him when I got home from Pepito's—which was a little after midnight—I was very concerned."

"Jack's cell phone didn't show any calls or texts from your number after seven that night," Wade said. "If you were concerned, why didn't you try to reach him?"

Kat glared at Wade and then Powell, and her face flushed pink. "I thought you guys said you had arrested someone for Jack's murder. Why do I feel like I'm still under investigation?"

"Because you are the victim's wife and you are Bully Calhoun's daughter," Powell said. "Any defense attorney for Newton will come at you and your father hard under an alternative theory, and we don't want there to be any surprises." Powell paused and leaned his elbows on his knees. "Are we clear?"

"Crystal," Kat said. Then she looked at Wade. "Jack didn't like to be bothered when doing business. He always said he had no room in his life for a 'nervous ninny.' I had left him a voice mail and a text from earlier in the day to call me. I'm sure the records will reflect that." She turned to Powell. "Satisfied?"

"You stand to collect three million dollars in life insurance proceeds on account of Jack's death, true?" Powell asked, ignoring Kat's question and hitting hard with the heart and soul of any defense theory that Jack Willistone's wife murdered him.

"Damn right," Kat said. "And being that man's wife for seven years entitles me to every penny of it."

Powell was surprised and impressed by the defiance in Kat's voice. "Why do you say that?"

"Oh, let's cut with the bullcrap, Mr. Conrad," she said, standing from her chair. "Jack Willistone was a ruthless son of a bitch and a serial cheater. A 'man of the flesh,' as my daddy would say. I was seduced by Jack's money and charm, but the only reason he married me is because of my daddy's wealth." She smirked. "Ironic, huh? I got played just like so many others who dealt with Jack. But that life insurance money is mine. It's the only thing Jack had left of value, and I intend to collect."

Powell glanced at Wade, who took the cue to change gears. "When I met with you before," the detective began, "you told me that you were at Pepito's with Callie Sanderson, Melanie Towry, and Breck Johnson."

"That's right. We all work out at Don's Gym around the same time each day and have become friends."

"Did you work out this past Tuesday?" Powell asked.

She nodded. "I work out most weekdays at 6:00 p.m., same as Callie, Mel, and Breck. The gym has women's and men's locker rooms, and we shower there on Tuesdays and head to Pepito's."

She has an alibi from six o'clock until past midnight, Powell thought to himself. *With three witnesses . . .*

"What about your father?" Powell asked.

"What about him?"

"Where was he the night of the murder?"

Kat gave a half smile. "I assume he was back home in Jasper."

"Did he stick around after he dropped Jack off?"

"No, he did not. He gave me a hug and a peck on the cheek and headed back to the Sipsey Wilderness."

Powell reviewed his notes. "Ms. Willistone, there's one more thing I'm curious about. The visitor's log for the St. Clair County Correctional facility shows that you never went to visit Jack while he was in prison." Powell paused and looked up from his notepad. "Jack's ex-wife, Barbara, visited several times. Her and Jack's son, Danny, did as well. But in eighteen months you didn't come to Springville a single time to visit your husband. Why?"

"Because he told me not to," Kat said, folding her arms. When no further response came, Powell closed his notepad and stood from the couch. "Thank you for your time, Ms. Willistone. We'll be in touch."

Powell cranked the ignition on the Charger as he and Wade gazed through the windshield at Jack Willistone's mansion. For several seconds, the only sound was the whirring of the air-conditioning and the crickets chirping from outside. Finally, Powell grunted.

"I know," Wade said. "Too clean. But it doesn't change the fact that Wilma Newton is our killer."

"All the same," Powell said, putting the Charger in gear, "after we talk with Jack's ex-wife again, I think we're going to need to take a road trip."

Wade sighed. "Jasper." Even the name of the town made the hairs on the detective's neck stand up. "Make sure you pack your revolver."

Powell grunted as he turned onto McFarland. "No need. Once you pass the Walker County line, if you're aren't packing, they hand you a gun."

When the front door was safely closed, Kat Willistone reached into her purse and took out her cell phone, which was on during the entire interview. "Well?" she asked, keeping the device on speaker.

"Perfect," a man's deep voice said. "Dead solid perfect."

Kat Willistone let out a sigh of relief. "Thank you, Daddy."

16

Tom arrived back at the office at nine o'clock. As he trudged up the stairwell, he found a familiar face waiting for him on the top step.

"Where's your dog?"

Tom stopped and squinted at her. Tonight she wore a red "Tuscaloosa Middle Soccer" T-shirt, black athletic shorts, and white tennis shoes with a red Nike swoosh. Her hair, which she'd done up in a ponytail, was matted on the sides from dried sweat, and her face was red from exertion. "You just get out of practice?"

She nodded. "Then I came here."

Tom continued up the stairs and unlocked the door. This time Laurie Ann's visit wasn't a surprise. She had called him on his way home from Henshaw. Tom needed to drop by the office to look over a few files that had deadlines looming, so he had reluctantly agreed to talk with her for a few minutes.

They passed into the air-conditioned office, and Laurie Ann plopped down on the couch in the reception area. "So you met with Mom?"

Tom took a seat in a straight-back chair across from her. He placed his hands in his lap and tried to catch his breath from the walk up the stairs and the overall fatigue of the day. It had been a while since he had worked a day like this. *Not since Pulaski,* he knew, feeling a sense of exhilaration mixed in with the aching of his back muscles.

"I did."

"And?" For the first time since he'd met Laurie Ann Newton, her voice contained a trace of fear. The ball was in his court now. If he said no, then Wilma Newton would likely be represented by the public defender. *And we have a good one,* Tom knew. But given the evidence that Wade had mentioned in the parking lot and the stacks of files in the PD's office, the public defender couldn't possibly give Wilma's case the time it would need.

"It's OK," Laurie Ann finally said, her tone a mixture of disappointment and bitterness. "It was a pipe dream expecting the great Professor to take this case." She began to walk toward the door.

"I didn't say no," Tom said as he forced himself to rise from the chair.

"But you didn't say yes either. Mom's case is going to need someone to go all-in with it. No testing the water with your feet." She paused with her hand on the doorknob and glared at him. "Her attorney will have to jump."

Tom shook his head. "Where did you learn to talk that way?"

She rolled her eyes. "I've been on my own since I was twelve years old. I didn't have a choice. When we were ripped away from Mom, I wasn't given the option of testing the water. I was thrown in the deep end, and me and Jackie were either going to swim or drown. Mom's cousin Tawny has the intelligence of a box of hammers, and her husband, Sam, is even dumber. I'm the one who makes sure Jackie has her lunch money before school and I'm the one who helps her with her homework. If I need a ride after practice, I get it myself. If I can't line one up, then I run."

"Is that how you got here?"

She nodded.

"That must be a three-mile hike from the school."

She shrugged. "It's five miles from the school to Tawny's house. You want to ask me how many times I've run that?"

Tom didn't answer, and Laurie Ann pulled the door open. "Adios, Professor. Thanks for the memories, old man." She continued to talk as she descended the stairs. "I ought to let you kick me in the knee before I head home. You know, just for old times' sake. Your whole existence has just been one big size-fourteen boot in my family's ass."

Tom caught up with her halfway down the stairs. When he reached for her shoulder, she wheeled on him with fists raised. "I was just joking about the kick in the knee."

For several seconds, he gazed down at her, unsure of what to do. Then, shaking his head and cursing under his breath, he walked past her. He'd have to look at his other files in the morning. "Come on."

"What are you doing?"

He spoke without turning. "You're not running home tonight."

Ten minutes later, Tom pulled to a stop in front of a double-wide trailer in a mobile home park in Northport. On the way, he had gone through the Taco Casa drive-through, and the smell of burritos and refried beans filled the interior of the Explorer.

"Thank you for the ride and the food," Laurie Ann said, grabbing the to-go sack and opening the door. Tom rolled down the passenger-side window, and Laurie Ann leaned her head back in, piercing him with her brown eyes. "I appreciate you going to the jail today, Professor. You didn't have to do that." She extended her hand through the window and Tom took it. "Thank you," she said.

"You're welcome," Tom managed.

She let go and took a step back, and Tom gazed over the steering wheel at the other trailers that lined the park.

"Well . . . bye," she finally said, and began to walk toward the front door of the mobile home.

"When do you get out of school?" Tom yelled, and Laurie Ann turned and continued to walk backward.

"Next week."

"Would you like to work in my law firm as a runner this summer? We could use the help." He paused. "Especially if I'm going to be handling a murder case."

She stopped and placed her hands on her hips, smiling down at the ground. When she looked up at him, tears streaked her cheeks and merged with the dried sweat. Her face shone in the light from the half-moon above. "Really?"

"Really. You can come in after school next week as soccer practice allows and then full time once you're out."

"S-sounds good," she said as her voice cracked with emotion. "Thank you so much."

"You may not be thanking me when this is over. We've got a huge hill to climb, and the Tuscaloosa district attorney is as good as they come."

Laurie Ann approached the Explorer and placed her hands on the window seal. Her face was all business. "So what's our first step?"

Tom squinted at her and then leaned back in his seat, gazing over the wheel again. "Pulaski," he finally said. "I've got to go back to Pulaski."

Laurie Ann wrinkled her face in confusion. "Why?"

"Because there are some things I need to know about your mother." He paused and cracked a weary smile. "And I need to recruit some more help."

PART THREE

17

Just past the Giles County Line on Highway 64 is a dilapidated building that a person would probably miss if they weren't looking for it. Tom put his right-turn blinker on and pulled his Explorer into the barren gravel lot. The front door was boarded up, and "For Sale" signs adorned the entrance and exit to the place, but Tom could still read the faded letters on the side of the structure: "The Sundowners Club."

Tom climbed out of his vehicle for a better look. Last year, a wealthy Pulaski businessman and landowner named Andy Walton had been murdered in this parking lot. Two shotgun blasts from close range. The corpse was then moved a half mile down the road to his farm, where it was hung from a tree and set on fire. In his younger years, Walton had been the Imperial Wizard of the Tennessee Knights of the Ku Klux Klan, and his brutal killing had garnered a lot of press. Tom and Rick had represented the man accused of the crime in a week-long trial that ended with the charges being dismissed and ten members of the Klan being brought to justice for the 1966 hanging of a black sharecropper named Roosevelt Haynes. One of the ten Klansmen was Larry Tucker, the longtime owner of the Sundowners.

Shortly after the trial, Tucker was murdered himself before he could be arrested. His club closed a week later.

Good riddance, Tom thought, squatting and scooping a handful of gravel. He gripped the pebbles in his right hand and let them slowly run through his fingers. The Sundowners Club closed its doors in early November, 2011. Unfortunately for his new client, the club was very much open during the spring and early summer of 2010. He raised his eyes to the upstairs windows, which weren't boarded up. Inside one of them, he could see what looked like a recliner. In his consultation with Wilma at the jail, she had told him that Jack Willistone wouldn't agree to Wilma's price to perjure herself on the stand in Henshaw until she had sex with him in one of the VIP rooms on the second floor of the Sundowners. Tom trudged toward the front door, gazing upward through the dusty glass at the room that had been a house of horrors for his client.

For him to effectively represent Wilma, he had to understand her motives, and he knew that this place had been a turning point for her. A place of no return. She had made a deal with the devil and been burned.

Wilma had told Tom that she had almost killed herself in the aftermath of the trial and losing custody of her children. She said she'd even shot out a mirror in her rental home. But she hadn't done the deed because she couldn't give up on her daughters. Tom had yet to meet the younger one, but he sure had met Laurie Ann, and there was a fierce determination that he felt the girl must have inherited from her mother. *"Nothing for me. Everything for them."* Tom whispered Wilma's mantra out loud and nodded his head as he ran his hand over the two-by-fours that ran crossways over the front door. She'd told him that she would say those words over and over to herself in the dark days before the trial in Henshaw and even more so during her incarceration for twelve months in the Giles County Jail. Tom glanced around the building one last time, trying to envision the place as it had once been, with its neon signs and the marquee at the entrance, which had long since been removed, advertising "Exotic Dancers" in red flashing lights.

Wilma had subjected herself to the evils of this place so she could put her girls in pretty clothes and provide more opportunities for them. Her reasoning for lying on the stand in Henshaw was one and the same, and she didn't defend herself on the prostitution charges because she couldn't risk the repercussions for Laurie Ann and Jackie. Jack Willistone and JimBone Wheeler had threatened that they would kill her daughters if she ever came forward with the truth, so she had kept her mouth shut. "Nothing for me. Everything for them," Tom repeated.

For all of her faults, Wilma didn't feel like a revenge killer to Tom. Murder would be too costly for her daughters, and Wilma was actively pursuing regaining custody of them.

Then how come Jack was murdered with her gun?

Tom sighed and shook his head. Assuming Wade was correct—and Tom had no reason to doubt his old friend's veracity—explaining the gun would be critical to a viable defense. When he returned to Tuscaloosa, he would need to have a come-to-Jesus talk with his client about the murder weapon.

As the afternoon sun beat down on his neck, Tom squinted toward Highway 64 as a familiar car approached and put its blinker on. To have any chance of winning this case, he would either have to discredit the state's forensic report concluding that the murder weapon was Wilma's pistol or . . . convince a jury that someone else killed Jack with Wilma's gun.

Tom's spirits began to sink as he went through the analysis in his head and thought of the steep uphill climb ahead. Then he smiled as a white Toyota Sequoia pulled into the gravel lot and a large black man emerged from behind the wheel. He wore gray athletic shorts, a crimson "A-Club" T-shirt, and combat boots, his bald head glistening with sweat. Even at fifty years old, standing six feet four and weighing well over two hundred pounds, the man still resembled the college linebacker he had once been. But as his old friend walked toward him, Tom noticed that his left leg was still gimpy and caused him to limp. Lines of worry were etched in his once-smooth face. He looked like he'd been to hell and back, and Tom knew that wasn't far off.

"Well look who's back in God's country," the man said, extending his hand, which Tom shook. When he did, his friend pulled him close for a hug and whispered a few more words in his ear. "Tell me something, Professor. Have you lost your mind?"

Despite the pain that engulfed his shoulders and lower back from the embrace, Tom managed to chuckle. "It's good to see you too, Bo."

Bocephus Aurulius Haynes was born in Pulaski, Tennessee, in 1961. At the age of five years old, he had watched his father hanged from a tree by ten members of the local chapter of the Ku Klux Klan. Less than a week later, his mother had disappeared, and Bo was raised by an uncle who lived nearby. As he grew up, Bo was blessed with freakish athletic talent, which was harnessed by an enormous chip on his shoulder to one day bring the men who destroyed his family to justice. He went to the University of Alabama on a football scholarship and played on Coach Paul "Bear" Bryant's last national championship team in 1979. Then, after blowing out his knee his junior year, Bo decided to go to law school after shadowing Tom for a semester at Coach Bryant's request. As a law student, Bo shined, and he was a member of Tom's second trial team to win the national tournament. After graduation, Bo spurned numerous big-firm offers to return to Pulaski, where he became Giles County's only African American trial lawyer and one of the most successful plaintiff's attorneys in the state of Tennessee. He had also renewed his quest for vengeance on the men who lynched Roosevelt Haynes.

That journey culminated last fall when Bo was charged with the capital murder of Andy Walton, the leader of the mob. After a week-long trial, the charges were dismissed as the truth behind both Andy's and Roosevelt's murders finally came out. With Tom and Rick's help, Bo had fulfilled his lifelong mission. The Klansmen who had participated in Roosevelt Haynes's murder were now either in prison or dead.

But victory had come with a heavy cost. Based upon the deep lines that Tom saw in his friend's forehead and his ever-present limp, Bo was still paying the physical toll that the trial and its aftermath had taken. And Tom knew that the emotional scars from the revelations of last fall ran even deeper. Bocephus Haynes had spent his life believing in one reality, and that vision had been turned upside down.

After meeting at the Sundowners, Tom followed Bo a half mile down the road to the turn-in for what had once been Walton Farm. The once-proud W that adorned the front wrought-iron gate had been taken down, but Tom noticed as he drove up the winding path that the farm still appeared to be in good shape and the great lawn in front of the mansion that Maggie Walton had referred to as the Big House was neatly mowed. After they'd parked their vehicles, Bo motioned for Tom to sit in a rocker on the wraparound porch while he went inside. A few minutes later, he returned with six beers in a bucket of ice. Tom was well into his second cold one as the sun made its descent over the rolling acres of soybeans.

"I still can't believe that this is all yours," Tom said, waving a hand over the railing at the farm.

Bo took a sip of beer. Then he placed his bottle on the wooden deck and gazed down at it. "That makes two of us. But Andy's will was pretty clear. The farm went to Maggie and, upon her death, to 'my surviving issue.' That's me, dog."

"Have you decided what you are going to do with it?"

Bo grabbed the bottle and leaned back in the chair. "Not yet. Gonna let Booker T keep farming it for now, and then . . ." He took another sip of beer.

"What does Jazz think?"

Bo shook his head. "That I've lost my mind. She begged me to just hire a realtor and sell it."

"Why didn't you?"

"Don't know. Just couldn't part with it yet. A lot of water under the bridge, you know."

"This land hasn't brought you anything but pain, Bo. Why would you want to keep it?"

"You sound like Jazz."

When Bo didn't say more, Tom leaned forward and spoke in a lower voice. "How are things between you two?"

Bo shook his head again. "The same. She's put up with a lot over the years, Professor. I haven't been the easiest person to live with."

"But everything seemed so good after the trial. She came back. We won. It just seemed like—"

"And they lived happily ever after," Bo interrupted, killing the rest of his beer in one gulp and cracking open another one. "That's the way it ends in fairy tales, but not here in the real world. Sure, everything was great for a few weeks. I stayed with her and the kids in Huntsville and commuted the hour to work each morning. I was so excited to get back to working my cases."

"Wide ass open," Tom said, remembering Bo's catchphrase for how he liked to practice.

"Damn right." He stood and leaned on the railing, gazing into the twilight. "Then the State Bar of Tennessee sends me a letter saying that I'm on indefinite probation until they can investigate my actions prior to and during the murder trial. A month later, they hand down their verdict."

"One-year suspension, right?" Tom asked, already knowing the answer.

"Complete bullshit." Bo spat the words. "The General dismissed all the charges, but the board suspends me for 'behavior unbecoming of the virtues of a lawyer in this state.' I appealed the decision, but you know how that goes. The bar is judge, jury, and executioner. They weren't going to change their mind."

"How long does the suspension run?"

"Next April," Bo said, taking a sip from the bottle. "April 22 to be exact."

"Did Alabama also suspend you?" Tom knew that Bo had been planning to open a satellite office in Huntsville since Jazz had started teaching at Alabama A&M.

"Yep. Everything's on hold until next April." He spat over the railing. "My whole damn life is on pause."

Tom stood and leaned against the railing, gazing sideways at his old friend. "None of that explains why you and Jazz are having problems."

Bo continued gazing at the farm that he'd once worked as a field hand and to which he now owned the deed. "Jazz is never going to move back to Pulaski. Her folks are from Huntsville and the separation allowed her to reimagine life for her, T. J., and Lila there. She can teach art history at Alabama A&M, and the kids can go to Huntsville High, her alma mater. So far she's doing great in her job, and the kids are both adjusting well to school."

"But you don't want to move?" Tom offered.

"It's not just that. I've got no problem with Huntsville. It's a cool place. And while I was able to work, I didn't mind the commute. But . . ."

"Spit it out," Tom finally said.

Bo turned and gazed at Tom with eyes that burned with intensity. "Professor, everything that I am is here." He waved his arm over the railing at the farm. "On this land. In Pulaski. My entire identity for fifty years has been wrapped up in being from Pulaski and coming home to bring the men to justice who murdered my . . . who hanged Roosevelt Haynes."

"You did that, Bo," Tom said softly.

"Yeah." He snickered. "And in the process I learned that my real father was once an Imperial Wizard of the Klan. The man I despised my whole life was my blood, and the man I thought was my daddy was just a damn sharecropper trying to feed a mouth that didn't belong to him." He sighed. "And now I own all this land and I don't know what the hell to do with it."

For several seconds, neither man spoke. Truth be known, Tom didn't know what to say. He wished he had been able to spend more time with Bo over the last few months. "Have you thought about seeing a therapist?" Tom finally asked. "That is a lot to have dumped on you at one time."

"Did you talk with Jazz before coming out here?" Bo asked, not hiding the accusatory tone in his voice.

"No, but she's a smart woman and you've been through hell and back. Talking to a professional is a good idea regardless of who suggests it."

Bo grunted but didn't respond.

"When did you move out?" Tom asked.

"Back in February. I was going crazy at the house with nothing to do. Once Andy's will was probated and the land became mine, I moved back here to clean things up."

"Are you really living in this house?" Tom asked.

"No, I couldn't do that. I'm staying at the office until I can figure out my next move."

"Has Jazz filed for divorce?"

Bo shook his head. "Not yet."

Tom nodded but didn't say anything. It was now pitch dark outside, and the sound of crickets and the blinking of lightning bugs filled the air.

Finally, Bo returned to his rocking chair and leaned back. "Well, I've caught you up on my sad state of affairs, but that's not why you're here." He paused and squinted up at Tom. *"Wilma Newton?"* He held out his palms. "I'll repeat what I asked at the Sundowners. Have you lost your mind?"

Tom crossed his arms and gazed down at the deck. Before making the trek to Pulaski, he had called Bo and said that he had just taken a new case and wanted to discuss it. He hadn't wanted to give any details, but Bo had pressed him and he'd finally broken down and given a bare-bones sketch.

"Professor, you still there?" Bo asked on the porch after Tom had remained silent for almost a minute.

"What did you just say about happy endings, Bo?" Tom asked, still looking at the deck.

"Only in fairy tales."

Tom met his friend's eyes. "Things haven't exactly been a bowl of cherries at our firm since your trial."

Bo creased his eyebrows. "Rick still hasn't come back."

"No, and I don't blame him. He worshipped his father, and his mom really needs help running their farm right now. And he never says this, but I suspect it keeps his mind off Dawn."

Bo let out a low whistle. "What's the latest on Ms. Dawn?"

"Moved to Birmingham and took a job with a midsize insurance defense firm."

"Still giving Daddy the trial run?"

Tom nodded. "As far as I know. Funny how life goes. Rick was about to ask Dawn to marry him. Was even carrying the ring around in his pocket, and they'd planned a weekend getaway to the coast. He was going to ask her at the Marina Cafe, a fancy restaurant in Destin. Had it planned out all the way to the dinner reservations. He's got his car packed and is stopping at her apartment to pick her up, and voilà. There's Daddy." He paused and took a swallow of beer. "The guy's name is John and he says he wants another chance to be a father to Julie, the daughter he has with Dawn."

"Which put my believer in a no-win situation." Bo had called Rick "my believer" since the trial last year because of the kid's genuine sincerity when he spoke to the jury.

"Exactly. He decided to take a step back and give Dawn some space." He sighed. "And a month later, she tells him that she wants to give John another chance. For the child's sake."

"How did he take that?"

Tom smirked. "Rick has matured a great deal in the last few years, but . . ."

"How bad?"

"He told Dawn he understood and managed to get through their conversation pretty well. But once she was gone, he basically destroyed his office and went home. According to Powell, the rest of the night was even uglier."

Bo whistled again. "When did his dad die?"

"Ten days later."

"Jesus. Any word on the hit-and-run driver?"

Tom shook his head. "Rick says it's a dead end. They'll never find him."

For several seconds, the only sound on the deck came from the crickets. Then Bo broke the silence with the question that had been hanging in the air all night. "Why'd you come here, Professor?"

"Because I need a lead investigator on the capital murder case I just agreed to take and"—he paused and looked around the deck—"you need something to do."

In the darkness, Tom couldn't make out Bo's features. All he could tell was that the big man had crossed his arms and begun to rock in the chair. Bo rose and walked around Tom to the front door. He reached inside and flipped on the porch light and an overhead fan. Then he took a place next to Tom by the railing and leaned his elbows on it. "Lead investigator, huh?"

"That's right. I'm not asking you to practice law, just help me dig up some information. Kinda like you did in the Henshaw trial a few years ago, but in a more official capacity."

Bo continued to peer out at the darkened fields. "This case is going to put you against your boy Powell, right?"

"Right. And you against Wade." Tom paused. "If you're in."

"You're breaking up the band, Professor. Wade and Powell helped us in Pulaski last year. We all could've bitten the bullet if they don't take down JimBone Wheeler on the square." He stopped and looked at Tom. "You really want to do that?" When Tom didn't answer, he pressed. "Is this case really worth that?"

Tom held Bo's gaze but didn't say anything.

Bo leaned closer and spoke in a low voice. "Wilma Newton is a convicted prostitute. She's also a liar. She perjured herself on the stand in Henshaw, and most of my investigation was aimed at helping you cross-examine her because your gut told you that she was going to do exactly what she did." He licked his lips. "I can't imagine why you would want to help her under any circumstances, much less in a case that pits us against our friends."

"She saved Dawn's life," Tom whispered.

"No, dog," Bo said, poking his index finger lightly in Tom's chest, "*I* saved Dawn's life."

"If we hadn't gotten the warning call from Wilma, then we might not have acted with such urgency. You might not have arrived in time to save Dawn."

"How can you be sure that Wilma Newton made that call?"

"Who else could it have been?" When Bo didn't answer, Tom knew he'd made his point. "Remember Darla Ford?" Tom volunteered.

"Andy's favorite dancer at the Sundowners. Testified for us in the trial last year. Now running an oyster bar on the coast."

"That's right," Tom said. "Well, after I spoke with Wilma at the jail, Darla called and all but begged me to take the case. Said Wilma was a lost soul in need of a break. She even offered to contribute to her defense fund." When Bo remained silent, Tom added, "Darla didn't have to testify for us last year, but she came of her own accord."

"I know that, Professor, and I agree that we owe Darla a debt of gratitude, but Powell and Wade are our brothers. Do we owe her that much?"

"No," Tom said. "No, we don't. But it is a factor."

Finally, Bo slammed his fist down on the railing and glared across the porch at Tom. "Stop giving me factors and *tell me the deal*. Why did you take this case?"

Tom slumped into one of the rockers and looked past Bo into the darkness. "Because of the girl," he finally said.

"What girl?" Bo asked.

"Wilma's oldest daughter, Laurie Ann. She's fourteen years old. It wasn't Wilma who asked me to represent her. It was Laurie Ann. She showed up at the office and told me about everything that had happened to her and her sister since the accident in Henshaw."

"So *you feel sorry* for Wilma's daughter? Is that the deal? This is a pity mission?"

"No, that's not it," Tom snapped, feeling heat on the back of his neck.

"It sure as hell sounds like it," Bo said.

"That's not it," Tom repeated, his voice firm. Then he whispered, "Nothing for me. Everything for them."

Bo wrinkled his eyes in confusion. "What?"

"'Nothing for me. Everything for them.' The phrase that Wilma Newton would say to herself to keep her going while she was doing all these things. Becoming a stripper. Doing the deal with Willistone to lie on the stand. Not defending herself once she was charged with prostitution. The year in jail. All of her actions . . . all motivated by her daughters."

"OK, so . . ."

"She's not a revenge killer, Bo. Killing Willistone might give her vengeance, but it would end any chance of being reunited with Laurie Ann and Jackie. That doesn't fit."

"People are crazy, Professor. You know that. I don't think it's a stretch to suggest that Wilma might have snapped and killed the man who ruined her life and cost her the custody of her daughters."

"Well, that will certainly be Powell's argument, but he doesn't have privy to the most damning information. The deal that Wilma cut with Jack to commit perjury isn't something he could prove independent of Wilma telling him, and there'd be no way to prove that Jack was behind the loss of her children. That's all information I got directly from Wilma, and as far as I know, she's the only person who could testify to such an arrangement who's still alive other than JimBone Wheeler."

"Who is on death row in Nashville," Bo added.

"And would have no reason to help Powell prove his case. Our sandy-haired friend is who put him there."

"OK, so they may be weak on motive. You said the physical evidence was bad over the phone. What is it?"

"Ballistics hasn't confirmed this yet, but it appears that the state will be able to prove that the gun that killed Jack Willistone was registered to Wilma Newton and only had her prints on it."

"Where'd they find it?"

"Underneath the dock where Willistone was shot and killed."

Bo raised his eyebrows. "Now how are we supposed to get around that?"

Tom held out his palms. "I don't know. I need an investigator to dig around a little and see if we have an angle."

Bo smirked. "It sounds like you need Jesus of Nazareth."

"Him too," Tom said. "But I'll settle for now on Bocephus Haynes." He paused and extended his right hand. "You in?"

Bo blinked his eyes, but a smile pursed his lips. He shook Tom's hand. "When can I start?"

18

Jackie's Lounge is a dive bar on Paul W. Bryant Drive. For years, it has been the saloon of choice for law school students at the University of Alabama needing to blow off steam. At 11:30 p.m. on Monday night, the law school crowd had already deserted the place, and it was almost empty except for a middle-aged couple playing on one of the pool tables in the back.

Detective Wade Richey nodded at the couple as he entered the dimly lit bar and squinted his eyes toward the bartender, a twenty-something blond who wore a pink cap with "Bama" embroidered in white along the front. She rolled her eyes and cocked her head toward the ancient jukebox that rested against the far wall. In the darkened corner nearest the music machine, Wade saw the shadow of a man, and the detective strode toward it. As he walked, the opening chord of Willie Nelson's "Whiskey River" rang through the overhead speakers. Wade took a seat next to the man.

"So it's a 'Whiskey River' night."

"Yep." Powell Conrad's voice was flat and he raised a glass of whiskey over ice to his lips.

"How many times did you push it?" Wade asked, nodding at the jukebox.

"Fifteen," Powell said, his tone still flat as a week-old keg.

"How many times has it played so far?"

"Seven I think."

"Any complaints?"

Powell shook his head. "I think Weezy likes it."

Wade chuckled. The bartender's name was Louisa, but she insisted that everyone call her Weezy. Judging by the look she gave him when he walked in the door, Wade doubted that she was as enthralled with hearing the redheaded stranger's tune over and over again. But Powell had helped convict the bartender that Weezy replaced for skimming off the top of the business's profits, and since then the owner had let the prosecutor have the run of the place. Occasionally, that meant dealing with a "Whiskey River" night.

"What's up?" Wade asked.

Powell reached into his pocket and pulled out a folded piece of paper. He slid it across the table and took another sip of whiskey. "This."

Wade unfolded the page and his skin immediately turned cold as he recognized the style of the case: *The State of Alabama v. Wilma Christine Newton* and, underneath the style, the title of the pleading: "Notice of Appearance of Counsel for the Defendant." *No,* Wade thought, skimming the stock language of the notice until he reached the signature at the bottom of the page. "Thomas Jackson McMurtrie," he said out loud, his voice rising above the nasal twang of Willie on the jukebox.

"Yep," Powell said, draining his glass and holding it up and nodding at Weezy for a refill.

"Make that two," Wade yelled as he reread the official entry of Tom McMurtrie into the case. After the bartender had placed the glasses of Jack Daniel's Black on the table, Wade looked at his friend. "You OK?"

Powell shrugged. "It's a free country. The accused in a capital murder case is entitled to a defense. That's what our legal system is founded on."

"That sounds good for TV. I like it. Now"—Wade leaned forward over his glass and gritted his teeth—"how do you really feel about it?"

Powell glared at Wade with bloodshot eyes but didn't respond. On the jukebox, the song was fading out. But three seconds later, the opening salvo restarted, and Willie began to sing about drowning in a whiskey river again. Wade looked at Weezy, who threw up her arms in frustration and held up both hands, mouthing the words "That's ten."

"You sure this is the eighth time the song has come on?"

"Could be nine." He grunted, and his red-rimmed eyes blazed with intensity. "I love the Professor, but I have a job to do for this county and state. This is a capital murder case, and I don't intend to let up until Wilma Newton is put to death by lethal injection. If Professor McMurtrie gets in the way, then I'm going to run over him. Plain and simple." He paused. "You good with that?"

Wade nodded. "I warned Tom to walk away and I told him what would happen if he got in our way. We don't have a choice, brother."

Powell sighed and started to take another sip, but Wade grabbed his hand. "I need to show you something. You got a computer in your car?"

Powell smirked. "Yeah . . . but I'm kind of in the middle of getting drunk. What is it?"

Wade stood from his chair. "Come on. Once I show you this, you're going to feel a lot better about our chances of taking Tom to the woodshed." He glanced at Weezy. "And despite all the capital you've built up with this place, I'd say you're two more playings of 'Whiskey River' away from being thrown out."

Powell glanced at the bartender and took a last swig from his glass. "Fair enough."

Twenty minutes later, they were back at the Sheriff's Office, with Powell's computer propped on the middle of the conference room table. After watching the video one time in Powell's Charger, they had left Wade's truck parked on the curb outside of Jackie's, and Wade had driven the district attorney back to the office and made a pot of coffee. Since then they had watched the seven-minute tape at least four more times, and Powell had drunk three cups of joe. The prosecutor was now stone sober and hyperalert. "This is pure gold, brother," he said, pressing play once more.

On the screen, four black-and-white images of the inside and outside of the Oasis Bar & Grill came into focus. Having no audio, the video showed two angles inside the bar as well as views of the front door and back visitor's entrance. Under the cube of images was a scroll that read "5/8/12" and next to it the time: 17:23. After twenty seconds, 17:23 turned to 17:24.

"Jack Willistone was murdered on the night of May 8 sometime between ten o'clock p.m. and twelve o'clock midnight," Powell narrated in a loud voice, his eyes focused on the computer.

Wade pointed to the left-hand corner of the cube of images, and Powell clicked pause and enlarged the picture. "And that's our victim sipping on a cold one at the Oasis at 5:24," Wade said. "Five to seven hours before he sleeps with the fishes."

Powell nodded. On the screen, Jack faced the camera and sat at a table near the bar. He appeared relaxed, with one leg crossed over the other, while he occasionally took a drink from a Bud Light. The woman across from him bobbed her head up and down while she talked and occasionally used her hands to gesture. She had medium-length hair and was wearing some type of blouse, but with her back turned to the screen, it was impossible to tell who she was. The image wasn't clear enough to make out Jack's facial expressions, but he didn't appear upset. After three minutes, Jack stood and threw a couple of bills down on the table. He placed a cap on his head and appeared to say something to the woman.

Wade pressed pause on the keyboard. "The bartender, Toby Dothard, told me this afternoon when I watched the tape with him that Jack says 'You crazy bitch' right here." Wade then clicked the play icon, and Jack walked out of view. For a second, the woman sat still at the table and put her face in her hands. Then she slammed her hands down and followed Jack out of view. When she turned to face the camera, the image froze.

Wade having again paused the video, the two men gazed at the screen. There was now no question of the woman's identity. "Wilma Newton," Powell whispered. He hit play and pointed to the bottom-right camera angle, which at the moment showed no one. Two seconds later, the door opened and Jack stepped through. He almost walked out of view but then stopped, as if someone had yelled at him from behind. Wilma then appeared and was pointing at Jack. She stuck her index finger in his chest, and Jack grabbed her arm and twisted it, causing Wilma to fall to a knee. He leaned over her and said something, but then Wilma slapped his face with her other hand. She tried to slap him again, but Jack blocked the blow and covered his face with both arms while Wilma wailed on him with her fists. The door swung open again, and a man wearing an apron stepped between them. Wilma still swung her arms, yelling something.

"Toby," Powell said, having ordered food and drinks from the bartender on numerous occasions. With his right arm wrapped around Wilma, Toby Dothard turned his head and motioned with his left arm for Jack to go. Jack Willistone stepped backward out of view of the camera. Toby tried to lead Wilma toward the door, but she broke out of his grasp and ran in the direction that Jack had gone.

Toby paused for a second or two and went in the bar. For almost a full minute, the screen showed only the gravel parking lot. Then Toby returned with a large muscular man wearing a tank top and sporting a mullet crew cut.

"Toby get a new bouncer?" Powell asked, his eyes locked on the screen.

"Yeah. Big Mike finally quit. This kid hired on about three months ago. I can't remember his real name—I wrote it down—but Toby calls him Drago because he looks kind of like the big Russian in *Rocky IV*."

"I don't remember Drago having a mullet."

Wade pointed at the screen. The bartender and the bouncer walked out of view and, for another minute and a half, the image was barren of people. Then Toby and Drago reappeared with Wilma between them. Drago had his arm up under Wilma's to steady her, while Toby had a hand on her back. Powell clicked pause, and the screen froze with Wilma staring blankly toward the door. "Anything else of note on the tape?"

"I haven't combed through all of it, but the only thing else you see is Wilma drink three Jack and Cokes alone at the bar." Wade paused. "She leaves around 6:30 p.m."

Powell hit rewind on the computer, the screen shifting back to Wilma screaming at Jack and thrashing her arms while Toby held her back. "Tell me again what Toby said she was yelling."

"'You're going to pay me my money or I'm going to kill you, you son of a bitch.'" Wade paused. "Some version of that over and over again."

Powell stood and paced the floor of the conference room, occasionally taking a sip from a Styrofoam cup of coffee. He looked at Wade and smiled. "I'd say we're doing better on motive, brother. Great job tracking this down."

"You want me to make a copy of this for Tom? He might plead her to life after seeing this."

Powell shook his head. "Make a copy of the video but let's not give it to him until he serves us with discovery. No freebies, Wade. He may be our friend, but he's representing a killer, and this tape seals the deal." He paused. "I'm not sure I'd agree to a life plea after seeing that. Wilma Newton threatened to kill Jack Willistone four to six hours before he was murdered with her gun. I think she sat at that bar and decided on how she was going to do it."

Wade rubbed the whiskers on his chin. "We still going to Jasper?"

"Hell yes," Powell said, beginning to pace again. "Any defense lawyer, much less one as good as the Professor, would be crazy not to focus on Jack's family as alternative suspects, and we need to know if there are any soft spots." He pointed at the computer. "But that tape changes the dynamic. We know Bully is dirty, but it's going to be hard for any defense theory aimed at him to overcome what we just saw on the screen."

"Or the gun."

"Or that," Powell said. "Do we have an absolute confirmation yet from ballistics?"

"No, but we should soon. They know it's a rush."

"Good."

For several seconds, silence filled the conference room as both men went over their internal to-do lists. Then, rubbing his whiskers again, Wade spoke in a hushed voice, almost as if he were talking to himself. "I still can't believe Tom would get involved in this case. It's a no-win."

Powell took another sip of coffee. When he spoke, his tone was solemn. "Same reason Ali fought Holmes. Or why Joe Willie played that season for the Rams." He sighed. "The great ones never know when to quit."

19

The Riverbend Maximum Security Institution, in Nashville, is where the State of Tennessee houses its inmates on death row.

After being checked through security, Tom followed an armed guard along the long corridor that led to the consultation room. "The prisoner is waiting for y'all," the guard said, turning her head slightly as she spoke. She was a statuesque woman at just a shade under six feet. Biceps toned by weight lifting bulged out of her short-sleeve button-down shirt. The name tag above her lapel read "Cpl. Stone."

"Thank you, Corporal," Tom said.

"No problem," she said, turning her head full around to smile at the woman walking beside Tom. "When the General asks us to jump around here, we don't ask why. We ask how high."

Tom also smiled and shot a quick glance at his companion for this trip. Helen Evangeline Lewis was the district attorney general for the Twenty-Second Judicial District of the State of Tennessee, which included the counties of Giles, Maury, Lawrence, and Wayne. At sixty years old, Helen had pale, almost ghostly skin and jet-black hair, dyed even darker than its original color, which fell to her shoulders. Her lips were painted with bright-red lipstick, and she wore a sleek black suit and high heels that, with her thin figure, made her appear even more imposing and intimidating. Though her face had begun to show signs of age and she was no stranger to Botox, Tom had always found Helen to be a strikingly attractive woman. The utter confidence with which she carried herself had broken many a defense lawyer in her over twenty years as a prosecutor. Tom thought it fitting that one of the nuances of Tennessee law was that state prosecutors were referred to as "General" in the courtroom, since outside of Coach Paul "Bear" Bryant, no one in his life had commanded as much authority as Helen Lewis.

When they reached the end of the hall, Corporal Stone began entering numbers on a keypad. After a couple of seconds, a sealed door slid open, and the three stepped through the opening. Tom blinked his eyes, noticing that this hall was a little darker and not as long.

"He's in the second door on the left," the corporal said, leading the way down the dimly lit hall. "His hands are chained to a bar that runs along the middle of the desk and his feet are shackled." Tom felt his heartbeat speed up as he gazed at the metal door behind which sat one of the country's foremost killers, a man who murdered one of Tom's oldest friends, not to mention countless others. He felt a hand on his wrist and glanced at Helen.

"You ready?" she asked, her eyes narrowing with concern.

"Thank you for setting this up," Tom managed, giving her a quick nod.

Helen scoffed and signaled for Corporal Stone to unlock the door. "You saved my life last year, Tom. If I can help you, I will. But . . ." She leaned close to him and spoke so that the corporal couldn't hear. "I can't imagine how this bastard can help you in your case. He's a stone-cold psychopath, and you know it."

"I'm just doing my due diligence, General," he said, gesturing toward the door. "He's a big part of why my client's life went off the rails, and he was a confidant and right-hand man of the victim in my case."

"He won't talk," Helen said as the door slowly opened.

"We'll see," Tom said, motioning for Helen to enter first and then following the prosecutor inside.

James Robert "JimBone" Wheeler peered at Tom through slit-like eyes, but his expression remained neutral. His dirty-blond hair was longer than Tom remembered, falling halfway down his neck, and the similarly colored stubble that Tom had seen on his face had now grown into a full-fledged beard. With his ruddy skin and flat eyes, everything about the man reminded Tom of a copperhead snake. In the South, though rattlesnakes are the more famous species, copper-heads are the meanest and, in Tom's opinion, the deadliest. Living on a farm in Hazel Green, Alabama, Tom had seen his fair share of the viper. While rattlesnakes usually warned you to stay away with their sound, copperheads blended in with the dirt and grass and just bit the crap out of anyone who got near them.

Tom and Helen took a seat in the two chairs that faced JimBone, while Corporal Stone stood behind them with her arms folded. For almost a full minute, silence filled the small square-shaped room. Finally, glancing at Helen, Tom leaned forward and spoke. "Mr. Wheeler, I'm sure by now that you've heard about Jack Willistone."

JimBone blinked but didn't say anything. His face gave away nothing.

"He's dead," Tom said. "He was murdered a week ago. Two days after he was released from prison."

JimBone glanced down at the desk as if he was thinking through something, his face engulfed by shadow. Finally, he raised his eyes. "How?"

Tom felt goose bumps on his arm. He had never heard the man talk before, and his voice had an ever-so-slight Louisiana twang. "Three gunshot wounds from a small handgun." Tom paused. "His body was found on the banks of the Black Warrior."

JimBone gazed down at the table again, blinking his eyes. For a moment, he gritted his teeth and then his face relaxed. Still looking at the table, he spoke in a barren voice. "Why are you here, old man?"

Tom glanced at Helen, who nodded at him. This was the opening that he'd hoped for. "I represent the person accused of killing Jack." Tom paused. "I believe you know her."

JimBone raised his head and looked at the attorney. Even the man's hazel eyes gave off a yellowish, reptilian tint.

"Wilma Newton," Tom said, looking intently at the killer to gauge his reaction.

JimBone's face broke from neutral into a wide grin. "Is it April Fools'?"

Tom again glanced at Helen, who gave an impatient roll of her eyes. Then he squinted back at JimBone. "It's May 15, Mr. Wheeler, and I'm not joking. Wilma Newton has been charged with murdering Jack Willistone, and the state has asked for the death penalty."

JimBone shook his head. "I still don't believe it."

"What do you not believe, Mr. Wheeler?" Tom asked, venturing in with as much caution as he could muster. "That she was charged . . . or that she did it?"

"Either one," he said. "I can't believe either one."

"Why?" Tom asked, hoping that he could keep him talking.

The smile on JimBone's face slowly faded and his eyes hardened. "I agreed to this little meeting because I have to admit that I was curious as to why you would come here, McMurtrie. But now that you appear to be on a fishing expedition, I have to ask, What's in it for me?"

"Nothing," Helen said, her voice stern and ice cold. "You have been convicted of the murder of Raymond Pickalew and the attempted murder of Bocephus Haynes, as well as numerous other felonies, for which you've been sentenced to death. I have no authority to give you any kind of reduced sentence. If you don't want to participate any longer in this meeting, then let Corporal Stone know, and we'll be on our way. This meeting was arranged as a favor to Professor McMurtrie, who as you well know had a hand in putting you where you are now."

JimBone smirked. "Bullshit. That loudmouth prosecutor Conrad is who put me here. He and that crazy detective."

"They wouldn't have been in Pulaski that day if it weren't for Tom." She paused. "What's it gonna be, Wheeler?"

"I'm still here. What do you want to know, old man?" He turned his slit-eyed stare to Tom.

"Why can't you see Wilma Newton as Jack's killer?"

"Because she's a doe, old man. I spent a good deal of . . . *quality time* with Wilma leading up to that trial in Henshaw a couple years ago. I believe you saw me in the courtroom, did you not? You even asked Wilma about the man who drove her to court."

Tom waited for more.

"Well, the Wilma I knew would never have the sand to take down a man like Jack. She would never risk losing her daughters."

"What if she had already lost custody of them? What if a crazy psychopath left an answering machine message at her rental home that made her sound like a whore, and that tape got in the wrong hands?"

JimBone cocked his head to the side. "No way."

Tom ignored him and continued. "What if she was then charged with prostitution and was too scared to defend herself so she pled guilty and spent a year in jail?" Tom paused and watched the killer's face, which gave away nothing. "Is this new information to you, Mr. Wheeler?"

"Yes, it is. But I have to say I'm enjoying hearing it."

"After all that, you still don't see her for the murder?"

JimBone rubbed the whiskers on his chin. "I guess it's possible, but only if she did it to protect herself or her kids." His voice left nothing to doubt. Tom creased his eyebrows.

"Why so sure?"

"Because she had her chances. I know she carried a gun in her purse when me and Jack would *visit* her. If she'd wanted to bad enough and had the sand for it, she could've taken her shot then." He paused. "Believe me, we gave her every reason to want to kill us."

Tom rubbed his chin. Everything that JimBone Wheeler had said so far matched his own conclusions. It was time to change direction.

"Mr. Wheeler, you worked with Jack Willistone for many years, correct?"

"No comment," JimBone said. "I'm not going to answer stupid questions."

"OK then, let me get right to it. When you learned that Jack Willistone had been killed, were there any names that popped into your head as possible suspects?"

JimBone shook his head. "I don't think that way. My only thought was that I'm sorry I didn't do it."

Tom felt goose bumps break out on his arm. "Why is that?"

"Because Jack owed me money. *A lot* of money. I also think he gave Conrad and that detective information about my whereabouts last year that helped them spoil my party in Pulaski. I was so close to killing your black friend. I guess Pickalew was a nice consolation prize."

Tom's hands balled into fists and he felt heat on his face.

"Ray Ray is what you called him, right? Old law school buddy of yours?"

Tom gritted his teeth. "He was also my teammate at Alabama."

"That's right. One of Bear Bryant's boys. Well . . . Roll Tide." He cackled, and Tom felt Helen's hand on his wrist, which he now noticed was shaking. "Easy," she whispered.

"Oh hell," JimBone continued. "I'm sorry, McMurtrie. I guess I got carried away."

Tom clasped his hands together to keep them from trembling and drew a short breath. It was hard to shake the image of Raymond "Ray Ray" Pickalew as he'd seen him last. At the Hillside Hospital emergency room, two bullet holes in his gut, eyes with a frozen gaze as a hospital technician pulled the sheet over his head. Tom cleared his throat and glared at JimBone. "If I put a gun to your head and asked you to guess Jack Willistone's killer, who would you say?"

JimBone leaned back in his chair and gazed up at the ceiling. "Do you know where I was born, McMurtrie?"

Tom squeezed his hands together and glanced down, trying to hold his patience. *Keep him talking.* "No, I don't."

"You ever been to the Sipsey Wilderness?"

Tom felt a flutter in his heart. "Yes. Went camping there with my family one fall. Pretty country."

JimBone scoffed. "I guess. We never paid much mind to the scenery. I was born in a trailer on the edge of the national forest. My daddy drove a log truck and was gone for months at a time when I was a kid. I had an older sister, and she and my momma would entertain men during the day when daddy was on a haul." He chuckled bitterly. "Sometimes I'd be in the main room of the single wide watching *Scooby-Doo* on our black-and-white set and I'd hear momma panting like a dog in the bedroom while some mechanic from Hamilton bent her over the foot of the bed. Marcy would be in her closet of a room doing the same thing. I'd turn the volume up full blast, but

I could still hear what was going on." He smiled. "When they were done for the day, they'd sit out on the wooden deck in back of the trailer and smoke weed or do lines of coke or any other drugs the men left as payment in addition to the paltry cash they made for being whores." He stopped, still gazing up at the ceiling. "Daddy left on a haul in 1981 for Jackson, Mississippi and never came back. I can't say I blamed him."

"Your mother and sister were both killed during a trailer fire in 1992, right, Mr. Wheeler?" Helen asked. Tom figured this was information she'd dug up during her investigation after Wheeler's arrest.

"Yep. Bodies burned beyond recognition."

"The Walker County fire chief ruled the blaze arson, but no arrests were ever made." She stopped. "You know a bit about arson, don't you, Mr. Wheeler?"

Tom remembered the fire that had engulfed the Ultron Gasoline Plant in Tuscaloosa after the accident in Henshaw. That fire hadn't been ruled arson, but it had been suspicious.

"I was in the army at that time, General Lewis. Fort Benning." He spoke with a trace of humor in his voice that left Tom no doubt who had set the fire that killed his mother and sister.

"Where are we going with this, Mr. Wheeler?" Tom asked, trying to get the conversation back on the murder of Jack Willistone.

JimBone lowered his gaze and focused on Tom. "As you might imagine, I didn't enjoy being home much as a kid. I spent a lot of time roaming the streets of Jasper. Eventually, I got caught stealing a Hershey bar at a grocery store. The store owner was about to call the cops, but a man there stopped him." JimBone's eyes flickered at the memory. "This man had salt-and-pepper hair with long Elvis-like sideburns and wore a damn leisure suit. He told the grocery store manager that he'd handle it, and that was that. The manager walked away, but not before I saw the fear in his eyes." JimBone smiled and squinted at Tom. "Ever hear of a man named Marcellus Calhoun, Professor?"

Tom held JimBone's stare, but his heartbeat had sped up. "Goes by Bully, right?" Tom asked. "Bully Calhoun."

"That's right. Back in the '80s Bully still wore wild suits that made him stand out like a sore thumb. I hear he's a lot more conservative these days."

"How long did you work for Bully?"

JimBone shrugged. "Pretty much full time from the age of nine up until I graduated high school. Then for a few years after I got out of the army."

"We found nothing on you after you were discharged," Helen chimed in.

"Better for business to be invisible."

"If you worked for Bully for so long, how did you get mixed up with Jack Willistone?" Tom asked.

"Bully owned a lot of businesses that required the use of long-haul trucks. Some of these operations required secrecy. If the price was right, Jack didn't care about breaking the law. You found that out, didn't you, old man?"

Tom ignored the question. "How—?

"I'm getting there," JimBone interrupted. "Patience, old man. After a while, Bully loaned me out to Jack when their joint deals required someone to be silenced. I had learned a lot about *silencing* folks in the army."

"Special Forces?" Tom asked.

"Ranger. Anyway, after a while I started being hired by Jack for solo jobs."

"Did Bully mind?"

JimBone scoffed. "No, I think Bully was relieved to have me on someone else's payroll. That is until his daughter decided to become the second Mrs. Jack Willistone."

"I take it Bully wasn't happy with that development," Tom said.

"He was pissed," JimBone said, a devilish gleam in his eyes. "Like every daddy in the world, he'd wanted his little girl to marry a doctor or a lawyer, but lo and behold, little girls always end up marrying their fathers, and Jack and Bully were two sides of the same coin. Bully saw Jack's courtship of Kat as a betrayal. A crossing of an invisible line in the sand. You asked me who I thought would kill Jack if I had a gun put to my head. Well, that's easy. Bully has wanted Jack dead from the minute the preacher said, 'You may kiss the bride.'"

"If that's true, then why didn't he kill him a long time ago? Jack married Kathryn Calhoun in 2005. That was seven years ago."

JimBone shrugged. "Bully has always been cool as a cucumber. Despite how he felt about Jack, he wouldn't kill his baby girl's husband unless she wanted him dead. Initially, I think Kat was pretty happy living in the Big House with Jack. Even more so than Bully, Jack was flashy with his money, and Kat didn't lack for anything. Course that all changed when Jack was arrested after the trial in Henshaw." JimBone stopped and raised his shackled hands at Tom. "That was you, too, you son of a bitch. Conrad got credit for the arrest, but just like with me, it was you that put him there. Anyway, once Jack was sentenced to prison and went bankrupt, I suspect Kat's feelings about her husband changed a great deal." He licked his lips. "I'm sure you've checked to see if there was a life insurance policy."

"I just took the case, so I haven't verified that yet."

"Well, mark it down. He had a policy to the tune of several million dollars and, last I heard anything about it, the sole beneficiary was Kathryn Calhoun Willistone."

"How do you know this?" Tom asked, genuinely impressed.

"It was my business to know. When you work for the people that I work for, knowledge is power."

Tom shot Helen a glance. The prosecutor raised her eyebrows, her curiosity, like his own, clearly piqued. Tom had known that Bully

Calhoun was Jack Willistone's father-in-law and he had known Bully's history as a player in the Jasper mob. That was why he'd needled Wade back at the jail. Given Bully's history, you'd have to give him a look.

But JimBone's story had struck deeper. "Mr. Wheeler, do you think Bully Calhoun would have the ability to have Jack Willistone murdered and then frame a doe like Wilma Newton?"

JimBone smirked. "Are you kidding? Bully could do that and still bet on the horse race at night."

The rest of the interview was uneventful as Tom asked several questions about JimBone's own activities in the past few months since being sentenced to death. He was primarily interested in any visitors who might have said anything about Jack or Wilma. But the line of inquiry went nowhere.

"I'm sure they'll let you check the visitor's sheet," JimBone said. "But I know for a fact that it's as empty as church on the Sunday after Easter. Ain't nobody come to see the Bone."

Tom looked at Helen, who nodded her agreement with JimBone's summary. Then he gazed across the table at the killer. "Mr. Wheeler, I appreciate your time. The information you've provided has been helpful."

JimBone's face remained neutral as he looked back at Tom with his copperhead eyes. He said nothing. Tom felt a hand on his arm and saw that Helen had risen to go. He did the same but kept his eyes on JimBone. "Why did you talk with me today, Mr. Wheeler?" Tom asked after a moment. "According to General Lewis, you've barely said a word since your arrest at the courthouse square."

For several seconds, the two men just looked at each other. Tom wondered if JimBone had any rhyme or reason for opening up. "Well, thank you," Tom said, and followed Helen to the door.

As Corporal Stone began to unlock it, JimBone's voice caused the hairs on Tom's neck to stand up. "Come here."

Tom and Helen looked at each other and then both started to approach the table.

"Just you, McMurtrie," JimBone said, lowering his sights. "The two bitches can stand by the door."

Helen shook her head. "*Let's go,*" she whispered, but Tom held out his hands and made eye contact with both Helen and the corporal.

"It's fine," he whispered. "I want to hear what he has to say."

Tom took two steps toward the table and returned to his seat, while Helen and Stone waited by the door. "OK," Tom said.

JimBone leaned forward and rested his chin on his shackled hands. He raised his eyes and spoke in just above a whisper. "Do you know what the word 'reckoning' means, McMurtrie?"

Tom felt the goose flesh that had sprung up on his neck spread down his arms. "Revenge," Tom said. "Another word for revenge."

"It's more than that," JimBone said. "It's a balancing of the scales. A making of things right. A day . . . *of reckoning.*"

"So what?" Tom asked, beginning to tire of the games.

"Your day is coming, old man. And if you mess with Bully Calhoun, it may come sooner rather than later. I hope that isn't the case."

"Why?"

"Because when I get out of here, I intend to give you your day." He paused and his voice went so low that Tom strained to hear it. "I'm going to kill you, McMurtrie, and everyone you hold dear. Your son the doctor and his wife. That grandson of yours and his baby sister. Your whole family. I'm also going to kill your partner, Drake, and his family. Your nigger friend Haynes and his wife and kids. Conrad and that crazy detective. I'm going to bring a day of reckoning on you and everyone you hold dear, McMurtrie."

Tom's skin had gone cold as visions of this psychopath attacking Jackson and Jenny flooded his brain. He swallowed and when he spoke, he was surprised that the words came out calm and deliberate, reminding Tom of the way he had once advised his son to hold steady before bringing the head of a shovel down on a snake that had gotten in the garage. "Let me remind you that you are on death row, Mr. Wheeler. You're going to be put to death by lethal injection." Tom hesitated, before adding, "Your threats mean nothing."

"Really?" JimBone asked. "How is your partner's daddy doing?"

Tom leaned forward, sure he had heard him wrong. "*What?*"

"How is Billy Drake doing these days? I seem to recall hearing something about him having an accident."

Tom felt light-headed. "How could you—?"

"Who have we spent most of this meeting talking about?" JimBone interrupted.

"Bully . . . Calhoun?" Tom asked, his voice distant, his body numb with fear.

JimBone squinted at Tom with eyes that danced with delight. Then he slowly nodded. "After I left Bully's employ, he eventually found need for a person with . . . similar talents. I knew someone that would fit the bill very nicely." JimBone patted the desk with his fingertips. "Let's just say that my replacement was grateful for the job, and over the years we've helped each other out from time to time."

Tom leaned over the desk and forced his voice to be calm. "Are you saying that Bully Calhoun has a hit man that killed Billy Drake as a favor to you?"

JimBone grinned. "You must be hearing things, old man."

"I hear just fine," Tom said, his legs wobbly. "Why Rick's father? Why not me or Bo or even Rick himself?"

"I'm saving the rest of you for me," JimBone said, his voice just above a whisper. "But while I'm stuck in here, I thought I'd have a little bite. An appetizer before the main course."

Tom glared down at the psychopath, anger quickly replacing shock. "You're a crazy son of a bitch. When I do investigate Bully Calhoun, I'm going to tell him that *you* led me to him. That his old employee, James Robert Wheeler, is who flashed the light on him." Tom paused. "How'd that be?"

The grin widened on JimBone's face. "Bully is too smart to ever mess with me. I'm that stray dog you're not quite sure of. That dog that never barks. That you see sneaking around your back porch at night and in the morning. After a while, your own dog turns up pregnant or dead, depending on whether I want to fuck or kill it, and your garden don't have any food left. I'm a dog that only bites, Professor. A man like Bully Calhoun knows to leave me well enough alone."

Tom stood to leave. When he looked at Helen, her eyes were wide with worry, but Corporal Stone's face was bored. Just another day on death row.

When Tom reached the door, JimBone spoke in a clear, brittle voice from behind him. "Remember what I said, old man. Your day of reckoning is coming."

Tom didn't look back at him, but as Corporal Stone opened the locked door, the killer's words, an octave higher and with more menace, rang out above the jangle of keys.

"Courtesy of the Bone."

20

After Tom hadn't said a word for the first thirty minutes of the trip back to Pulaski, Helen finally nudged his elbow. "Hey, you OK? Your face is white as a sheet. What did that crazy bastard say to you before we left?"

Tom gazed out the window at the rolling Tennessee hills that dotted both sides of I-65. "Just crazy talk," Tom said, still thinking about what JimBone had said about Rick's father. He shivered and rolled down the window for air. Was it possible that the story JimBone Wheeler had just shared was true? Tom's heart was racing and he felt sick to his stomach, giving him his answer. He'd call the Henshaw County sheriff in the morning and he'd eventually have to tell Rick. Tom cringed as he envisioned his partner's reaction to this news. *How much more can he take?*

"Hey, stranger," Helen said, nudging Tom a little harder. When she did, he felt a ripple of agony run down his back and he winced. "I'm sorry. Are you OK?"

"Fine," Tom said, his teeth clenched in pain. "Just got a bulging disc or something."

"Well, what did you make of that back there? I was impressed that you got him to talk."

"Don't be," Tom said. "I didn't do anything special. He wanted to talk." Tom sighed, forcing his thoughts away from Billy Drake's death and back to the defense of Wilma. "But he did give us a few things. He confirmed that we should look at Bully Calhoun as an alternative killer, and, if Kathryn Willistone is in fact the beneficiary of the life insurance policy, then Bully would have motive to do the deed." He exhaled. "It was definitely worth the trip." Tom leaned his body against the passenger-side door, trying to get in a position where his back didn't hurt.

"Are you OK, Tom?" Helen repeated, and Tom glanced at her.

"I'm fine. Why do you ask?"

She focused her eyes over the steering wheel. "I don't know. This case just doesn't seem right for you. I mean, I understood why you took on Bo's defense last year, but why represent Ms. Newton?"

"I think she's innocent," Tom said. "And my actions during the case in Henshaw hurt her and I want to make things right." He thought of JimBone's words from the prison. "Balance the scales."

"You just represented the victim's family in an awful trucking accident. You didn't do anything wrong."

"I know, but Wilma Newton and her daughters were victims of that accident too. I want to help them."

"Is that it?"

Tom thought of his last encounter with Judge Braxton Poe and all of the case files in his office that would never end with a jury verdict. "Pretty much."

"Come on." She touched his shoulder. "Tell me."

Tom rolled up the window and then peered at Helen. "I don't know how many trials I have left in me, and . . . I'm a trial lawyer."

Helen slowly nodded. "OK, I get it now."

As she turned her blinker to get off on the Highway 64 exit, she spoke softly. "There's still something I don't get."

"What?" Tom asked.

"Why didn't you ask me out after Bo's trial last year?"

As she turned right onto Highway 64, Helen shot a look at Tom, whose face had turned a bright shade of red.

"Counselor, there is a question on the floor," Helen pressed, but her voice had a singsong tease to it.

Tom sighed. "I don't know. Do you think the Legends Steakhouse is still open?"

"Maybe," Helen said, her voice remaining playful.

"Can I buy you dinner?"

Helen chuckled and grasped Tom's hand, giving it a squeeze. "I thought you'd never ask."

21

Highway 69 is a curvy, mostly two-lane stretch of asphalt that runs through the Alabama towns of Tuscaloosa, Jasper, and Cullman. Though portions of the fifty-two miles from Tuscaloosa to Jasper are beautiful—especially the part that borders the river—other stretches exist where a person is glad to be in a moving vehicle with a gun in the glove compartment. As he passed a collection of single-wide and double-wide trailers, several of which proudly flew the Confederate flag in their yards, Bocephus Haynes was grateful that he'd decided to make the trek during the day. As a black man living in Pulaski, Tennessee, the birthplace of the Ku Klux Klan, Bo was used to seeing the battle flag of the Confederacy, and he thought the scenery on Highway 69 wasn't much different than Highway 31 going north toward Nashville. But Pulaski was his home and he knew the terrain. He very much felt like an outsider as he passed a green sign indicating "Walker County."

An African American law school classmate of his once said that either in Cullman or Walker County—he couldn't remember which—there used to be a handwritten sign next to the county line that read,

"Nigger, don't let the sun set on your back." Bo wasn't sure if that was true or just some hocus-pocus, but either way he planned to be on I-65 once darkness descended on Jasper.

It was Wednesday morning and he was expecting a call from the Professor any minute. Despite Bo's advice to the contrary, Tom had visited JimBone Wheeler on death row in Nashville yesterday. Bo doubted the killer would talk to anyone, much less Tom, but he was curious nonetheless. If he were honest, he was also still trying to get a read on why the Professor would want to get involved in Wilma's case. He hadn't met Laurie Ann Newton, nor had he spoken with her mother, as Tom had done, but the whole affair still didn't make much sense to him. Regardless, Bo was grateful to have a job to do. He had been so restless since his license was suspended that he had forgotten what it felt like to have a mission. As his Sequoia hurtled down Highway 69, his body hummed with excitement, as it had on so many cases over the past twenty-five years practicing law. *Wide ass open,* he thought, his mantra when a case began to heat up.

While Tom was in Nashville yesterday, Bo had driven in the opposite direction to Tuscaloosa, where he'd met with Detective Wade Richey at the Sheriff's Office. The meeting was tense and awkward, as Wade was none too thrilled with his friends' involvement in the Wilma Newton matter. Nonetheless, consistent with Powell's open-door policy with defense counsel, Wade made a copy of the state's file on Wilma and also provided Bo with a copy of the surveillance tape from the Oasis Bar & Grill in Cottondale.

As he passed through the tiny town of Oakman, Bo remembered Wade's last warning: "I've been a detective for over three decades, and it doesn't get more open and shut than this one, Bo. It was her gun, and she threatened to kill him less than six hours before he bought the farm." He had then placed one of his palms on Bo's shoulder. "We all went through a lot in Pulaski last year," he said. "Try to talk him out of this."

Bo had holed up at the Hotel Capstone on Paul W. Bryant Drive last night and reviewed the investigative report, all of the witness statements, and watched the Oasis video on his laptop. If he were a jury of one, Wilma Newton would ride the needle based on what he had seen so far.

But while Wade Richey had spent his life on the prosecution side, Bocephus Haynes had taken quite a few murder cases to a jury verdict and come out victorious on the other end. Things weren't always as black and white as prosecutors and detectives made them out to be. Based on his review of the evidence, Wilma Newton looked almost *too* guilty. The gun being dropped under the dock with only her prints rang hollow to him. If she had killed Jack Willistone, as the evidence suggested, with three shots from a handgun at a close distance, and then dumped his body into the Black Warrior, would she really have just dropped the weapon for the police to find? He could already hear Wade's response. *"Murderers do stupid things. That's why most of them end up being caught and sent to prison."* Still . . . it didn't fit to Bo. There were also the aggravators that made the case a capital one and not just first degree. Jack Willistone's pockets had been emptied, his wallet pilfered, and his vehicle, which was left parked in Greg Zorn's garage, had been looted. All of this screamed that the killer had been looking for something. That it wasn't just a revenge killing.

Again, Bo tried to play devil's advocate. The tape at the Oasis clearly showed Wilma demanding "her money" from Jack. Therefore, the cleaning out of Jack's pockets, wallets, and glove compartment all fit. Wilma was searching for the money he owed her. Her motive for murder was dual. Revenge *and* greed. She had sat at the Oasis for an hour and worked up the courage to murder Jack and take whatever she found on him.

Bo sighed, still not buying it. The murder looked more like a hit to him. Or more like a threatened hit gone wrong, since in a true mafia operation he doubted the body would have just been lazily rolled into the river. But . . . *perhaps the whole idea was for the body to be found.*

Bo had a whole lot more questions than answers, but one thing was clear from reading the file: if Wilma Newton didn't kill Jack Willistone, then whoever did had likely framed her. *Who would have the ability to do that?* he asked himself, already knowing the answer.

All roads lead to Jasper, Bo thought, feeling a sense of dread come over him as he put on his right-turn blinker to stay on Highway 69. Wade's investigative report contained a brief summary of the detective and Powell's interview of Kathryn "Kat" Willistone, Jack's widow. Though the report concluded that Kat had a stone-cold alibi for the time of her husband's murder, two sentences nonetheless held Bo's attention. *"Mrs. Willistone is the presumed beneficiary of a three-million-dollar life insurance policy owned by the victim. Mrs. Willistone is the daughter of Marcellus Calhoun."* Bo quoted the words from the report out loud. Then he reflected again on the part of the report that was missing.

There was no interview with Kat Willistone's father.

Bo figured Marcellus Calhoun wasn't likely to just drive up to Tuscaloosa for an interview. *Especially if he ordered the hit . . .*

There was also the matter of the overwhelming physical evidence connecting Wilma Newton to the crime. Why fool with a trip to Jasper to interview a mob boss if there was no need? But such reasoning didn't feel right to Bo. He figured that a seasoned detective like Wade Richey and a talented prosecutor such as Powell Conrad would know that any defense theory would eventually put Bully Calhoun in its crosshairs. *They just haven't gotten around to it,* he concluded, clicking his right-turn blinker on as the yellow and black colors of the Waffle House became visible ahead. As he slowed the Sequoia for the turn, Bo's cell phone began to buzz in the passenger-side seat. Seeing "Professor" pop up on the screen, he clicked the answer button. "How did it go?"

"He talked," Tom said, his voice hoarse from sleep.

"And?"

"It was just like I thought. Wheeler fingered Bully Calhoun for it. He called Wilma a 'doe' and said that this type of job was something Bully could do with no sweat. Especially if he had a good reason."

"How about three million reasons?"

"You've seen the life insurance policy?"

"No, but Wade's report indicates that Willistone had a three-million-dollar policy and Kat Willistone is the '*presumed beneficiary*.'"

Silence for several seconds, and then Tom's voice came through strong and clear, but the trepidation in his tone was palpable. "I need you to go to Jasper."

As he turned into the Waffle House on Highway 69, Bocephus Haynes smiled. "I'm already here." Then before the Professor could go into a "be careful" rant, Bo added, "I'm about to meet with someone that may have an angle on Bully. I'll report back at the end of the day," and clicked off the phone.

As he made his way toward the entrance, the dread that he'd felt back in the car began to set back in.

All roads lead to Jasper . . .

22

Santonio "Rel" Jennings sat in the corner booth of the Waffle House chewing on a toothpick. An almost empty plate of what looked to have once been several waffles, eggs, and bacon lay in front of him. The only thing left was a film of syrup in the middle of the plate.

"Forgive me, brother, but I started without you," Rel said, standing and shaking Bo's hand.

There were few people in the world that a man of Bo's physical size had to look up to, but Rel Jennings was one of them. At six feet, seven inches tall and a shade under two hundred pounds, Rel was, as the saying goes, "skinny as a rail." During his basketball-playing days at Shelton State Community College, in Tuscaloosa, Rel had been what today's broadcasters would have called a point forward, routinely dribbling the ball up the court and setting the offense from the wing. He'd averaged twenty-five points a game during his senior year in 1979, good enough to get him invited to try out for several teams, including the Los Angeles Lakers. Unfortunately, the Lakers were about to be good at the point for the next decade, as they had their eyes on a six-foot, ten-inch prodigy from Michigan

State named Earvin "Magic" Johnson. After bouncing around Europe for a couple years with several teams, Rel played for six weeks with the Philadelphia 76ers in 1982. Though he only logged a few minutes of actual game time backing up Maurice Cheeks, Rel did get in five games, and his favorite memory was throwing an alley-oop from half-court to Julius Erving. Doctor J. caught the ball midway up the backboard with one of his enormous hands and brought down a thunderous jam. Rel thought he'd played his way on the team, but he was let go right before the playoffs. After that, he'd returned home to Jasper, because that's where his momma was, and took some private investigator classes at Bevill State. For the next twenty years, he was one of the best private investigators in Walker County. Along the way, he'd married and divorced his high school sweetheart and had a couple of kids, who had now flown the coop.

Bo took the seat across from his old friend. Rel had a lighter skin tone than Bo's, and his once-dark beard was now solid white. Though mostly bald, he had close-cut white hair on his sides. Grinning, he looked Bo up and down and scratched his beard. "You dressed down today, Counselor? I thought all you attorney types had to wear coats and ties."

Bo smirked and assessed his clothing, a black T-shirt over dark jeans and combat boots. A crimson cap with the script *A* covered his bald head, and he hadn't bothered to shave. "Just trying to blend in," he said.

Rel belly-laughed. "In this county? Good luck with that, brother. Last census I heard, Walker County was over ninety percent cracker. Don't look now, but we're the only two brothers in this fine establishment."

Bo smiled. He hadn't seen Rel in at least five years—not since he'd represented him on his last DUI charge in Birmingham and got the sentence reduced to reckless driving. Some friends existed in the world who, regardless of the passage of time, you just picked right up with as if you hadn't been away from them for more than a few days. Rel Jennings was like that. Bo knew he could shoot the bull with Rel all day long and not get tired. Unfortunately, there was business to discuss and time was limited.

"I need your help," Bo said, motioning for the waitress to bring him some coffee.

"So you said on the phone." Rel's voice had a playful catch to it. "But you wouldn't tell me what you needed. Why all the secrecy? I feel like I'm on *Law & Order*."

Bo ignored the joke. "You ever hear of Marcellus 'Bully' Calhoun?"

The smile immediately evaporated from Rel's face and he slid the plate in front of him out of the way. Jutting forward on his elbows, Rel swept his eyes around the restaurant before returning them to Bo. "What do you want with Bully?"

Before Bo could respond, the waitress set a cup of steaming coffee in front of him. "Something to eat, sugar?"

"No, ma'am," Bo said. "Just the coffee is fine."

She gave a thumbs-up and walked away. Ignoring the mug and taking Rel's cue, Bo edged forward so that their heads were only a few inches apart. "I'm helping a friend investigate a murder case in Tuscaloosa. The victim was Bully's son-in-law."

Rel furrowed his eyebrows and gazed down at the table. "Heard about that. Jack Willistone, right?"

Bo nodded.

"I remember seeing his trucks run through here all the time. Highway 69 and 78." Rel paused. "Aren't you suspended from practicing law?"

Bo hadn't told Rel this little nugget of information and he was impressed by his friend's knowledge. He knew he shouldn't be. Despite being an average student through high school and college, Rel Jennings was one of the smartest people he'd ever met. He absorbed information like a sponge, regardless of whether it was online, in a newspaper, or from the street, making him a superb private eye. And that was why Bo was here.

"Yes, but I'm not acting as a lawyer right now. Just being an investigator for an old friend."

"That old friend wouldn't be Professor McMurtrie, would it?"

"Yes, it would."

"Guess you owe him big-time after that trial last year in Pulaski, huh?"

Bo squinted at Rel, but he didn't lean back. "He's my best friend in the world. I would have walked through hell and back for him *before* he represented me in that trial. But yeah, I owe him. Just like you owe me."

Rel lowered his eyes. "Fair enough. What do you need?"

"You still got your PI license?"

Rel smirked. "I do, but I never use it anymore. I don't even keep it in my wallet. Make more money managing McDonald's, and it's a lot less stressful."

"Well, I may need you to dig it out. Jack Willistone got out of jail on Monday, May 7 at nine o'clock in the morning. He was murdered on Tuesday, May 8 between the hours of 10:00 p.m. and midnight." Bo took a sip of coffee and winced as the hot liquid burned his throat. "I need to know what Bully Calhoun was doing during that stretch of time."

Rel raised his head and scratched his beard. "The Professor is representing the lady accused of killing Willistone, right?"

Bo nodded.

"The articles online don't sound too good for her. Convicted prostitute whose husband died driving trucks for Willistone." He grunted.

"The Professor believes she was framed for the crime," Bo said. "And he visited with an old employee of Bully's yesterday, who said that Bully could have pulled something like that off without a hitch. Easy as pie."

"Who was the former employee?"

"JimBone Wheeler. That name ring a bell?"

Rel's eye's widened, the fear unmistakable. "Loud and clear. Never met the man, thank Jesus, but I know he's from this area. He's not exactly Walker County's favorite son. On death row, right?"

"That's where the Professor interviewed him."

"Damn," Rel said, letting out a low whistle. "Going to be tough to get that kind of information on Bully. You're asking for a lot."

"I know," Bo said. "But I figure if anyone can find out, it would be you."

"What's in it for old Rel?" He smiled sheepishly.

"You owe me, dog. If it wasn't for me, you wouldn't have driven up here. You would have walked. Not many jobs you can work these days without being able to drive."

"I know, Bo, but digging up information on Bully Calhoun is a dangerous game. He's been mostly legit since getting out of the joint back in the '90s, but still. He owns too many businesses in town. We talking laundromats. A storage facility. Two restaurants. A bar. Lumber company. You name it in Jasper, Alabama, it's got Bully Calhoun's fingerprints on it. He also owns at least a thousand acres of land on the edge of the Sipsey Wilderness, and you know who the newly elected sheriff of Walker County's biggest campaign contributor was."

"Bully."

"You got it. Bocephus, I seen this man go to the farmers market on Airport Road, and the ladies selling tomatoes and peaches is handing him free sacks of produce like he's Don Corleone in Brooklyn."

Bo leaned back in his seat and eyed his old friend. "Is what I've asked you to find impossible?"

Rel shot a quick glance around the restaurant before looking at Bo. "No."

"How?"

Rel moved closer and kept his voice just above a whisper. "I got a contact on the inside."

Bo folded his hands into a tent. "And this contact would know what I've asked."

Rel bobbed his head. "He would, but Bo, I don't owe you this much. You're my friend and I want to help you because you've gotten me out of several jams. But if I'm going to cross Bully Calhoun, I have to get paid."

Bo rubbed his own chin. Tom hadn't given him any kind of budget to work with, and he worried that the Professor was handling the case pro bono. But Bo had spent two decades trying personal injury cases in Tennessee and had built up quite a war chest of his own. *All roads lead to Jasper,* he thought again. *If we can't find out what Bully Calhoun was doing during the time of the murder, then we are sunk.*

"How much?" Bo asked.

Rel blinked and rubbed his hands together, an obvious tell that he hadn't given the question much thought. "Ten thousand dollars," he finally said.

Bo smirked and said nothing.

"Times are tight, brother, and you've asked for the moon," Rel pressed.

"Five," Bo countered.

Rel didn't answer and abruptly stood from the table. "Been nice seeing you, Bo. I've got to run now. This information obviously doesn't mean much to you."

Bo let Rel go, placed a five-dollar bill on the table, and followed him out the door. As Rel began to unlock his vehicle, a black Cadillac Escalade, Bo finally caught up to him. "Times don't look that tight," Bo said, stepping into the crack that the open door had made and blocking Rel's entry.

"Boy, I've worked hard for everything I've got, and I'm putting my little girl through Alabama right now. I'm the manager of the

McDonald's in Walker County. You want to guess who owns the franchise?"

"Bully Calhoun," Bo said.

"One of his various LLCs." Rel's shoulders sagged. Before he could say more, Bo put a hand on his friend's shoulder.

"Relax, dog. I'll pay ten."

Rel grimaced, his face immediately registering that he should have asked for more. He gazed down and cursed under his breath.

"Your contact?" Bo asked, his voice soft. "Do you think he would help us?"

"I know he would," Rel said, glaring at Bo.

"How so? Me and you been friends for thirty years and you wouldn't help me without being promised ten thousand dollars, and I can already tell you think you'll regret it."

"I'm afraid I will," Rel said more to himself than Bo.

Bo let several seconds pass. Then he pressed further, feeling the same sense of dread that he'd first noticed when he saw the Walker County Line sign. "How can you be so sure of your contact?"

"Because he's my brother."

Bo laughed. "Everyone's your brother, Rel. I'm your brother."

Rel's smile was tight and the fear in his eyes was palpable. "It's not like that, Bo. I'm talking about blood." He paused. "I'm talking about my little brother."

Bo felt his heart rate quicken as an image came to mind. He and Rel playing basketball at the rec center at the University of Alabama in what must have been 1978, and a younger boy—maybe five years their junior—tagging along. He had been shorter but had a pure outside jump shot. "Alvie?" Bo asked, surprised that the name had come to him.

Rel hung his head. "I should have asked for more money."

23

Marcellus "Bully" Calhoun was not what Powell or Wade had been expecting. Stories abounded regarding the alleged mobster's tendency to dress in powder-blue leisure suits with long slicked-back silver hair and thick eyebrows that he curled up on the ends. But the man sitting across from Powell and Wade in the nineteenth hole of the Jasper Country Club looked like any other old man who liked to play golf and bet a little money on the outcome on Wednesday afternoons. Bully was clad in a white Under Armour golf shirt, khaki shorts, and a pair of golf shoes. A black Titleist cap with a gold magnetized ball marker on the bill was propped on the corner of his chair, and his sweat-soaked silver hair was cut short on the sides. The only thing odd about this scene, other than Wade and Powell being there, was the presence of a uniformed officer sitting next to Bully at the corner table.

Sheriff DeWayne Patterson was a wiry man with steel-blue eyes that shined just under his police hat, which he had yet to remove since meeting Powell and Wade outside the clubhouse and ushering them to the nineteenth hole lounge. Sheriff Patterson had arranged the meeting, and instead of holding it at his office, he said that Mr. Calhoun suggested they meet at the club for a late lunch. At 1:30 p.m., the once-crowded dining area had cleaned out as most of the patrons had either gone back to work or were out on the course for an afternoon round.

Bully took a sip from a mug of beer and squelched a burp. Wrinkling up his face, he glanced at Wade and then Powell. "Heard what you boys done in Pulaski." He shook his head. "You both got brass balls, I'll give you that." His voice was a husky baritone that had no doubt been enhanced by a combination of whiskey and tobacco over the years.

"I believe you were acquaintances with Mr. Wheeler." Wade smiled. It wasn't a question.

Bully nodded. "A man makes a lot of choices if he lives long enough. Some good. Others bad." He grimaced. "Bone was one of my bad ones."

"How do you mean?" Powell asked, his voice loud enough to cause Sheriff Patterson to slightly jump back from the table. Bully didn't budge, and his mouth curved into a grin.

"That boy is where he belongs thanks to you two. Now . . ." He slapped both hands on the table. "My time is short. The big team tees off at two and I'd like to hit a few balls on the range before we play. You didn't come here to ask me about JimBone Wheeler, did you?"

"No, sir," Wade said, glancing at Powell. "We're investigating the murder of Jack Willistone, your son-in-law, and we wanted to ask you a few questions."

Again Bully grimaced. "What do you want to know?"

"You picked him up at the Springville prison on the morning of May 7?"

"I did." Bully leaned back in his chair, his shoulders relaxed and his arms hanging by his side, the posture of a man who had nothing to hide.

"Why you?" Wade asked.

"What do you mean?"

"I mean why did you pick him up and not your daughter, Kathryn?"

Bully narrowed his gaze. "I didn't want Kat within thirty miles of that place and neither did Jack. I volunteered to pick him up, and she was fine with it."

"Mr. Calhoun," Powell waded in, removing a slip of paper from the briefcase at his feet, "we have the visitor's log for Mr. Willistone's incarceration at the St. Clair Correctional Facility. For the first sixteen months, you didn't visit him at all." Powell paused, gauging Bully's response, but the man's face registered nothing. "Then in the last two months"—Powell made a show of counting the columns—"you came five times." Powell stopped, but Bully's expression remained neutral. "Can you explain that?"

"I knew Jack was getting out after eighteen months, and I wanted to know what his plans were. My little girl had stood by her man while he was behind bars, and I wanted to make sure that Jack was going to be able to provide for her when he got out."

"Why no visits prior to this March?" Wade chimed in.

"Because there was nothing to be accomplished, and I wasn't going to give him a conjugal visit."

"Speaking of that, why didn't your daughter ever visit the prison?" Powell asked, ratcheting up the intensity in his voice.

"You'll need to ask her that," Bully snapped.

"You visited him twice in March, twice more in April, and once in May, not counting May 7, when you picked him up." Wade recounted the times, gazing down at the log. "What did you learn from your visits?"

Bully shrugged. "Jack was determined to get back into trucking. He told me he still had contacts in the business and that he was going to try to rebuild his company."

"Did you believe him?"

Bully chuckled. "You boys were around Jack a good bit, weren't you?"

"I arrested him in Henshaw and then prosecuted him for witness tampering and blackmail," Powell said. "I also interviewed him last year in connection with the murder of Andy Walton in Pulaski."

Bully drained the rest of his beer. "Then you know how he was." He stared wistfully at the empty glass. "I've never met a more cock-sure man in my life. Jack didn't just want to make a living again. He wanted *all* the way back. He told me he could have a hundred trucks rolling in two years." Bully snorted. "I was like Jack once. Used to dress flashy and talk big like he did." He jiggled the handle of the empty beer mug. A few seconds later, a barmaid placed a full mug on the table and took away the empty one. Bully took a long sip and wiped his mouth. "Prison changed me. When I got out, I gave up the fancy clothes and the big talk. I stopped making myself a target." He jerked his head. "Incarceration didn't have the same effect on Jack."

Wade glanced at Powell and they shared a look. "Mr. Calhoun, I appreciate that, but it doesn't really answer my question." Powell moved his eyes back to Bully. "Did you believe that your son-in-law would be able to provide for your daughter?"

"Provide for her? Yes. Have a hundred trucks rolling in two years? I think he was in for a rude awakening about that."

"Did Jack ask for your help during any of your visits?" Wade asked.

Bully rubbed his chin and suppressed a grin. "Oh hell yeah. Jack was not shy about asking for money. I was going to give him some too. Not enough to bankroll his operation, but some to get him started." He took another sip of beer. "Never got the chance, though."

Powell again glanced at Wade. So far the interview had gleaned nothing, which was a relief in some ways. Still, as Powell began to take the interview in a different direction, he was wary of the man sitting across from him. If anything, the lack of flash made Bully Calhoun seem even more dangerous. "Mr. Calhoun, tell us everything you did after picking up Jack at prison."

Bully looked up at the ceiling of the lounge, appearing to think out loud. "Well, we picked him up around nine or so that Monday."

"We?" Wade asked. "Did you have someone with you?"

"Yes. My driver. I don't do any driving anymore except around town. Back gets too stiff and my eyes ain't what they used to be."

"What kind of car?"

"Gray four-door Crown Victoria."

Powell was expecting him to say a limousine, but then he remembered what Bully had said about not making himself a target. "Then what?"

"We stopped at the Cracker Barrel in Bessemer on the way to Tuscaloosa so Jack could get a meat and three. Arrived in T-Town around one."

"Did you stick around?"

"Just long enough to give my baby girl a kiss. Was home that afternoon."

"Did you see Jack again?" Powell asked.

"No. I got a call from Kat on Wednesday morning that Jack had been killed."

"Did you go back to Tuscaloosa anytime between May 7 and May 8?"

Bully shook his head. "Only to drop Jack off. That was it."

"And what about the night of Tuesday, May 8? What were you doing that night between ten o'clock and midnight?"

Bully drank from his mug. "Well, I played big team that afternoon until four o'clock. Then because the bets were all screwed up, we played an emergency nine, and that finished up around six thirty. Then there was the poker game in the back room here till around eight thirty or so . . ." He motioned with his hand at the young waitress cleaning mugs behind the bar. Powell turned to look at her. She had brown hair done up in a ponytail and had caked on a little too much eye shadow. "About nine o'clock, Layla there drove me home and"—he made a show of looking at his watch, which Powell noticed was a plastic Casio—"at approximately ten o'clock that evening, I believe I was putting Mr. Johnson inside of Ms. Layla. After those ninety seconds were up, we watched old *Cheers* reruns on the tube before falling asleep."

"So, you were with . . . Ms. Layla from 10:00 p.m. until midnight on May 8?"

"Literally and biblically." He finished off the rest of his beer and stood up. "Are we finished, gentlemen? I need to warm up if I'm going to play big team."

Powell and Wade also stood, but Sheriff Patterson remained seated. "Mr. Calhoun, how many businesses do you own in Walker County?" Powell asked, knowing he had no authority to hold the man any longer than he desired to stay, but not half-finished with the questions he'd wanted to ask.

"Too many to list, boy."

"Are you aware of any of your employees being in Tuscaloosa on the night of May 8?" Wade asked.

"No, I am not," Bully said. "But hell, that don't mean none of them weren't there. I've got hundreds of employees, and some of them probably have relatives in that area." He turned to go.

"Mr. Calhoun?" Powell stepped in front of him to block his path. "We believe that the woman we've arrested, Wilma Newton . . . killed Jack Willistone on the night of May 8. We have arrested Ms. Newton and charged her with murder."

"Congratulations," Bully said, scowling at Powell, his face flushed red with irritation. "Now get out of my way."

"Ms. Newton's lawyers are sure to try to investigate you given your . . . history."

"So what? They'll hear the same thing I just told you. At the time my son-in-law, God rest his soul, was murdered, I was at my house near the Sipsey Wilderness with that fine piece of tail by the bar."

"And the people who work for you?"

"I had provided no instructions to any of my employees to go anywhere near Jack Willistone."

"That will be your testimony."

"That's a fact." Bully brushed past Powell and made his way for the door.

"Mr. Calhoun?"

Bully stopped with his hand wrapped around the doorknob. He glared back at Powell. "What?"

"What's the name of your driver? The guy that drove you and Jack from the prison to Tuscaloosa?"

Bully sighed. "I have a security detail that does that. It could have been any number of people."

Powell approached Bully. "Think, Mr. Calhoun. Whoever it was is likely to be interviewed by the defense. We'd like to talk to him first."

Bully rubbed his chin. "You really think they'll be fool enough to go after me for this?"

Powell took a step closer. He could smell the scent of beer and grease on the man's clothes. "You're a convicted felon, and though all of your businesses appear to be legitimate now, you were once considered to be one of the biggest figures in organized crime in the Southeast. Not only that, but your daughter indicated that she was the sole beneficiary of a three-million-dollar life insurance policy on Jack's life." Powell paused. "If I were them, I'd go after you with both barrels."

Sheriff Patterson grabbed Powell's arm and spoke in a whisper. "Listen, son, if you want to talk with Bully anymore, we'll set up another meeting. But let him go now. He's told you enough today."

Powell ignored the sheriff and kept his eyes on Bully, who had stayed glued to his position. Then his mouth curved into a grin. "I hope they do, boy. Because I'm as clean as Ms. Layla's shaved honey-pot, you hear?"

Bully swung the door open, and Wade's voice rang out from behind Powell. "Mr. Calhoun, can we get the name and contact information for your driver on May 7?"

Bully stopped in the opening. "C&G Security. They've got an office on Highway 78. That's my detail and they'll know."

"You really can't remember the name of your driver that day?" Powell asked. "Awful long trip . . ."

Bully spat on the sidewalk outside and turned back to them. "I think Alvie was driving the Crown Vic that day."

Before Wade or Powell could say anything else, Bully stomped toward a golf cart with a set of clubs hooked to the back. Seconds later, he was driving up the hill toward the first tee.

"Well . . . that was interesting," Wade said as they watched the cart fade into the distance. "Want to interview Ms. Layla now?"

"Yeah. Then we need to head over to C&G Security."

"You think the driver will have a different memory than Bully?"

"No," Powell said, turning to walk back into the nineteenth hole. "But we need to make sure."

24

The interview with Layla Perkins was short, sweet, and full of embarrassment. The barmaid was thirty-four years old and she had worked at the Jasper Country Club for seven years, first as a cart girl delivering drinks on the course, and then moving up to a bartender in the nineteenth hole. Layla was a divorced single mother with two kids, the oldest of which was already seventeen. Her daughter kept her youngest at night when Layla needed to work late at the club. She remembered the night of May 8. Bully and the other big teamers played cards until nine, and then she drove Bully to his house out on Sipsey Canyon Drive. She stayed the night with him, and between the hours of ten and midnight they were in his bedroom together.

As he and Wade were about to leave, Powell made the mistake of asking her if she was "in a relationship" with Bully, and Layla contorted her face in confusion. "Well, I wouldn't say that. But we do have sex almost every Tuesday night, so . . ."

Powell's face turned crimson red. "Thank you, ma'am," he said, and they left the lounge, with Wade giggling as they exited the door.

In the parking lot, they noticed that Sheriff Patterson was leaning against Powell's Charger. He had said he needed to make a few phone calls before the interview with Layla began, and Powell had assumed the lawman had left. But here he was, hat still on and hands resting over his gun belt. "Sheriff, we appreciate you arranging for us to meet with Mr. Calhoun," Wade said as he and Powell paused in front of the car. The sheriff remained propped against the driver's-side door, blocking their path.

"Glad to do it," Patterson said, but judging by his tone he had been anything but happy to help. "I hope that will be the end of it. It sounded to me like he had a rock-solid alibi for the time of Mr. Willistone's murder."

"We caught that too," Powell said, smirking at the sheriff. "We may need to talk with Bully again as the case moves forward, and we still need to interview some of his security detail."

"The driver?"

Powell nodded. "Did you recognize the name he gave. Alvie?"

"Alvin Jennings," Patterson said. "Goes by Alvie. Good Jasper boy. Black as the ace of spades and a hell of a basketball player in his day. Coaches ball at Jasper Middle during the school year, and I guess he works for that security firm too."

"You didn't know that?"

"I did not. But that's not surprising. A lot of the coaches and teachers around here work a second job to make extra money."

For several seconds, none of the men spoke, and Sheriff Patterson made no move to get out of their path. "Something else on your mind, Sheriff?" Wade asked.

"Just that it seems clear that Bully Calhoun has nothing to do with your case, and I'd appreciate it if y'all would stay away from my county."

Wade took half a step forward and spoke in a growl. "You sure seem jumpy to help a convicted felon, Sheriff. By the way, who was your largest campaign contributor in the last election?"

Patterson raised the bill of his hat and his eyes blazed with fury. "Screw you, Detective."

"No thanks," Wade said.

Again, awkward silence. "We got places to go, Sheriff," Powell said. "You want to get out of our way."

Patterson didn't move. "Boys, I realize y'all are just doing your job, and I appreciate that. And I understand that Bully Calhoun has quite a reputation in this state, and it's not all good."

"None of it's good," Wade spat.

"Maybe in Tuscaloosa County that is so. Hell, maybe in the rest of the state too. But here in Walker County, Bully's rep has changed. That conviction you're making a big deal about happened in 1988. He spent four years in the pen and got out in 1992, *twenty* years ago."

"What's your point, Sheriff?" Powell asked. "I want to get over to that security place."

"My point, Mr. Conrad, is that Bully Calhoun has been a model citizen in this county for the last two decades. He owns a lot of land in Walker County and at least six local businesses, with hundreds of employees. Since getting out of the joint, he's been good for the county."

"Huh," Wade said. "That's interesting, because my sources tell me that he's running one of the largest methamphetamine operations in the Southeast and using those *businesses* as a front. My sources say that he's damn near untouchable now because the local law enforcement officials are all in his back pocket."

Patterson glared at Wade. Powell would have tried to push past him if he wasn't blocking their entry to the car.

"Your sources are full of shit," Patterson said, speaking through his teeth.

"Thirty thousand," Wade said.

"What?" Patterson asked, crinkling his eyebrows.

"That's how much Marcellus 'Bully' Calhoun and his *businesses* contributed to your campaign. Thirty thousand dollars. I think your total contributions were around forty grand, so that's seventy-five percent. That's a whole hell of a lot of motivation to look the other way, huh, Sheriff?"

"I want you two turds to get the hell out of my county. If you want to meet with Bully again, you won't get any help from me." He stepped out of the way, and Powell unlocked the door and climbed inside the Charger. Wade walked around to the passenger side, watching Patterson like he might be a coiled-up rattlesnake.

"Sheriff, we think we have Jack Willistone's killer in custody. The only reason we requested this meeting is to find out what Bully knows, because we expect the defense lawyers are going to investigate him hard. But if Bully Calhoun starts doing any *business* in Tuscaloosa County, he won't get the VIP treatment that he gets here."

Patterson's eyes continued to burn. "I'll be sure to let him know. Now get out of this parking lot before I arrest you for loitering."

Wade opened the door and climbed inside, still watching Patterson through the windshield.

"Well . . . it's always nice to be in the good graces of the local police," Powell said, putting the Charger in gear.

"To hell with him," Wade said. "Bully Calhoun is still running meth, and that son of a bitch is his lead blocker."

"Let's stay focused, brother," Powell said, turning out of the parking lot and pushing the accelerator. "Wilma Newton killed Jack Willistone, and Bully Calhoun was hundreds of miles away with an alibi that's been corroborated. That's one of the reasons we came here, and we've accomplished that objective. Now, obviously a man of Bully's power and influence would have the means to hire someone to kill Jack, and that's probably how he would go about it, so Bully's alibi doesn't end the inquiry, but it's a necessary first box that had to be checked."

"So on to the security place?"

Powell nodded. "Due diligence. If I know the Professor, he'll turn over every one of these rocks looking for reasonable doubt, and I want to know what's under them."

"Alright, but watch your speed. If we get a ticket, I don't think we'll be getting any favors from the Sheriff's Office."

"You think?" Powell asked, and both men laughed as the Charger headed toward downtown Jasper.

25

The third hole of the Jasper Country Club is a dogleg-right par four with houses lining the left side of the fairway. After bungling his way to a double bogey, Bully noticed a figure standing under a tree behind the green. *Right on time,* he thought, placing his putter in his golf bag and telling his playing partner to take the cart on around to the next hole. As he approached, he saw that the woman wore black pants, a light-blue button-down, and flats. Aviator sunglasses covered her eyes, which Bully knew were the color of coal.

"Thanks for coming so fast, Manny." Bully couldn't remember her real name anymore. He called her Manny because she was from the Philippines and he'd made a good chunk of money betting on the famous Filipino boxer Manny Pacquiao. Bully thought of the nickname as a term of endearment. "You know that job you did for me a couple of weeks ago in Tuscaloosa?"

She nodded.

"I had a prosecutor and a detective from Tuscaloosa County ask me some questions about it earlier today. I think I convinced them that I didn't have anything to do with it myself, but they're going to poke around the security detail and maybe some more of my companies. I called Harm and let him know what to expect and to advise his staff accordingly, but I want you to have your ears and eyes open. If someone needs to be reminded to keep their mouth shut, I expect you to advise them accordingly."

"Anything else?"

Bully's eyes rotated toward the fourth-tee box. Ralph Harwell hit a blistering draw down the middle of the fairway. Ralph was the A player on the team. Bully smiled, continuing to watch the tee shots as he spoke softly to Manny. "The prosecutor said that the lawyer for the lady they arrested is going to come after me with both barrels as an alternative suspect." Bully paused as his B player, Ronnie Corlew, smashed a low worm burner into the right-hand rough. "I want you to find out who's representing the woman and follow him around. Learn as much as you can without being outed. I bet her lawyer has an investigator that he'll dispatch over here to dig up stuff on me, and you'll want to make sure that he doesn't find anything we don't want the world to know about." Bully turned and looked at Manny. "Understand?"

"*Sí.*"

"Good." Bully took a step toward the tee box, where the other men were now waiting on him, but Manny hadn't moved. He looked back at her. "Is there a problem?"

"What if this investigator does find something he shouldn't?"

Bully blinked. "Then remove the threat." He took a step closer and spoke just above a whisper. "Are we clear?"

Manny lowered her sunglasses so that Bully could see her black eyes. "*Sí.*"

26

Alvin "Alvie" Jennings held a basketball under his arm and barked out instructions to his team. He waved when he saw his brother but didn't come over.

Bo and Rel took a seat on the bleachers and watched the action.

Alvie was just under six feet tall and probably weighed two hundred pounds. He had darker skin than Rel, and his head was bald like Bo's. He had a barrel chest, and by the grace with which he moved around the court, Bo guessed he still played a little pickup ball on the side. Subconsciously, Bo rubbed his left kneecap, which had been shattered by a buckshot from a twelve-gauge shotgun the previous fall. He knew his pickup-basketball-playing days were over.

Ten minutes after they arrived, Alvie blew a whistle and the team huddled at center court. Bo noticed ten white players and only two blacks, which, based on what Rel said about the county census, was pretty representative.

"Break it down!" Alvie yelled, and the players put their right hands together and chanted "One, two, three, team."

As they filed off the court, Alvie said, "Open gym tomorrow afternoon if anyone wants to shoot." Then he approached the bleachers. "Who you got with you, Rel?" he asked. Then his eyes widened and his mouth curved into a grin that showcased all of his teeth. "Bo!"

Bo stood and the two men bear-hugged while Rel continued to sit and chew on a toothpick.

"How you been, man?" Alvie asked, still smiling. Before Bo could answer, Alvie patted his shoulder and added, "So glad that trial in Pulaski went your way."

Bo touched his left knee. "I paid for it."

"I heard about that," Alvie said, stealing a glance at Rel. "You got shot, didn't you?"

Bo nodded. "Won't be playing any one on one with you anymore."

"Well . . . that's good," Alvie said, grinning again. "You could never beat me, so it saves you the disappointment."

Rel finally stood from the bleachers. "Enough grab-assing, boys, let's get down to business." Bo glanced at Rel, whose anxiety was palpable. His eyes darted around the now-empty gymnasium, and he rolled the toothpick end over end in his mouth like a Ferris wheel.

Alvie sensed his brother's nervous energy. His smile faded. "What's up, Bo?"

Bo looked at Rel, who gave an impatient nod. "Tell him."

Bo stepped closer to Alvie and spoke in a hushed voice. "I'm working a case. Helping my friend Professor McMurtrie defend the woman accused of murdering Jack Willistone, Bully Calhoun's son-in-law."

"Uh-oh," Alvie said, taking a step away from Bo and giving Rel a worried look. "What'd you tell him, bro?"

Rel rubbed his neck and gazed up at the rafters of the gym. "That you work security for Bully and might know something about his whereabouts the last couple of weeks. Specifically, on May 7 and May 8."

"I ain't telling this nigga nothing about that," Alvie said, scowling at Bo. "Are you crazy, Rel? You know who Bully is and what he's capable of."

"I owe Bo a favor," Rel said, his voice a mixture of regret and angst. "And . . . he's offered to pay me ten thousand dollars for any information you can provide."

Alvie lunged at Rel and grabbed the taller man up under the arms, lifting him off the ground. "You trying to ransom my future, bro? You'd sell me down the river for ten K?"

Bo watched the scene play out, knowing better than to get in the middle of the brothers' quarrel and surprised by the strength of Alvie. He had remembered Alvie Jennings as scrawny, smaller, but the boy he knew was now a full-grown man taking his older brother to task.

"It's not just the money," Rel said, scratching the words out. "I owe him a favor."

"Fuck him," Alvie said, letting go of his brother and wheeling to face Bo. "You hear me, nigga? Fuck you."

"I hear you, dog," Bo said, taking a step toward Alvie and putting his left foot in front of his right in a fighter's position. "I hope you know better than to try that with me."

Alvie remained still and then scoffed. "You boys are crazy. You been into the Boone's Farm or something today, Rel?" He glanced at his brother, who had dropped to one knee to catch his breath. When he did, Bo grabbed Alvie by his T-shirt and pulled him into a headlock.

"You son of a . . ." Alvie flailed his arms and tried to elbow out of the hold, but Bo's grip held firm.

"Now, I just want to ask you a few questions. Your brother was convinced that you would know Bully Calhoun's whereabouts, and he *does* owe me a favor, so why don't you tell us what you know and I'll be on my merry way?" Bo loosened his grip around Alvie's neck and pushed him hard to the floor. Alvie rolled but didn't get up when he saw Rel and Bo both standing over him. Instead, he leaned forward and grabbed his knees with his arms.

"Hey, Coach, you alright?" a white kid with a flat-topped haircut wearing maroon sweats yelled out from the door to the locker room, where a number of the other players were heading for the exit. They all stopped when they saw their coach sitting on the floor of the gym and the other two men hovering over him.

"Fine, Sam," Alvie yelled back, climbing to his feet. "This here's my brother Rel and a friend of his. We're good."

Sam hesitated for a second but then waved. "See you tomorrow, Coach. Who you got in the game tonight?"

"The Heat," Alvie said. "Big three too much."

"Naw, unh unh," Sam said, walking toward the exit and shaking his head as a couple of the other boys laughed. "The Knicks gonna take 'em tonight. Melo gonna light Lebron up."

"Dream on, Sammy," Alvie said, forcing a smile. When all of the kids had left the gym, he spoke to the other two men without looking at them. "I need to turn off the lights and lock up." He started to walk toward the locker room, and Bo called after him.

"I'll be back," Bo said. "This ain't the end of it."

When Alvie ignored him, Bo walked over and blocked Alvie's path to the door.

"Come on, Bo," Alvie said, looking over his shoulder for his brother. Rel was sitting down on the bleachers, rubbing underneath his arms where Alvie had grabbed him.

"No, you come on," Bo smiled. "Why is Rel so sure that you know what Bully's been up to?"

Alvie sighed. "Because I'm his driver."

"What?"

"I work for a security firm called C&G on the weekends and part-time during the summer. We do the security detail for Bully. Some of the guys are stationed at his house out on Sipsey Canyon Drive and there's at least one guard stationed at each of his businesses." He looked at the wooden floor. "I'm his driver when he goes out of town or needs to conduct meetings in his car."

Bo raised his eyebrows. *His driver . . .* He looked over Alvie's shoulder to Rel, who gave him a knowing salute. Trying to hide his excitement, Bo returned his focus to Alvie. "The prison records from the St. Clair Correctional Facility show that Bully Calhoun picked Jack Willistone up the morning of May 7. Were you his driver that day?"

Alvie kept his eyes on the floor, fists clenched. "Yes."

"Did you drive him and Jack all the way to Tuscaloosa?"

Alvie nodded.

"Can you tell me everything that happened on that trip? Every phone call Bully made. Any conversations you overheard. Anything and everything."

Alvie lowered his chin and gave his head a slow shake. "I can't, Bo. I'm sorry. I'd like to help you. I'd like to help Rel too, but I can't."

"You know something, don't you?" Bo was sure of it, but he wanted confirmation.

"I'm not going to say more. I've already said too much." He took a step forward. "Now let me be, OK?"

Bo stepped away from the door but caught Alvie by the forearm as he passed. "What are you so afraid of?"

"I'll lose my job, Bo. We're supposed to protect our clients, not rat them out. We sign a confidentiality agreement when we hire on."

"Come on now, Alvie. Your job is coaching middle school basketball. This security thing is just a part-time gig. I bet I've offered Rel more money for this information than you'll make all summer, and I'm sure I can talk him into splitting it with you."

"I said I can't," Alvie said, his voice firm. "Now let go of me."

Bo released Alvie's forearm and stepped backward, still eying him. "Why won't you talk?"

With the door cracked open, Alvie hesitated, his eyes peering down at the hardwood floor. "Because he'll kill me. Bully will kill me and never think twice."

27

"Can you believe this mess?" Wade asked as he and Powell gazed through the windshield at the two men approaching one of the only other cars left in the gymnasium parking lot. They had recognized the vehicle, a white Sequoia with a Tennessee license plate, but seeing their old friend amble toward them was still a jolt.

Powell grunted and grabbed the door handle. "Well . . . I guess we should say hello."

They exited the Charger and leaned against the driver's side with arms folded. When the two men were within ten feet, Powell stepped toward them. "Bo, how the hell are you?" he asked.

Bo stopped and blinked before his mouth broke into a cautious grin. "Well . . . I'm still above ground." He paused, moving his eyes from Powell to Wade. "And I owe a lot of that to you two." He walked toward them and shook hands, and then introduced Rel as an "old Walker County friend."

Awkward silence engulfed the four men as they faced each other. Finally, Bo cleared his throat and asked, "You boys are a good ways away from Tuscaloosa, aren't you?"

Wade scoffed. "Last I checked, Pulaski was a hell of a lot farther from Jasper than T-Town. I'd ask what you're doing here, Bo, but bullshit seems a bit inappropriate given what the three of us have been through together." He glanced at Rel. "No offense, Mr. Jennings."

"None taken, Detective," Rel said. Then he walked around the Charger to Bo's Sequoia. "I'm goin' let you boys catch up while I check a few emails." He held up his phone for show. Bo smiled, knowing that Rel might have walked away but he was close enough to hear everything. His old friend would be listening like a hunting dog.

"Is he in there?" Powell asked. "Alvin Jennings?" Powell and Wade had left the Jasper Country Club and gone straight to the offices of C&G Security. After an hour-long wait, they finally spoke with Harm Twitty, the owner and president of the company. At first, Twitty had refused to give them any information, but after reaching "Mr. Calhoun" on the phone and obtaining approval, he reluctantly told them that they could probably find Alvin Jennings at the Jasper Middle School gymnasium. Now here they were, and Powell was trying hard to hide his irritation. He hadn't been all that surprised that the Professor had enlisted Bo's help for this case. But seeing him here in person—Bocephus Haynes, one of the finest trial lawyers in the state of Tennessee and one of the toughest and most intimidating men that Powell had ever been around—and one step in front of them rankled him in an unexpected way.

Bo nodded. "Alvie's locking up the gym now."

"You know him?" Powell asked, noting that Bo used the same familiar nickname that Bully Calhoun had.

"He's Rel's brother, and me and Rel go way back to when I was playing ball in Tuscaloosa."

More silence ensued, as none of the men quite knew what to say. Powell spoke up first. "It's our understanding that Alvin Jennings was Bully Calhoun's driver when Mr. Calhoun picked Jack Willistone up from the St. Clair Correctional Facility on May 7. Mr. Jennings drove the two of them to Tuscaloosa, where Jack was dropped off at his home, and then he returned Mr. Calhoun to Jasper."

Bo rubbed his chin. "That's good to know. You get that from Bully?"

Powell nodded.

"Then why do you want to talk with Alvie?"

"Due diligence."

"Did Mr. Jennings say any different?" Wade asked.

Bo cut his eyes to the detective. "Alvie wouldn't say nothing other than agreeing he drove Bully to pick up Jack and take him to Tuscaloosa."

"Wouldn't or couldn't?" Wade asked. "Maybe he doesn't know anything."

"He's scared. He knows something about that trip, but he's too scared to say."

Wade and Powell looked at each other, and then Powell noticed a man walking through the exit and locking the door. "Well," Powell said, "I guess we need to see for ourselves." He grunted and walked past Bo without looking back.

Wade started to follow but paused when he was shoulder to shoulder with Bo. "It's good to see you, Bo, though I wish to hell it was under different circumstances."

Bo remained quiet, knowing there was more the detective wanted to say.

Wade brushed back his hair and tugged on his mustache. Then he looked Bo directly in the eye. "I've been a detective for over thirty years, Bo, and I've closed over a hundred homicide cases during that time. Let me tell you something that I've learned over the years. Most of the time, the simplest and easiest answer is the right one." He spat on the asphalt. "Conspiracy theories are fun to talk about over a few beers and they make for great movies, but at the end of the day it's usually the person you find with the gun who did the deed. Lee Harvey Oswald killed Kennedy, and the person who murdered Jack Daniel Willistone is sitting behind bars at the Tuscaloosa County Jail. Wilma Newton is our killer. I wish you would steer Tom clear of this dumpster fire."

"The simplest and easiest solution? Is that what I hear you saying?"

"That's it."

"In the murder of a wealthy individual, isn't that person's spouse normally the first place you look?" Bo paused. "Especially when the spouse is the sole beneficiary of a three-million-dollar life insurance policy."

Though dusk had begun to fall and the parking lot was dimly lit, Bo could still see that the detective's face had reddened. "Kathryn Willistone was drinking margaritas at Pepito's when Jack bought the farm. Three witnesses were with her." Wade paused. "She has an airtight alibi. It's all in the file I copied for you yesterday."

"Sounds pretty convenient," Bo said. "As a seasoned investigator, wouldn't you expect the daughter of a convicted felon and noted mobster to cover her tracks?"

Wade exhaled a deep breath, clearly trying to hold his temper in check. "Bully Calhoun was screwing the barmaid at the Jasper Country Club at the time of the murder, and *said barmaid*, Ms. Layla Perkins, corroborates Bully's story."

Bo snickered. "Tell me something. When you met with Mr. Bully Calhoun, did he look like someone that would do his own killing?"

"You're just as crazy as Tom is," Wade said, starting to walk toward Powell, who had begun to talk with Alvie Jennings by the door to the gymnasium. "Y'all keep chasing your windmills."

"If Wilma Newton is so guilty and Bully Calhoun is so clean, then why is Alvie Jennings scared to death to tell me what happened on his trip from the prison in Springville to Tuscaloosa?" Bo took a couple steps backward. "And why are you and the district attorney still in Jasper?"

Wade stopped and studied the asphalt. Even from twenty feet away, Bo could hear the detective's sigh of exasperation. Finally, Wade looked at Bo over his shoulder and spoke through clenched teeth. "Due diligence."

28

Alvie Jennings arrived home at 8:30 pm. He had stopped and picked up a pizza at Domino's and bought a six-pack of Yuengling at the convenience store next door. To calm his nerves, he'd drank one of the bottles of beer on the ten-minute trip, and he was well into his second by the time he pulled into the driveway. Alvie cut the ignition but didn't immediately get out of the car. Despite the air-conditioning being on full blast, he still felt sweat on his bald head. He wiped at the moisture with the palm of his left hand while taking another sip from the bottle with his right.

Inside his one-story rancher, he could see the flashing lights of the television that he'd mounted in the family room through the crack in the blinds. Smiling, he watched his wife, LaShell, walk into the room and say something to their son, LaByron. The boy was just six years old but could already dribble a basketball between his legs and around his back. Alvie couldn't see LaByron but could discern the basketball rising up toward the ceiling and falling back toward the floor. Then again. And again. The boy was lying in front of the TV and practicing his form by shooting the ball up toward the ceiling. Just like Alvie and Rel had done as kids.

Alvie drained the rest of the beer and grabbed the pizza and remaining portion of the six-pack from the passenger side of his pickup truck. Then he began to walk toward the garage. The electric door was up, but the overhead light wasn't on. Alvie thought that was a little odd but figured LaShell had just gotten busy with laundry or something and forgotten. As he neared the threshold, he heard a voice from the shadows.

"*Hola.*"

Alvie wheeled toward the sound but couldn't see anything. Then, after blinking several times, he saw the figure leaning against the side of the house. Despite the mugginess in the air, Alvie felt goose bumps break out on both forearms and his neck. The woman had a pistol stuck in the front of her black pants.

"How are you?" Alvie asked. He had met the woman that Bully Calhoun called Manny on several occasions since taking the security job, and he knew enough to be terribly afraid. He glanced behind himself to the refrigerator that he kept in the garage for beer and sodas and the door that led to the house. Other than his older brother, all he cared about in the world was behind that piece of wood.

Be cool, he told himself.

"It is a nice night, no?" Manny asked. Her accent was exotic and seductive, but there was also a hint of menace in its smooth and melodic tone.

Alvie nodded. "A little hot."

"Your wife is a beautiful woman," Manny said, looking over Alvie's shoulder to the door that he had just gazed at himself. "And your son. Your *hijo*, he is strong to be so young. He gonna be a basketball player like his *padre*?"

Alvie felt his heart constrict, as if the witch had reached into his chest and was squeezing it. "He's coming along pretty well if he keeps practicing."

"And I see that your wife is pregnant." Manny gave a faint smile. "Perhaps another son. Or . . . maybe a little girl."

"We don't know yet," Alvie said. "Still too early to determine the sex." Alvie took a cautious step toward the woman. "What can I do for you?"

The smile remained on Manny's face. "Mr. Calhoun wanted me to find out what you told the prosecutor and the detective. You spoke with them at the gym about thirty minutes ago."

Alvie felt his heartbeat begin to race, but he forced himself to speak in a steady voice. He would have been more worried if Manny had asked about Rel and Bo.

"They asked a bunch of questions about me driving Bully to Springville to pick up his son-in-law in prison and then driving them to Tuscaloosa."

"And what did you tell them?" Manny's tone was seductive and dangerous, and Alvie was reminded of those old *Wild Kingdom* shows he'd watched as a kid with the women who could charm king cobra snakes.

Alvie licked his lips and carefully chose his words. "I told them that I drove the Crown Victoria, and Bully and Jack rode in the back seat. I didn't see anything suspicious. I couldn't hear nothing, and Mr. Calhoun didn't tell me nothing." Alvie forced his face to take on a beatific look. "See no evil. Hear no evil."

Manny's smile vanished, and she tapped the handle of the pistol stuck in her pants. "You sure that's all you said?"

"Positive."

"*Muy bien.*" Manny took a couple of steps backward, and Alvie wondered where she had come from. He saw no other cars on the street, and there was nothing behind the house except a wooded area that he'd never explored.

"One more thing, *señor.*"

"What?"

"There were two black men at the gym. I recognized one of them as your brother. You call him Rel, right?"

Alvie's stomach tightened. "Right."

"Who was the other man?"

Alvie knew if he lied, Manny or Bully would find out and the repercussions could be disastrous. "That was Bocephus Haynes, an old friend of Rel's. He's a lawyer and he's helping a friend of his defend the woman accused of murdering Bully's son-in-law."

"What did he want with you?"

"Same thing that prosecutor and detective wanted."

"And what did you tell him?"

"Nothing. Same as with the law dogs."

"See no evil. Hear no evil."

"That's right," Alvie said.

"Make sure you keep it that way," Manny said. Then she turned and walked toward the woods, her pace neither slow nor hurried. She glided like a water moccasin on the river, her head up, afraid of nothing above or below.

"*That was cool,*" Alvie whispered to himself. Then he let out a long sigh of relief.

"Alvie, what are you doing?"

His wife's voice startled him and he nearly dropped the pizza box and what was left of the six-pack. He turned to see LaShell standing in the cracked doorway. "I thought I turned this light on," she said to herself, and then flipped a switch. Alvie's eyelids fluttered as he adjusted to the sudden brightness. When he looked at her, his focus immediately went to the bulge in her stomach, which was barely noticeable given the loose nightgown she was wearing.

"You alright, honey? You look like you've seen a ghost or something."

Realizing his mouth was open, Alvie closed it and trudged into the garage. He handed the pizza box to his wife.

"They just selling four-packs at the store now?" she asked, smirking at the carton of Yuengling that Alvie cradled in his other hand.

"Long day."

"Well come on. LaByron has the game on and has been waiting for you to come home for an hour."

"Be there in a second." He put the beer in the fridge and grabbed another bottle. He twisted the top off and gazed back at the wooded area where Manny had disappeared. *That was cool,* Alvie thought, taking a long swig of beer and wishing for all the world that he had just seen a ghost and not Bully Calhoun's enforcer.

29

Manny's real name was Mahalia Blessica Reyes.

When she had first been introduced to Mr. Calhoun seven years earlier, she had given her name, but the old man said it was too big of a handle. He'd looked her up and down and smiled. Then he had said, "Manny will do."

Manny hailed from Manila, the capital of the Philippines, and one of her heroes was the great boxer Manny Pacquiao. She rather liked the nickname that her employer had bestowed on her.

As she walked through the woods behind Alvie's house, she knew that her ambush of Jennings had accomplished two objectives. One, she had identified a member of Wilma Newton's defense team. The name Bocephus Haynes sounded familiar, but Manny couldn't place why. When she got back to her office, she would get on the internet and learn all about him.

Two, she had scared Alvie Jennings to death. Based on the fear she saw in his eyes, Manny doubted that he would ever talk. The man had too much to lose. He was vulnerable, which made him weak.

Manny had learned early on in life that you could never show your enemies what you cared about.

Manny walked two miles through the woods, surrounded by trees and brush on all sides. Eventually, she stepped through a clearing and saw the highway. Carefully, she made her way down a steep embankment and waited. Five minutes later, a brown Chevy Monte Carlo pulled to a stop beside her and she climbed in the back seat. The front seat was occupied by two Mexican brothers who had crossed the border five years ago hidden under the back axle of a dump truck. The driver, who called himself Pasco, looked at Manny through the rear mirror. "On time?" he asked, his English broken.

"*Sí,*" Manny said. "*Gracias.*" Manny's parents had spoken Chavacano, a Spanish-based Creole language, and, as a child, she had grown up around Filipino and English-speaking people. By the time she reached adulthood, she was fluent in multiple languages and dialects, which was a skill she'd found to be quite valuable in her line of work.

"*No hay problema,*" Pasco said. In Manny's profession, it also paid to have a couple of hired hands to help her make clandestine trips on her boss's behalf. Pasco and his brother Escobar were foremen on two of Bully Calhoun's Mexican-only construction crews. They lived in a two-bedroom house with at least ten other men and women and worked like dogs from sunup until well past sundown Monday through Saturday. Despite the heavy workload, the brothers enjoyed the extra cash they made doing Manny's bidding, and Manny knew that neither man would ever talk to the authorities and risk being deported back to Mexico.

Fifteen minutes later, the brothers dropped her off at the Jasper Mall. Manny went inside and ate a sandwich in the food court and then walked through the crowd of shoppers to the parking lot in front of J. C. Penney. Her car, a gray Honda Accord, blended in with the other vehicles like she was just another patron. Manny opened the driver's-side door and put her pistol in the glove compartment. She pulled out of the lot.

She waited until she was on the highway to make the call. Bully picked up after only one ring. "Talk to me."

"The message has been delivered," Manny said.

"And?"

Manny remembered the look of fear in Alvie Jennings's eyes. "See no evil. Hear no evil."

PART FOUR

30

The courtroom can be a lonely and scary place. Especially when you are a criminal defense attorney representing a client who appears to be guilty as sin. Even more so if you are handling the case without a partner.

Tom sat alone at the defense table with his legs crossed and gazed at the yellow pad in his lap, which was blank now but by the end of the day would be filled with notes summarizing the witnesses called by the prosecution. He was leaning slightly to the right in his chair, which seemed to be the only position he could sit in that wasn't painful. The back pain that had started a couple months earlier with a few spasms was almost ever present now, and he knew he would eventually have to follow his son's advice and get it x-rayed. For now, though, with a capital murder case in full swing, there simply wasn't time. He'd have to stick with his regimen of several Advil a day and pray that the ibuprofen alleviated the pain enough so that he could function.

He raised his eyes and looked at the clock behind the judge's bench. It was 8:55 a.m., and the preliminary hearing was supposed to start at nine. In all capital murder cases in Alabama, the court is required to schedule a preliminary hearing within thirty days of arrest to determine if there is probable cause that the defendant committed the crime. Though many times "the prelim," as it is typically referred to amongst lawyers, is extended by mutual agreement, the state had not asked for an enlargement. Today was June 11, 2012—exactly thirty days since Wilma Newton was arrested for the murder of Jack Willistone.

"Professor, how you doin'?"

Tom looked up and saw Powell Conrad standing in front of him. The prosecutor wore a navy suit, white shirt, and red tie. His sandy hair, which appeared to have recently been trimmed, still looked like a mop on his head. "My back is killing me," Tom said. Then, as gingerly as he could manage, he stood and shook hands with his former student.

"We got the final ballistics, autopsy, and DNA reports back yesterday afternoon," Powell said, holding up a manila envelope and flipping it onto the defense table. "Those are your copies. I put a rush on them so that we could have them before the prelim."

Tom felt his stomach tighten. "Can you give me a sneak preview?"

"Ballistics analysis confirms that shell casings found on Zorn's dock as well as the bullet dislodged from the victim's sternum are a match for the nine-millimeter Smith & Wesson pistol discovered underneath the dock. As you know already, that weapon was registered in your client's name and had only her prints on it."

Although it was jarring, Tom had already assumed that the ballistics report would match, given what Wade had told him on his first visit to the jail. "And the DNA?"

Powell's eyebrows creased. "Remember the cap found on the dock? It's mentioned in Wade's investigative report, and Willistone is wearing it in the video at the Oasis."

"Yes." In his mind's eye, Tom visualized the hat as seen on the tape and described in the detective's summary. White with the block letters "WTC" in crimson on the front and "Willistone Trucking Company" in smaller crimson lettering underneath.

"Well, saliva matching the sample provided by the defendant was found on the bill." Powell hesitated. "There was also a very small strand of saliva located on the victim's collar, which must have hung out of the water enough for it to stay on. It also matches the defendant's sample."

Tom felt his heart constrict, and he was too stunned to speak.

"She spat on him, Professor," Powell continued. "After she put three bullet holes in him . . . she spat on him."

A few seconds of silence passed as the prosecutor allowed Tom to appreciate the gravity of this finding. Though his stomach was turning, Tom forced himself to speak in a calm, measured tone. He knew there might be other explanations for the saliva, but Powell's conclusion certainly made sense, and the image that he had just painted would be powerful in front of a jury. "Anything else?"

Powell's grim expression reminded Tom of the way a dog owner might gaze at a long-suffering pet a couple minutes before the veterinarian puts the animal down. "We also have a video from the guardhouse at the entrance to Zorn's neighborhood for the night of May 8." Powell pointed at the envelope on the table. "There's a DVD in that package with a copy of this recording on it."

Tom raised his eyebrows. "I take it my client is on there."

Powell slowly nodded. "Coming and going." He took a step closer and leaned his head forward, his bloodshot eyes resonating intensity and conviction. "She killed him, Professor. I was sure of it before we had those things, but now I know I can prove it beyond any shadow of doubt." He started to say more, but then the bailiff swung open the door to the judge's chambers. "ALL RISE!"

As they waited for Her Honor to emerge from the opening, Powell leaned closer and spoke into Tom's ear. "If you ever decide to withdraw as counsel, I won't oppose it and I'll make sure Ms. Newton has enough time to retain a new attorney or have the court appoint her one. You have my word on that."

Tom gazed at his former student in disbelief. "When have you ever known me to quit?"

Powell's face darkened but he didn't blink. "You're gonna want to at the end of this hearing."

"The State of Alabama v. Wilma Christine Newton." The Honorable Leah Combs banged her gavel once on the bench and gazed down at the attorneys. Combs was a district court judge elected three years ago after the more popular candidate, who had been expected to win in a landslide, failed to list all of his campaign donations and was disqualified from the race. As a lawyer, Combs had been a solo practitioner who had forgotten none of the hard knocks she had suffered during fifteen years of private practice battling spoiled attorneys from silk-stocking firms and overworked assistant DAs. In her three years on the bench, she had a reputation for starting on time, not fussing with much pomp and circumstance and, first and foremost, entering rulings, whether right or wrong, in a timely manner. Her quick and decisive judgments made her a favorite of the local bar, as the other two district judges, both of whom had much more distinguished careers as attorneys, had grown lazy in their years wearing the robe. Not Leah Combs. With her face full of freckles, petite stature, and curious eyes, she still looked like the awkward, inquisitive student who had sat on the front row of Tom's Evidence and Torts classes almost two decades earlier.

Still standing, Combs looked over the attorneys' heads to the gallery, which was filled to capacity with spectators, many of whom were reporters for local, state, and even national news outlets. Tom had noticed the cameras in the hallway as he entered, and he knew that whatever the results of today's hearing, there would be full coverage in the newspapers and online publications within hours of its conclusion. Not too long ago, Jack Willistone had been one of the richest businessmen in the country, whose trucks lined interstates and highways from Alabama to California. His fall from grace and subsequent incarceration were big news two years ago, and his brutal murder just thirty-six hours after being released from prison had galvanized the news media's zest for scandal. The defendant's being an attractive former prostitute whose husband had been killed driving a Willistone rig did nothing to quell the reporters' interest. Finally, Tom knew his own involvement in the case had also stirred the pot. The *Tuscaloosa News*'s Sunday edition had even published a photograph of him below the front-page story announcing the date and time of the prelim with an article entitled "Local Legend McMurtrie Representing Another Capital Murder Defendant." The story hit on Tom's career as a professor and return to the courtroom in Henshaw two years earlier to bring Willistone down, but the majority of the article focused on the televised trial of Bocephus Haynes in Pulaski the previous fall. The last sentence posed a question that Tom himself had asked several times since visiting Wilma Newton at the jail three weeks ago: "Given his age and the stress of litigation, could this be Professor McMurtrie's last trial?"

Judge Combs cleared her throat and spoke in a strong voice. "I realize that this case has gotten a lot of attention in the press, but I expect quiet in the courtroom today. Anyone who cannot respect the decorum of this court will be removed by my bailiff." She then placed both hands on the bench and leaned forward, looking at Powell first. "Mr. Conrad, is the state ready to begin?"

"Yes, Your Honor."

She then looked at Tom and gave him a warm smile. "Professor McMurtrie, are you ready?"

Tom gave a slight bow. "Yes, Your Honor."

Combs's face flushed a slight pink, which Tom remembered had happened in class when she was able to answer a question correctly after being called upon.

"Very well," the judge said, the smile now gone as she turned to her bailiff. "Benny, please bring in the defendant."

Wilma Newton was escorted into the courtroom by two sheriff's deputies, with the judge's bailiff, Benny Passon, leading the way. Wilma wore a black blouse and matching skirt that she said was the most professional outfit she owned. As she passed the front row of the gallery, where her daughter Laurie Ann sat alone, Tom stole a glance at the teenage girl who had gotten him into this mess. Laurie Ann Newton wore dark jeans and a burgundy blouse, and her dirty-blond hair was done up in a ponytail. She raised her eyebrows, and Tom could tell that she was holding her hands together to keep them from shaking. He gave her a thumbs-up sign as the officers removed her mother's handcuffs and left her with Tom at the table.

"Are we ready?" Wilma whispered, raising her eyebrows in much the same way her daughter had just done as she and Tom both took their seats.

Tom nodded. "Like we discussed yesterday, today we see the state's case against you. We don't call our own witnesses. Our goal is to learn as much about the prosecution's case as possible."

"How bad do you think it will be?" she asked.

Tom had strategically chosen not to disclose the information provided thus far by the prosecution to his client. He wanted her to see everything fresh without his poisoning the well. He looked across the room at Powell, who was hovering over the prosecution table and looking over some notes on a yellow pad. His focus and intensity were palpable. Tom then moved his eyes to the end of the table, where Detective Wade Richey sat with his legs crossed. He wore a navy suit and maroon tie and held a notebook in his lap. It had been years since Tom had seen Wade dressed for court, and he almost didn't recognize his old friend, whose normal dress was a black T-shirt and jeans.

With his salt-and-pepper hair and matching mustache, the detective bore an eerie resemblance to Sam Elliott's portrayal of the lawman Virgil Earp in *Tombstone*. Wade caught Tom's eye, and his expression was grim. Tom figured Wade had given this same look to many criminal defense attorneys in his years as a homicide detective. Tom also assumed this was the expression Wade saved for those same lawyers' clients right before he watched them ride the needle.

"Professor?" Wilma grabbed Tom's arm, and he mercifully broke free of Wade's stare. He looked at her and tried to keep his expression neutral as she repeated her question. "How bad?"

Tom glanced at the unopened manila envelope that Powell had dropped on the defense table a few moments ago. "Worse than we think," he said, squeezing her hand and steeling himself for what was about to come.

31

The first and only witness called by the state was Detective Wade Richey. As the threshold in a preliminary hearing is probable cause and hearsay is admissible, Wade was allowed to summarize the witness interviews, expert reports, and video evidence gathered by the state. The picture painted was dire for the defense of Wilma Newton.

Powell began with motive, having Wade describe Jack and Wilma's encounter at the Oasis Bar & Grill a few hours prior to the murder. He hit the high points from the video and the handwritten statement of the bartender, Toby Dothard, including showing footage of the altercation outside the bar and reading the part from Dothard's statement where Wilma yells at Jack, "'You're going to pay me my money or I'm going to kill you, you son of a bitch.'"

Next came evidence establishing Wilma's opportunity to do the deed, and Powell wisely had the detective start with the discovery of the corpse and work his way backward. The body of Jack Willistone was found on the banks of the Black Warrior River a quarter of a mile west of the Cypress Inn Restaurant. Two fraternity brothers from the university, Todd Shuman and Happy Caldwell, found the corpse while trying to hit a golf ball across the river. Caldwell called 911 at 2:37 a.m. on May 9, 2012, and a group of sheriff's deputies, led by Roland Lusk, arrived on the scene at 2:50 a.m. Wade was there before 3:15 a.m.

At just after 4:00 a.m., Jack Willistone's Toyota 4Runner was discovered in the garage of a lake home owned by Gregory Zorn, Willistone's attorney. Willistone's cell phone was located on the dock attached to Zorn's boathouse. Upon investigation, the only calls that Jack had received on the phone, which he had purchased earlier in the day from Verizon, were from his wife, Kathryn, and his ex-wife, Barbara, in addition to a number registered to Wilma Christine Newton. The last communications were an exchange of text messages between Wilma and Jack. The first was from Wilma at 9:30 p.m. on May 8, 2012: *I want to see you again.*

Jack replied at 9:34: *Have you reconsidered my proposition?*

Wilma at 9:35: *Yes. Where can we meet?*

Jack at 9:45: *My attorney's house on the river. 1400 Rice Mine Road. Bent Creek subdivision. Tell the guy at the guardhouse you're visiting Greg Zorn. His place is at the bottom of the hill nearest the water. Let's meet here in thirty minutes.*

Wilma at 9:46: *C u then.*

Powell then handed the detective a document with several pages stapled together. "Detective Richey, was an autopsy of the victim's body performed?"

"Yes. Ingrid Barnett, chief medical examiner for the State of Alabama, performed the autopsy."

"And did Dr. Barnett prepare an autopsy report?"

"Yes. I'm holding it right here."

"What did she determine to be the approximate time of death?"

Wade flipped the pages until he reached the section he wanted. "It was Dr. Barnett's conclusion, based upon her examination and analysis of the body, that Jack Willistone died during the two-hour period from 10:00 p.m. to midnight on May 8, 2012."

Powell finished this sequence by having Wade read from the witness statement of Othello Humphrey, the security guard at Bent Creek, who remembered seeing a woman driving a white Mustang Coupe come through the entrance at just after 10:00 p.m. When shown a picture of the defendant, Humphrey identified Wilma Newton as the driver. Humphrey said the Mustang exited the subdivision approximately thirty minutes after arrival. Wade then summarized the surveillance tape from the guardhouse, which showed a white Mustang registered to Wilma Newton entering Bent Creek at 10:07 p.m. and exiting at 10:38 p.m.

"So, Detective, for clarity's sake, we have a time of death from 10:00 p.m. to midnight, and the defendant is seen on video coming into and out of the subdivision where the crime occurred during the operative period."

"That is correct."

Powell took his time walking to the witness stand, where Wade handed him the videotapes from the Bent Creek subdivision and the Oasis. Tom glanced at Judge Combs, who was writing notes on a pad she kept at the bench. He figured Her Honor was probably marking off the necessary boxes needed for the crime of murder. *Motive, check. Opportunity, check.* He remembered one of the lessons he had drilled into his trial teams. *When you've made a key point, oftentimes the best way to emphasize it is to say nothing and let the information sink in.* Powell Conrad, one of Tom's finest former students, had just illustrated the effectiveness of this tactic, and despite his adversarial role in these proceedings, it was hard for Tom not to feel a trace of pride.

That feeling quickly changed to apprehension when the district attorney strode back to the prosecution table and retrieved a clear plastic baggie. Holding it from the ends, he turned and showed the package to Tom.

Inside the ziplock container was a nine-millimeter pistol.

Next to him, Tom heard a sharp intake of breath. Tom forced himself not to look at his client, but he could hear her legs shaking underneath the table. Calmly, he placed his own foot over hers, and after a few seconds the shaking stopped.

Powell then made a show of presenting Wade the baggie on the prosecution table, who in turn held it up so the judge could view the gun. During this demonstration, Tom looked behind his shoulder to where Laurie Ann Newton sat in the front row. She was still squeezing her hands together, her face pale. He wondered if she knew the full extent of the evidence against her mother. If not, she was seeing it now in all its glory.

He tried to give her a reassuring nod, but he doubted it worked. Laurie Ann gazed back at Tom like he was holding the only life preserver on the *Titanic*.

Powell then took Wade through the most devastating part of the state's case. "Detective, were you able to determine the identity of the owner of this weapon?"

"Yes. Using the serial number, we learned that the gun was last purchased at Willie's Pistol & Pawn in Fayetteville, Tennessee, on February 22, 2010. The purchaser was Wilma Christine Newton."

"Is the gun registered?"

Wade nodded. "The registered owner of the weapon is Wilma Christine Newton."

"And did you find any prints on the gun?" Powell asked, his voice rising to the far walls of the courtroom.

"Yes," Wade said. "There were four prints on the handle of the weapon."

"And were you able to identify to whom those prints belonged?"

"We were," Wade said, turning and looking at Judge Combs. "The only prints on the gun were identified as belonging to Wilma Christine Newton."

Tom could hear his client's shallow breaths next to him. Stealing a quick glance, he saw Wilma scribbling a note on the yellow pad in front of her. Without looking at him, she slid the pad ever so slightly so that Tom could read the words she had written. "I need a break. I'm going to be sick."

Tom turned his head back to the witness stand, knowing he couldn't ask the judge for a halt in the action right now. As subtly as he could, he grabbed the notepad and wrote his response. "Five minutes?"

He slid the pad back over and stole another glance at Wilma, who was biting her lower lip. Her face was ashen. When she saw what he had written, she looked at Tom and gave a quick nod.

Tom forced his focus back to the witness stand, where Powell had slipped another clear plastic evidence pouch in front of Wade.

"Detective Richey, could you please identify the evidence in this container?"

"These are two shell casings that were found a few feet to the right of Greg Zorn's dock."

"Was a firearms analysis performed on the gun and shell casings?"

"Yes, we received the ballistics report back yesterday."

"What was the conclusion?"

"Based on the retractor marks left on the used shell casings and a comparison study of sample shells fired from the gun, it was the conclusion of the firearms and tool markings specialist that the shell casings found on the side of the dock came from this gun." Wade held up the evidence bag with the weapon for emphasis.

"Detective Richey, going back to Dr. Barnett's autopsy, what did the medical examiner determine to be the cause of death?"

Wade again pulled out Barnett's report, flipping pages until he reached the end. "The cause of death was two bullet wounds to the decedent's sternum and another bullet entry above the right temple of the victim's forehead. The combination of these shots led to the victim's immediate demise."

"Was she able to determine the type of bullet?"

"Yes." Wade flipped the page of the report over. "A portion of a nine-millimeter slug remained in the victim's thoracic cavity as well as one fully intact bullet."

"Were these also tested by ballistics?"

"Yes. The damaged slug could not be tested, but the intact bullet was put through a ballistics analysis."

"And what was the final deduction of that testing?"

Wade again lifted the bag with the pistol, but this time his eyes strayed toward the defense table. Tom remembered his old friend's warning back at the jail. *You want me to tell you how many cases I've lost in thirty years in the Sheriff's Office when we have the murder weapon and it belongs to the defendant?*

Tom tried not to wince as Wade rammed home the final nail in the state's murder case.

"Ballistics traced the bullet directly to this gun."

Wilma almost didn't make it to the bathroom. After Judge Combs granted Tom's request for a short recess, a uniformed guard escorted her down the middle of the courtroom and into the hallway. During the trek, Wilma's stomach clenched several times and she thought for sure that the vomit she was holding in her mouth would spew out. Mercifully, she made it to the stall and the bile flooded the inside of the toilet bowl. As the smell hit her nostrils, she hurled again, eventually losing count of how many times her stomach heaved.

"Everything alright in there, Wilma?" the guard's voice came from behind the stall door.

"Fine," Wilma managed. "My stomach is just in a knot. Must have been something I ate."

The guard's snicker might have made her mad if she didn't feel so awful. Finally, she wiped her mouth and flushed the remnants of the vomit down the toilet. Then she sat on the commode seat and leaned against the metal pipes.

Images of the pistol she had bought at the pawn shop in Fayetteville flashed through her mind like an old black-and-white projector film. She had kept it in her purse when she'd made the deal with Jack at the Sundowners, and she'd left it there during the torture she'd endured from JimBone in those dark days before the trial in Henshaw. Hell, up until May 8, 2012, the only thing that gun had ever shot was the mirror in Ms. Yost's rental house.

I am so stupid, she thought as her mind's projector flashed new images. These were snowy and unfocused, like a television channel having a hard time picking up the signal. Jack Willistone, sneering at her from the across the gravel parking lot of the Oasis. Toby Dothard pouring Gentleman Jack over ice in a glass and telling her that things couldn't be that bad. That if she waited until nine, when his shift ended, he'd take her to his place and they could split a pizza and watch a movie. His mouth had formed those friendly words, but despite her inebriated state, Wilma knew that the bartender's lustful gaze telegraphed what he really wanted.

Then as she squeezed her eyes tight and swallowed the sour taste of bile, the images became smaller and even less focused. The drive-through of Taco Casa. A checkout guy with yellow teeth. Stumbling through her apartment after wolfing down half a burrito. Digging through her bottom drawer until she found the gun.

Wrapping her hands around its steel handle . . .

Three loud knocks on the stall door caused Wilma's eyes to fly open.

"Wilma, what are you doing in there? The judge said she wanted everyone back in the courtroom in ten minutes, and we're almost late."

"I'm sorry. I'll be right out."

"Whatever. You've got sixty seconds, or I'm going to take the door off its hinges."

"I'm coming," Wilma said. She ripped some toilet paper off the roll beside her and blew her nose. When she was finished, she threw the tissue into the bowl and, using the walls of the closely confined stall for leverage, raised herself to her feet. Her legs were shaky and she kept a hand on one of the sidewalls as she pushed down on the flush handle. As she watched the shriveled paper do three turns before sucking through the bottom, she knew that her future was less promising than the tissue's destination.

I am so stupid . . .

32

Eight hours later, at just after 7:30 p.m., Tom sat at a table on the bottom deck of the Cypress Inn Restaurant. He gazed out over the water of the Black Warrior and gulped from an ice-cold bottle of Samuel Adams Boston Lager, his third. The sun was setting over the Hugh Thomas Bridge, which connected the towns of Tuscaloosa and Northport, but Tom's eyes were focused on a dock a half mile closer—the place where Jack Daniel Willistone was murdered. Based on the evidence submitted by the prosecution earlier today, he could barely imagine anyone at the other end of that gun barrel besides Wilma Newton. *"She killed him, Professor."* Throughout the hearing, Tom's thoughts were pounded by Powell's words, loud and intense, like a train rolling down the tracks. *"She killed him."*

That vibe only increased after seeing his client's reaction to the gun introduced by the prosecution as the murder weapon. As an experienced trial lawyer and teacher of courtroom advocacy, Tom knew that juries responded to nonverbal communication and body language as much or more so than to actual testimony. It didn't take Clarence Darrow to understand how a jury would have interpreted

Wilma's pale skin and nervous fidgeting during Wade's breakdown of the ballistics analysis. And though she said she was fine after the recess, Tom caught a sour smell on her breath and person, deducing that her break had included a round of nausea. Adding it all up, Tom was grateful that today's proceeding had been the prelim and not the actual trial.

Tom stretched his back, which was mercifully beginning to loosen up due to the alcohol. Unfortunately, his head still throbbed from the stress of the day. He rubbed his temples and took another long sip of beer.

"You OK, Professor?"

Tom looked across the table at Bo, who had picked him up from the courthouse after the obligatory press interviews were completed.

"You ever taken a case you didn't think you could win?" Tom asked, turning his eyes back to the river.

"No," Bo said, but there was warmth in his tone. "But I've gotten into a few cases and wanted to pull out for that reason."

"Did you?"

"No," Bo said, any hint of humor gone. "I learned the game of life from the same man you did. Guy that stadium over there is named after." Bo pointed across the river. Though Tom couldn't see it, he knew that just beyond the lights of Jack Warner Parkway was the campus of the university and, beyond that, Bryant-Denny Stadium. Named in part for their football coach, Paul "Bear" Bryant. "We don't quit," Bo continued. "Ever. It's OK to lose. It ain't OK to quit."

Tom nodded. "Damn right." He stood and leaned over the railing of the deck. At this time on a Monday night, no other patrons were on the bottom floor of the restaurant, and Tom was grateful for the privacy. "So, since we both agree that quitting isn't an option, how the hell can we win this thing?"

Bo, who had watched the preliminary hearing from the back row and who had had no communication with Tom during the

proceeding—Tom didn't want there to be any implication that Bo
was practicing law, in violation of the terms of his suspension—put
his feet up on one of the empty chairs and stretched his arms over his
head. He yawned, but then he spoke with the quiet resolve of a seasoned criminal defense attorney. "They're weak on the aggravators."

Tom tended to agree but wanted the benefit of his friend's analysis. "How so?"

Bo set his feet back on the ground and leaned forward in his chair,
slowly rocking back and forth and thinking the problem through.
"Our boys are trying to make it a capital case by saying that Wilma
Newton intentionally murdered Jack Willistone during a robbery. So
robbery is the aggravator, correct?"

"Correct," Tom said, still gazing at the river. After the recess,
Powell had completed his presentation by taking Wade through the
physical evidence demonstrating that the victim had been robbed
either just before or just after his murder. "And today, Powell showed
that Jack Willistone's wallet was pilfered of at least three hundred
dollars, the glove compartment of his 4Runner was looted, and a
briefcase was stolen from the back seat." He paused and took a sip of
beer. "I'm not seeing the weakness."

"Bear with me and let's play this thing out."

"Play it out."

"They got Wilma's fingerprints on the murder weapon and no
one else's, right?"

"Yep."

"They got her saliva on Jack's cap and shirt collar." Bo paused
and stood from his chair, gesturing with his beer bottle. "Ladies and
gentlemen of the jury, she spat on the victim!" Bo mimicked Powell's
high-arching voice.

"OK."

Bo walked over to Tom and leaned his back against the railing,
nudging Tom's elbow. "Where are the prints on the wallet?"

Tom looked at him. "When I asked Wade about that on cross, he said there was a smudge on the billfold, but it wasn't clear enough to do a definitive test."

"Doesn't matter what the detective says. It's a seed of doubt, and that's not all. Where are the prints on the 4Runner? If our girl was digging all through that vehicle searching for money, why aren't any of her prints on the back seat where the briefcase was located? Or on any of the door handles? Or on the latch of the glove compartment? Or any damn where?" Bo took a quick gulp of beer. He again nudged Tom's elbow. "And how come there's none of her DNA anywhere in Jack's vehicle, Zorn's house, his boathouse, or even the dock? None of Ms. Wilma's blood, saliva, or hair was found anywhere on Zorn's property."

"The saliva—"

"On Jack's person," Bo interrupted. "Not Zorn's property."

"That's not enough, Bo, and you know it."

"I agree, but it is something. And something is better than nothing." He took another sip from his bottle. "Little seeds of doubt can grow into fruit if we have a story to attach them to."

Tom drained the rest of his bottle in one long gulp. "So what's our story then?"

Bo set his beer on the railing. "What does our client say?"

Tom sighed. "I don't know."

Bo wrinkled up his face. "What do you mean you don't know?"

"I mean I haven't gone over all of the state's evidence with her. I wanted her to see it all today."

Bo grabbed his nearly empty bottle and took one last swig. He rubbed his chin and looked out at the river. "That's not a bad strategy. I've actually used that myself a few times." He peered at Tom. "Especially when I thought my client might have committed the crime. Is that what you think?"

Tom rubbed his eyes, which burned with fatigue. He had cross-examined Wade for nearly four hours on the stand, confirming that the state had produced all witness statements and expert reports and meticulously going over each piece of physical evidence. By the time he told Judge Combs he had nothing further, he was literally leaning against the podium by the defense table to keep himself upright. If a day in court took this much out of him, he wondered how in the world he'd be able to handle a full week of trial with the pressure of the death penalty hanging over his client's head. "I don't know what I think yet, Bo. But my gut feeling was that I needed to hear the prosecution's story before I heard Wilma's."

Bo leaned his forearms on the railing. "A trial lawyer has to trust his gut. That was one of your mantras, Professor. When are you going to have your come-to-Jesus with her?"

"First thing in the morning."

"Good." Bo stuffed his hands in his pockets and walked back toward the table, but Tom remained by the railing, his eyes back on the Black Warrior. "Professor, can I ask you a question?"

"Of course."

"Are you OK? You seem to be wincing a lot and you were limping pretty bad on the way in here."

Tom rubbed his neck and looked at his friend. "I think I've got a bulging disc or something. I hurt it walking with Lee Roy a couple months ago. Damn dog lunged for a squirrel."

"Have you gotten it x-rayed?"

Tom shook his head. "Not yet. Haven't had time. Besides, there's no way I'm going to do any type of extensive back surgery at my age. All those lead to is more surgeries."

"Have you spoken with Dr. Davis about it?" Bo had taken Tom to some of his scans and treatment after he'd been diagnosed with bladder cancer two years ago, and he was familiar with Bill Davis.

"Yeah, a little. He just scanned my bladder in April and it was clean. He also said it was incredibly rare for bladder cancer to spread to the back." Tom sighed, tiring of talk of his health. "He did say he wanted to do an X-ray, but I haven't called to schedule one yet."

"Does he know you've taken this case?"

Tom scoffed. "Yeah, and he's not happy about it. Neither is my son or my daughter-in-law. Hell, even my grandson told me to be careful after his last ball game."

Bo stifled a laugh before asking, "How old is Jackson now?"

"Twelve." Tom shook his head. "Nobody thinks the old man should have taken this case."

"And what does the General say?" Bo raised his eyebrows and his smile turned into a wide grin.

Tom glared at Bo. "I took her to dinner. One damn dinner. We aren't dating or anything." He sighed. "But I think that she probably thinks I've lost my marbles too."

Bo's smile faded and he took a few steps toward Tom. The last light of the sun was now gone and the water was only illuminated by the cars going down Jack Warner Parkway and across the Hugh Thomas Bridge. "None of that matters. The only thing that matters . . . is what you think."

Tom moved his eyes back to the river but didn't say anything.

"So . . . what do you think, Professor?" Bo finally asked. "You've had something on your mind ever since we got out here. Spit it out."

"I think I've got one more trial left in me," Tom said, still looking at the river. "And I don't plan on losing it."

"That's good to hear. And even though we need an explanation for a lot of things, I don't see Wilma for this crime. What did JimBone Wheeler call her?"

"A doe."

"Well, I agree with the crazy bastard. We've got to know the whole story, but no prints or DNA at Zorn's property or in Jack's vehicle doesn't fit. It's a head-scratcher, and I'm betting the answer to the riddle lies in Walker County."

"You're thinking that Bully Calhoun wanted Jack dead so that his daughter could collect the insurance proceeds, that Bully was probably following Jack, and that Wilma Newton gave him an opportunity to do the deed and leave her as the patsy."

"Something like that," Bo said. "I think Bully has someone on his payroll doing the dirty work for him. Didn't JimBone say he had found someone for his old boss who had similar talents? And didn't he also insinuate that this hit man is the one who ran my believer's father off the road?"

When Tom didn't answer, Bo continued, his voice soft and low. "You told him, didn't you?"

Tom closed his eyes, a sense of guilt and dread creeping over him. "When I got back from Nashville, I called Jimmy Ballard, the sheriff of Henshaw County, and relayed what JimBone had told me."

"What about Rick?"

"I called him too."

"And?"

"I told him that Wheeler had implied that he had something to do with the hit-and-run and to make sure he took extra precautions."

"Did you say anything about Bully Calhoun's new enforcer?"

Tom's eyes flicked open. "I didn't get into the details. Rick's been through hell the past few months, and I don't want to send him over the edge. The kid's always been volatile. You know about him punching me after that trial competition in law school?"

"Are you kidding? I've seen the YouTube video. It was a good lick."

Tom rubbed his jaw and looked at Bo. "It was. He's come a long way since then. I mean, you saw how effective he was in the courtroom in Pulaski."

"I couldn't have asked for a better legal team than you and Rick."

"Well, he's gotten even better. Up until the hit-and-run, Rick had really taken over the office and was transitioning into more of a first-chair role." Tom stopped and turned back to the river. "I just don't want to hurt him or his mother any more than they've already been hurt."

For a while there was silence, and then Bo's voice, deep and strong, filled the void. "You can't protect everyone, Professor. This case we got going here . . . it's like the Alabama-LSU game these past few years. It's a knife fight in a ditch."

Tom squinted back at his friend. "What are you trying to say?"

"Rick is young and I know his heart is wounded, but he's also a country boy from Henshaw County. He's smart, tough, and he ain't afraid to fight. Plus he's got skin in the game . . . his daddy's blood. He shouldn't be on the sidelines."

Tom continued to gaze at the river, pondering Bo's words. *I can't protect everyone . . .* Finally, giving his head a jerk, he turned to Bo. "How are you coming with the driver? Jennings?"

"Alvie is still stonewalling me. Not answering calls, and when he does, only staying on the line long enough to tell me to leave him alone."

"And his brother?"

"Rel hasn't been much help either. I think something happened when I went up there that spooked them both. I think Bully has gotten to them in some way."

"Keep trying," Tom said. "I don't know that we have any other angles right now." Abruptly, Tom stepped back from the railing and began to walk down the steps that led to the river.

"Where are you going?" Bo asked, following after him.

"You'll see," Tom said.

Three minutes later, they were standing on a wooden dock directly in front of the restaurant. "See Zorn's dock?" Tom said, pointing at the larger structure half a mile down the river, illuminated by a fog light on top of an adjacent boathouse.

"Those two frat boys found the body halfway between where we are standing and that dock, right?" Bo said.

"Yeah. In the daytime, you can see a trampled path of brush where the cops have walked back and forth from the restaurant to where the body was discovered and then to Zorn's dock." He gestured across the river to the other side. "Bo, it is hard to see right now, but there's a walkway that runs about two miles down the Black Warrior on the opposite side of the shore. There's a couple of restaurants, Another Broken Egg Cafe, and a froufrou place."

"They'd be closed during the time of the murder, wouldn't they?"

"Yes, but I bet there are probably some students and maybe even locals that like to walk along the Riverwalk at night. It's possible they may have seen something. It's only three hundred yards or so across the water. That's why the kids come down here and try to hit a golf ball over the expanse."

"Professor, you know I love you, but that seems like a huge long shot. Zorn's boathouse does have a light, but to think that a walker might have seen the murder of Jack Willistone is a stretch."

"I'm not thinking so much about an eyewitness," Tom said. "I agree that would be highly unlikely."

"Then what are you thinking?"

Tom breathed in the muggy air coming off the dirty water. "What did you say when we first began discussing Bully Calhoun as an alternative suspect for the murder?"

Bo smiled. "All roads lead to Jasper."

Tom snapped his fingers, and he could feel his heart rate picking up speed. "That's right, but the highway is not the only path to Jasper." Tom motioned with his head toward the river. "If you head south by boat on the Black Warrior, then you'll reach the mouth of the Tombigbee. But if you head north . . ."

". . . you'll hit Jasper. You want to know if anyone on that side of the river might have seen a boat or some activity on the water around the time of the murder."

"Exactly. I also want to talk with those two frat boys again and see if they noticed any boats that looked suspicious. We obviously need to watch the entire surveillance video from the guardhouse of the Bent Creek subdivision—hopefully there's more on the tape than what they played today—and determine if there is anyone else who came through the gate that could be a suspect. But my gut tells me that Bully Calhoun would be too smart to send his enforcer right through the gate. Too much risk that he'd leave a trail." Tom licked his lips. "The water doesn't have those limitations."

"I like it," Bo said.

Tom took one last look at Greg Zorn's dock before turning to his friend. "Bo, you hit the nail on the head. No prints or DNA in the car or on the property gives us a seed of doubt to plant on the robbery charge. It doesn't fit with the story that the prosecution is trying to tell."

"We just need to find the story it does fit," Bo said.

Tom pointed at the waters of the Black Warrior. "If there is one, we'll find it on the river."

33

The lights in the district attorney's office were still on when Wade stepped through the door. It was past ten o'clock at night, and the whir of telephones and fingers pattering on computer keyboards had given way to the sobering melancholy of the Delta blues. Wade smiled and walked toward the conference room. He entered without knocking and saw Powell pacing the vinyl floor in a white undershirt, khaki pants, and bare feet. His jacket, button-down, and tie were draped over one of the chairs, and his black Johnston & Murphy lace-ups had been kicked to the corner. Wade couldn't see the socks anywhere and didn't ask. The room smelled like sweaty feet and coffee.

Spread across the length of the conference room table were the physical evidence and expert reports introduced at today's hearing. The only nonevidentiary item was an iPod box belting out Robert Johnson's greatest hits. Wade held up a bag of Golden Flake salt and vinegar chips in one hand and a six-pack of Miller High Life in the other, and Powell, finally taking notice, hit the stop button on the iPod.

"Your order, Mr. Prosecutor."

"Just in time," Powell grunted.

Wade snagged a bottle out of the carton and handed it to Powell, and then he got one for himself. Powell opened the bag of chips and popped two in his mouth. He twisted the top of the beer and tilted it back. Wiping his mouth, he saluted the detective with his other hand. "Thanks, brother."

"No problem. I like the soundtrack." Wade nodded toward the iPod. "You think Johnson really sold his soul to the devil?"

Powell rubbed his chin and bit into another chip. "I don't know whether there was an official transaction or not, but I do believe this." He pointed at Wade with the chip, and the detective could tell his friend was wired on caffeine. "I believe that *Johnson believed* he had sold his soul to the devil." He took another long sip of the champagne of beers. "And that's all that really matters."

"What?"

Powell cocked his head. "What do you mean, what?"

"I mean, you said that's all that really matters. *What* is it that matters?"

Powell plopped down in one of the chairs. "What a person believes." He squinted at Wade with eyes that were as red as Alabama's home jerseys. "In a court of law, what a jury believes."

Wade slowly took a seat next to him. "What's on your mind, boss?"

"We're weak on the aggravators."

"*We are damn not,*" Wade said, slamming his fist down on the table. He had expected this complaint and it pissed him off. "Robbery is an aggravator, and the evidence clearly shows that the victim was robbed of a good bit of cash, his briefcase, and whatever was in his glove compartment."

"It's all circumstantial," Powell said, taking a sip of beer.

"I know that, damnit, but sometimes an eyewitness and a confession don't just jump in our laps." He sighed and took a pull from his beer bottle.

"The Professor scored some points today." When Wade flung up an arm to protest, Powell held up his palm to stop him. "Hear me out. No prints or DNA of the defendant in the victim's car is puzzling given that there were prints on the murder weapon, don't you think?"

Wade took another sip of beer and tried to keep his temper in check. "Yes, but easily explainable. She didn't want to shoot Jack with gloves on. Her nine-millimeter is a thin pistol, and she may not have felt comfortable using it with gloves on. She intended to wipe the gun after she shot him, but she dropped it."

Powell rose from his chair and began to pace again. "That's what I think too, OK? A very plausible explanation. But why no DNA in Zorn's home? Or the boathouse? Or the dock itself?"

"We got it where it matters, son," Wade said. "DNA on the victim's body."

"I know, but the absence of it in the car and on the property gives them an angle."

Wade set his bottle down on the table. "Have you ever had a murder case built on circumstantial evidence that was perfect?"

"No," Powell admitted, continuing to pace.

"Me neither. Everything is always simpler when you have a confession or a murder with several eyewitnesses."

Powell stopped pacing and grabbed his beer. "Any response to those flyers we put up at the Riverwalk?"

Wade shook his head. "None."

Powell took a sip and gazed at the detective. They were now on opposite sides of the long conference room table. "You ever been to the Park at Manderson Landing at night?"

"I went there every night for the week after the murder. Me and two deputies. We stopped and talked to everyone we saw. It's all in the file."

"There was an astronomy professor who was out running the night of the murder, right?"

"Yeah. Can't remember his name off the top of my head, but he lives near campus and runs just about every night along the Riverwalk. He teaches a class on Tuesday and Thursday nights, so on those evenings he runs after the class is over."

"What time?"

"Well, the class is from eight to nine, so normally he goes from nine fifteen to ten."

"Which is just outside Ingrid's time of death."

Wade took a sip of beer. "Yes, but he said he would have gone later on the night of the murder, because he took the students in his class, all of whom are twenty-one or older, to Buffalo Phil's for a couple of three-dollar pitchers of Bud Light on the outside patio to celebrate the end of the semester."

Powell winced. He and his best friend, Rick Drake, had enjoyed three-dollar-pitcher night at Phil's throughout law school. Powell felt a twinge of sadness as he thought of Rick. He hadn't seen him since his father's funeral and hadn't talked with him since the arrest of Wilma Newton. He'd started to call him a couple of times, but with the Professor representing Newton, he'd stopped. The conversation would've been too awkward.

"Anyway," Wade continued, "the guy"—Wade snapped his fingers—"Sean Newell is his name. Dr. Newell said he wouldn't have gone running until around ten on May 8 and would have finished up around elevenish."

Powell creased his eyebrows. "He went running after drinking beer and eating wings?"

"You'd have to see the guy. He's north of fifty years old but a total health nut. Runs every day and big into triathlons. He said he couldn't miss a run or it would throw off his training."

"So he would've been there within Ingrid's time-of-death range."

"Yeah, but he didn't see anything. Says when he runs, he zones out. He also had ear buds on and was listening to his iPod playlist, so he didn't hear anything either."

Powell began to pace again, holding his almost empty bottle by his side. "Newell couldn't be the only runner on the Riverwalk that night."

Wade sighed. "It was late, brother. I agree that there's a lot of foot traffic along the Riverwalk through the day. Runners, kids, and adults walking their dogs, nature lovers, you name it. But at that time of night on a Tuesday . . ."

"Any word on the panties y'all found by the railing?"

"You'll never believe this, but no one has come in to claim them."

"Big surprise," Powell said. "Did Newell mention any other frequent flyers? Folks he would always see when he would run at night?" He paused. "Coeds knocking boots on the benches nearest the shore?"

Wade shook his head and sipped from his bottle. "None of the above."

Powell cursed and grabbed a handful of chips. "So it's a dead end."

"Looks like it. I guess it's possible that someone could see the flyer and come forward, but that would be highly unlikely at this point in the game. I mean, if there was somebody out there that did see something, why haven't they already come forward? Besides, we are talking about a distance of about three hundred yards across the river. Even if there was a witness, would that person be able to identify Wilma Newton as our killer from that far away?"

Powell didn't say anything. He plopped down in the closest chair and Wade did the same. For a few minutes, the two men drank in silence. Finally, Powell leaned back in his chair and gazed at the ceiling. "How did it feel being cross-examined by the Professor?"

"Weird," Wade said. "Very weird. I didn't like it."

"Me neither," Powell said, still gazing at the ceiling. "Wade, I don't want to lose this case. But I'm not sure how happy I'm going to be if we win it."

"I feel the same way, but we have a job to do and we are going to win. We may not get the death penalty—it's hard for a jury to put someone to death without direct evidence—but we'll get her on murder, you can take that to the bank. Tom may have scored some points today with the prints and DNA that we don't have, but we made a pretty damn convincing case with what we do have. He knows he's got an uphill climb."

Powell nodded and cracked open another beer. "I'm worried about Jack's family."

"The widow?"

"Not just her. Did you see Jack's son today?"

"Yeah, he was sitting in the back row with his mother. Jack's ex-wife. We had made room for them on the row behind us, but Barbara said she didn't want to disrupt the hearing if Danny needed a break."

"You think that was the only reason? Did you see how she looked at Kat?"

"I suspect her . . . *feelings* toward Jack's widow had something to do with it too."

"Has Kat collected the life insurance benefits yet?"

"No, but her claim was approved. She should be receiving the money in a few weeks."

"Keep an eye on her. Jack Willistone is not a sympathetic victim, but he will be even less so if his widow is out gallivanting around, spending money like it's going out of style." He sipped the beer. "We should probably have her come in for a talk once she does receive the proceeds."

"I agree. What about Barbara and Danny?"

Powell rubbed his chin and again gazed at the ceiling. "Danny has severe autism and resides at a facility in Birmingham, right?"

"Right. Glenwood I think is the name. His mother lives here in town on Queen City."

Powell began to flip through a notebook of documents. When he found what he wanted, he motioned to Wade. "Come here, I want you to look at something."

Wade stepped over and glanced at the page. "Visitor's log for the St. Clair Correctional Facility."

Powell went through the sheets of paper, counting with his fingers. "I count twenty-two visits by Barbara Willistone during Jack's eighteen months of confinement. Some with Danny and some without."

Wade wiped his eyes and looked at his watch. It was now past eleven o'clock and the detective was ready to hit the hay. "So what?"

"So his ex-wife visits on a regular basis while he's in prison and his current wife doesn't come to see him at all. Not a single time."

"Break it down for me, brother. What are you getting at?"

Powell rubbed his own bloodshot eyes and flipped through the notebook to another tab. "Have you had a chance to read Ingrid's final autopsy report cover to cover?"

"Twice," Wade said. "Come on, brother, give me more credit than that."

"I'm sorry. We just got it yesterday and I didn't want to make any assumptions."

"Ingrid did a thorough job and the cause of death matched what we've known from the beginning. What's the problem?"

Powell licked his fingers and turned the pages until he found what he wanted. When he did, he tapped the sheet with his index finger. "This."

Wade peered down and read the two sentences below Powell's finger. "OK, I repeat, What's the problem?"

"He was *dying*," Powell said, his voice dripping with intensity. "At the time of the murder, Jack had prostate cancer that had spread to the liver and lymph nodes. Don't you think that changes the dynamic a little?"

"No," Wade said. "Why don't you break it down for me?"

Powell closed the notebook and began to pace again. "Look, I know Jack Willistone was a hard son of a bitch, but it doesn't make sense to me that his autistic son wouldn't be at least a partial beneficiary on his life insurance policy. Especially with him knocking on death's door."

"You think that's why Barbara came to visit so many times?"

"Why else? I don't think she was giving him hand jobs. Conjugal visits are limited to a current spouse. And based on everything we know, their divorce was nasty. He left her for a younger, richer woman."

Wade rubbed his eyes again. "OK, I see your point, but why are you worried about it? So Barbara was trying to get Jack to change the beneficiary on his life policy before he bought the farm, and he ended up screwing her over. That sounds like Jack to me."

"I guess," Powell said, putting both hands over his face and rubbing them up and down. "There's also Bully Calhoun's handful of visits to Jack in the two months before his release. When we met with Bully in Jasper, he didn't say anything about Jack being sick."

"Maybe he didn't know."

Powell pursed his lips. "Seriously?"

"Yeah. It wouldn't be that uncommon for a person not to broadcast his health problems. Who knows? Jack may not have even been aware he was sick. We'll need to obtain the prison medical records, if there are any, to be sure."

"Let's do that ASAP, OK? I'm sure the Professor will request them after he has time to digest Ingrid's report."

"Ten-four."

Powell collapsed into his chair and took a long sip from his beer bottle.

"You want some advice?" the detective asked.

"Not really, but I'm sure that won't stop you."

"Don't worry so much. Let Tom and Bo try to make a case out of some life insurance conspiracy. We both know that there's no physical evidence connecting anyone else to this crime but Wilma Newton." He slapped the prosecutor on the back. "We're in good shape, brother. Kat Willistone. Bully Calhoun. Barbara Willistone. They're all windmills that I'm sure our good friend will chase, but we're sitting in the honey hole with as rock solid a circumstantial case as you can have in this business." Wade grabbed the carton of Miller High Life and headed for the door. "If your mentor wasn't on the other side of this case, you wouldn't have your panties in such a wad. Don't even try to argue different."

Powell didn't. "Anything else, Dr. Phil?"

Wade put the carton under his arm and turned the knob. Then he looked back at his friend. "Yeah. Get some sleep, partner. These cases are marathons, not sprints."

Once Wade had left, Powell put on another pot of coffee and resumed his review of the file. Despite his friend's admonition, he knew that Wade was just as worried as he was. Circumstantial cases were based on a story, and the lack of the defendant's DNA and prints in Jack's 4Runner and Zorn's property didn't fit the prosecution's version of events. Could it be explained? Yes. Would that explanation weaken the case? Absolutely. Would the Professor shine a light on these omissions at the trial in a few months? Most definitely.

Would the absence of this evidence provide enough reasonable doubt for the jury to acquit Wilma Newton?

"No," Powell thought aloud.

The Professor would need more to win the case, but as Powell again perused the prison visitor's list and thought about the wives of Jack Willistone, he wondered, *Is there more?*

34

If her ex-husband weren't already dead, Barbara Willistone was sure that she would have killed him tonight. She pressed the joint to her lips and inhaled deeply before blowing smoke over the top of the steering wheel. Closing her eyes, she relished the taste of the marijuana as it filled her lungs and mouth. Like almost everything bad in her life, pot was introduced to her by Jack. She had her first hit in Jamaica on their honeymoon and, over the years of stress that she had endured both with Jack and without him, she'd found that marijuana was the only substance that gave her any kind of relaxation. Alcohol just made her tired. She liked cigarettes but had quit before trying to have kids. And the one line of cocaine she had done in her life—in the spring of 1973 while watching Elvis's *Aloha from Hawaii* special on the tube with Jack—resulted in her waking up naked in the shower the next morning covered in her own vomit.

But a few hits of pot almost always calmed her down. Tonight, unfortunately, was the exception: she was already on her second joint and there was no relief in sight. She again snatched the letter she had folded and placed in the passenger-side seat. She had read the correspondence at least fifteen times since finding it in her mailbox upon returning home from the courthouse, hoping each time that it would say something different. That it wouldn't confirm her greatest fear. The letter was clearly a form, with only her son's name added to the salutation blank. In the close confines of her Toyota Camry, she read the words aloud:

"To Mr. Barton Daniel Willistone, your claim for death benefits has been denied. You are not a covered beneficiary under this policy."

There was more mumbo jumbo in the letter and an offer to accept a phone call if Danny wanted to talk about the rejection. But Barbara glossed over that part, unable to get past the first two sentences. *He told me he had changed it,* she thought. *He even showed me the form he had signed.*

Barbara set the letter back in the passenger seat and took another hit off the joint. She raised her eyes to the third-floor loft apartment and glared at the shadow of the woman through the open blinds. From this vantage point, you could only see her silhouette. With her back arched and pelvis moving forward and back, it was clear that she was enjoying the prick inside her. Barbara flipped the latch on the glove compartment of the Camry and gazed at the pistol inside.

I ought to kill the bitch right now. If they're gonna leave the blinds open so that all of Tuscaloosa can see them, then the door is probably not locked. I could just walk in and shoot her twice in her head. If she's having an orgasm, I can put one of the bullets in her open mouth.

Barbara inhaled more pot and enjoyed the image, but any sense of satisfaction evaporated as she glanced again at the letter in the seat next to her.

It wasn't fair, she thought, hating herself for such a childish sentiment. If she knew anything, the former Barbara Grace Atkins knew that life was anything and everything but fair. Her daddy had been a banker in Tuscaloosa for forty years, and her momma had taught Sunday school at the First United Methodist Church. She hadn't had a hard childhood by any stretch, and she'd been a "catch" when Jack Willistone proposed to her in the fall of 1970. She came with a dowry, and it was her father, Ollie, who gave Jack his first loan to start his business. She still remembered helping him place the sign out in front of the work trailer on a hot July day in 1971. "Willistone Trucking Company." Jack had chosen the crimson and white colors on purpose, saying that in Alabama those shades personified winning and "that's what our brand is all about." After the placard was up, they had admired it in the hot sun for several minutes, with Barbara snapping a number of Polaroids, one of which she still kept in an old shoebox at home. Then they had gone inside and had rough sex on the metal desk in the un-air-conditioned trailer. Afterwards, they had sat naked on the edge of the desk, their bodies sticky with sweat, smoking cigarettes and listening to Janis Joplin sing about Bobby McGee. Patting her thigh, Jack told her that he didn't know what he would ever do without her.

They were twenty-seven years old, and Barbara didn't think it was possible to be happier.

It wasn't.

Barbara's fingers trembled as she placed the joint to her lips. Sucking cannabis into her lungs and trying to shake off the old memories that scarred her soul, she again looked up to the third-floor apartment. The light in the room was off.

Seconds later, Kat Calhoun emerged from the front door on the ground level of the complex wearing a white tank top and purple athletic shorts. Her face, illuminated by the streetlamps on the sidewalk going into the entrance, was flushed red from the exertion of the workout she had just finished upstairs.

Barbara took a last pull on the joint and clicked the latch on the glove compartment. She grabbed the pistol and opened the door of her car. "Hey, b-bith . . . bitch!" she yelled, and she heard the lisp in her voice and knew that she was high as a kite. Barbara didn't care. She stomped out the joint and stumbled toward the younger woman. She gripped the pistol tight in her right hand. "What did you do?"

Kat Calhoun stopped and looked at her accuser, squinting into the darkness. When she recognized who was coming her way, she continued to walk to her car.

"Stop, bitch!" Barbara yelled after her. "You whore. You like that y-y-young dick you got upstairs?"

Kat took her keys out and clicked the keyless entry. The headlights to her silver Range Rover snapped on and off. She opened the driver's-side door, but Barbara grabbed her by the arm before she could climb inside.

"I said stop, you little b—"

A forearm caught Barbara right under the nose and rocked her backward on her heels. She felt the gun slip out of her fingers, and then a sharp pain in her right knee as Kat Calhoun's sneaker crushed into it. Barbara fell hard on her right shoulder and felt the sting of asphalt on her cheek. Then the air went out of her chest as Kat kicked her in the solar plexus.

Barbara fought for breath and finally coughed a gasp of air and then another. She rolled over on her stomach, her right shoulder throbbing in pain, and propped herself on her left forearm. She gazed up at Kat Calhoun.

"You're drunk, Ms. Barbara. Or maybe high is the better word."

Barbara blinked, remembering how Kat had called her "Ms. Barbara" as a little girl when the Willistones and Calhouns would get together. "What did you do?" Barbara managed, coughing the words out. "My son was supposed to get the life insurance proceeds. Jack"—she coughed again—"told me so."

Kat gave her the same pitying smile she had given her when Barbara caught her screwing Jack in the office eight years earlier. "Oh,

Ms. Barbara, I think Jack must have been joshing you." She squatted next to Barbara. "You didn't promise him a blow job or something, did you?"

Barbara ignored the jab and gritted her teeth. "What did you do?"

"I took what was rightfully mine," Kat said, standing up and trotting over to the pistol on the ground. She ejected the bullets in the weapon and walked back to Barbara. "Nine-millimeter," she said. "Interesting choice, Ms. Barbara."

Despite the pain in her shoulder, Barbara felt her pulse quicken.

"You didn't happen to use one of these about thirty days ago on my husband, did you?" She licked her lips. "Oh, Ms. Barbara, you have to feel so stupid."

"You were at the h-hearing today," Barbara said, pushing up off the asphalt into a sitting position. "That stripper killed Jack." She paused. "And if she didn't, your daddy framed her for it."

Kat shook her head and chuckled. "It doesn't really matter, does it?" Her voice was so cold that it made Barbara shiver despite the muggy heat.

"What are you . . . t-talking about?" Barbara slurred her words, the marijuana and the beating that she had just received working to jumble her thoughts. She felt dizzy.

Kat again squatted and spoke in a low voice. "The only thing that matters is all that money"—she paused and gazed wistfully at the night sky—"three million big ones. It's all mine. My claim was approved and I'll be receiving the check shortly. I may have to buy a new Range Rover. The new smell is wearing off that one." She stood up and pointed the gun at Barbara. "My daddy didn't have anything to do with Jack's death." She grimaced, showing her teeth. "But if you ever threaten me again, you're going to spend the next night in a morgue, you understand? Poor Danny will have to fend for himself."

As adrenaline pulsed through her body, Barbara made a move to get up, but youth and athleticism won out. Kat hit her with the butt end of the gun just above the temple, and Barbara fell to her knees. She never saw the kick, only felt the toe of the sneaker catch just under her nose.

She was out cold before her face hit the ground.

Once she was back in her vehicle, Kat thought about dialing 911 and reporting Barbara for stalking and trying to attack her. See how that hag liked waking up in a jail cell. Based on the woman's smell, a possession-of-marijuana charge might ride along with the attempted assault on Kat. But gazing up at the third-floor window, she thought better of it almost immediately. She didn't want to bring any attention to her friends-with-benefits relationship with Breck, which had started while her now-dead husband was rotting away in the St. Clair Correctional Facility.

Instead, she called her father, telling him everything but the part about having sex with Breck.

"I think you handled it fine," Bully said, and Kat could hear the pride in his voice. "Let her complain to the police. Maybe she can get herself arrested."

"Dad, she knows about the form. She knows Jack tried to change the beneficiary."

When silence filled the line, Kat's heart thudded with the first traces of panic. Then her father's baritone filled the airwaves, enveloping her like a fleece blanket.

"I know, darling. Unfortunately for the former Mrs. Jack Willistone, there's not a damn thing she can do about it. Jack is dead, and that money is ours."

Kat caught herself about to say "mine," but the words never came out. She knew better than to bite the hand that fed her. She had crossed her father by marrying Jack and had learned her lesson well.

So had Jack . . .

"Thank you, Daddy."

Barbara opened her eyes to rain pelting the side of her face. As she propped herself on her forearms, a wave of nausea came over her and she vomited. *Concussion,* she thought as the smell of the bile hit her nostrils and she threw up again. She rolled away from the mess and sat on her bottom, wrapping her arms around her knees and rocking back and forth as the rain began to pick up steam. Her nose throbbed from where she had been kicked, and when she gingerly touched it, she heard a slight crackling sound and knew it was broken. After a few seconds, her tears began to mingle with the rainwater. *I am such a fool,* she thought, squeezing her eyes shut and trying to stop herself from crying to no avail. She sobbed as thunder crackled above her.

Finally, her right shoulder began to ache and, using her left arm for leverage, she rose to her feet. When she did, she felt a piercing pain at her temples and, seeing stars, placed her hands on her knees and waited for the next round of nausea. When it came, she heaved several times, grateful for the darkness so that she couldn't see the color of her vomit.

Feeling shaky but a little better, she walked gingerly back to her Camry. The driver's-side door was still open, just as she'd left it when she had taken after Kat. *"Oh, Ms. Barbara, you have to feel so stupid."* She could hear the little bitch's voice ringing in her ears. Barbara collapsed into the driver's-side seat. For a second, she couldn't find her keys and wondered if Kat had thrown them somewhere. Then, mercifully, she saw them lying on the floorboard just under the accelerator. She bent down to grab them, but before she had them in her grasp, another wave of nausea hit her. Unable to move fast enough, she turned to her side and hurled a stream of bile onto the passenger-side seat of the Camry. She closed her eyes and took several deep breaths, waiting for the attack to pass. When her stomach finally felt stable, she opened her eyes and saw that some of the vomit had gotten on the rejection letter from the insurance company. She picked it up and wiped the residue off with her thumb, leaving an orangish-yellow smudge on the side. *At least I can still read it,* she thought, but then the tears came as she heard Kat Calhoun's confident voice fill her ears again. *"It doesn't really matter, does it?"*

Barbara placed the letter on the dashboard and, more carefully this time, bent to retrieve her keys. She placed them in the ignition and prayed that the battery wasn't dead due to the door staying open for so long. When the Camry fired to life, she said a quiet "thank you" to a God she wasn't sure she believed in anymore.

Ten minutes later, she pulled into her driveway on Queen City and parked in the one-car garage. When the electric door had come all the way down, she got out of the car and took all of her clothes off at the landing by the side entrance to the house. As her filthy blouse hit the floor, she felt a strong sense of déjà vu. She had done this very thing almost thirty days ago, in the wee morning hours of May 9 after she had seen her ex-husband for the last time. She had immediately put the garments and tennis shoes she had worn that morning in the washer and hadn't rested until she had washed and dried them twice. Tonight there was no reason to be so careful, and she had just had the crap kicked out of her. She left the clothes by the door.

She entered the two-bedroom house and was greeted by her white toy poodle, Coconut, who was probably starving, having not been fed all night. After putting three scoops of dog chow in the animal's bowl, Barbara limped to the back of the house, her right knee throbbing from where Kat had kicked her. She went into the bathroom, flipped on all the lights, and looked at herself in the mirror.

Dried blood covered both of her nostrils and there was a large bruise above her right eye. Her chin looked swollen. Placing her hand to it, she winced and wondered if it was broken. Barbara turned on the shower and knew the water would sting her wounds but that she would feel better afterwards.

Gripping the counter with both hands, she gazed into the mirror at brown eyes that had seen more than their fair share of sadness in her sixty-eight years. Despite Kat's mockery, Barbara Atkins Willistone knew that she was anything but stupid. And when it came to her son, she would do anything to secure his future. She had proved that to herself thirty days ago. The problem now was what to do about Kat still being the beneficiary of Jack's policy.

Barbara didn't believe that Jack had lied to her about sending in the change form. Jack wasn't living at home at the time of the murder, and he had to know that Kat was probably screwing around on him. He also knew that his time on earth was in short supply; he hadn't even thought he'd be alive when he was finally released from prison. Jack was not a good man by any stretch—Barbara knew that he had done terrible things to many people on his climb to the top of the trucking industry. But she had seen something in his eyes when he had showed her the copy of the change form. *Regret? Pride at doing the right thing?* Barbara wasn't sure what it was, but whatever the emotion, it felt genuine and good to her. *He believed he had changed the beneficiary to Danny.*

She sighed, knowing that Jack Willistone could con a con man. It was foolish to believe in him when he had let her down so many times, but she had no other choice. She had seen the copy of the form with her own eyes. She had seen Barton Daniel Willistone listed as the intended beneficiary of Jack's three-million-dollar policy. She could not quit.

Taking a deep breath, Barbara stepped into the shower and winced as the hot water burned the bruise on her forehead and the cut on her chin. She couldn't go to the police; too much risk. And there was no way that Greg Zorn would talk with her.

That left only one option.

Feeling better, Barbara turned off the water and grabbed a towel from the hanger. After drying herself off, she dug in one of her drawers for Neosporin and applied the ointment to her chin and forehead. Then she slipped on a bathrobe and walked to the kitchen. After fixing herself a cup of hot tea, she booted up the laptop on her table.

Two minutes later, she googled the name of the one person in the world who might be able to help her and Danny. The irony made her smile. In order to fulfill Jack's dying wish, Barbara would have to rely on the man whom Jack blamed for his incarceration and financial demise. But as the results of her search filled the screen, her smile faded as she thought of the danger she was about to invite into her life.

If she wasn't careful, she could be ruined too.

That is a risk I'm going to have to take. Then, focusing on the screen and swallowing hard, she wrote down the phone number for Thomas Jackson McMurtrie.

35

The morning after the preliminary hearing, Tom sat across from his client in the consultation room of the Tuscaloosa County Jail. The top button of his shirt was undone, and he had wrapped his suit coat around the back of the plastic chair. His back ached from the effort exerted at the hearing, and though he could hear the whir of the air-conditioning unit, he still felt hot in the small, stuffy room.

"You didn't sugarcoat it," Wilma said. She was dressed in the green sweat pants of a pretrial detainee, which made her look younger than her thirty-eight years. Tom was again struck by the resemblance between this woman and the teenage girl he had first encountered on the top step of his office a month earlier. Wilma looked down at the chipped wooden table and fidgeted with her hands. "It was worse than I could have ever imagined." She looked up from the table. "What happens next?"

"The case gets bound over to the grand jury," Tom said, hearing the fatigue in his voice. "The prosecution will put on the same song and dance they did today, and if the grand jury finds probable cause, which they will, an indictment will be handed down. The judge will then set a hearing date for your arraignment, where you will enter your plea of guilty or not guilty. Then the case will be set for trial."

"At least the judge seemed nice. Did you teach her when you were a law professor?"

Tom nodded. "I did, but Leah Combs won't be our judge going forward. In Alabama, a district judge like Leah typically handles the prelim, but a circuit court judge will preside over the trial."

"Who will we get then?"

"There are three. Williams, Baird, and . . . Poe." Tom almost winced at the possibility of Braxton Poe being assigned to this case.

"Are they good?"

"Pretty much." He didn't want to scare her by giving his true feelings on Poe, so he decided to shift gears. "Wilma, I expect the grand jury will hand down its indictment within the next thirty days and, since the prosecution already has its DNA and ballistics reports, I'm figuring this case will be tried by the end of the year."

She rubbed her arms and looked down at the table. "OK. Do you think we have a snowball in hell's chance of winning?"

Tom peered at her. "That depends."

Wilma looked at him and held out her palms. "On what?"

"We haven't talked much about the night of the murder."

"You haven't asked."

"I know. I didn't ask on purpose, because I wanted you to hear the state's case against you first."

Wilma grimaced. "You think I'm guilty, don't you?"

"No," Tom said, though he wasn't entirely sure what he thought at this point. "It's just a defense strategy."

"Whatever," Wilma said, irritation creeping into her voice. "Well, are you asking now?"

"Yes. I need you to tell me everything you did on May 7 and May 8."

Wilma looked down at the desk and began to rub her hands together. "May 7 was a Monday, right?"

"Right." Sensing that she was struggling with where to begin, Tom added, "Why don't you start with how you ended up at the Oasis Bar & Grill the afternoon of May 8?"

Wilma let out a breath and picked at her thumbnail. "I saw on the news that Jack had been released from prison. I had gone searching for work that morning and had come up empty again. Not much of a market for convicted prostitutes. Came home around noon and was going through my bills and realized I wasn't going to be able to make the rent if I didn't get a job soon. Then I saw the story about Jack getting out of prison, and I looked through the contacts in my phone. I still had his cell number saved—he had given me it before the trial in Henshaw. Like I've told you, he owed me a hundred thousand dollars. I took a shot of Jim Beam and made the call." She smiled and looked down at the table. "You know what he said after I told him who I was?"

"What?"

"He said, '*Jesus Christ Superstar, if I were given a thousand guesses as to who would be the first person to call me after getting out of the joint, I wouldn't have guessed you.*'"

Tom smiled. She did a pretty good imitation. "What did you tell him?"

"That he owed me a lot of money."

"How did he respond?"

Wilma smirked. "How do you think? He laughed. Told me that he had filed bankruptcy and didn't have a pot to piss in. Well, I just lost it. I told him that he was a son of a bitch who had cost me my whole family and that he owed me. I said some other things I don't remember." She shook her head. "A lot of cussing. I figured Jack had hung up, but I could still hear him breathing on the other end of the line. Then he surprised me."

"How so?" Tom asked.

"He said he was sorry. That he had made a lot of mistakes and his biggest was the way he handled me during the trial in Henshaw. Then he said that he had an idea of how I might make some money and invited me to meet him at the Oasis for a drink."

"Did he say what he had in mind?"

"Not over the phone. He said if I wanted to hear his proposition, I'd have to come see him at the bar." Wilma gritted her teeth and glared down at the desk. "I told him to go to hell and hung up. Then I paced my apartment for thirty minutes second-guessing myself. I had been back in Tuscaloosa for three months and hadn't sniffed a job. With my criminal record, I was worried I'd never get one, and the court wouldn't let me have my girls back if I didn't find employment." She raised her eyes. "I was desperate. Finally, I decided it wouldn't hurt to hear what Jack had to say. Before I could change my mind again, I grabbed my keys and drove to the Oasis."

"What happened?"

"I got there and he acted like I was an old friend. He bought me a drink and told me how much he missed the trucking business and the drivers, like Dewey, who had made things run. That all he had ever wanted to do was work hard and make a dollar for it, but that the Feds didn't want folks to make a living. It sounded like he was trying to justify his life or something, but I didn't care." She shook her head. "After I finished my drink, I asked him about his proposition."

"What was it?"

"Sex. He said he'd pay me four hundred dollars for the real thing, and half for a blow job."

Now it was Tom who shook his head. "How did you react?"

"You saw it all on the video. I was furious. I thought a man who had made the type of money that Jack had in his life might actually have an idea that would allow me to profit that didn't involve me dropping my panties." She scoffed. "But nope. The once all-powerful

Jack Willistone hadn't been laid since being sent to prison and was willing to pay me top dollar to let him wet his whistle. Can you believe that?"

Unfortunately, Tom could. "Did you ever tell him you were going to kill him?"

"I'm sure I did. Honestly, I can't remember everything I said. I was blind mad."

"Do you remember anything Jack said?"

She chuckled bitterly. "Yeah, I do. I followed him to his car, cussing him the whole way. Before he had quite made it to the 4Runner, he wheeled around and grabbed me by the waist. Before I knew what was happening, he was kissing me rough on the mouth. Then when I tried to break his hold, he let go and I fell backward on the gravel and scraped up my butt pretty good. When I looked up, he was hovering over me, laughing."

"Did he say anything?"

"Yeah," Wilma said. "He asked me if I had changed my mind yet."

"What did—?"

"I climbed to my feet and spat on him."

Tom felt his pulse quicken. "On his cap?"

"Right in his face. I suspect some got on his hat and collar."

That explains the saliva, Tom thought, jotting notes down on a yellow pad. "What happened next?"

Wilma slapped her hands on the table. "You saw it today on that video. Toby came and dragged me back into the bar and I proceeded to get hammered."

"Based on Detective Richey's testimony today at the hearing and the statement of Toby Dothard, you left the Oasis at approximately 6:30 p.m. Where did you go?"

"The ABC store on McFarland for a pint of Smirnoff and then the Taco Casa drive-through."

Tom's heart rate was beginning to pick up as they got closer to the time of the murder. "Then what?"

"I drank most of the vodka and ate my food."

"And after that?"

Wilma folded her hands and placed them under her chin, eyes down. She began to rock to and fro in her chair.

Tom couldn't tell if she was thinking or stalling. "What happened next, Wilma?"

Her lower lip began to tremble, and when she finally looked up, Tom saw tears in his client's eyes. "I'm sorry, but I can't tell you," Wilma said.

"Can't or won't?" Tom asked, his voice firm.

Wilma Newton wiped her eyes with the palms of both hands. Then, sitting up straight in the chair, she cleared her throat and crossed her arms. "Both."

36

"So where does that leave us?" Bo asked after Tom relayed the substance of his conversation with Wilma. They were seated across from each other in the conference room. The Newton file covered almost every square inch of the table.

"I'm going to keep trying," Tom said. "She was very emotional, and she has a great distrust for lawyers and the law. Neither have been very kind to her in life."

"I can understand that, but how can she expect us to defend her if she won't tell us what happened?"

Tom peered at his friend. "There is no us, Bo. When I try this case, you'll be a spectator."

"I was speaking figuratively. Any word from Rick?"

Tom shook his head.

"You can't try this case by yourself, Professor. You're gonna have to get him involved at some point. You know that, don't you?"

"Have you heard anything yet from your friend in Jasper?" Tom asked, ignoring Bo's question.

"I sent Rel another text this morning and left him a voice mail too. If I don't hear anything by the end of the day, I'm going there tomorrow. Now"—Bo stood up from the table and glared at his former teacher—"let's get back to my question. You know you can't try this case by yourself, right?"

Before Tom could respond, he was mercifully interrupted by the telephone intercom. "Professor?" the voice of the firm's receptionist, Frankie Callahan, blared through.

"Yes?"

"There's a Barbara Willistone on the line for you. She says it's urgent."

Tom looked across the table at Bo, who raised his eyebrows. Then he walked toward the phone. "Put her through."

"Yes, sir," Frankie said. She clicked off, and the phone began to ring.

Tom grabbed the receiver. "This is Tom McMurtrie."

For several seconds, all Tom heard on the other end of the line was heavy breathing. "Hello? Mrs. Willis—"

"I need to see you." The woman's voice was throaty, her words followed by several coughs.

Tom held the phone away from his ear until the coughing stopped. Then, trying to think of an appropriate response, he went with simplicity. "Why?"

"Because I know why Jack was murdered."

37

Thirty minutes later, Tom pulled into the driveway of Barbara Willistone's cottage on Queen City Avenue with Bo riding shotgun. "Give me the rundown again of what we know about her," Tom said.

After Barbara's cryptic phone call, Tom had Bo review the witness statements from Jack's ex-wife that were in the prosecution's file.

"Married Jack in 1970 and stayed hitched for thirty-four years. They had one child together—a son named Barton Daniel Willistone that goes by Danny. Kid is autistic and resides at an adult facility for autism in Birmingham. Worked primarily for Willistone Trucking Company as a receptionist and secretary until the divorce in 2004."

"How soon after the divorce did Jack marry Kat Calhoun?"

Bo looked down at the timeline he had written on a pad. "Five and a half months."

"Hmm . . . And where was Barbara on the night of the murder?"

"According to Detective Richey's statement, she was home alone."

"So she has no alibi."

"Nothing corroborated."

"What about jobs since the divorce?"

Bo again looked at his pad. "Belk in McFarland Mall. Works full-time in the women's shoe department."

"Salary?"

"It's not on here, but it can't be much. Thirty-five thousand a year I'd guess."

Tom cut the ignition. "Anything in there on how much a year that autism facility costs?"

"No." Bo gave him a curious look. "You thinking she's a suspect? Would be kinda odd for her to call you out of the blue if she was the killer, don't you think?"

"Yes," Tom agreed. "I've just spent so much time thinking about Bully Calhoun that I haven't even considered Jack's ex-wife." As he grabbed the door handle, he turned to look at his friend. "You know, when we were defending you last year and going over the visitor's list to the St. Clair prison, I always assumed that Barbara was Jack's current wife. No other woman with the last name Willistone came to see him. Have you noticed that?"

Bo nodded. "No record of Kat Willistone on the visitor's log. Only Barbara."

"Doesn't that strike you as odd?"

"It does."

"Did you see Barbara Willistone at the hearing yesterday? I only saw Kat."

"There was a stocky woman sitting on the back row opposite me with a man who looked to be in his thirties or forties next to her. They left the courtroom a couple of times, always together. I'm pretty sure that was her."

"So she would have heard all the evidence?"

"Most of it," Bo said. Then he chortled. "Professor, I could be wrong, but my gut tells me that the sun is about to finally shed its light on our vitamin D–deprived asses."

Tom climbed out of the Explorer. *We are due a break,* he thought as he trudged up the cobblestone walkway and rang the doorbell.

When Barbara Willistone answered the door, Tom could see why she wanted their meeting to occur at home. The woman's right eye was black and had swollen shut. Her lower lip was puffed out and the side of her forehead was tinted reddish purple. Her nose appeared unnaturally flat. *Broken,* Tom thought. *What the hell happened to her?*

"Please come in," she said, and ushered them both in the house. As Tom and Bo followed her through a den with an old box-style television set propped on an armoire, the smell of coffee hit Tom's nostrils. Not fancy Starbucks java, but old-school Maxwell House or Folgers. The scent reminded him of the teacher's lounge at the law school.

Once they were seated around a circular table in the kitchen, Tom opened with the obvious. "Ms. Willistone, are you OK? You look like you've been—"

"Run over by a bus," Barbara interrupted, her throaty voice, like on the telephone, followed by a coughing fit. "Excuse me. I honestly wish that was it."

"What happened?" Bo asked, and Barbara turned her eyes to him.

"You're Mr. Haynes, aren't you? The lawyer from Pulaski?"

"Yes, ma'am."

"I watched your trial on C-SPAN last year. I'm glad you won."

"Me too," Bo said. Then he nodded at Tom. "I had a pretty good lawyer."

Barbara moved her gaze to Tom and then abruptly stood up from the table. "Where are my manners? Can I fix y'all a cup of coffee?"

They both accepted her offer. As she prepared three steaming mugs, she spoke with her back to the duo. "Professor McMurtrie, did you know that Jack blamed you for ruining his life?"

"Yes. He so much as told me last year when I visited him at the prison."

Barbara turned and placed mugs of coffee in front of them. "I didn't realize you had come to see him."

"Yes. You came to see him quite a bit yourself."

She gazed into her coffee cup. "I took Danny . . . our son, to visit. Danny is autistic."

"When was he diagnosed?" Tom asked.

"Officially, not until he was four, but we knew something was wrong at eighteen months."

A solemn silence enveloped the small area. Tom and Bo had both been fortunate that none of their children and, for Tom, grandchildren had been born with any birth defects or had developed any serious conditions or disorders. Tom couldn't imagine the strain that could put on a family. Still, his defensive coach at Alabama, Gene Stallings, had raised a child with Down syndrome, and he always said that he never had a bad day in his life afterwards because his son, Johnny, despite his condition, never complained about anything. Tom knew that not everyone could handle that situation with such grace and patience, and as he thought about what a ruthless man Jack Willistone had been, he realized that the woman sitting across from him had likely raised her son on her own.

"Is Danny the only reason you visited Jack in prison?" Bo asked, and Tom winced at the forward nature of the question.

"You are direct, aren't you, Mr. Haynes?" Barbara asked. Then, not letting him respond, she said, "Yes. Though I admit that quality father-and-son time wasn't the intent."

"What was?" Bo pressed.

Barbara leaned forward and looked inside her purse, which she had set in the middle of the table. She pulled out a single sheet of paper and placed it in front of Bo. Tom scooted his chair closer to his friend so that he could read what appeared to be a letter. The right-hand edge of the paper had an orange smudge on it and there was a sour odor that Tom couldn't place.

Tom felt his stomach jump when he saw the letterhead: "New York Life." He and Bo quickly scanned the contents and then looked at each other.

"Danny filed a life insurance claim?" Bo asked, sliding the letter to Tom so that he could have a better look. It was only two paragraphs, a short rejection-of-benefits notice signed by "Walter Beasley, Claims Representative."

"Yes," Barbara said. "I filed it for him. The main reason that I came to see Jack so often at the prison was to try to convince him to name Danny as the primary beneficiary of his life policy." She took a sip of coffee. "Jack was bankrupt. *You* bankrupted him." She looked at Tom, but there was no anger or menace in her eyes. "He had nothing left, and he was dying."

Tom felt his heart jump. He looked at Bo, and his friend's eyes grew wide as saucers. "He was dying?" Bo repeated.

"Prostate cancer that had spread to the liver," she said. "I think that was the main reason he was released from the prison. So that they could avoid the costs of treatment." Barbara looked from one to the other. "You didn't know that, did you?"

Tom's heart was now pounding and he felt a surge of adrenaline. "No, ma'am. We just received the full autopsy report yesterday, and there were no medical records in the file produced by the prosecution."

"You said you went to the prison to persuade Jack to change the beneficiary to Danny?" Bo asked, back on point. "Were you successful?" He stole a glance at Tom. Both men knew that Kat Willistone had also filed a claim for the three million in benefits, which had been approved.

"I thought so. On my last visit before his release, he said he had changed it to Danny. He told me that he had sent the form in." She glared past Tom to some unseen spot in the distance. "Then after he was out, he came by the house and showed me a copy of the form he had completed listing Danny as the beneficiary."

Tom held up the stained letter. "But his claim was denied."

Barbara nodded and continued, her jaw tight. "After I learned that Jack had been murdered, I went down to Max Conchin's office on Skyland. He was Jack's insurance agent for thirty years. One of the life insurance company's most successful agents. Max said that he had received nothing from Jack. That he hadn't even talked to him since he was sentenced to prison." Her voice began to shake with emotion. "I couldn't believe it. Jack had lied to me before, but he had shown me the copy of the form. I had seen it with my own eyes. I asked Max for a claim form anyway and I sent it in. I thought maybe Jack had gotten cross with Max and decided to send the change form directly to the insurance company." She pointed at the letter. "That's what I got in response."

"Ms. Willistone, what happened to the copy of the change form that Jack showed you?"

She held up her palms. Tears now streaked her bruised and swollen face. "I don't know. He put it back in his briefcase and left the house. The next morning I heard about his murder on the news."

Tom thought back to the Bent Creek subdivision video that Powell had played at the preliminary hearing the day before. There had been a leather briefcase in the back seat of Jack Willistone's 4Runner. *Which the state claims was stolen by his killer.*

"Do you think Max Conchin lied to you about getting anything from Jack?" Bo asked, and Tom could hear the excitement in his friend's deep voice.

Barbara snorted. "I wish I believed that, but I don't. Max is a deacon in the First Methodist Church and I've never seen him without a Bible in his hand or nearby." She stared at Tom with eyes haunted by years of hurt and sacrifice. "I know that doesn't mean much, but Max is not a hypocrite. Jack always said that Max could walk into a Baptist revival and wrap a diamondback rattler around his neck like a shawl." She paused. "No, he didn't lie to me."

"What about Jack? Was the copy you looked at a fake?"

Tears filled Barbara's eyes again. "I know you probably think I'm a fool. Jack could be . . . such a horrible man, I know. I witnessed it with my own eyes. But he wasn't always so bad. Before Danny . . ." She stopped and started to sob. Tom saw a box of Kleenex on the counter and grabbed them, offering her a tissue. "I'm sorry," she said. "It's just . . ." After stifling a sob, she folded her arms tight around her chest. When she spoke again, her voice was so hushed that Tom had to lean close to hear her. "Jack had wanted a litter of kids, but my body wasn't made for that. I had three miscarriages—*three*—before Danny was born in April of 1975. Jack had been so proud. I had given him a boy. A *son* to carry on his name and one day run his business. Jack was giddy for those first few months after the birth. But it wasn't too long before we realized something was wrong."

Tom glanced at Bo across the table and could tell that his friend was about to say something, and he held his hand up to stop him. *We need to let her get this out,* he tried to convey with his eyes.

Barbara stared at the wall. "Jack came home from work after a particularly long day when Danny was eighteen months old. He had a cussing fit when I informed him that dinner would be fish sticks and fries." She chuckled despite her tears. "Times were still tight then. Jack was two years away from landing the deal with Andy Walton in Pulaski that would change the future of the company. Jack had a loud voice, and even though I was used to it, it still scared me when he blew his top. But Danny just sat at the kitchen table and didn't even whimper. He hardly ever cried or made sounds. When Jack was through cussing, he looked at Danny for a long time. I . . . I've never seen such an expression of disappointment and shame. It *burned my soul.*" She wiped her eyes. "I took Danny to see the pediatrician the next morning and, after two-and-a-half years of tests, the doctors concluded that Danny had a form of severe autism. He would never be 'normal.' He would never play football. His father would never be able to hand him the keys to Willistone Trucking Company." Barbara let out a long sigh and looked at Tom, her eyes distant, looking back through the hourglass. "Something just broke in Jack after that. He had always cheated on me. A year after we were married, I began to smell a scent of perfume that wasn't mine. But the world was different back then. My momma told me that some men needed a little strange on the side to be a good husband at home. You ever hear such a thing?"

Neither Tom nor Bo answered, knowing that it was a rhetorical question.

"Now, Momma didn't so much as say that my father had taken some strange in his time, but I could read between the lines. Daddy was a rounder, and I had married one too. So I looked the other way. At first because of what Momma said. And after Danny, because I . . . I felt like I had failed Jack by not having a healthy child. I took care of Danny, made sure that he was in the right kind of facility, and visited him every day. And Jack built an empire and . . . pretty much humped everything with a vagina in Tuscaloosa County. I stopped putting up with it when I caught him with Kat."

"Why?" Bo asked, his tone startling Tom out of the trance that Barbara's sad tale had put him in.

"I don't know. I guess I had never really walked in on him before, and Kat was just a child, for God's sake. When she was twelve years old, she had tagged along when Bully and his second wife, Janice, and me and Jack and several other couples had all taken Bully's yacht down the Tennessee River for the Alabama-UT game. She wore a precious 'Bama cheerleader outfit and had pigtails and called me Ms. Barbara. When she was eighteen, she had stayed at the Big House with us so she could go through rush at the university. We . . . *I* had been good to her and I had almost looked to her like a daughter." She paused. "About eight years ago, I came to the office one night with a pot of homemade spaghetti. I was going to surprise Jack. I hadn't done anything like that in years and was excited. But when I walked in the door, Jack was bending Kat over his desk." She scoffed. "He was so into the act that he hadn't even noticed I was there. But Kat had. She was in her late twenties then with tan skin, a perfectly toned body, and perky frat-girl breasts. The ungrateful little bitch had looked right at me, but instead of screaming at being caught, she *smiled*. I swear to God she looked like she had just won the blue ribbon at a beauty contest and I was the unlucky girl that came in second." Barbara slammed her fists on the table, and Tom and Bo grabbed their coffee mugs to keep them from spilling. "Can you believe the gall? She felt *sorry for me*." Barbara stood from the table and walked back to the coffeepot, making a show of pouring out the liquid in her cup and then refilling it. "I couldn't stand for that, so I told Jack I wanted a divorce." She snickered. "Jack looked at me like he was Brer Rabbit and I had asked him to jump in the briar patch. I was damaged goods, and Kat was heir to Bully Calhoun's dynasty. He filed the next day and married Kat a few months later."

Barbara returned to her seat and blew her nose into another Kleenex. "I think . . . when he was in prison, something changed in him. I'd like to believe it was my visits, but it was probably the cancer. Jack always thought he was ten feet tall and bulletproof. Having to deal with his own mortality really shook him." She gazed up at the ceiling. "I know that form was real. I know he changed the beneficiary to Danny." She lowered her eyes to Tom and this time there was no distance in her gaze. Her pupils bore into his like lasers. "*I know it.*"

For almost a minute, no one said anything. Tom wanted to give Barbara a moment to gather herself, and Bo furiously jotted notes. Finally, Tom cleared his throat and leaned his forearms on the table. "Ms. Willistone, what happened to your face?"

She winced and brought a hand to her forehead. "That bitch."

Tom glanced at Bo, who asked the next question. "Kat?"

Barbara nodded. "I shouldn't have done it, but I just couldn't help myself. She had been so prim and proper all day during the hearing, wearing black and playing the role of the grieving widow. When I got that letter, I went over to the Big House—Jack's house—and parked down the road. I followed her to an apartment in downtown Tuscaloosa and saw her having sex with a man in the upstairs loft. It was the guy that was at Pepito's with her."

"Breck Johnson?" Bo asked, and Tom was grateful for his partner's near-photographic memory of the evidence produced by the prosecution.

"That's the one. He met her in the parking lot, and I saw them walk to the elevator together." She gazed bitterly at her mug. "He left the blinds cracked just enough that I could make out her shadow."

"How . . . ?" Bo started to ask another question but stopped himself.

Barbara chuckled. "I may be old and saggy, Mr. Haynes, but I remember what sex looks like."

"Yes, ma'am. What happened next?"

"When she came outside, I went after her. I was so mad. I wanted her to know that I knew that Jack had changed the beneficiary on his policy."

"What was her reaction?" Tom asked.

She touched her nose. "She beat the crap out of me."

"Did you call the police?"

Barbara shook her head. "I couldn't. I started it. I grabbed her from behind. She would say that she was defending herself, and she'd be right."

Bo looked Jack Willistone's ex-wife up and down and let out a low whistle. "Looks to me like she did more offense than defense."

Tom tapped his pen on the table and took a sip of joe. Finally, he looked Barbara straight in the eye. "Ms. Willistone, why are you telling us all of this?"

She didn't blink. "Because I know that Jack intended to change his life insurance policy to make Danny the beneficiary. I know he sent the form somewhere. And I think his bitch widow and her father did something that prevented the change form from going to New York Life."

"And then they killed him before he could figure out what they had done," Bo added.

Barbara wiped her tear-streaked face. Then she gave a quick nod. "Exactly."

As they walked toward Tom's Explorer, Bo said, "You feel that?"

"Feel what?" Tom asked.

"The sun on our asses," Bo said, slapping his hands together.

"Let's not get too excited," Tom said. "All we have right now is the ramblings of a bitter woman."

"You know it's more than that," Bo said.

Tom did, but he didn't say so. Instead, he started the car and headed east on Queen City.

"Where to now?" Bo asked.

Tom took a deep breath and tried to calm his rapidly beating heart. He had been so engaged in the meeting with Barbara Willistone that he had forgotten about the ache in his back, and he wanted to keep the momentum. "I think it's time we pay Jack's Bible-toting insurance agent a visit."

In the passenger seat, Bocephus Haynes smiled. "Wide ass open."

Inside the house, Barbara watched them leave through a crack in the blinds. She had told them everything but the part about her being high and carrying a pistol during the altercation with Kat. She closed her eyes and said a silent prayer that she'd done the right thing. That she'd done right by her son.

"Please, Lord," she said out loud. *"Hear me this time."*

38

They found Max Conchin at the City Cafe in Northport sitting by himself and eating a plate of fried green tomatoes. His receptionist said that Max would be there until the restaurant closed at three thirty. "It's a Tuesday," she had said, as if that explained everything.

The insurance agent had thick white hair that was combed in a tight part and wore a navy-blue suit. Even on a ninety-degree day in June, he still wore his jacket.

"Mr. Conchin," Tom said, extending his hand just as the other man was lifting his fork to eat. Max stuck half of the fried vegetable in his mouth and chewed furiously while rising to his feet. He smiled as if on autopilot and extended his hand. "Max Conchin." The man's voice boomed out the words like a televangelist.

"Tom McMurtrie," Tom said, and then gestured to Bo. "This is my friend Bo Haynes. Would you mind if we joined you?"

"Not at all," Max said, gesturing to the two seats across from him. "I have a lunch meeting in about . . ." He made a show of looking at his watch, and Tom guessed the man was probably pushing eighty years old. "Forty-five minutes. Maybe I can talk you fellas into exploring a life insurance policy."

"We didn't come here to talk about insurance," Tom said, taking the seat directly across from Conchin, while Bo took the one catty-corner.

"Oh," Max said, wiping his mouth with a white paper cloth napkin. "Then what gives me the pleasure?"

Tom glanced at the empty seat next to Conchin and noticed a rather large briefcase. On the placemat above the seat was a white notebook, filled with the insurance agent's chicken-scratch handwriting. Underneath the notebook was a worn leather-bound copy of the Holy Bible.

"Mr. Conchin, I was hoping to ask you a few questions about Jack Willistone."

Max blinked but his face remained pleasant. "Longtime customer of mine. Thirty years at least. I hated to hear about what happened to him. Why do y'all want to ask me about Jack?"

"I represent the woman accused of murdering Mr. Willistone," Tom said. "And Bo here is my lead investigator. We wanted to ask you some questions about Jack's life insurance policy."

"What do you want to know?" The man's eyes held no trace of hostility, and his lack of discomfort rattled Tom. He was expecting someone who would be irritated or annoyed at having his lunch interrupted. But Max Conchin appeared to be enjoying the interaction. *Probably why he sells a lot of policies,* Tom thought.

"How much was the policy worth?" Bo asked, lobbing an easy question over the net to get things started.

"Three million," Max answered, the smile still plastered to his face.

"And who was the beneficiary at the time of his death?"

"His wife, Kathryn, or Kat as she likes to be called."

"When did Kat file her claim?"

"When? I can't remember the exact date. But I know she came in and requested the death benefits form a couple of days after Jack was killed."

"Did anyone else request a death benefits form?" Bo asked.

"What?" Max asked, and for the first time he looked uncomfortable, his perma-smile growing tight.

"Did any person besides Kat request a death benefits form?"

Max wiped his mouth with his napkin, clearly stalling. "Well . . . as a matter of fact . . . Jack's ex-wife Barbara did come see me and ask about that."

"Tell us about that," Tom said.

The shine finally faded from the insurance agent's voice. "Say, you fellas want to tell me what this is about? Am I in some kind of trouble? I'm a God-fearing man that's always tried to do right by people. I love the Lord and Jesus loves me, just like the children's song goes."

"You're not in any trouble, Mr. Conchin," Tom said. "At least none that we are aware of." He paused. "What happened when Barbara came to see you?"

Max laid his napkin down and gazed at his half-eaten plate. He looked at Tom with genuine empathy. "Barbara was under the impression that Jack had changed the beneficiary on his life policy to their son, Danny. She told me that Jack had told her that he had sent in a change form. I wish that he had, I really do. I know Barbara has been through hell with that boy, and three million dollars would have taken care of his expenses for life. But I never received anything from Jack or his attorney. Hell, I hadn't even talked with Jack for at least two years before he died."

"Mr. Conchin, do you know Kathryn Willistone's father, Marcellus Calhoun?" Bo asked. "Also goes by the name of Bully Calhoun."

Max's eyes went wide but he shook his head. "No, sir. I do not know the man."

"Have you heard of him?"

"No, I have not, and based on his nickname I'm glad I haven't." Conchin's expression was Boy Scout earnest, and Tom had a vision of a diamondback rattlesnake curled around the agent's neck. *If you truly believe, the snake won't bite,* Tom thought, imagining Conchin preaching these words in a one-story church in rural Alabama.

"Mr. Conchin, if Jack Willistone did want to make a change to his life insurance policy, would you have expected him to contact you?"

The perma-smile returned. "Yes, I would. In fact, when Jack decided to change the beneficiaries from Barbara and Danny to Kat after he remarried, that's exactly what he did." He stuck his fork in a fried green tomato and pointed the silverware at Tom. "I most certainly would have expected either Jack or, since he was in prison, his lawyer to call me if he wanted to make a change." Max slipped the fork into his mouth and chewed with vigor.

"And that didn't happen," Bo said, a statement, not a question.

"No, it did not," Max said, taking a sip of coffee.

Tom gazed at the ancient insurance agent, thinking that the man was in remarkably good health for the age he appeared. "I'm curious, Mr. Conchin. How old are you?"

"Eighty-three and eleven months. I'll be eighty-four next month."

"Well . . . you certainly look a lot younger," Tom lied.

"Thank you," Max said, nodding at Tom and then Bo.

"Your receptionist said that you come here every Tuesday," Bo said. "That true?"

"Yes, it is. I spend Monday morning at the Waysider and the afternoon at Piccadilly. Tuesday is the City Cafe for the duration. Wednesday is the Cracker Barrel in Cottondale. Thursday I'm back at the Waysider, but I skip the afternoon and play golf at Hidden Meadows. Friday I'm back here. Saturdays I spend fishing on Lake Tuscaloosa, and Sunday is for the Lord."

"Are you ever at your office?" Tom asked.

"Not if I can help it," Max said, wiping his mouth with a napkin. "Gentlemen, I've sold life insurance policies for a half century, and I have never closed a deal, not a single one, in my office." He waved his hands and looked around the crowded restaurant. "This is my place of business."

"The City Cafe?" Bo asked.

"No, sir," Max responded, his arms still outstretched. "The world."

Bo gave a sidelong glance to Tom, who got the message and stood up. "Mr. Conchin, thanks so much for your time."

Max also rose to his feet and shook hands with both men. He smiled even wider than before. "I've got a few more minutes. Are you sure I can't discuss your options with you? It's never too late to protect your most valuable asset." He pointed his right index finger at Tom and his left at Bo. "*You*," he said, and Tom wondered how many times that same spiel had worked on a potential customer.

"Thank you, Mr. Conchin," Tom said. "But we are very bus—"

"At least tell me a little more about yourselves," Max interrupted. Then his smile was gone and his eyebrows creased. He placed both hands on Tom's shoulders. "I'd like to know you . . . so I can love you."

Before Tom could respond, he felt a rough hand on his back and hot breath in his ear. "Time to go," Bo whispered, nudging Tom sideways and away from the table while looking at Conchin over his shoulder. "Maybe some other time." But as he started to walk away, Bo wheeled on the insurance agent and asked one last question.

"Mr. Conchin, can you think of anyone who Jack might have spoken to about changing the beneficiary of his life insurance policy?"

Max had returned to his seat and took a few seconds to consider the question. "Well . . . no. I mean no one other than the obvious."

"The obvious?" Bo asked, and Tom stepped closer so that he could hear better.

"His lawyer, of course," Max said. "What's that young fella's name? He's a client of mine too. Greg . . ."

". . . Zorn," Tom said, turning from Conchin to Bo. "Greg Zorn."

39

Tom and Bo rode back to the office in silence. Neither had to say out loud what the other was thinking. Greg Zorn was a dead end. Tom had left him at least fifteen voice messages since taking over the defense of Wilma Newton, and all of his calls had gone unreturned. Tom had met the attorney last year at the St. Clair Correctional Facility when he and Powell had interviewed Jack Willistone in connection with Andy Walton's murder. Tom had thought this familiarity might lead Zorn to be cooperative.

I thought wrong, Tom knew. Though it didn't make him feel any better, Tom also was aware that Zorn hadn't been all that forthcoming with the prosecution. The witness statement attributed to Zorn in the file ended with Wade noting that, outside of admitting that he had offered his waterfront home for Jack to stay in while he was handling a trial in Birmingham, Zorn refused to discuss anything further about his conversations with the victim pursuant to the attorney-client privilege. There were no follow-up attempts by Wade documented in the file, which wasn't all that surprising.

What does he add to their case?

"Nothing." Tom whispered the answer to himself.

"What?" Bo asked.

"Nothing," Tom repeated. "When are you going back to Jasper?"

"Unless I hear something back today, I'll head there first thing in the morning."

"Then what?"

"If the trip produces any leads, I'll follow them. If not, I'll probably head home for a couple days. I suspect that Lee Roy is getting tired of sharing your guest room with me, and as much I love that dog, his snoring is starting to wear a little thin."

Tom laughed. "Home to Pulaski or home to Huntsville?"

Bo sucked in a breath and slowly exhaled. "That's a good question."

"Have you told Jazz about all this?"

Bo nodded. "She was actually relieved to hear that I was doing something besides working on that Walton land. Told me to give you her regards."

"Be sure to give her mine. She's a good woman, Bo, and . . . you know that she loves you."

"I do," he said, gazing down at the floorboard. "And she knows that I love her. I wish—" The ringtone of Bo's cell phone interrupted whatever he was about to say, and he pulled the device out of his pocket. He gazed at the screen. "No caller ID," he said. Then he pressed the phone to his ear.

"Yeah." Bo listened for several seconds and hung up without saying anything further. "That was Rel. I think he was using a pay phone."

"What did he say?"

"He wants to talk," Bo said.

"When?"

"Now."

40

Twenty-five minutes later, after retrieving his vehicle at the office and telling Tom he'd regroup with him soon, Bo pulled his Sequoia to a stop in front of a white cinder-block shack on Martin Luther King Jr. Boulevard in Northport. Though the street sounded like it might be a large thoroughfare, it was actually a nondescript road in the middle of nowhere and, even though Bo had been to the place hundreds of times in his life, he still had a hard time finding it.

Bo smiled at the structure like it might be an old friend. Tuscaloosa was known for its barbecue, and for Bocephus Haynes's money, the best pork in town was made by the man inside this shack.

George and Betty Archibald opened their tiny barbecue joint in 1962, and though Bo couldn't be sure, he doubted the place had changed much in the past five decades. Now run by George Jr., Archibald's was a Tuscaloosa institution. A person wanting his fix could go through the drive-through and take the food back home or to the office. Or if you really wanted to get the full ambience, you could order inside and sit at one of the picnic tables in the yard. As

Bo climbed out of his vehicle, he breathed in the aromas of burning hickory wood and slow-cooked barbecue. He walked toward the
building and saw that Rel Jennings had already ordered and taken his
place at one of the tables.

"You start without me again?" Bo yelled.

Rel held out sauce-stained palms. "I'm sorry, brother, but I
couldn't resist."

Bo waved at him and walked inside. Five minutes later, he was
seated across from his friend at the wooden table, which had been
spray-painted a crimson red. He brought a forkful of pulled pork to
his mouth and savored the taste.

"Still as good as ever, isn't it?" Rel asked.

Bo nodded and moved his eyes from the picnic tables toward the
shack. Adjacent was the old barbecue pit, and Bo saw an older man
with gray-specked stubble putting more hickory wood on the fire. "If
it's possible, it may be better," Bo said. Then his eyes narrowed and he
gazed at Rel. "What phone did you call from?"

"Pay phone at a gas station on McFarland."

"Why all the secrecy?"

Rel took a sip of sweet tea. "Alvie's convinced that we're being
followed."

"Really?"

"Really. He says Bully has this Filipino woman that does his dirty
work for him. He says he's seen her five or six times since your visit
last month."

"Coincidence?" Bo asked.

"No chance," Rel said. "Alvie says this woman is too good to be
letting him see her. He says she wants to be seen so that he knows
he's being watched."

"What does he know? If he's being watched, then he must know
something that Bully doesn't want to get out."

Rel gazed down into his paper plate full of ribs and white bread. "You need to understand something about my little brother, Bo. Alvie's not like me, you understand?"

"What are you talking about, Rel?"

"He's a family man. Got him a nice wife who doesn't bitch at him too much. Got him a boy to carry his name on and another one coming." Rel fingered a piece of bread but didn't eat it. "He's got a lot more to lose than me."

"You're selling yourself short," Bo said.

"No, I'm not. I am what I am and I'm proud of what I've done. I've put my kids through college here at the university and I've worked hard all my life. Old Rel has done OK, but Alvie . . . he's got a chance to have it all. Good job, loving wife, kids. He can come as close to the American dream as a black man can in this county." Rel looked up from the plate at Bo. "He can be like you, brother."

Bo felt a pang in his heart, knowing that Rel was wrong but not having the energy to correct him. "Why are you telling me all this, Rel?"

"So you'll know what's at stake."

"I know you got ten thousand dollars on the line."

"I don't care about that anymore. You can keep your money. When Alvie told me about that woman following him, I blamed it on your coming last month. I told him to just keep his mouth shut and forget about you, but Alvie set me straight. He said if it wasn't you, it would have been someone else. That he saw something he shouldn't have seen and would have been viewed as a threat regardless." Rel put a rib in his mouth.

While his friend chewed the pork, Bo watched him. He tried to be patient but could feel his heart beating hard in his chest. Finally, as Rel washed the bite down with a sip of tea, Bo asked, "What did Alvie see that made him such a threat?"

Rel swept his eyes around the outside of the shack.

"We're alone," Bo said. "There's no one here but us and ain't no one watching. What did he see?"

"Alvie was Bully's driver for that trip," Rel finally said, and Bo could hear the stress in his friend's choppy delivery. "He drove Bully to the prison in St. Clair. They picked up Jack, and he drove them to Tuscaloosa. On the way, they made one stop at the Cracker Barrel in Bessemer, and then they dropped Jack off at his house around one o'clock in the afternoon."

When Rel stopped, Bo gritted his teeth in frustration. "This is all information that I already know, and none of it should give Bully anything to worry about. Detective Richey's summary of his interview with Bully mentions all of this."

Rel looked up from the plate. "Did Detective Richey mention the stop Bully made on the way back to Jasper?"

Bo felt his stomach flitter. "No. Wade's report indicates that Bully said that there were no stops on the way home."

"Wrong," Rel said. "There was a stop. Right after they dropped Jack off, Alvie says that Bully asked him to drive downtown to the old First National Bank Building."

"That's the big historic building, right?"

"Yeah, ten stories I think. Bully said he needed to run an errand and Alvie waited in the car. Well, Bully was gone a long time—longer than an hour—and Alvie got worried. He tried to call him on his cell phone and Bully didn't answer. Finally, Alvie got out of the car and went inside. He didn't want anything to happen to Bully on his watch, you know?"

Bo didn't say anything. He knew Rel was close to the punch line.

"Once he was inside the bank, he tried to call again, but there was still no answer. He went to the directory sign in the lobby and tried to guess where Bully had gone. After scanning the names, only one looked vaguely familiar, and it was on the fourth floor. Alvie took the elevator up to four and, as he was stepping out of the doors, Bully was getting on. He had a manila envelope in his hand and his head was down. Bully damn near walked right over Alvie as he came in, but once he saw who it was, his face turned red and he asked Alvie what the hell he was doing. Alvie started to say something but stopped when he saw the man in the hallway watching them. The fella had dark greasy-looking hair and wore glasses, and his eyes were wide, as if he had just been caught with his hand in the cookie jar." Rel hesitated, before adding, "Alvie had seen him before."

"When?" Bo asked, but he could feel the pieces to the puzzle beginning to come into place.

"At the prison. Bully visited Jack several times earlier this year, and on a couple occasions that fella was there. One time, Bully and the guy talked for a few minutes in the visitor's parking lot, with Alvie waiting in the car."

"Who?" Bo asked, but he already knew the answer.

"Zorn," Rel said, and Bo had an eerie sense of déjà vu. "Gregory Zorn."

41

Bo called Tom on his way to the First National Bank Building. "I'll meet you in the lobby," Tom said after getting the full debriefing.

Ten minutes later, Tom and Bo rode up the elevator together. "There's no way he's going to talk with us," Tom said.

"Probably not," Bo said. "But since he won't return our calls and emails, we don't have any other options."

When the elevator reached the fourth floor, the doors opened and Tom and Bo stepped onto the landing. They came to a standstill when they saw the movers carrying a large leather sofa out of the glass doors leading into the law office of Gregory Zorn, PC.

"Damnit," Bo whispered under his breath as the two men carrying the furniture walked past them.

"What's going on here?" Bo asked.

"What does it look like?" one of the men grunted. "Moving day."

Tom and Bo watched as the movers walked swiftly down the hall, where the door to the stairwell had been propped open. A few seconds later, the workers disappeared down the stairs.

"Let's take a look," Bo said, and without waiting for Tom to respond, he walked through the doors of the office. Tom hesitated, but only for a moment, as he followed Bo inside.

The office was mostly deserted, walls bare except for a few nails where pictures had once hung. Tom saw only a few stray pieces of furniture.

When the moving crew returned a few minutes later, Tom noticed that one of them was wearing a cap that said, "Two Men and a Truck."

"Where is Mr. Zorn?" Bo asked the man with the cap.

"Not here." He began to walk down a hallway, and Bo and Tom followed him.

"Where is he?" Bo persisted.

"I have no idea, sir," the man said. "All I know is that we're supposed to load up this office and move it today."

"Where are you moving it to?" Bo asked.

The man smirked. "Now you know I can't tell you that." Then he barked at his partner: "Looks like we got three tables left, Steve, and then we can hit the road."

Bo glanced at Tom. "Try the phone number."

Tom couldn't remember the digits offhand, so he googled "Gregory Zorn" on his phone and, thirty seconds later, clicked on the telephone number. After six rings, the answering machine picked up, offering the same message that Tom had been getting for the past month. There was no mention of a move.

"Sir," Tom called after the man with the cap, "when were you guys called to do this job?"

"Yesterday," he answered, his impatience palpable. "Look, I don't know what you guys are doing here. I'm assuming you have legal business with Mr. Zorn and weren't aware that he was leaving town."

"That's right," Bo said.

"Well, I can't help you. All I can tell you is that, in the words of Jerry Reed, we got a long way to go and a short time to get there and you two speed bumps are slowing us down."

"Mr.—"

"If you don't leave now, I'm calling the police."

Tom held out both hands. "OK, we're going. I just have one question. We do have legal business with Mr. Zorn and it is urgent that we speak with him. We had no idea he was moving offices and he hasn't answered his calls. Can you give us any clue as to his new location?"

"Hey, Chuck, quit yapping and help me with this last table," the other man yelled from down the hall. "They stop serving food at the Flora-Bama at nine, and I don't want to drink my dinner."

Chuck took off his cap and gazed at the carpeted floor. Then he gave Tom a sidelong glance. "That's the only hint you're going to get."

42

"Bad news, *señor*." Manny spoke into the cell phone as she watched the two lawyers from a bench across from the bank. "It appears that your driver has loose lips."

"How can you be sure?" Bully barked back.

"I just saw the investigator, Mr. Haynes, meeting with the driver's brother at a barbecue shack in Northport."

"Archibald's?"

"*Sí*. Mr. Haynes drove directly to the bank after talking with Mr. Jennings for about twenty minutes. Mr. McMurtrie met him there and they went up to the fourth floor."

"Zorn has already moved out, hasn't he?"

"*Sí*, but these two are very resourceful. I suspect they will locate him soon, perhaps even tonight."

Silence filled the phone line. When Manny felt enough time had passed for her employer to appreciate the situation, she uttered the question hanging between them. "Do you want me to remove the threat?"

More silence, followed by an exasperated groan. "I was having such a good day." Then, his voice turning matter-of-fact, he answered the question: "Yes."

43

There wasn't a whole lot of discussion about what to do next. "When they get to where they're going, I'll call you," Bo said, watching from the driver's seat of the Sequoia as the movers closed the back of the truck. Tom climbed out of the passenger seat and then leaned through the open window. "Don't make it obvious you're following."

"I won't," Bo said.

Moments later, the brake lights of the truck flared on and it pulled away from the bank parking lot. Bo waited a few seconds and put his vehicle in gear. "If you learn anything useful about Zorn, call me," Bo said.

"I will." Tom slapped the side of the truck and took a step back. "Hey, Bo?"

"Yeah."

"Be careful."

Thirty seconds after Bocephus Haynes pulled his SUV out of the bank's parking lot, Manny Reyes followed suit driving her unassuming gunmetal-gray Accord.

Turning onto I-20/59 North toward Birmingham, she smiled as she saw the moving truck a hundred yards ahead and the Sequoia half that distance. What was the English saying for this? She had heard Mr. Bully say it a few times over the years; something from a movie, she thought. What was the film? *Smokey and the Bandit*? Or was it a country music song?

Regardless, she chortled when the phrase came to her and mimicked her boss's Southern accent as she uttered it out loud. "We got us a convoy."

44

Tom kept his cell phone in his pocket the rest of the afternoon, but he heard nothing from Bo and didn't expect to if the hint the moving crew had given was on point. *The Flora-Bama is in Orange Beach, and that's a good four-and-a-half hours away.*

Tom called the clerk's offices for Tuscaloosa, Jefferson, and Shelby Counties, figuring those were the most prominent jurisdictions Zorn practiced in. Though each of the clerks was familiar with Greg Zorn, none were aware of a move or any change in the attorney's contact information. When that turned up a dead end, he fired off his fifteenth email to Zorn in the past month. He knew the message would probably be ignored but sent it anyway. Then, straining to think of other options, he asked Frankie to pull up Zorn's website and social media pages on the internet and had her send private messages to his Facebook, Twitter, and Instagram accounts. She also completed the prospective client form on his firm website, and in the "How can we help you?" box asked that he call Tom as soon as possible.

By five thirty, Tom let Frankie go for the day and resolved that he had done all he could do regarding Zorn. On his way home, he decided to pay Barbara Willistone a visit.

She answered the door before he could ring the doorbell, as if she had been waiting on him by her window. "What is it?" she asked, her voice a panicked whine. "Did you find the change form?"

"Not yet," Tom said. "But we have a lead." He noticed that her bruised chin and forehead were less swollen than the day before. "Can I come in?"

Barbara opened the door and ushered him inside.

"Of course," she said after Tom had relayed the substance of his and Bo's conversation with Max Conchin and their trip to Zorn's abandoned office. They were again sitting around the circular kitchen table with coffee mugs placed in front of them. "Jack was too smart to involve a loudmouth like Max, but any communications he had with his attorney would be confidential, right?"

"Yes, they would be protected by the attorney-client privilege."

"So Jack sent the change form to Greg Zorn and told Zorn to send it in."

"Ms. Willistone, we don't have any idea what Jack said or did, but . . . that's the theory we're working under."

"And then Bully Calhoun came by Zorn's office right after he dropped Jack off at the Big House."

"And left an hour later with a manila envelope."

"Which contained the original of the change of beneficiary form."

"Again, we have no way of knowing, but that feels right."

"Then Jack is murdered, the change form is never sent in and probably destroyed, and my Danny gets screwed and that whore Jack married gets the three million."

Tom didn't answer.

"You know her daddy had him killed," Barbara continued, banging her fist on the table. "Jack was smart as a whip and just as mean, if not meaner, than Bully. If Jack found out that Zorn and Bully had double-crossed him, he would have brought hell down on both of them."

"More importantly," Tom added, "he would have first made sure the change form was sent in, which would have cut out Kat and, by association, Bully."

"They had to kill him," Barbara said, her voice breathless.

Tom nodded but didn't say more. He felt a cold chill that made the hairs on his arms stand up. If they were right and Bully Calhoun did kill Jack to ensure that his daughter collected the three million in life insurance proceeds, then what would a man like that do to keep the truth hidden?

"Have you eaten dinner, Professor McMurtrie?"

The question interrupted Tom's chain of thought and he blinked. "What?"

"Dinner?" She pointed behind her to the stove. "I was going to make some spaghetti. Would you like some?"

Tom thought about Bo, who could call any moment from the coast, and the other stop he needed to make before going home. "Uh, not tonight, Ms. Willistone. I have a good bit of work to do."

As he turned to leave, she called after him. "I'm sorry," she said. "I . . . don't know what I was thinking. It's just . . . it's been a long time since I've had a man over to my house at this time of night."

Tom looked down at her, wincing at how broken the woman appeared, both in body and spirit. "No apology necessary. I'll let you know if and when we are able to track down Greg Zorn."

"Do you think he'll talk?"

Tom considered the question. "I don't know, but I'll tell you one thing I'm certain of." He met her eye. "I bet he's scared to death."

45

Ono Island is a barrier island at the mouth of Perdido Bay, in Baldwin County, Alabama. Stretching almost six miles, it's bordered on the north by Bayou St. John and to the south by the Old River. A quarter mile farther south and just across Perdido Key Drive sits the Gulf of Mexico.

Bocephus Haynes sat at an outside table at the Ole River Grill. From his vantage point, he could see across the river to the house on the island where the moving truck had stopped. With light traffic and a little luck, he had been able to creep along Perdido Key Drive, which ran parallel to the main drag through the island, and watch the truck until it stopped at a house catty-corner from the restaurant. Bo quickly parked and obtained a seat on the back deck.

Gazing across the water, he was struck by the similarities between this scene and the place where Jack Willistone was murdered. *Zorn must have a thing for waterfront property,* he thought. Then another thought crossed his mind. *How the hell can a solo practitioner specializing in criminal defense afford to own a house on the Black Warrior and one on Ono Island?* To Bo's knowledge, Greg Zorn handled no personal injury cases, which, as Bo knew well, could result in huge cash verdicts and settlements that could fatten a lawyer's bank account. *He didn't get this rich being Jack Willistone's criminal lawyer, so how?* Bo thought about the envelope that Bully Calhoun had carried out of Zorn's office the day that Jack Willistone was murdered. *How much did you get for selling your soul, you greasy SOB?* Bo wondered as he spied the moving truck back out of the driveway.

He remained in his seat and watched the vehicle with "Two Men and a Truck" etched on its side move toward the guardhouse to exit the island. Walking to the edge of the railing and leaning forward, he saw the truck flick on its left-turn blinker and turn onto the highway. A few hundred yards up, the truck had its blinker on again, and for a second Bo worried that the movers were going to eat here. But instead of turning left into the Ole River Grill, the truck turned right into the gravel parking lot of the Flora-Bama, right across the street.

True to their words, Bo thought, gazing down at his watch and noticing that it was 8:30 p.m. *And just in time for dinner.*

Bo walked back to his seat and resumed watching the house on Ono Island. The lights were on, so he assumed someone was inside. He also assumed that the security guard wouldn't just let a moving truck on the island if someone weren't at the house where the truck was going. *He's there,* Bo's gut told him.

While he waited, Bo sent Tom a text, updating him on where he was and what he was doing. He also ordered a fried shrimp basket and a Red Stripe. He figured that if there was no further activity tonight, he'd get a hotel room and think of an excuse to get on the island in the morning. An hour later, after he'd finished his food and beer, and searching on his phone for suitable accommodations, he saw a convertible sports car ease out of the driveway of the house. As darkness had now descended over the island, Bo couldn't tell the make and model, but he figured he could catch the vehicle if he hurried as it turned onto the highway.

He quickly set several twenty-dollar bills down on the table, leaving an ample tip, and strode through the restaurant to the parking lot. A minute later, he was on Perdido Key Drive, squinting toward the guardhouse leading into the island. "Boom!" he yelled as he saw a red Porsche with the top down pulling out of the gate.

Seconds later, the sports car turned onto the highway in front of him. Bo saw that the driver had curly brown hair and fit the picture he'd seen on the firm's website.

"Where are we going, Mr. Zorn?"

46

Tawny Ford was Wilma Newton's first cousin on her mother's side. Wilma's mom and Tawny's dad had been sister and brother. At fifty-three years old, Tawny was fifteen years older than Wilma and at least fifty pounds heavier. As Tom gazed at her across the living room of the double-wide trailer she and her husband Sam shared in Northport, it seemed inconceivable that she was related to his client. Tawny had a cigarette dangling from her mouth, and the volume on the television was so loud that Tom could barely hear the woman talk.

"Like I was saying, sir, I appreciate what you're doing for my younger cousin, but she's a lost cause if you ask me. Been a train wreck ever since her Dewey died, God rest his soul." Tawny rocked herself in a worn rocking chair that had several cigarette burns on it. Next to her, Laurie Ann and Jackie sat on the couch. Unlike her older sister, Jackie Newton looked nothing like their mother. The twelve-year-old had dark, almost black, hair and brown eyes, and her skin coloring was more olive than her sister's. Based on a younger photograph of Dewey that Tawny had shown Tom when he entered the house, he thought Jackie resembled her father. "Some folks can never get over the loss of a spouse, you know what I mean?"

Tom knew exactly what she meant, and he subconsciously glanced at the third finger of his left hand. He didn't wear his wedding ring anymore, but he could still feel it sometimes. Just like he could feel Julie when he was on the porch at his house at night. Or when he put flowers on her grave at the Hazel Green farm. "Yes, ma'am, I do. I lost my wife several years ago."

Tawny took a drag and blew a cloud of smoke above her head. "I'm sorry." Then she came forward and grabbed the remote control off an old suitcase that apparently doubled as a coffee table. "Is it time for *Modern Family* yet?" she asked while pointing the remote at the television.

Tom glanced at Laurie Ann, who rolled her eyes. "Not until eight o'clock, Aunt Tawny."

"Oh, well OK. I don't want to miss it. Those two queers make me laugh so hard I 'bout pee my pants."

"Professor, you want some ice cream?" Laurie Ann asked as she shot up from the couch and walked toward the refrigerator. The living area and kitchen merged into one main room, and Tom watched as the girl grabbed a pint of Blue Bell from the freezer and two spoons from a drawer. "You need a bowl?" she asked, and shook her head to let him know the correct response.

"Uh, no. That won't be necessary." He stood and coughed as a blast of secondhand smoke hit his nostrils. "It's a nice night out tonight. How about we talk on the steps?"

A minute later, Tom stuck a plastic spoonful of vanilla ice cream in his mouth and breathed in the hot, muggy air. Anything would be better than the smoke-filled room he had just left. "Is it like this every night?" he asked, handing the carton to Laurie Ann, who gave it right back to him.

"I don't want any. I was just looking for an excuse to talk with you away from Tawny. And to answer your question, yes. It's like this every night. Tawny sits in that chair and smokes two packs of cigarettes. Sam works the night shift at the water treatment plant and doesn't get home until we're off to school. I hardly ever see him except on the weekends, and he sleeps most of those. When he's not sleeping, he sits on the couch and drinks Natural Light out of cans. He probably goes through a case every Saturday." She reached into her pocket and brought out her own pack of cigarettes. Before Tom could say anything, she lit one and walked down the two steps into the weed-riddled yard. "What can I say?" she continued, blowing smoke toward the street. "It's like living with Cousin Eddie and Catherine from the *Vacation* movies, except worse."

Tom creased his face in confusion.

"Sorry," Laurie Ann said, taking another drag off the cigarette and, to Tom, looking more like a college sophomore than an eighth grader. "Tawny is addicted to movies from the '80s. She still has a damn VCR for God sakes, and unless it's *Modern Family* night, you can bet she has a VHS tape playing in the damn thing, and you can also bet it's either *Vacation*, *Footloose*, *Raising Arizona*, or *Top Gun*. She also likes the *Back to the Future* movies and *Silverado*."

"Who doesn't?" Tom asked, and Laurie Ann frowned at him. "Sorry," he added.

"Why'd you come here? I was planning to work tomorrow." Laurie Ann had started her job as a runner for the firm once school had been let out and since then had been busy hand delivering mail, getting lunch, going to Office Depot for supplies, and doing anything else that Frankie asked her to do.

"This couldn't wait," Tom said. "And I thought it was time I met the rest of the family."

"Aren't you glad you did?" Laurie Ann asked, her voice dripping with sarcasm.

"I noticed that your sister barely said a word," Tom said. "Is that normal for her?"

"Depends on your time frame," Laurie Ann said, taking another drag on the cigarette. "Before Daddy died and Momma abandoned us, Jackie was a regular chatterbox. She drove me crazy she talked so much." She flung the cigarette down, stomping it hard. "But since those two events happened, she's damn near been a mute."

"Has she seen a counselor?"

Laurie Ann laughed bitterly. "Oh yeah. Both of us did. That bitch prosecutor in Giles County made sure we were thoroughly examined by a shrink before signing off on that hag in there"—she pointed at the trailer—"taking custody of us."

"Tawny is your only living blood relative," Tom said, trying to keep his voice as neutral as possible. He didn't want to argue. "There weren't many available options."

Laurie Ann lit another cigarette. "Well, that about sums up the life of Laurie Ann and Jackie Newton. Hell, just put that on top of a VHS tape cover. *There Weren't Many Available Options.* I can see it now. Me and Jackie, wearing overalls and holding a pouch of Beech-Nut between us, sitting right where you are in front of this trailer." She waved her arms in the air and spoke in a theatrical tone. "Come relive the true story of two country girls who lost it all when their Dad wrecked a tractor-trailer rig and their mom became a whore." She kicked at a weed. "It's either a bad '80s movie or a good David Allan Coe song, whatever your pleasure." She ended her tirade. "Tell me why you're here."

"I need you to talk with your mom."

"About what?"

"She won't tell me what she did the night of the murder."

"You mean who she did."

Tom's stomach tightened. "What?"

"Have you talked to some of the other patrons of that apartment complex she rents in?" Laurie Ann asked, her voice now a combination of sarcasm and bitterness. "My bet is she was screwing somebody on site for rent money. Probably her landlord."

Tom stepped off the porch. "You aren't being very helpful, Laurie Ann. You got me into this mess, remember? You're the one who said your mother was innocent and begged me to represent her."

She puffed on her cigarette and Tom snatched it out of her mouth. "You have to be a monumental idiot to smoke this cancer stick," he said, dropping it to the ground and stomping on it.

"Oh come off it. I bet you smoked at my age. Hell, everyone smoked in the '60s, didn't they?"

"I did not smoke at your age, but I did in my twenties and thirties and I regret every bit of it."

"Thanks for the public service message, old man. I'm just shooting straight with you. My bet is that Wilma was doing one of the other renters at her apartment complex and doesn't want to say anything for fear of losing any chance of getting her girls back." She placed a palm on her heart in mock sympathy.

"You're in a mood, aren't you?" Tom asked, stepping away from her. "What's wrong with you?"

In the glow of the overhead light on the trailer's front stoop, Tom saw Laurie Ann's lip begin to quiver. "I hate my life, that's what's wrong. I'm embarrassed by what you just saw in there. I wish my sister would talk more. I wish my daddy hadn't died driving that rig. I wish my momma hadn't turned to stripping and whoring. I wish you had never set foot in that courtroom in Henshaw. I wish, I wish, I wish. I pray, I pray, I pray. *And ain't nothing changes.*"

Tom approached the young woman and placed his hands on her shoulders. "None of that is your fault."

When she didn't say anything, he shook her gently. "You hear me? It's not your fault."

"You're wrong," Laurie Ann said.

"I'm right," Tom said. "It's not your fault." Thinking it was time for him to go, he began to walk toward his truck. "Please tell your sister and aunt that I was pleased to meet them."

When he reached the door, he heard footsteps behind him and turned.

Laurie Ann Newton, with fresh tears in her eyes, stood before him. "I'm sorry, Professor. Sometimes I get a little"—she pointed back to the trailer—"overwhelmed by everything."

"It's OK," Tom said. "I want you to know something. I took this case because of you. Because of the hurt and brokenness I saw in your eyes and that I feel when I'm around you. I know I played a role in making things the way they are for you and your sister, and I want to help." He quickly grabbed his back, as it felt like a thousand little pinpricks were rolling down his spine.

"Are you alright, Professor?"

Tom nodded and gnashed his teeth against another current of pain. "Yeah, but I don't know how much longer I'm going to be doing this. Your mom's case may be my last jury trial." He looked at her tear-streaked face. "And I damn sure don't want to lose it."

"I'll talk to Momma," Laurie Ann said, her voice stronger and determined.

"That's more like it," Tom said, patting her shoulder. He opened the door and was about to get in when he called after her. "You know that scenario you just described?"

She squinted at him, not understanding.

"You said your mom was probably having sex for money with one of the other lessors of that apartment complex on the night of the murder."

"I was just ranting," Laurie Ann said.

"Were you?" Tom asked, not quite believing her. Rant or not, the statement had a ring of truth. "If she was doing what you described between ten o'clock and midnight on May 8, then you know what that gives her?"

Laurie Ann wiped her eyes and her lips curved into a cautious smile. "An alibi?"

"Bingo," Tom said, relishing the word that Coach Bryant used to say on his weekly television show when someone made a big hit. Tom liked the sound of it so much that he said it again. "Bingo."

47

The Pink Pony Pub is a dive bar in Gulf Shores, Alabama. It's a little more than twelve miles from Ono Island. True to its name, the exterior of the tiny building is hot pink and has a pony painted under the sign.

Once Zorn walked inside, Bo called Tom on his cell phone. It was now 10:00 p.m., but he figured the Professor wouldn't go to bed without hearing from him.

"About damn time," Tom said after the first ring, forgoing any salutation. "Tell me."

Bo did. After he was through with his summation, Tom began to pace his house, thinking. Finally, he said, "I wish you had called me when the movers were on the island. I could've gotten you across the bridge."

"How?"

"I know a guy who used to live there. He may still own a house on the island. Even if he doesn't, he could have gotten you through the gate."

"Do I know this fella?"

"The pride of Foley High?" Tom responded. "I would hope so. At one point, the whole world knew him."

Then it clicked for Bo. "Snake? I can't believe I didn't think of that."

Tom smiled. Kenny "the Snake" Stabler, a Foley High School legend, had played on Coach Bryant's 1964 and 1965 national champions and went on to be a Super Bowl–winning quarterback for the Oakland Raiders. "Don't sweat it. He's more my generation than yours anyway. My bet is that Zorn is running scared and probably won't talk."

"I think you're right, but there may be some value in letting him know we're onto him."

"I agree. Bo, watch your back in there. Didn't Mr. Jennings say his brother is convinced he's being followed?"

"Yeah." Bo went over the conversation at Archibald's again in his mind. "He said Bully uses a Filipino woman to do his dirty work, and that Alvie had seen her five or six times in the last month watching him." As he looked past the pink bar and out into the dark waters of the Gulf, Bo felt the skin on his arms begin to prickle.

"Call me when you're through," Tom said. "And promise me something. If things get crazy, get the hell out of Dodge, alright?"

"Ten-four." Bo clicked off the phone and grabbed the door handle. Then, thinking about Bully Calhoun's enforcer, he undid the latch of his glove compartment and grabbed the Glock from inside. If things did get crazy, he didn't want to be bringing a knife to a gunfight. He stuck the pistol in the back of his pants and put a sports jacket over his button-down shirt. Then, closing the door, he ambled toward the entrance to one of the most famous watering holes on the Gulf Coast.

Tom kept his cell phone in his hand and walked out on the back porch of his Tuscaloosa home. He plopped down in one of the rocking chairs. Below him, Lee Roy lay on his stomach, dead asleep. The only sound in the yard besides the dog's snoring was the whirring of a fan above and a few stray crickets.

"Don't let me disturb you, boy," Tom said, and Lee Roy didn't budge. The bulldog could sleep through a tornado and almost had when the F-5 hit Tuscaloosa in April 2011. Tom leaned over and petted Lee Roy behind the ears and, even with his eyes remaining closed, the dog's stub of a tail began to shake back and forth. Tom smiled, but his mind was still with Bo in Gulf Shores.

Tom had been to the Pink Pony Pub on at least a half-dozen occasions in his life, usually during the day. It was a little crazy at the bar on the water after dark, and he'd only been there once at this time of night. *I should've gone,* he thought, unable to escape his feelings of fear and worry. Bocephus Haynes was one of the smartest and most resourceful men he'd ever known. He was also tough as nails. If there was a chance in hell of getting Greg Zorn to talk, Tom knew Bo was the man for the job.

But as his dog snoozed below him, Tom felt the same cold chill he'd had earlier in the day at Barbara Willistone's house. The case was taking on a dangerous tenor, and Tom had a premonition that something terrible was about to happen. He felt it the same way he used to sense a trick play coming from the offense during his football days. It was the same vibe he'd experienced last fall when, after the trial in Pulaski and the shooting on the square, he'd felt compelled to drive out to the clearing on Walton Farm, arriving just in time to thwart Bo's death. Now his whole being throbbed with the same frequency.

With adrenaline flooding his veins, Tom began to pace along the porch. He soon heard a low growl. He glanced down. Lee Roy was baring his teeth, and the dog's white and brown coat shook. *He feels it too,* Tom thought. He smiled down at the friend that Bo had given him as a gift two years earlier.

"Easy, boy," Tom said, looking at the phone in his hand. In times of stress, Tom often went back to the teachings of Coach Bryant, and one of them came to him now. Loud and clear, as if the gravelly voice were speaking right in his ear.

Leave it on the field. Hold nothing back.

Nodding and feeling the same steely calm he had in Pulaski eight months earlier, Tom clicked on the four digits that unlocked his mobile device. One . . . nine . . . six . . . one.

Before he could change his mind, he made the call.

48

Bo found Greg Zorn belly up to the bar in much the same position as the painted pony on the side of the building. For a weeknight during the middle of summer, the bar was hopping, and on the stage to the right of the bar, he saw a bleached-blond fortysomething holding a microphone and doing a scratchy-voiced rendition of "Delta Dawn" by Tanya Tucker.

Karaoke night, Bo thought. *Wonderful.*

As he walked toward the bar, Bo noticed the glances and double-takes that he always received. When a six-foot-four-inch, two-hundred-forty-pound, bald-headed black man walks into a dive bar in south Alabama where the patrons are all lily white except for the suntan or sunburn on their neck and arms, he's unlikely to go unnoticed. Bo ignored the looks and murmurs. He took a place on the stool next to his target and waited. When the attorney finally turned and took notice of him, Zorn shot off the stool and tried to walk away.

Bo grabbed the man's arm and spoke in a firm voice above the screechy sounds of the karaoke singer. "Sit down, Zorn. I'm going to buy you whatever you're drinking and we're gonna have us a conversation."

"The hell we are!" Zorn's eyes were bloodshot and his voice slurred. He was half-drunk already, which told Bo that he had started hitting the booze at his house or in the car on the way.

Bo tightened his grip. "Greg, I followed a moving van four hours to find you, and I'm going to buy you this drink and have my say."

"Or what?"

"Or I'm going to kick your ass from here to Foley."

"You're crazy, man. I know you. Bocephus Haynes, right? Well, I'm going to call the Tennessee bar tomorrow and tell them about this little conversation. Who knows? Maybe that'll result in a suspension of your license."

Bo didn't let go. "You're a little late to that party, dog. I'm already suspended and, generally speaking, I've been in a bad mood for the last nine months. Don't let me take it out on you."

Zorn opened his mouth, but no words came out. Sweat beads pooled on his forehead.

"Sit down, Greg," Bo continued. "I want to tell you a little story, and I want you to tell me how it ends."

"Everything OK, gentlemen?" The bartender's voice broke through loud and deep as the karaoke singer mercifully finished butchering Tucker's classic.

"We're good," Bo said. "I'll have a Red Stripe, and please set my friend up here with another of what he's drinking." He pulled out his wallet and slid his credit card across the bar. "Put them both on my tab."

"Yes, sir," said the bartender, a twentysomething man wearing a hot-pink shirt with the name of the bar adorned on the front, giving Bo a mock salute.

Bo pushed Zorn onto his stool, and the lawyer finally relaxed, either too drunk or weak to fight any longer. "That's my boy," Bo said.

When the bartender set their drinks down, Bo glanced at Zorn's glass. "That a Long Island Iced Tea?"

The attorney nodded and took a sip. Zorn wore an untucked white golf shirt over khaki shorts and flip-flops. He had a two-day growth of beard, and for all the world he looked like a local beach bum. "You're kinda fitting in to this beach life, huh?" Bo asked.

"Can we get to the point?" Zorn asked. "You said you had a story to tell me."

"That's right," Bo said, rubbing his chin and watching the other man. "You're in trouble, aren't you, Greg? That's why you're on your way to a ten-gallon hangover, right? You're scared shitless. You've made a choice you can't take back, and you don't know what to do about it. Based upon the people you been making deals with, I bet you cringe every time you start that sweet Porsche too. Am I right?"

"What do you know?" Zorn asked, but he didn't look at Bo. Instead he focused on the mirror behind the bar.

"I know that on the day he was released from prison, your client, Jack Willistone, was picked up at the St. Clair Correctional Facility by his father-in-law, Marcellus 'Bully' Calhoun. I know that Bully dropped Jack off at his house in Tuscaloosa and then went directly to see you. I know that Bully Calhoun spent north of an hour with you in your office some eight hours before his son-in-law and your longtime client was murdered on the dock of your house on the banks of the Black Warrior River." Bo licked his lips and pressed closer to the other man. Zorn stunk of alcohol, and there was a slight twinge of body odor coming from him. Bo wondered when the man had showered last. "I know that Jack Willistone intended to change the beneficiary of his three-million-dollar life insurance policy from his wife, Kat, to his autistic son, Danny. I know that he had already completed the form and sent it to you to process with New York Life so the change would be finalized."

Though Zorn continued to look at the mirror, Bo noticed that the attorney's knees were knocking each other and his hand shook slightly when he raised his glass to his lips.

"And I know that this change of beneficiary form somehow never made it to New York Life, and that Bully Calhoun left your office eight hours before Jack Willistone's murder carrying a manila envelope in his hand. Now I would bet my newly inherited farm in Giles County that the change of beneficiary form that Jack had completed at the jail and sent to his attorney for safekeeping was in that envelope, and I would further wager that said form has been burned to ashes and spread somewhere along Highway 69 in Walker County." He took a sip of Red Stripe and nudged Zorn with his fist. "How am I coming?"

Zorn snickered "That's a hell of a story, but you can't prove any of it."

"Wrong, dog. I can actually prove every bit of it except the part about the change form being in the envelope. I'm going to need you for that, Greg, I won't lie to you. I'm going to need you to suck it up and turn state's evidence, and maybe your sentence won't be too bad if you put a noted mobster who's running one of the largest meth operations in the Southeast behind bars." He took a pull off his beer. "Hell, maybe your suspension will be less than mine."

For at least a minute, Zorn just looked at his reflection in the mirror and drank. When he had taken down the last of the Long Island Iced Tea, he finally turned to Bo. "Bully's driver, right? That's how you know all this."

Bo smiled. "Ask no questions. Tell no lies. Keep your mouth shut. Catch no flies."

"If you won't talk, I won't talk," Zorn slurred. "But I don't need you to answer that question, because it's a no-brainer. Your source is Alvie Jennings. Head coach of the Jasper Middle School basketball team. Wife's name is LaShell. Son's name is LaByron." Zorn paused. "He should probably be a little more careful about leaving his garage door up during the day. I don't think LaShell is always good about locking that side door."

Bo grabbed the man under his arms and lifted him off the stool so that the Zorn's feet dangled a foot off the ground. "How do you know that?"

"Routine background check for the job and names," Zorn managed. "I can't tell you how I gleaned the other stuff because it's protected by the attorney-client privilege."

Bo placed Zorn roughly back on his stool. "You're Bully's lawyer too?"

Zorn coughed as he struggled to catch his breath. "There's nothing wrong with an attorney representing multiple members of the same family."

"What about when there's a conflict of interest?" Bo asked.

Zorn held up his index finger and motioned for Bo to come closer. The lawyer leaned into Bo's ear, and when he breathed, Bo's nostrils burned with the scent of liquor. *"If Alvie Jennings is your source, then he's a dead man,"* Zorn whispered. *"Dead, you hear me?"*

Bo pulled away and looked at his own reflection in the mirror. He could see the fear in his own eyes. *Alvie . . .*

"I'm sorry," Zorn said.

Bo turned his head and glared at Zorn. "You should be. You don't look like an idiot to me, Greg, so let me ask you one more thing."

Zorn held up his empty glass and the bartender took it. When it was returned to him full, he gazed at Bo with dead eyes. "Shoot."

"Did you keep a copy of the change form?"

Zorn blinked, and Bo knew the answer without him saying a word.

"You aren't as dumb as you look, Greg." Bo took a sip of his beer. "That's your leverage, right? That's why you're not a dead man too."

Zorn tilted up his glass, and after smacking his lips, he motioned Bo to lean toward him again.

Bo held his breath and did as instructed.

"If the wrong person ever heard what we were just talking about . . ." He gave his head a jerk and swept his eyes over the bar. "Then we're both dead."

49

The wrong person had heard.

Manny Reyes waited at one of the picnic tables outside the restaurant. She had a clear view of the Gulf of Mexico but paid the shadowy water no mind. Instead she listened to the recording device she'd placed in the woman's purse sitting next to Greg Zorn. She'd caught the woman in the gift shop and pulled her aside and asked if she could do her a small favor: "I'm a private investigator for that man's wife"—she pointed at Zorn around the corner—"and I think the black guy is a pimp that runs prostitutes to him."

For $500 cash, the woman, who had been through her own nasty divorce, was happy to oblige. As she listened to the conversation on earbuds, Manny knew that things had already gone too far. When her boss heard the tape, he would agree with the actions she was about to take. He had already approved the removal of Zorn, but she now viewed the investigator as a threat too. She removed the knife from the holster clipped to her right thigh and, after casually glancing around the dimly lit parking lot, slashed the four tires on Zorn's Porsche. Then, sauntering over to Haynes's Sequoia, she quickly did the same to his wheels. She returned the knife to its holster and resumed her position at the picnic table.

Manny wore a yellow sundress that was cut just below the thigh and a white cap with the words "Pink Pony Pub" embroidered on the front that she'd bought at the gift shop. Spreading her dress over her knees, she felt for the bulge on her left thigh and ran her fingers along the barrel of the pistol. Since the gun had a silencer, no sound would be heard when she killed the two men. Even better, given that there were only a few lights in the lot, a witness to the shooting would be highly unlikely.

See no evil, hear no evil, Manny thought as she leaned her back against the picnic table and waited.

50

Four hours later, at just past 2:00 a.m. and approaching closing time, Greg Zorn said he was ready to leave. While the inebriated attorney was in the bathroom, Bo paid the tab and assured the bartender that he would see to it that "his friend" had a ride home.

"Well, I guess this is goodbye," Zorn said once he had returned from the head. He didn't bother to extend his hand, and he brushed past Bo toward the exit. "Thanks for the drinks."

"Wrong, Greg. Not yet. I'm going to drive you home, alright?" Bo followed on his heels, noticing that Zorn was having a hard time walking in a straight line. "I promised the bartender."

"F-f-fuck him," Greg said, his voice a drunken mess as he pushed the door leading outside.

The two men stepped into the salt air, and Bo was grateful for the gentle breeze he felt coming off the Gulf. He grabbed Zorn by the arm before he could take another step. "Greg, that barkeep has already notified the traffic cops on Perdido Key Boulevard to be on the lookout for your Porsche, which, by the way, stands out like me in this bar."

Zorn smiled. "It's a sweet ride, isn't it?"

"Yeah, it's sweet alright," Bo said, pulling the man forward. "Come on. I'm going to take you home and you're going to tell me where you keep the copy of that change form."

"The hell I am," Zorn said. Then, realizing his gaffe, he whined, "I don't know what you're talking about."

Bo heard faint footsteps behind him and looked over his shoulder, but no one was there. *The wind,* he thought, but he still felt an inner chill as he pondered the information he had just gleaned from Zorn and what Bully Calhoun might do to keep it hidden. *If I can get my hands on that change form. Even if it's a copy . . .*

Bo clicked the keyless entry and the brake lights to the Sequoia flashed on. When they did, he saw that the front left tire was flat as a board. "Damnit," he said. He had parked in enough gravel lots today to pick up a nail. Then he noticed that the back left tire was likewise flat.

"Shit, man, sss-someone did a number on your tires," Zorn slurred, walking around the back of the vehicle. "The ones over here are slashed too."

Bo knelt down and shined the light on his cell phone at the front tire. He immediately noticed the puncture mark and he felt gooseflesh break out on his neck and arms. He shot to his feet. "Greg!" he yelled, but the lawyer was now stumbling across the lot toward his Porsche.

"You ever driven a 911, Haynes?" Zorn said behind his shoulder. "It's like sticking your prick in a virg—" He stopped dead still with his voice caught in his throat. When his vocal cords began to work again, the scream came out like the wail of a child. "No!" Zorn lunged forward and knelt on his knees in the gravel by the back tire.

Bo swept his eyes in all directions and walked in a crouch toward the drunken lawyer. Whoever cut their wheels might still be out there, and they were easy prey at this time of night. *Ducks on the pond,* Bo thought.

"Is everything alright?"

Bo wheeled toward the voice. A tan-skinned woman wearing a yellow sundress and a white cap was walking toward him. "Why is he screaming?" she asked.

Bo glanced at Zorn, who was still on his knees by the Porsche looking like he was about to pass out. "His tires were slashed," Bo said, moving his eyes back to the woman. "So were—"

He stopped talking when he saw the muzzle of the gun rising upward.

Bo reached for the Glock tucked in the back of his pants but knew it was too late. His instincts had failed to fire when he'd seen the sundress. As his hands latched around the handle of the pistol, the woman pointed her gun, a nine-millimeter if Bo had to guess, at his head.

Bocephus Aurulius Haynes closed his eyes and an image of his wife Jazz holding T. J. and Lila's hands on the first day of second grade and kindergarten popped into his mind. He held the vision and waited for his lights to be turned out forever. But instead of a pistol firing, he heard the unmistakable blast of a twelve-gauge shotgun.

Bo's eyes flew open and the tan-skinned woman—Bully Calhoun's enforcer, no doubt—was gone. He slowly turned to his right, his heart pounding in his chest, as he searched the darkness for the person who had just saved his life.

A half second later, he saw a figure in a T-shirt, jeans, and work boots approaching cautiously. The man had at least a week's worth of stubble on his face and wore a dark cap pulled low over his eyes. As the man entered the light, Bo met his gaze while at the same time reading the letters on the hat.

Drake Farms.

"My believer," Bo said, hearing his voice catch in his throat and never being so happy to see someone in his whole life.

Richard William Drake, holding a Remington 1100 shotgun in shooting position, looked past Bo to the restaurant and, beyond it, the beach. "I missed," he finally said, the frustration in his voice palpable. "I had her in my sights . . . and I missed."

51

After Bo and Rick scoured the beach and surrounding properties for thirty minutes without finding any clues as to where the sundress woman might have gone, they finally called the police. Two hours later, after Rick and Bo had completed handwritten statements, the investigating officer took their numbers and said he would call if they developed any leads. They thanked the policeman for his time, but both knew that any investigation would be a dead end. Bully Calhoun's enforcer was gone.

Dust in the wind.

They crashed for the night at a beachside Hampton Inn. Turned out Zorn didn't own the house on Ono Island. His ex-wife did, and Zorn had bequeathed almost all of his office furniture to her in the divorce property settlement. The attorney had met the moving crew at the house, assisted in getting the couches and tables to the upstairs den his teenage sons were using, and then split a pizza with the boys before heading to the Pink Pony Pub. On the way, he belted half of a pint of Jack Daniel's he kept in his glove compartment in case of emergencies. Apparently, any time he had to spend more than fifteen minutes with his ex-wife, Jill, qualified as an emergency.

Once Zorn had safely passed out on one of the double beds in the room they'd rented, Bo and Rick sat in plastic chairs on the deck overlooking the ocean. To the east, the sun rose over the Gulf of Mexico. For several minutes, neither man spoke, the only sound the crashing of waves on the shore below. Finally, Bo slapped Rick on the back. "When did Tom call you?"

"About ten fifteen."

"*Last night?*" Bo asked, not believing it.

Rick nodded. "He filled me in on Bully Calhoun's enforcer and how she might have been the one who ran my dad off the road. Then he said he was worried that she might be following you, so . . ."

"You came."

"Yep. I got into a similar scrape down on the coast last year and Wade bailed me out. Just paying it forward I guess."

"Well . . . I owe you." Bo yawned and rubbed his hands over his face, trying to fight off the fatigue that was beginning to set in. "How well did you see the woman?"

"Pretty well. Good enough to have a clear shot, but everything happened so fast."

"Could you pick her out of a lineup?"

Rick frowned. "I'm not sure. Maybe . . . I can't believe I missed that shot."

Bo stood and placed his elbows over the railing. After a few seconds, he turned toward Rick. "Son, you were almost fifty yards away in a dimly lit parking lot shooting with a twelve-gauge that must be at least three decades old. You may not have killed the woman, but you sure as hell kept her from killing me. Thank you." He leaned down and looked Rick in the eye. "You hear me? Thank you."

Rick nodded but didn't say anything for several seconds. Then, with his voice rising just above a whisper, he said, "It was my dad's."

"What?" Bo asked.

Rick stood and squinted at Bo as the sun rose behind them. "The gun. It was my father's."

"Well, he'd be damn proud." Then, smiling, Bo added, "I'm really . . . really glad you finally decided to join this party."

Rick's face broke into a smile, made even brighter by the emerging sunlight. "Better late than never."

52

Manny called her boss from a gas station in Pensacola, some thirty-five miles northeast of the Pink Pony Pub. She had changed out of the sundress and now wore jeans, a blue blouse, and a painter's cap. As she recounted the events at the bar, she watched the road, looking for any hint that the police were on her tail.

It took a lot for Manny Reyes to be shaken, but she was having a hard time regaining her composure after botching the hit at the bar and almost being killed herself. But for the reflexes she'd learned as a soldier, she'd be in a morgue.

"Are you absolutely sure that's who it was?"

"Positive. He looked a little different with the scruffy face and cap, but it was McMurtrie's partner, Drake. I've seen enough pictures to recognize him."

"Lord have mercy," Bully said. "Did either Haynes or Drake see you?"

"*Sí.* I was wearing a hat pulled low over my eyes, but . . . they saw me. Drake almost killed me."

"Damnit," Bully said.

Silence filled the phone line for almost two minutes as Manny waited for her instructions. When Bully finally spoke, she was again reminded of her boss's ingenuity and flat-out nerve. The kills that had eluded her tonight would be hers in good time. She would just have to exercise one of her strongest virtues.

Patience . . .

53

At his two-story ranch house on the edge of the Sipsey Wilderness, Bully Calhoun gazed at a portrait that hung in his basement. Bear Bryant, wearing a white hat with a crimson *A* instead of his signature houndstooth, flanked on one side by Joe Willie Namath and on the other by Kenny "the Snake" Stabler.

Bully sipped from a glass of single-malt scotch poured neat and groaned. He was too old for this mess. He didn't enjoy it as much as he had back in the day when he wore the powder-blue leisure suits and curled his eyebrows. He was seventy-four years old and, if he hadn't ended up with a son-in-law that was pushing seventy and just as mean and ornery as he was, he'd probably be driving a grandson around in a golf cart and buying the kid Gatorades from the cute little cart girls.

Instead, his daughter had married the meanest rascal in the state, only a few years younger than Bully himself and long past the point that his junk could swim. And Bully was still chasing pickle tickles from the cute little cart girls anytime he thought one might be interested.

He was also dead broke, and he had spent the last year and a half holding off his creditors. His meth operation, which had boomed in the 2000s, had stalled as the cooks and suppliers he had relied on for years had died off or quit the business. Bully was out of options and needed a miracle.

And it came in the form of his son-in-law's three-million-dollar life insurance policy. *Like manna from heaven.*

Bully smiled and sipped his scotch. Kat's claim had been approved last week and she should receive the check in a few days. He had already had his attorney in Jasper draw up the dummy corporations for Kat to funnel two of the three million into. His daughter would still keep a cool million for herself, which would be ample enough money to ride on until she was able to latch on to another man with a sack full of cash.

With the two million he was taking, Bully could settle all his debts, pay Manny the money he owed her, and still have a go-to-hell fund if the meth business took longer to kick back up than he was expecting. It would all work out so long as he could keep Greg Zorn and Alvie Jennings quiet.

Things hadn't been as clean as Bully had hoped. Life had stepped in and thrown a couple of curve balls, but Bully Calhoun had always been able to handle surprises. He could adapt and overcome as well as a Marine in the field of battle. He had made three fortunes and would make a fourth before he met his maker. He had survived four years in prison and five decades of being the alpha dog in one of the roughest and meanest counties in the state of Alabama.

And I'll survive this too, he thought, draining the rest of his scotch. It would be messy and might lead to some temporary discomfort—the good things in life normally did—but he knew he would survive and thrive.

At the end of the day, Wilma Newton was going to be convicted of the capital murder of Jack Daniel Willistone, and Bully and Kat

Calhoun would be three million dollars richer. There wasn't anything that Tom McMurtrie, Bocephus Haynes, Rick Drake, or any damn body else could do about it.

As he walked upstairs, Bully was pleased with the plan he'd just communicated to his executioner.

"You must always remember the golden rule," he whispered, chuckling as he recounted the soundest advice his late father had ever given him. "He who has the gold makes the rule."

In Jasper, Alabama, where his own daddy had been a strip miner all his life and died working for the man, Marcellus "Bully" Calhoun had the gold. Sometimes he lost it, but never for long.

My town. My county. My gold.

My rule.

54

At 10:55 a.m., Rick dropped Zorn and Bo off at a Goodyear tire place in Foley.

"You sure you want me to head back?" Rick asked, tapping his fingers on the worn steering wheel of his fourteen-year-old Saturn.

Bo didn't speak until Zorn had exited the car. "Yeah. Our cars should be ready in an hour, and it'll give me a little one-on-one time with Mr. Zorn."

"Ten-four," Rick said, and Bo hopped out of the car. Leaning his head back through the passenger-side window, Bo winked at him. "Thanks again, kid."

"No problem."

As he watched the rusty gold sedan pull onto the highway, Bo heard Zorn's voice next to him. "That's one more piece-of-junk car."

Bo looked at Jack Willistone's onetime lawyer out of the corner of his eye. "Maybe. But the driver saved our asses last night."

"I know," Zorn said. "Kids these days have no respect. Slashing tires on both of our cars. You'd think the punks could get their rocks off like we used to do. Sex, drugs, alcohol."

"Speak for yourself," Bo said, glaring at the dull-eyed Zorn, who was clearly still feeling the effects of the whiskey and Long Island Iced Teas he'd drowned himself in the night before. "And I'm not talking about the tires. I'm talking about the woman who was about to shoot us both in the head before Rick fired his shotgun."

"What?" Zorn turned and looked Bo straight in the eye. Sweat beads had formed on his forehead, and Bo had a feeling they weren't just from the heat and his hangover.

"You were so drunk you don't remember any of it, do you?" When the cops had arrived, the investigating officer had agreed with Bo and Rick that Zorn was too hammered to write a statement, so the lawyer had stayed in Rick's car.

"Remember what?" Zorn asked.

Bo sighed. "There was a woman. Very tan. Yellow sundress. When you were crying over your tires, she pointed a nine-millimeter pistol at me and was just about to blow my head off when Rick saved the day."

"What did she look like again?" Zorn's eyes were now moving back and forth. He was coming out of his fog fast.

"Dark complected. Long legs. Exotic looking with a foreign accent." Bo stopped, deciding to test Zorn. "I'd say she could be Mexican, but if I had to bet, I'd put money on her being from the Philippines."

Zorn grimaced and the sweat on his forehead was now a clear sheen. "Mr. Calhoun is rumored to use a Filipino woman to"—he licked his lips—"do certain kinds of jobs for him."

"Yeah," Bo said. "The kinds of jobs where a coroner or medical examiner gets called in after she's done."

Zorn didn't say anything. Instead he walked over to a bench and plopped down. Behind him and to the left, Bo saw his Sequoia and Zorn's Porsche inside the covered garage being raised up on pulleys while the mechanics installed brand-new Goodyear tires.

Bo turned his attention to Zorn, whose eyes were closed. "How'd you get messed up in this, Greg?" Bo asked, his voice soft as he took a seat next to the lawyer.

"Two words. Crystal meth."

"Uh-oh."

"Yep. Have you ever tried that stuff?"

Bo shook his head. "Not planning on it."

"Don't, 'cause once you do . . . My paralegal Robin is who got me on it. We'd just won a big trial over in DeKalb County."

"Fort Payne?"

"Yep. I have a cousin over there who referred me a murder case. After a week-long trial, the verdict came back at five thirty on a Friday afternoon. Not guilty. Me and Robin went nuts. It was one we weren't supposed to win. You ever had one of those?"

Bo suppressed a smile. "I'm helping a friend with one of them now."

Not getting it, Zorn continued. "We stopped in Birmingham on the way back and splurged at Bottega's. Drank two bottles of wine and got too drunk to drive home. I got a room at the DoubleTree and texted my wife that I was still in Fort Payne and would have to stay the night because the jury hadn't come back. It wasn't a big publicity trial, so I didn't think there was any way that she would find out I was lying. When me and Robin got to the room, we ordered another bottle of wine from the hotel bar and she broke out the crystal meth." He raised his eyes. "Jesus . . . Christ, that stuff messed me up. The next twenty-four hours were a haze. I woke up the next day at four o'clock in the afternoon on the carpet floor of the hotel room."

"Did you and your paralegal—?"

"We had sex," Zorn said. "Not that either of us remember much of it. For the next week or so afterwards, I dabbled a couple more times with meth at the office with Robin. When she said her supply had run out, she mentioned that her dealer was from Jasper."

"You bought from Bully?"

Zorn shook his head. "Not directly from him but from one of his minions. He tape-recorded the transaction and, about three months before Jack was released from prison, he showed me the tape and told me what he wanted."

"If Jack ever said anything about changing the beneficiary of his life insurance policy, you were supposed to tell Bully," Bo offered, trying to keep him talking.

"More than that," Zorn said. "Bully was worried that Jack would make the change. He knew Jack's marriage with Kat was on the rocks and that Jack's ex-wife, Barbara, was putting a lot of pressure on him to change the beneficiary to their son. Bully told me in no uncertain terms that I could not let that happen. If I did, he would release the tape and I'd lose my law license and be sent to jail." Zorn took in a deep breath and then stood from the bench. He took a couple of steps to the left and puked on the pavement.

"You alright?" Bo asked, putting a hand on his shoulder.

"I'm screwed is what I am," Zorn said.

Feeling his pulse quicken, Bo squatted and held his breath so he wouldn't inhale the scent of vomit. "Greg, if you have a copy of that change of beneficiary form, I need you to give it to me. That alone might be enough reasonable doubt for Wilma Newton to walk."

"And just give up my future?" Zorn dry-heaved. "No way."

"If you aren't going to give me the copy, why did you just tell me your sob story?"

"Because I'm a dead man." Zorn whirled around to stare at Bo, eyes wild with fear. "If Bully's wench tried to kill us last night, then she'll try again, *dog.*"

"We can hire you a security team. They'll watch you 24/7."

"For what?" Zorn said, spitting bile on the pavement. "So I can happily spend twenty carefree years in jail?"

"You can cut a deal. Turn state's evidence. Tell Powell Conrad everything, see what he can offer you."

"I violated the attorney-client privilege. Hell, I trampled all over it. I helped Bully Calhoun defraud an insurance company. What deal could Conrad offer me?" Zorn spat again. "I'm not an idiot, Bo. I'm a lawyer. Don't you think I've played out these scenarios in my mind a million times?" He rocked back on his heels and gazed up at the cloudless South Alabama sky. "I was a dead man the minute I gave the original of that change of beneficiary form to Bully Calhoun."

Bo chewed on the problem, and his head hurt from the various possibilities. He agreed that none were particularly appealing for Zorn.

"Greg, come with me back to Tuscaloosa. We can see Powell together. He's a friend of mine. He'll listen."

"No chance," Greg said, walking toward the garage. "Hey, are you guys finished?"

A mechanic patted the Porsche, which was back on the ground with four brand-new tires. "Hell of a nice ride, sir."

"Thank you. Are we done?"

"Yes, sir. If you've already paid, I'll drive it out of the garage and you'll be ready to roll."

"Greg," Bo called after him, but the attorney ignored him and brushed past him to where the mechanic was backing the Porsche out.

"That's good," Zorn said, and the mechanic jumped out of the car.

Zorn handed him a twenty-dollar tip and climbed into the driver's-side seat.

"Wait!" Bo yelled, and placed both hands on the open window seal. "Greg, if you won't come with me, at least tell me where I can find the copy of the change form."

Zorn looked over the wheel for several seconds before gazing up at Bo with dead eyes. "I can't," he said. "I don't know where it is." Then, before Bo could respond, Zorn clicked a button and the window began to roll up.

Bo stepped back and watched as Greg Zorn pulled the Porsche out onto Highway 59, heading south toward the Gulf of Mexico.

Five minutes later, Bo pulled his Sequoia out of the Goodyear store and turned in the opposite direction.

Due north toward Tuscaloosa.

As he pressed the accelerator to the floor, he looked in his rearview mirror as Baldwin County receded into the distance.

Bocephus Haynes had a strong feeling that he would never see Jack Willistone's lawyer again.

55

"He doesn't know where it is?" Tom asked, not disguising his exasperation.

"That's what he said." Fatigue dripped from Bo's voice.

"Where are you?"

"Getting on 65. About four hours out."

"OK, no need to come in today. I know you're worn out."

"Thanks," Bo said. "I think I'm going to go see Jazz and the kids. I almost orphaned them last night."

Silence filled the line and Tom closed his eyes, thanking God that his friend was OK. "So, you're glad I brought Rick in?"

"That decision saved my butt, Professor. Second time I've been staring down the barrel of a gun in the past year, and both times you've pulled me out of the fire."

"We were lucky. I didn't expect Rick to leave immediately when I called, but if he hadn't—"

"You'd be picking me out a coffin."

They said their goodbyes, and Tom walked back into the conference room. It was almost eleven thirty and he had kept the young man sitting at the end of the table waiting long enough. Frankie had scheduled the meeting for eleven, and the kid had showed up fifteen minutes early. But Bo had called just as Tom was about to go in, and catching up on his investigator's near-fatal trip to the Gulf Coast took priority.

"I'm sorry, Mr. Caldwell," Tom said as he entered the room.

Happy Caldwell stood and gave a slight bow with his head. "No worries, Professor McMurtrie. It's an honor to meet you."

"Thank you," Tom said, gesturing to the chair. "Please, sit down."

Caldwell did as he was told.

"You had indicated on the phone that your friend, Mr. . . ." Tom paused and began to flip through the Newton file, all of which had been stacked in boxes on the conference room table. He pulled out the folder with Wade's investigative report, but before he found the name, Caldwell blurted it out.

"Shuman. Todd Shuman. Pledge name is Screech. I called and texted him several times and tried to get him to come with me, but he's a pansy . . . er, I'm sorry, he's a little gun-shy about all this."

"And you're not?"

Caldwell's face turned a slight shade of red. "A little," he admitted. "But I'm also curious. I'm prelaw at Alabama." He looked Tom right in the eye. "You're one of my heroes."

Tom didn't know what to say and felt his own face beginning to flush as well. Then, shaking off his embarrassment, he met the young man's gaze. "Mr. Caldwell, have you read the witness statement that Detective Richey prepared summarizing his conversation with you and Mr. Shuman a couple hours after you and your fraternity brother discovered the body of Jack Willistone?"

Caldwell nodded. "I read it and signed it a few days later. It's dead on."

"Have you read it since then?"

"No."

Tom again looked for the summary. After thirty seconds, he located it in a manila folder in the investigative file jacket. "Would you mind looking at it again?"

"Sure."

Tom slid the statement over and watched as Caldwell took several minutes to read through the contents. When he was done, he looked up from the page. "It's all there."

"Is there anything else you remember that's not in there? Anything at all?"

Caldwell didn't say anything.

"Mr. Caldwell? Is there something else? Did you see any boats in the distance? Any strange-looking people down by the shore or in the parking lot of the Cypress Inn?"

"No," Caldwell said, but he sounded less cocksure than he had a few moments earlier.

"Are you sure?" Tom asked. "My client's life is on the line here, Happy."

His face reddened again and he looked down at the table. "I'm sorry, Professor McMurtrie, but I can't remember anything else. I'd . . . really like to help."

Tom watched him, trying to read whether he was telling the truth. Then he slid his business card across the table. "If you do remember something, call me, OK?"

"Yes, sir," Happy said.

Happy Caldwell met Todd Shuman at Innisfree fifteen minutes later. Happy did two shots of Jim Beam before he was able to say anything. "We need to come clean," he said, looking his fraternity brother dead in the eye.

"Are you crazy? We'll be kicked out of school. Out of Phi Delt. My parents will kill me."

"Screech, that woman's life is hanging in the balance. How can we just—?"

"We can't, alright, Happy? You can't, you hear me? All for one and one for all, right, brother?"

Happy flinched at the sound of the fraternity slogan. "This is bigger than us, Screech."

"No, it's not," Shuman said. "Nothing we say is going to stop the prosecution from convicting that woman of killing Jack Willistone. We add nothing. You read the article yesterday. He was killed with her gun. Her prints were on it. She spat on him." He flung his hands up. "Your hero and his client are going down, Happy. And we don't need to go down with them."

56

Raina Farrell didn't even line up the putt before she proceeded to yank it left. *And eighty-seven becomes eighty-eight,* she thought, backhanding the remaining one-incher in and retrieving her ball from the cup.

"Bogey?" her playing partner Michaela Jackson asked, trying not to sound obnoxious as they walked off the green.

"Yep. The bogey train rolls on. Double snowman today. I'm really on a tear."

"Just a slump," Michaela said. "You'll get it back."

In the parking lot, the two teammates hugged, and Raina put her clubs in the back of her Mustang hatchback. "Thanks for meeting me, Michaela. Are you home the rest of the summer?"

Michaela nodded. "Good old Hunts-Vegas," she said, her pet name for Huntsville. "How about you? Home?"

Raina's mom lived with her boyfriend in a two-bedroom shack in Bagdad, Florida, and her dad had been dead since she was five years old. Home didn't sound all that enticing. "No, I'm gonna take some summer classes and try to get ahead."

"Well, let's do this again," Michaela said. "Birmingham is only an hour and a half away from Huntsville, and with Eagle Point letting the team play for free on weekdays, you can't beat the rate."

Raina forced a smile. "Sure thing."

As Michaela opened the door to her Cherokee jeep, she glanced over her shoulder at Raina. "Hey, what did you make on your astronomy final? I got a freaking C minus. Can you believe that douchebag Newell? Acting all cool and buying us beers before the exam and then he lowers the boom with such a ridiculously hard test."

Raina felt heat on the back of her neck and in her chest. "I . . . I got a B," she said.

"You what?" Michaela asked, cocking her head.

"I got a B."

"But we studied together. You didn't know that stuff any better than me. How could you have gotten a B?"

Raina knew her face had turned bright red, but she kept her voice neutral. "I studied on my own too, and I . . . I went to see Dr. Newell a few times for extra help."

Michaela smirked. "I bet." Then she held out a fist, which Raina touched with her own. "Girl's gotta do what a girl's gotta do, huh?"

Raina took a step closer to her teammate. "I worked my ass off studying for that test. I'm sorry you didn't make what you wanted, but I deserved the grade I received."

Michaela tilted her head, obviously not buying it. "You and Newell were awful chummy at Phil's that night."

Raina blinked back tears and turned toward her car. "Have a nice summer, Michaela."

"Raina, wait."

But Raina already had the keys in the ignition.

"Raina, I'm sorry!" Michaela beat her fists on the driver's-side window, but Raina ignored her. She pressed the accelerator to the floor and burned rubber out of the golf club.

Forty-five minutes after leaving the course, she turned into the Tuscaloosa Public Library on Jack Warner Parkway. Instead of going inside, however, she walked to the edge of the street, looked both ways, and crossed. Twenty paces later and she was on the Riverwalk.

She never parked at Manderson Landing anymore because she didn't want to take a chance that Dr. Newell would see her car. She had blocked his cell phone number, and the one time he'd caught her walking on the Quad, she had literally run away from him. She never wanted to see that bastard again.

The affair had lasted all of a month and they had only had sex three times—four if you wanted to count the thirty seconds on the bench the night she saw the murder.

The prior times had all been in his office after class. She would act like she was leaving with the other students and then, feigning that she forgot something, walk back up the stairs. He'd lock the door, and five minutes later, if not less, they were done. She had never reached orgasm—there wasn't time for it—but she had turned a failing grade into a solid B.

By the time she reached the bench looking over the river, she was weeping. She sat down and wondered if anyone had ever found the panties that she had forgotten in her panic to leave after witnessing the shooting. She had packed up the telescope but forgotten her damn underwear.

Despite her tears, she managed a laugh at the absurdity of it. She had told no one about what she had seen and no one had asked.

She had noticed the flyers the police had put up at the park, but she hadn't called.

Dr. Newell may be a douchebag, as Michaela had called him, but he was right about what he said that night. If anyone learned that she had given her fiftysomething astronomy teacher sex in exchange for a passing grade, she would lose her golf scholarship and probably be kicked out of school. Best case, she'd earn a healthy suspension.

I may lose my scholarship anyway, she thought. Raina, a scratch player whose scores almost always hovered between 68 and 74 had not broken 80 since May 8. Her other classes, which she hadn't needed to screw the teacher to pass, also suffered, and she barely ground out Cs.

Raina had never been a good student. Her gifts lay in her physical talents. She was a hell of a golfer and knew how to please a man. When she was fourteen years old, she broke par and lost her virginity in the same summer and never looked back.

The tears began to fall again as her conscience ate away at her. She was trapped. If she did nothing, then she would keep her golf scholarship, assuming her game came back, and would still have a future at school and in the game she loved. *But a murderer may walk free.*

If she came forward and told what she had seen, justice would be done. *And my life is ruined.*

Raina placed her head in her hands. There was no way out.

57

Visiting hours at the Tuscaloosa County Jail ended at 4:00 p.m. By the time Laurie Ann got out of school and made the twenty-minute bike ride, it was 3:40. She sat across a plexiglass wall and held a telephone receiver tight in her right hand, waiting for the guards to bring in her mother. By the time they did, it was ten till four.

"Make it quick," a guard snapped behind Laurie Ann, but she didn't turn around. Instead she looked through the glass at the woman smiling back at her.

"You're a sight for sore eyes," Wilma said. "It's not the weekend yet, is it?"

Since her mother's incarceration, Laurie Ann had come every Saturday morning to see her, bringing Jackie each time. "No, it's Thursday," Laurie Ann said.

Wilma nodded, but her gaze was unfocused. Leaning closer to the glass, Laurie Ann noticed that her mother's eyes were bloodred. She looked like she hadn't slept in weeks.

"How's your sister?" Wilma asked.

"The same. Still doesn't say much."

Wilma looked down at her hands. "How are you?"

Laurie Ann ignored the question. There was no time for small talk. "Professor McMurtrie asked me to meet with you."

Wilma raised her eyes and folded her arms across her chest. "Oh?"

"He said you won't tell him what happened the night of the murder."

Wilma looked behind her to see if any guards were in the vicinity. Then she gazed up at the ceiling. When she lowered her eyes, they were full of tears. "You sure have grown up, you know that?"

Laurie Ann rolled her eyes. "Momma, we don't have time—"

"When I'm in the cell at night," Wilma interrupted, beginning to rock her shoulders in the plastic chair, her arms still wrapped tight around her sternum, "and the lights are off and the only thing I can hear is the guard in the hall whistling . . . I think about how things were. How Dewey used to mow the grass on the weekend so that he could grill steaks in the backyard. Do you remember our old house? The little rancher in Northport with the patio in back. Do you remember that last November? I guess that would have been 2008. I took all those pictures of your daddy and you two girls playing in the leaves. Lord Jesus, that man loved his children." A sob escaped Wilma's lips. "It's all my fault, Laurie Ann. All of it. If I had just let Dewey quit trucking, none of this"—she flung an arm out to the side and looked around her—"would have happened. If I hadn't been so greedy. So starved for money. If I had just let him walk away like he wanted, he'd still be alive. We'd still have our house. Jackie would . . ." She bit her lip. "Jackie would still be the happy-go-lucky kid she was." Wilma stopped and a strange smile came to her lips. "Do you know what your daddy really loved to do?"

Laurie Ann said nothing.

"He loved to cook." She giggled through her tears. "And he was good. Do you remember that chili he made every Halloween?"

Laurie Ann felt her own eyes begin to moisten as she saw a vision of her father as she remembered him best. White apron covering his flannel shirt and blue jeans, crooked grin on his face, stirring a huge pot of chili on the stove in their house and singing aloud the words of George Strait's "Baby Blue" as the real George's melodic voice poured out of the ancient transistor radio on the kitchen counter. "I remember," she said, wiping her eyes.

"It's all my fault," Wilma repeated, and she rapped her knuckles on the glass. "You remember that, and don't you ever forget it. *This is all my fault.*"

"Momma, you need to tell the Professor everything you did the night of the murder," Laurie Ann said. "He can help us."

When Wilma didn't say anything, it was Laurie Ann who hit the glass, tapping it several times with her index finger until her mother met her gaze. "Momma, please . . . he can help."

Wilma placed her palm against the barrier.

Laurie Ann thought back to the trip to Boone's Hill, Tennessee, after her father's death. How her mother had put her hand against the car window while she was pumping gas and waited until Laurie Ann, who was sitting in the back seat on the same side as the nozzle, stuck her own palm on the glass opposite. *We're gonna be OK,* Laurie Ann had thought at the time. *Momma is strong, and we're gonna be OK.* Wishing without hope that she could conjure up the same vibe today, Laurie Ann pressed her palm to the glass and looked into her mother's bloodshot eyes. "Please, Momma. Please tell him."

Wilma shook her head. "You know I can't."

Once her daughter had left the jail, Wilma Newton lay on her cot in the holding cell and scrutinized the ceiling. She thought through their conversation again, wishing for all the world that she could do what

Laurie Ann said. That she could tell McMurtrie everything; that he could somehow help her find a way out of this mess.

But as visions of the night of May 8, 2012 played in her mind, along with the videotapes that the prosecutor had showed at the hearing, she knew it was no use.

Finally, she began to cry, as what she had first told McMurtrie during his initial visit to the jail rang true in her heart.

Ain't nobody can help me.

58

For six weeks, Tom's life returned to some semblance of normal. With Rick back in the fold, the firm functioned like old times, with the two splitting duties on their civil files. Tom drove to Huntsville and caught the end of Jackson's Little League regular season and all-star tournament, and he spent a weekend taking care of some housekeeping matters on the farm in Hazel Green. The case of *The State of Alabama v. Wilma Newton* would be dormant until the grand jury issued its indictment, and Tom enjoyed the breather. His back pain had even gotten a little better, though it never entirely went away.

For his part, Bo returned to Pulaski while making regular telephone check-ins with Rel Jennings in Jasper and Greg Zorn in Gulf Shores. Zorn had bought a one-bedroom condo near Ono Island and, until he could lease some office space, was practicing law out of his car like the guy in *The Lincoln Lawyer*. Though Zorn answered Bo's calls—he said it wouldn't be right to ignore a man who, along with Rick Drake, had saved his life—he adamantly refused to go to the authorities with what he knew about Bully Calhoun and Jack Willistone's life insurance policy, and he said he'd plead the Fifth

Amendment if subpoenaed to testify. The bottom line was that Greg Zorn would not be a witness for the defense at trial. Bo had informed Wade of what Zorn had told him, and the detective had been lukewarm about the intel, saying that unless Zorn came forward himself or Bo found a copy of the change form, there was no use pursuing it.

Rel remained as jittery as a long-tailed cat in a room full of rocking chairs. He said that Alvie hadn't seen Bully's enforcer in a while and was beginning to think that maybe the worst was behind him, but Rel wasn't as optimistic.

"Feels like the calm before the storm to me."

59

The storm began on Friday, July 27, 2012.

Greg Zorn arose that morning to his alarm ringing at 6:00 a.m. and, after slipping on athletic shorts, tennis shoes, and a T-shirt, drove two miles up Perdido Key Boulevard to a public beach area a few hundred yards past the Caribe Resort. As was his habit since buying the condo, Zorn ran a couple miles along the coast, past the Flora-Bama Lounge and the Florida state line. He walked most of the way back and, before leaving the beach, stripped off his shirt and shoes and took a dip in the ocean.

He never made it out of the water.

Zorn was shot in the head with a sniper rifle, and his corpse washed out with the tide. The body wasn't found until a week later, and no suspects were arrested after his death was ruled a homicide. A rumor leaked that Zorn was a meth head, murdered in a drug deal gone wrong.

Bo Haynes didn't buy it. As he paid his condolences to Zorn's ex-wife and sons after the funeral service at the First Baptist Church of

Orange Beach, he knew who had killed Zorn. He had seen her with his own eyes in the shadowy parking lot of the Pink Pony Pub.

The storm came to Jasper a week later. Alvie Jennings came home after basketball practice to mow the yard. When he arrived, he noticed that the garage door was up, which might've put him on notice that something was wrong, as LaShell typically kept it down when she ran an errand.

But Alvie was distracted from a bad practice and stressed from watching his rearview mirror all the way home, wondering if Bully's enforcer was following him. Since Zorn's death, Rel was also checking in every six hours, and it was driving him crazy. LaShell's car wasn't in the garage, and Alvie figured his wife had just forgotten to push the button when she left for work that morning.

He never thought twice about starting the lawn mower. It never crossed his mind that someone might jimmy the garage door open while his wife was at work and his kid was at school and then plant a bomb inside the starter of his Toro model.

LaShell had just pulled in the driveway as Alvie was positioning the push mower in the grass to start it. When she got out of her car, he whistled at her pregnant frame and she rolled her eyes at him. Alvie gassed up the mower and checked the oil. Everything looked good. Then he pulled the cord. Nothing happened.

"I keep telling you that you need to get a new one," LaShell said as she walked out of his view and into the garage.

But LaByron watched his father. "Will you let me mow some today, Daddy?"

"Yeah, son," Alvie said, pulling back on the cord a second time with no luck. After the third unsuccessful try, he let out an exasperated scream and kicked the side of the machine.

"Can I try?" LaByron asked.

"Not now, son," Alvie said, grasping the cord again. "I'll let you mow the backyard once I get it going, OK?"

"OK, Daddy."

Alvie smiled and pulled the cord back. The last thought of his life was of shooting a few hoops with his son after the yard work was done.

The explosion tore Alvie Jennings's arms from his body. A trace of flame reached the house and, by the time the fire department arrived, the garage and kitchen had already been destroyed.

The firefighters found a pregnant LaShell Jennings in the first stages of shock, sitting on the curb holding tight to her six-year-old son, whose bloodcurdling screams could be heard over the blaring of the sirens.

In the woods behind the house, Manny watched the explosion and resulting blaze with satisfaction. The plan to sit tight and wait until Zorn and Jennings let their guards down had worked to perfection. After allowing herself a few seconds to enjoy the success of the mission, she walked down the embankment to where Pasco and Escobar waited in their car.

Once the vehicle was rolling down Highway 78, she called Bully, who answered on the first ring.

"Well?"

"The threats have been removed."

60

Alvie Jennings's funeral took place on August 15. Bo didn't go because the family forbade it. Rel actually warned Bo that if he didn't respect their wishes, they'd bury Bo in a box right next to his brother.

So Bo went to the Sheriff's Office instead. After demanding an audience with Wade Richey, he launched into a diatribe as soon as the detective appeared. When he finally ran out of breath, Wade spoke in a calm voice. "Bo, I'm sorry about your friend, I really am, but I don't see any connection between Alvie Jennings's death and the trial of Wilma Newton."

"I just told you the connection. Alvie was Bully Calhoun's driver. After he and Bully dropped Jack Willistone off at his house on the day Jack was released from prison, Bully stopped and talked for over an hour with Jack's lawyer, Greg Zorn. Zorn told me that Jack had wanted to change the beneficiary on his life insurance policy to his son, Danny, and that he'd sent the change form to Zorn to send to the insurance company."

"But Zorn never sent it in; he gave it to Bully. You've told me this story before, Bo, and I can't do anything with it unless Zorn and

Jennings were to come in and give statements, or if you could produce the copy of the change form you say Zorn kept somewhere."

"That's not possible anymore, Wade."

"That's not my problem," Wade said.

Bo eventually stormed away, throwing one last stone before he left. "I never thought I'd see the day that you and Powell cared more about winning a trial than doing the right thing."

A few hours later, at 4:30 p.m., the last of the storm arrived when Frankie rushed into the conference room holding a piece of paper.

"What is that?" Tom asked. Across the table, Bo held his face in his hands and didn't look up.

"The grand jury just indicted Wilma Newton for capital murder," she said, her voice clipped and anxious. "This is the order for the arraignment. It's set for August 27."

"Who's the judge?" Tom asked, holding his breath.

Frankie hesitated long enough for Tom to know that the news wasn't good. Then she spat it out. "Poe," she said, her eyes traveling to the bottom of the page. "The Honorable Braxton Poe."

PART FIVE

PART FIVE

61

On the last Thursday in October, four days before the trial of Wilma Newton was set to begin, Tom met Dr. Bill Davis at the Walk of Champions in front of Bryant-Denny Stadium. It was 6:00 p.m., and, with the days growing shorter, almost pitch dark. The path leading to the stadium, however, was well lit. Tom found his longtime physician and friend sitting on a concrete bench across from the statue of Coach Paul "Bear" Bryant.

Tom knew that the reason for this meeting couldn't be good. He had undergone his latest bladder scope ten days earlier and, while in Bill's office, had finally gotten his lumbar and cervical spine x-rayed. For good measure, Bill had thrown in an X-ray of his chest. Three days later, the doctor had asked Tom to go to the radiology center for a CT scan of his chest as well as a bone scan. When Tom had inquired about all the tests, Bill had said that he needed to know for sure what might be going on.

Tom felt his heart rate flutter as he took a seat next to Bill and gazed up at the statue of his mentor.

"Why'd you pick this place?" Tom asked, glancing at his friend. Bill Davis had a ruddy complexion and his once-carrot-top hair had thinned to a few gray patches on the sides. He had his arms folded and was looking down at the ground.

"I don't exactly know," he said. "It's just . . . I've known you for a long time, Tom, and I wanted to go somewhere that you would feel good. I know this is a special place for you. And . . ." His voice caught for just a second. "I guess I was hoping for a little inspiration myself."

Tom looked to his left at the stadium, where he had played on numerous fall Saturdays in the early '60s. Back then, Bryant-Denny only had around forty thousand seats. It was nothing like the hundred-thousand-plus-seat Death Star it was now. Tom gazed up to the top, where the red national championship flags flew all the way around the enclosure. Then, feeling the cool fall wind on his cheek, he moved his line of vision down to the plaques on the ground, which identified the players and coaches on each of the Crimson Tide's title-winning teams. He normally stopped at least for a second at the 1961 monument, but he'd been too distracted tonight to do so. Farther in the distance he saw the fraternity houses that lined University Drive. Though he couldn't see them in the dark, he knew that over the top of the houses and a mile to the west and north were the bulk of the faculty buildings that made up the University of Alabama. A person could drive a half mile through the campus and eventually dead end at Jack Warner Parkway.

Just beyond Jack Warner was the Black Warrior River.

"How bad?" Tom asked. When Bill didn't immediately answer, Tom added, "Look, I know you're about to tell me the cancer has come back, so just spit it out. How bad? Is the mass bigger than it was last time? Can you get it out? I'm a big boy, Bill."

"I know, Tom." Bill looked up from the ground and met Tom's eyes. "Your bladder is clean. There's been no recurrence."

"Well, that's good, right?"

"Yes." The doctor's voice was hollow.

"What's the problem then?"

Bill stood and walked over to the statue of Coach Bryant and leaned against it. He gave a quick jerk of his head. "I don't even know why I ordered a chest X-ray. The pain was mostly in your lower back, but when the X-rays didn't show anything obvious, I threw the chest scan in, thinking it couldn't hurt to take a look."

"What did you see?"

Bill pursed his lips and turned toward Tom. When he spoke, it was in the trained voice of a physician who had been forced to deliver bad news on so many occasions that he could remove emotion and just give the facts. "You have a mass in your right lung. It's about four centimeters long and three centimeters wide. The CT scan shows numerous spots throughout your chest cavity and lower back consistent with metastatic lesions. I entered an order an hour ago for a referral to an oncologist named Trey Maples in Huntsville. I know you have family in that area, and I thought you'd want to go through treatment close to home. Trey is the best in North Alabama, if not the whole state. I suspect he'll order a biopsy of the mass just to be sure and also a PET scan to see how active the lesions are."

Tom felt numb. Both of his legs had fallen asleep as he stared up at Bill Davis. "Can you get all of what you just said down where the goats can eat it?"

"Trey will have to make the definitive diagnosis."

"Cut the bullshit, Bill," Tom said, feeling anger rise in his throat.

Bill walked slowly back to the bench and placed his hands on his knees. He looked Tom directly in the eye. "You have lung cancer that's spread to the bone."

Tom bit his lip, not quite believing what he had just heard. "How is that possible if my bladder is clean?"

"Lung cancer normally doesn't come from the bladder. I suspect this is a new formation that you've had festering for a while with no symptoms. Probably stems from the cigarette smoking we all did back in the '60s and '70s. You didn't realize anything was wrong until your back started hurting."

"I thought you were going to tell me that I had a bulging disc," Tom said, speaking through clenched teeth.

"Me too," Bill said, plopping down on the bench next to him. "I'd give anything if that were the case."

Tom stood and shook the sleep out of his legs. He limped toward the statue of Coach Bryant and turned back to Bill.

The physician had tears in his eyes. He had delivered the news, and now it was OK to be human again. "I'm sorry, old boy."

"How long do I have?"

Bill wiped his eyes and sighed. "With treatment these days, folks are really doing well. Some folks live up to five years."

"What's the average?" Tom asked.

"Six months. A year if you're lucky."

"Even with treatment?"

Bill walked over to the statue. For almost a minute, he didn't speak. When he finally did, his voice shook with emotion and frustration. "What the cancer movement desperately needs is a man like this fella here." He ran his fingers along the concrete game plan that Coach Bryant held in his hand. "Somebody that understands what it takes to win. Someone with judgment who will use the millions of dollars donated to all the various cancer organizations for something besides Hail Mary miracle drugs." His lips trembled. "If you had received mandatory chest X-rays since you turned fifty, Tom, we would have found the mass in your lung before it spread and you'd be on your way to living to eighty. But doctors don't make money on chest X-rays. They aren't sexy. It's like the dive play on the goal line. Who wants to see the fullback get the ball behind the left tackle? It's just a meat-and-potatoes football play, but you know what?"

Tom didn't say anything.

"It scores touchdowns. This fella"—he pointed at the statue, his index finger shaking—"understood that. It ain't about Hail Marys and miracles. It's about winning. And we're losing the fight against cancer, Tom."

Tom grabbed his friend by both his forearms. "I appreciate the sentiment, but you didn't answer my question. How long do I have with treatment?"

Tom could feel his friend's helplessness when he finally resumed talking. "Since the mass has spread to the bone, surgery is not an option, so it's incurable. Trey may tell you different, but there's no guarantee that you'll live a day longer with chemo and all the newest miracle drugs than you would if you did nothing at all."

"Six months then," Tom said.

Tom could hear Bill's teeth grind. "That's the national average," he said. "But you're gonna top that. I know it." He beat his fist into his chest. "I know it right here. Where it counts."

Tom didn't reply. The numbness and shock were beginning to wear off. He'd never seen Bill Davis so shook up. "How is that?" Tom asked.

"Because you're the toughest cuss I've ever been around." Bill's lip quivered and he pointed back at the statue. "And because you played for that hard-ass son of a bitch." He waved his arm wildly toward the red flags flying high over the stadium. When his words came again, they sounded like the growl of a wounded and dangerous animal.

"Ain't none of you boys . . . that played for that man . . . ever been average."

62

For several hours, Tom drove the streets of Tuscaloosa. Up University. Down McFarland to Skyland Boulevard and then a right on Lurleen Wallace to head downtown. He traveled the length of Paul Bryant Drive. He passed the law school, where he'd spent forty years as an Evidence professor, and Sewell-Thomas practice field, where the Man had once stood high above the team on a tower and barked instructions.

Then he took Bryant Drive east past the city limits sign until it turned into Culver Drive. He ate by himself at Nick's Original Filet House, a one-room steakhouse affectionately known as "Nick's in the Sticks." He and Julie had eaten here on Friday nights, and for three decades Tom's order never changed. "Rib eye medium well, baked potato, and a salad with ranch."

Two hours after Bill Davis had handed down his death sentence, Tom pulled his Explorer to a stop outside the office. While exiting the vehicle, he saw a news crew several yards down the sidewalk. As he walked toward the staircase, a female reporter stepped in his path.

He recognized her as the same young journalist who had interviewed him after his and Rick's win in Henshaw two years earlier.

"I'm sorry, Georgi, not tonight, OK." Tom tried to step past her, but the reporter held her ground.

"Please, Professor, just one question."

"Will you leave me be if I answer it?"

Georgi took a small notepad out of her back pocket.

"Shoot," Tom said.

"Is this your last trial?"

Tom had expected a question about the defense of Wilma Newton, not one so personal to himself. But then again, he knew he was part of the story for the drama-craving media. Looking past the reporter to the lights of Bryant-Denny Stadium, where just a few hours earlier Bill Davis had told him he had approximately six months to live, and then to his right to the concrete facade of the Tuscaloosa County Courthouse, Tom saw no reason to quibble.

"Yes," he said. Georgi's mouth hung open in surprise. "This is my last trial."

63

At 8:59 a.m. the next morning, Tom pushed through the double doors of the courtroom. His eyes burned after a sleepless night, and he kept them focused on the floor as he trudged toward the defense table. When he set his briefcase down, he felt a light touch on his forearm and looked up. Rick Drake wore a gray suit, white shirt, and blue tie. He had finally shaved the thick stubble he'd grown on the farm.

Tom brought a hand to the kid's face and gave it a soft tap. "That's my partner," he croaked.

Rick gave a nervous smile and cocked his head toward the bench. Before Tom could turn in that direction, he heard the familiar rasp.

"Just get here when you can, McMurtrie."

Tom's stomach clinched as he met the contemptuous gaze of the Honorable Braxton Winfield Poe. "Am I late?" Tom asked.

The pretrial hearing had been set for 9:00 a.m., so Tom was not tardy. He knew he should probably apologize anyway, but he just didn't have it in him.

Poe's face turned beet red, but he didn't answer Tom's question. "I set this hearing for today to cover any pending motions before we start jury selection on Monday. Mr. Conrad and Mr. Drake have informed me that there is only one outstanding motion. Is that your understanding, McMurtrie?"

"Yes."

"Good." He turned to the prosecution table. "Conrad, please proceed."

Powell Conrad stood and buttoned his coat. "Your Honor, the defense has identified on its exhibit list a document described as Jack Willistone's change of life insurance beneficiary form. Despite our request, the defense has not produced a copy of this form or provided the original for inspection." He paused and looked at Tom. "Professor McMurtrie and Mr. Drake indicate that they do not have possession of the form, but it is now the Friday before trial. The state moves to exclude the document and to prohibit any mention of it by the defense in their opening statement."

"Response?" Poe rasped at Tom.

Tom, who had yet to sit down, peered across the courtroom at the prosecutor. "Your Honor, as the district attorney said, we don't have this document. However, we still have hope that we will obtain it before the close of trial, and we did not want to blindside the prosecution without notice. We understand from the victim's ex-wife, Barbara Willistone, that the form was signed by Jack Willistone several weeks before his murder and that it purported to change his beneficiary from his wife, Kathryn, to his autistic son, Danny." Tom paused. "Judge, the victim's life insurance policy provided that his intended beneficiary receives three million dollars upon his death. It is the defense's position that he was murdered because of his decision to change beneficiaries."

Poe crinkled his eyebrows and leaned back in his chair. "I've studied your trial brief, McMurtrie, and it reads like a Grisham novel. It's an entertaining theory, but one that isn't supported by tangible evidence."

"We would like for the jury to decide that, Your Honor."

Poe smirked. "I bet you would." He put on his bifocals and looked down at the paperwork in front of him, giving the impression that he was still thinking about what he was going to do. Then he peered at Tom. "I'm going to grant the motion. The form is excluded and there will be no mention of it by the defense."

Tom ground his teeth, trying to keep his cool. "Your Honor, if we are able to obtain possession of the document, we would ask for an opportunity to revisit this issue."

Poe coughed and cleared his throat. "*If* that happens, then I'm happy to hear what you have to say," he said, looking anything but happy.

"Is there anything further?" Poe asked, moving his eyes from Tom to Powell.

"No, Your Honor," Powell said.

"No," Tom agreed.

"Well, there is one thing further that I would like to discuss," Poe said, reaching behind him and grabbing a newspaper. He flung it in Tom's direction, the paper landing a couple feet in front of the defense table. Rick moved around the table and picked it up. His eyes widened. He handed it to Tom.

On the front page of the *Tuscaloosa News*, the headline read, "McMurtrie's Last Stand."

"You just couldn't do it, could you, McMurtrie?" Poe said, sneering at Tom.

"Couldn't do what?" Tom asked, skimming over the article, written by Georgi Perry, which documented their short interview the evening before and then launched into a summary of Tom's career as a trial attorney and law school professor.

"Couldn't try a case without turning it into your own little drama."

"Judge, I don't know what you're talking about. The reporter that wrote this article asked me one question and I answered it truthfully.

The inquiry didn't deal with any of the facts of this case and I saw nothing inappropriate about my response."

Poe scowled and pointed a finger at Tom. "Now you listen to me. I will not have my courtroom turned into a circus like what happened in Henshaw. You don't think that article might bring a few bystanders? Well, I'm not going to sit here and watch a parade of Alabama football legends like Lee Roy Jordan prance into my courtroom to show their support for you in your last foray. Such a spectacle will distract and prejudice the jury, and I'm not going to allow it. You hear me?"

Tom was unable to suppress the faintest of smiles. During the trial in Henshaw, ten members of the 1961 team, including Lee Roy, had shown up to support Tom in his first jury trial in forty years.

"You find this funny, McMurtrie?" Poe's scowl turned mock serious. "Why, I would think a man of your morals, a longtime law professor, would understand the unfair advantage you gained in Henshaw."

"My friends came to support me," Tom said. "I didn't ask them. They just came. It's a free country."

"It may be," Poe said, "but this is *my* courtroom, and I won't stand for any of those shenanigans." He shot a glance at Powell. "Since the prosecutor doesn't seem bothered by your impropriety, by motion of the court, I hereby initiate a gag order prohibiting either side from having any interview with the press about any topic until after this case has been disposed. Also, unless they have a role in this case or some professional reason to be here, it is the order of this court that any current or former member of the University of Alabama football team be excluded from these proceedings. I further rule that there be no mention made by the prosecution or the defense of Tom McMurtrie's history as a football player for Bear Bryant or Alabama." He slammed his gavel down. "Do I make myself clear?"

Tom gazed up at the bench in utter disbelief. During his career as a trial lawyer and professor, he had never intentionally used his position as a football player to gain an unfair advantage. The insinuation infuriated him.

"Yes, Your Honor," Powell said, his voice so loud that Tom's entire body tensed. Tom looked across the courtroom, and the prosecutor's face had darkened. "Perfectly clear."

Poe smirked. "I hope the state isn't prejudiced by your hero worship of opposing counsel, Conrad. Any prosecutor worth his salt would have made this motion without my involvement. You're an embarrassment to the title you hold."

"I respectfully beg to differ, Judge. I'm Powell Conrad, from Decatur, Alabama. By the time I could crawl, my momma had taught me to say three things: 'Yes, ma'am' . . . 'No, ma'am,' . . . and 'Roll Tide.'" He paused and, when he spoke again, it was with such intensity that Judge Poe's face went pale. "Without more reasons than the ones you've identified, the State of Alabama cannot back a motion to exclude the Crimson Tide football program from this courtroom." He paused. "However, my staff and I will abide by and follow the court's order."

Poe scoffed. "You're a real cowboy, aren't you, Conrad?"

"No, sir. I'm the district attorney."

Ignoring the answer, the judge turned his attention to defense counsel. "Does the defense understand the court's ruling?"

"Yes, Your Honor," Rick said.

Unsatisfied, Poe peered at Tom. "And what about you, McMurtrie? Will you abide by my order?"

Tom glared at him, not seeing the sixty-year-old version of the man but instead a twenty-seven-year-old who had started law school later than most. Poe had been what the other students called a "gunner," someone who sat in the front row, his hand shooting up every time Tom asked the class a question and seeming to enjoy hearing his own voice more than the Professor's. He had tried out for the trial team and come across as smart and prepared. Unfortunately, he had no talent for speaking to juries or thinking on his feet, and Tom had to choose the team based on merit. Desire, which Braxton Poe had in spades, mattered, but Tom owed it to the team to choose the best advocates.

When Poe didn't make the squad, he complained to the administration that his status as an editor on the law review and inclusion in the top 10 percent of his class made him overqualified for selection on the team. He argued that Tom played favorites and hadn't chosen him due to a personality conflict. Tom held his ground, and the school sided with him. When that year's team won the regional tournament and advanced all the way to the final match at nationals, Tom thought he had proven his point. Trial work was a different animal than writing briefs or memorizing legal theories; Poe wasn't entitled to a spot just because of his grades and writing skills. He had to earn it, and Tom didn't think he had.

The year had been 1979. Jimmy Carter was president. Bear Bryant still sat high on his tower at the Sewell-Thomas practice field, four years away from the heart attack that would take his life. And Tom McMurtrie had just started his second decade as an Evidence professor at the university.

"McMurtrie?" Poe rasped. "Has a cat got your tongue? Confirm that you will abide by my order, or I'm going to hold you in contempt."

Tom looked past him to the ancient clock attached to the far wall. He wondered how long the wooden time-telling device had been in that exact location in this very courtroom. Had it been here in 1979? Had it switched places in the thirty-three years since Tom had cut Braxton Poe from the trial team? One thing that hadn't changed was the hate that Tom saw in the eyes of his former student, now a circuit court judge whose ruling might sway the final trial of Tom's career.

Not to mention the future of Wilma Newton.

Tom felt his arm being squeezed, and he gazed into his partner's scared eyes. "Professor, answer him," Rick whispered.

"McMurtrie, this is your last chance, or I'm throwing you in jail. Are you going to follow my rule?"

Tom swallowed, his throat dry as sandpaper. Visions of other disappointed and dejected students passed through his mind. Kids who hadn't liked their grade in Evidence or who thought Tom had been too hard on them during class. Then there were the ones whom Tom had thought he had really helped. Kids like Jameson Tyler, who had been one of his finest pupils. Tom thought Jameson had grown into a great attorney and man, but the Big Cat had deceived him two years ago for money and fame. Tom hadn't reached him at all. How many others were there like Tyler? In forty years of teaching law, Tom knew he'd had a positive impact on molding the futures of throngs of legal minds, but it burned him that he'd also had a role in producing the likes of Braxton Poe and Jameson Tyler.

Finally, as Rick again pinched his arm, Tom spoke, his voice almost as scratchy as his nemesis on the bench. "Yes, Your Honor."

After Poe adjourned the hearing and had shut the doors to his chambers, Rick turned to Tom. "Are you OK, Professor? You kind of checked out on us there."

"I'm fine, son," Tom said, and he coughed to clear his throat. Since his talk with Bill Davis yesterday, Tom had noticed that he had been coughing more, which Bill had said to expect with lung cancer. "I just need some water."

"When were you going to tell me that this was your last trial?" Rick pointed to the newspaper, and Tom felt a sense of guilt.

"I'm sorry. I should have told you before you found out that way. I just . . ." He trailed off in another fit of coughing.

"Are you sure you're OK?" Rick asked, moving closer. "How did your appointment with Dr. Davis go yesterday?"

Tom considered his partner's hazel eyes. The boy had endured enough heartache in the last ten months to last a lifetime. *I'm not going to give him more today.*

"Fine," Tom said. "Bulging disc like I thought. Gonna treat it with pain meds and see how I do. Hopefully, I won't need surgery."

Rick looked at him, and Tom wondered if the boy could see through the lie. *I'll tell him the truth after the trial. I'll tell everyone . . . after.*

"Good deal," Rick finally said. "Meet you back at the office? I want to talk with Powell for a second."

"Sure thing," Tom said.

64

"Yes, ma'am, no, ma'am, and Roll Tide," Rick said, winking at his old friend as he approached the prosecution table. "I like it."

Powell grunted and then pulled Rick in for a bear hug. "It's good to see you, man."

"It's good to see you too."

Powell looked over Rick's shoulder to the defense table, where Tom had sat back down. "He OK?"

Rick glanced behind him and then back at Powell. "I think so. He and the judge . . . have a history."

"I know," Powell said, rubbing his chin. "If you guys want to file a motion for Poe to recuse, I won't oppose it." He stopped and glared toward the judge's chambers. "However, I don't think he likes me much better."

"It wouldn't matter," Rick said. "Poe would deny a motion to recuse, and we have no evidence of prejudice. At least not yet. If we find that change form, and he doesn't let it in, then—"

"Even if y'all come up with that document, it shouldn't come in," Powell snapped. "It's hearsay. You won't be able to authenticate it, and you have no physical evidence connecting Kat or Bully Calhoun to Jack's murder. I have to agree with Poe that y'all are in Grishamland with any theory that the Calhouns killed Jack because they knew they were about to lose the three million."

"I guess we'll see."

"She needs to plead guilty, Rick."

"Your offer still on the table? Life and eligible for parole in fifteen?"

"Yes, but all bets are off once the jury is in the box and we start opening statements."

"Understood," Rick said.

For a moment, there was an awkward silence as the two friends stared at each other. "Your mom doing OK?" Powell finally asked.

"Yeah, man. She's doing fine. Every day is a little better."

"I'm sorry I haven't called much, but once y'all got involved in this Newton mess . . ."

"No need to explain," Rick said. He started to walk away but then snapped his fingers. "Hey, Powell, I forgot to ask."

"What?"

"You got any opposition to my motion for trial by battle?"

In ancient times, in lieu of a jury trial, either party to a dispute could request "battle" as a remedy and could literally fight the other side with their bare hands or with swords or some other agreed-upon method. They could also hire someone to fight for them. When Powell and Rick had learned of this practice in their third-year civil procedure motion workshop, they had opened each mock hearing by stating, "Judge, assuming my motion for trial by battle is denied . . ."

The teacher never laughed and none of their classmates did either. But Powell and Rick thought it was hilarious.

Powell pursed his lips. "None. But I'll need to see if Ric Flair is available first."

"Sorry," Rick said. "I've already got dibs on the Nature Boy. Wooo!"

"Wooo!" Powell replied. He held out a fist, which Rick tapped with his own. "I hate this," the prosecutor said, glancing past Rick again to the Professor. "I hate being on opposite sides."

"Me too," Rick agreed.

"Y'all aren't going to plea, are you?"

Rick grimaced. "That's the client's call, and so far her position has been firm."

"All or nothing," Powell said, sticking his chin out.

Rick gave a short nod. "All or nothing."

65

By Sunday evening, the shock of Tom's lung cancer diagnosis had finally given way to the grim reality of his situation. Strangely enough, the first question that he began to panic about was so basic that it might have made him laugh if he wasn't so depressed.

Who's gonna take care of my dog?

After Tom had spent the morning practicing his opening statement for the Newton trial and the afternoon going over the jury list with Rick and Bo until his brain was scrambled, Tom packed up his briefcase and drove home. On the way, he began to stress about Lee Roy's future home.

He flung open the door and saw his bulldog sprawled out on the kitchen floor on his stomach. He walked over and knelt beside the animal, softly stroking his back until Lee Roy licked his hand. He went through the choices in his mind, knowing the thoughts were a defense mechanism for harder questions but unable to turn them off.

Tommy and Nancy already have a dog. Bo's current address is his office in Pulaski. Maybe Rick? His mother has the two chocolate labs at the farm. She'd probably be OK with another dog . . .

Finally, he went to the bathroom and splashed cold water on his face until he had control over himself. After he toweled off, he heard Lee Roy's whine below him. Tom squatted and the dog put a paw in his hand. "It's OK, boy," he said, scratching behind his ears. Then he took out his phone and pulled up the number for his son.

He hovered his thumb over the contact, wanting to talk with Tommy but knowing that as a doctor he'd want to discuss the scans that Bill Davis had done. He didn't want to have to lie to him too, but on the other hand he didn't want to hurt him with the truth. Tommy had taken his mother's death hard, and the boy had always been supersensitive. *Let's just get past the trial,* he told himself again. *Let's try this case and give the people I love one more week of peace before everything changes.*

Tom wiped his eyes, remembering how nine-year-old Tommy would sit in the front row of his classroom while he practiced his Evidence lectures. Tom would get so impatient when the boy would interrupt his flow with a question. *"What does hearsay mean, Daddy?"*

When Tommy was eleven, he had played rec league basketball. Tom had missed most of the games due to trial team practices, but he had come to the championship game. Tommy got fouled with two seconds to go and his team down one point. He had missed both free throws, the first one clanging off the back of the rim and the second an "airball," as the kids called it. He had cried all the way home, and Tom hadn't been able to console him. "You just need to keep practicing," was all he could manage for advice.

The boy never played basketball again.

Tom had so many wonderful experiences with his son, like throwing a football on the Quad, fishing on Lake Tuscaloosa, and teaching him how to eat a raw oyster for the first time at Sea-N-Suds, on the Gulf.

But the tired and lazy words that failed to build up his son's spirit after a setback haunted Tom's conscience even now. Despite all the good times since, irrespective of Tommy's growing up to be an accomplished orthopedic surgeon, Tom couldn't forgive himself.

Have I been a good father? Now that the faucet of regret had started running, he knew he wouldn't be able to turn it off. The hard questions, the ones that kept a person up at night, were coming fast and furious.

Tom looked at his phone, where Tommy's name was still illuminated, but he didn't make the call. He sat at the edge of his bed. On the dresser in front of him was the photograph of Julie from their engagement pictures. She wore a pink blouse and the pearl necklace Tom had given her their first Christmas together as boyfriend and girlfriend. Her blue eyes were youthful and full of life.

Was I a good husband?

He had been lucky and happy in marriage, but it was hard not to think of all the petty things they had spent so much time arguing and stressing about. Money. The nights and weekends he had been away from home for trial team tournaments. Silly spats with in-laws. None of it meant much when Julie's oncologist informed them about the lump in her breast. After that, Tom had cherished every second.

Time, precious time, he thought as he felt a tear roll down his cheek.

The next stop on the wheel of regret was his grandson. Jackson was twelve. Tom had hoped to watch him drive a car and see him graduate high school. To be there during those difficult teen years as a sounding board. Tom knew how hard it was to raise a boy. His own father had passed long before Tommy was a teenager, and there were so many times when Tom wished he could run a parenting question by his dad. Tom had wanted to be that extra set of ears for his own son. Perhaps he had not always had the right advice for Tommy, but he would make up for that with Jackson.

Now I've come up lame and failed them both.

Lee Roy placed his paws in Tom's lap and Tom bowed his head, rubbing his face against the bulldog's soft coat of brown and white fur. Tom had been an only child and had raised an only child. He had assumed that Tommy would just have Jackson.

But then came sweet Jenny. Spoiling that child with "slow cones" and other toys and goodies had given him the purest joy he had ever felt in his life. And there was another grandbaby coming.

Time, precious time.

He needed more of it with Rick. The boy was close to becoming a seasoned trial lawyer but wasn't quite there yet. Tom had wanted to practice for at least two more years, even if he had to cede all the trial work to Rick. He wanted there to be a gradual transition from the old dog to the young bull. He had it all planned out. *The best-made plans . . .*

And what about the General? He had taken Helen to dinner several more times since their meal at the Legends Steakhouse this past summer and enjoyed her company. She was smart, mischievous, and a hell of a lot of fun to be around. Tom would never marry again. He couldn't. Julie had been, and always would be, the love of his life. But by God, while he was still kicking on this earth, he liked spending time with Helen, and he knew the feeling was mutual.

Finally, there was Bo.

Tom's lip quivered as he thought of what his death might do to his best friend, whose family life had played out like a Greek tragedy. *He has always looked to me as a father.*

When the telephone rang, Tom released his tight grasp on Lee Roy and peered at the device like it might be an alien artifact. The name "Bocephus Haynes" was sprawled across the screen. *Telepathy,* Tom thought, smiling to himself. He coughed and cleared his throat. Then he gently put Lee Roy's paws back on the floor and answered the phone on the fourth ring. "Yeah?" he croaked.

"Professor, you've got to come down here."

Tom could feel the excitement in his friend's voice. "Down where?"

"The office."

Tom glanced at his watch. It was 9:30 p.m. He had been home for several hours, though it felt like only a few seconds. "Why?"

"Because your client's fourteen-year-old daughter just got off the phone with Robin Osborne."

Tom tried to shift his mind back to the trial, but he couldn't focus. "Robin who?"

"Osborne. Greg Zorn's paralegal. The woman we've been trying to find for the past four months." A pause. "The person who might be able to lead us to a copy of Jack Willistone's change of beneficiary form."

Tom felt a surge of adrenaline as his mind mercifully left the torture chamber of regret and returned to the trial of Wilma Newton. "I'm on my way."

66

Ten minutes later, Tom, Bo, and Rick stood behind Laurie Ann, who was seated at Frankie's desk and chewing a wad of bubble gum as if her life depended on it. The teenager wore gray sweat pants, a red Tuscaloosa High Soccer T-shirt, and tennis shoes. On the computer screen in front of her was a series of Facebook messages exchanged between Laurie Ann and a woman named Jeannette Osborne.

"Jeannette?" Tom asked.

"Middle name," Laurie Ann said, popping a bubble. "When she moved to Louisiana, she changed all of her identification to Jeannette. Driver's license. Car insurance. Facebook page. LinkedIn account. Everything."

"How did you find her?" Rick asked, and Tom heard the awe in his young partner's voice.

"I did a search with the last name Osborne and sent private messages to at least three hundred women. I told them who I was and that I needed to find a paralegal that went by Robin Osborne who worked for a lawyer in Tuscaloosa named Greg Zorn. I said my mother's life depended on it." She turned and looked up at him. "Jeannette responded tonight."

"Did she call you?"

"Yep. I told her the deal and begged her to meet with us. At first she said it was too dangerous, but when I started crying, she finally said she could meet tomorrow night."

Tom raised an eyebrow at Bo, who cocked his head toward Laurie Ann. "She's good, dog. Whatever you're paying this girl, you need to double it."

"Did you tell her the trial started in the morning?" Tom asked, peering back at Laurie Ann.

'Yes. She said tomorrow night at seven was the earliest she could meet, and I told her that Mr. Haynes would be there."

Tom and Rick shared a glance. Then Tom turned to Bo. "Can you go?"

"Hell yeah."

Tom rubbed his hands together and looked at Laurie Ann. "Did you ask her about the change of beneficiary form?"

"Yes."

"And?"

"All she would say is that she had what we wanted."

"Did she give you a phone number?"

"No, she refused to do that."

"Did you write down the number that she called you from?"

"Yes," Laurie Ann said. "It looks like a restaurant or something." She handed Tom a piece of paper, adding, "This is where she wants to meet."

He snatched it and read her cursive handwriting out loud. "Pat O'Brien's, New Orleans, Louisiana." Then he looked over the top of the paper at Rick and Bo, who were both grinning.

"There are worse places to have to go for work," Bo said.

Tom laughed, feeling alive for the first time since talking with Bill Davis on the Walk of Champions. He looked down at the firm's only runner, who had just gone well beyond her job description to track down a person who could end up being the defense's star witness. "Nice work."

67

"ALL RISE!" the bailiff's voice bellowed, and the Honorable Braxton Poe strode to the bench, his face already twisted into a scowl.

It was 8:45 a.m. Monday morning. Jury selection wasn't supposed to begin until nine, but Poe looked like he was ready to kick things off. *"State of Alabama v. Newton,"* he said, looking first at the prosecution table, where Powell Conrad and an older career assistant DA named Samuel Moody stood side by side, with Detective Wade Richey behind them.

"Is the state ready to strike the jury?"

"Yes, Your Honor," Powell said, buttoning the top button of his charcoal-gray suit.

Poe frowned at Tom with eyes that did nothing to betray his feelings. "Is the defense ready?"

"Yes, Your Honor," Tom said. Then, nodding to his right at Rick, who was wearing a navy-blue suit, he looked past his partner and winked at their client.

"Very well, everyone sit down." While Poe shuffled through some papers, Tom took a second to look around the near-empty space that was about to be full of potential jurors.

The only other people in the courtroom were the victim's widow, Kat Willistone, who sat in the first row of the gallery directly behind the prosecution table, Barbara and Danny Willistone, who sat in the same row as Kat but on the opposite end, and Bocephus Haynes, who was on the row immediately behind the defense table.

Poe put the papers down and gazed over the top of his bifocals. "I'm about to bring the jury pool . . ." He stopped when he noticed Bo. Then, scowling and pointing his gavel in Bo's direction, he continued, his voice even raspier than normal. "You're Bocephus Haynes, aren't you?"

Bo stood. "Yes, Your Honor."

"It is my understanding that you are suspended from the practice of law in the State of Tennessee and are not licensed to practice in Alabama. Is that true?"

"Yes, it is."

"You also played football for Coach Bryant, didn't you?"

"Yes, sir. Nineteen-seventy-nine national champions . . . *sir*."

"Then I would like you to leave this courtroom right now. Your presence is in direct violation of my pretrial order. If I see you in here again, then I will hold you in contempt of court and have my bailiff escort you to the Tuscaloosa County Jail. Have I made myself clear?"

"Your Honor," Tom interjected, astonished at the power play by Poe but knowing he shouldn't be. "Bo Haynes is our investigator for this case. He is in this courtroom in an official capacity, and there's nothing in his suspension from the practice of law that would prevent him from fulfilling that role for me."

"I think it's too close to the line and I also think you are thumbing your nose at the order I entered last Friday. I'm contemplating reporting him to the bar myself, and perhaps you too, McMurtrie, for actively participating in this fraud and violating the orders of this court."

The judge looked past Tom to Bo, who remained standing in the front row. "Now, Mr. Haynes, you can leave on your own or Henry here"—he gestured at his bailiff with his gavel—"can haul you down to jail. What'll it be?"

"I'm leaving now, Your Honor," Bo said, walking down the row. Before he left, he whispered in Tom's ear, "Good luck." Then he walked down the aisle toward the exit doors.

"Mr. Haynes," Poe said, "if I so much as see you in the bathroom of the courthouse, I'll hold you in contempt, you hear?"

"Yes, sir," Bo said. He opened the door and nodded at Tom as he disappeared from view.

Poe glanced down at Tom. "That holds true for you too, McMurtrie. If I see Haynes in the courthouse, you'll sit right next to him in the jail, you hear?"

"Yes, Judge."

"Alright then," Poe rasped. "Let's bring in the jury pool."

68

Though a little embarrassed by his grade school–style dismissal from the courtroom, Bo was grateful for the reprieve. As a citizen of Giles County, Tennessee, who had not resided in Tuscaloosa since he graduated from law school, he would likely prove useless in picking the jury. He could be of much more help on the outside, especially now that they had a lead. In fact, he would have had to skin out before jury selection was completed anyway in order to be on time for his appointment tonight.

After packing an overnight bag, Bo stopped at a gas station on McFarland and filled up the Sequoia. Then he pulled onto Interstate 20/59 east toward Meridian. Once there, he continued on I-59 to Slidell, Louisiana before looping onto I-10 for the last leg of the trip.

Six hours after he'd left the courthouse, as the sun began to descend over the Mississippi River and reflect an orange hue over the golden top of the Superdome, Bocephus Haynes rolled into the city of New Orleans.

69

By 4:30 p.m., the twelve people who would decide the fate of Wilma Newton were seated in the jury box. Neither Tom nor Rick was all that enthused. Ten men, all white, and two women, both black. Tom had hoped for an equal split of men and women, but the jury pool had been male heavy.

After giving his normal spiel to the jury about not doing any outside research, not talking with the attorneys, and not discussing the case amongst themselves until he instructed them to do so at the end of the trial, Poe dismissed them for the day. Then he advised the attorneys that they'd start with opening statements in the morning.

Thirty minutes later, Tom and Rick sat across from each other in the conference room of the office. "What do you think?" Tom asked.

Rick didn't hesitate. "I think Powell's plea offer sounds pretty good. If Greg Zorn had lived and been willing to testify, then we'd have a better story to tell."

"I agree, but the fat lady hasn't sung yet on that story."

"Maybe not, but she's warming up. Everything rides on getting a copy of that form."

"Bo will get it," Tom said.

When Rick didn't respond, Tom repeated the refrain, trying to make himself believe it. "If there is any way possible to get a copy of that document . . . Bo will find it."

70

Bo arrived in the French Quarter just after 5:00 p.m. Having a couple hours to kill, and famished after not eating anything on the road, he went to the Napoleon House on Chartres Street and grabbed a muffuletta and a Dixie beer. Once his stomach was full, he walked over to Bourbon Street, where the night was just beginning to gear up. On the balconies above the restaurants and bars, inebriated men and women hollered catcalls to the patrons walking below and threw beads at the women willing to expose their breasts and the men who dropped their drawers. Horse-drawn carriages transported tourists to and fro, and various street performers did everything from playing a musical instrument to acting like a statue.

As he took in the cornucopia of competing smells, which included beer, urine, seafood, horse manure, vomit, and cigarette smoke, Bo enjoyed the jazz music that poured out of different establishments.

At 6:50 p.m., he walked through the courtyard leading to Pat O'Brien's. Five minutes later, he entered the lounge area of the bar and gazed at the two dueling pianos on the stage. A blond woman belted out Elton John's "Tiny Dancer" on the piano to the left as a heavyset brunette rested while seated at the piano on the right.

A plump black man wearing a green sports coat escorted Bo to the table closest to the piano on the left and asked him what he wanted to drink.

"Hurricane," Bo said. *When in Rome . . .* Then he scanned the crowd, looking for Robin "Jeannette" Osborne. Before she had hung up with Robin the previous night, Laurie Ann had given her Bo's telephone number and told her to look for "a huge black man with a bald head." *Here I am,* Bo thought, subconsciously running a hand over his smooth noggin. He took out his phone and pulled up Robin's personal Facebook page, making a mental image of her profile picture. Brown hair. Medium height. There wasn't anything physically about her that stood out to him. He started to look around again and then felt a tap on his shoulder. He looked up, and a woman who was every bit of six feet, two inches tall with oversized breasts and gobs of blue eyeliner all over her face smiled down at him. "Are you Mr. Bocephus Haynes?" Instead of a woman's voice, the sound that came out of the stranger's mouth was a deep Southern twang.

"Yes . . . ma'am," Bo said.

"I have a delivery for you." The person handed Bo an envelope and then whispered hot breath in his ear. "If you're sticking around the Quarter tonight, sugar pie, come see me down at the Cat's Meow. I'm gonna sing 'Dancing Queen' sometime after eleven."

"I wouldn't miss it," Bo managed.

She giggled. "Anybody ever tell you that you look like that boxer Marvelous Marvin Hagler, only bigger?" She touched his arms. "Umm-hmmm. You ain't no middleweight, though, are you?"

Bo didn't know what to say and thought better of asking her if anyone ever told her that her voice sounded like Captain Woodrow F. Call in *Lonesome Dove*.

"Thanks again," Bo said, holding up the envelope.

"If you don't see me in the Cat's Meow, you ask the bartender if he's seen Desiree, you hear, sugar pie?"

Bo bobbed his head, and Desiree ambled out of the lounge. She blew him a kiss before disappearing behind the wall.

Bo opened the envelope as the waiter with the green sports jacket placed his hurricane on the table. His stomach twisted into a knot as he read the title of the xeroxed sheet: "Change of Beneficiary Form."

Bo quickly scanned the contents. On March 18, 2012, a month and a half prior to his murder, Jack Willistone signed a change of beneficiary form listing Barton Daniel Willistone as the beneficiary to his three-million-dollar life insurance policy.

Bo took a sip of his drink and wrinkled his face up as the alcohol burned his throat going down. He pulled out his cell phone and was about to call Tom when it began to ring in his hand.

"Hello," Bo said.

"Did you get it?" It was a woman's voice.

"Yes . . . Robin, wait! Give me thirty seconds." Bo slung a twenty-dollar bill on the table and shuffled as fast as he could through the mass of patrons until he reached the bathroom. Once inside a locked stall, he whispered into the receiver. "Robin, it's not enough. We need you to testify at trial. That still might not get us past the evidentiary objections, but we'll at least have a fighting chance."

When there was no response on the other end of the line, Bo closed his eyes and made one last plea. "Robin, Greg Zorn was murdered because of this form. We need you to bring Bully Calhoun to justice. Otherwise, the momma of that girl you spoke with last night is going to ride the needle. Please . . . I'm begging you."

"He'll kill me too," Robin said. "Why do you think I just had a transvestite hooker give you the form instead of meeting you myself?"

"We can protect you," Bo said.

"Like you protected Greg? No, thanks."

"Look, please—"

"No, you look. I don't even know why I'm doing this. I guess I feel sorry for Jack's son and that boy's momma. I had a cousin that was autistic. Plus the girl that called last night, Laurie Ann, she sounded so desperate."

"Robin, you won't be able to help Laurie Ann Newton save her momma or Danny Willistone obtain the proceeds of his father's life insurance policy unless you testify to this form in court." He spoke in an urgent whisper. "Robin, this has all been a complete waste of time unless you agree to testify. Greg died in vain. Danny won't get any money. Bully will get away with everything, and Wilma Newton will be put to death for a crime she didn't commit. This form is worthless without you there to testify about it. You might as well have wrapped up a plate of beignets from the Cafe Du Monde and stuck them in the envelope."

For almost thirty seconds, Robin said nothing, and Bo pressed the phone hard to his ear to make sure he didn't miss her response.

"When would I take the stand?"

Bo thought about all the witnesses for the prosecution. "Thursday afternoon or Friday morning. It's hard to tell this early on."

Fifteen more seconds passed before Robin replied. "See you Thursday."

71

On Tuesday morning at 8:30 a.m., Tom sat on a bench in the hallway outside the courtroom. Next to him, Laurie Ann Newton clasped her hands together to keep them from fidgeting. "Mom still won't talk," Laurie Ann said, looking at Tom with eyes filled with regret. "I'm sorry. I've really tried."

"Me too," Tom said. "She just won't budge. Me and Bo have talked with every single tenant at that apartment complex, and none of them can provide her with a credible alibi."

"She's not going to take the stand, is she?" Laurie Ann asked.

"That's her call, but I'm probably going to advise against it. If she can't remember what happened that night, then she can't rightly testify to things she didn't do."

Laurie Ann's chest heaved and she put her face in her hands.

Tom patted her shoulder to comfort her, noticing that she had lost a good bit of weight since he had first met her on the top step of his office back in May. He knew that Wilma had likewise lost weight.

"Laurie Ann, you did a hell of a job tracking down Robin Osborne, and your persistence paid off. We've got a copy of the change form, and Osborne's going to testify. That gives us a puncher's chance. I've just got to figure out a way to get that document in front of the jury."

"Well, you're the evidence guru, aren't you?"

"At one time."

"You'll get it in," Laurie Ann said.

Thinking that he would like his chances a lot better if anyone besides Braxton Poe were making the ruling, Tom tried to keep a positive outlook. "I hope you're right."

72

Two hours later, at just past 10:30 a.m., Powell Conrad concluded his opening statement with the theme of his case. "By the time Judge Poe turns this case over to you to render a verdict, we will have shown you that the defendant had the necessary motive for murder—she killed Jack Willistone because he owed her money. That she had the opportunity to commit the crime—she was seen entering and leaving the subdivision where the murder happened during the estimated time of the victim's death. And finally, and most significantly, she had the means to do the deed. *It was her gun.*"

Powell retrieved the evidence bag containing the nine-millimeter Smith & Wesson, holding it up for the jury to see. "As you sit through this case and hear all of the evidence presented, never lose sight of the undisputed fact that this gun was the means used to murder Jack Daniel Willistone." He turned and pointed at Wilma. "By the close of this trial, I am confident that you will find that we have proven beyond a reasonable doubt that the defendant intentionally murdered Jack Willistone, while also robbing his person and his vehicle. For these reasons, I know that you will reach the only just verdict, which is a finding of guilty on the charge of capital murder."

After Powell thanked the jury for their time, Judge Poe turned to the defense table. "McMurtrie, are you ready to give your opening statement?"

"Yes, Your Honor," Tom said, standing to his full height and clipping the top button of his coat. His back now ached on an ever-present basis, but he was wolfing down ibuprofen every four hours and he thought he could make it to Friday. "May it please the court," Tom began, coughing and clearing his throat. "Your Honor . . ." Tom glanced at Poe. "Counsel . . ." Tom nodded at Powell. Then he strode into the well of the courtroom, pausing just for a second to observe the packed gallery. He was relieved to see no former teammates; he had asked Bo to spread word of the court's order to all the former players he was still close to so that there would be no violation. Many of the spectators appeared to be reporters, and he recognized various lawyers and courthouse staff.

But sitting along the two rows directly behind the defense table was a group of people whose presence warmed Tom's heart. His son, Tommy, had taken the day off work to see the old man's last opening statement. He was dressed in slacks and a button-down, and when he met Tom's gaze, he gave the slightest of nods. Next to Tommy on the front row was Jackson; Number Forty-Nine wore a navy-blue blazer, khaki pants, and a red clip-on tie. He shot Tom a thumbs-up signal. His mother and sister had stayed home, as Tom and Tommy both agreed that Nancy, now eight months pregnant, had no business sitting on a hard bench for several hours, and Jenny was too young.

Rufus Cole, his loyal friend from Butler, Alabama, and retired circuit judge Art Hancock, a.k.a. "the Cock," Tom's mentor when he first started practice, sat side by side in the second row. Next to them, making her first trip out of Henshaw since her husband's death, was Rick's mother, Allie Drake. Finally, in the place nearest the aisle,

Helen Evangeline Lewis sat bolt upright with her hands in her lap. The General wore her trademark black suit with red lipstick. Her face was ghostly pale and her expression all business, giving Tom the nudge he needed to address his last jury.

"Ladies and gentlemen . . ."

Tom focused his presentation first on the heavy burden the prosecution bore to prove, beyond a reasonable doubt, that Wilma Newton was guilty of intentionally killing Jack Willistone. "If you have even a single doubt, a single question, as to the guilt of Wilma Newton, it is your duty to come back with a verdict of not guilty."

Then he launched into the defense story, first highlighting the discrepancies in the evidence. "As Mr. Conrad brings forth the state's case, ask yourself why there were no fingerprints belonging to Wilma Newton anywhere in Jack Willistone's car, on the dock where his body was found, or in Greg Zorn's boathouse or lake home. *None.* The only fingerprints were on the gun itself, and the only DNA to speak of was on Jack Willistone's clothing and cap. You will learn that Wilma Newton had an encounter with the victim several hours before his murder that concluded with an altercation outside the Oasis Bar & Grill. Ask yourself, as you listen to the testimony of the bartender Toby Dothard, whether this saliva mentioned by the prosecution could have gotten on the victim's clothing during this altercation as opposed to later on that evening. Do you have doubts?"

Tom ended by planting the crop that he hoped the court would allow Robin Osborne to harvest. He had to be careful, because it was fifty-fifty whether Poe would allow the change form into evidence. If Poe sustained the state's objections, then Tom didn't want to make a promise to the jury he couldn't keep. So he kept his theme general and vague, which he knew would be even more effective if the document came in, and less painful if Poe kept it out.

He walked to the defense table, remembering the instructions he had given forty different trial teams, spanning four decades.

"In your opening statement, always lay hands on your client. The jury has heard about the heinous things he or she has done, and it is important that they see you touch the defendant. It reminds them that your client is a human being capable of emotions and feelings."

Tom asked Wilma to stand, and he placed his hand on her shoulder. "Members of the jury, this is Wilma Christine Newton. She is a mother of two girls and a widow. She is also a convicted prostitute. She is not a saint, and you won't be asked to determine her moral character. Instead you will be asked whether this woman killed Jack Daniel Willistone on May 8, 2012. It is our position that she was framed for this crime. That others with much more to gain—*and much more to hide*—committed this atrocity." He tapped her shoulder, and Wilma returned to her seat. Then, ignoring the pain that throbbed down both his legs, Tom walked to the edge of the jury railing and moved his gaze over each of the twelve jurors. "It is not the defendant's burden today to prove that Wilma Newton was framed. The burden of proof never leaves the prosecution table." Tom turned and pointed at Powell Conrad. Then he looked again to the jury and spoke in a soft but firm voice. "We are not obligated to present a defense, but we will do so. And I'm confident that by the end of this trial you will have more than one doubt . . . *You will have many doubts* as to who really killed Jack Willistone on the night of May 8, 2012." He paused and took two steps backward, his eyes never leaving the jury box. "And when you do . . . it will be your sworn duty to return a verdict of not guilty."

73

Powell was meticulous and thorough in prosecuting the state's case in chief. On Tuesday afternoon, he called Detective Wade Richey to the stand to summarize his investigation, focusing primarily on the nine-millimeter pistol found below Greg Zorn's dock. Wade testified that the weapon was registered in Wilma Newton's name and only had her prints on it. He also summarized the cell phone texts and calls exchanged between the victim and the defendant leading up to the murder.

During Tom's cross-examination, Wade admitted that no fingerprints of Wilma Newton were found anywhere in the victims' vehicle or on Greg's Zorn's property.

"Can you explain those omissions?" Tom asked, breaking one of the cardinal rules of cross-examination.

Never ask a witness a question you don't already know the answer to . . .

But there was an exception to every rule, and Tom thought one applied here.

. . . except when the answer doesn't matter or is clearly asking for information the witness cannot know.

"No, I can't," Wade said. "I could only give my opinion."

Tom looked at the jury. "No further questions "

On Wednesday morning, the prosecution's first witness was the medical examiner for Tuscaloosa County, Dr. Ingrid Barnett, who testified that the cause of Jack Willistone's death was a combination of fatal bullet wounds to the head and sternum. She further provided her opinion that the victim's time of death was between 10:00 p.m. on May 8, 2012 and 12:00 a.m. on May 9, a period of two hours. Also, because he knew that Tom would bring this information out on cross, Powell asked Barnett to describe any existing disease processes going on with Mr. Willistone at the time of his death.

"Based on the autopsy I performed, it was my conclusion that Jack Willistone had a cancerous tumor in his prostate which had spread into his liver. I have also reviewed his prison medical records, which indicate that Willistone was diagnosed with stage four prostate cancer about eight weeks prior to his release."

Though Powell had softened the blow a little, Tom still managed to squeeze a sound bite into his one-question cross-examination. "Dr. Barnett, would you agree with the conclusion that as of May 8, 2012 Jack Willistone was dying?"

Dr. Barnett hesitated for several seconds before answering. "Yes, I believe Mr. Willistone's prognosis was grim."

"Thank you, Doctor."

On Wednesday afternoon, Powell called his specialists. First, his ballistics expert confirmed that shell casings found on the dock and the intact bullet taken from the victim's thoracic cavity matched Wilma

Newton's pistol. Then his DNA expert opined that saliva strands found on the victim's cap and shirt collar matched DNA samples provided by the defendant. During his cross-examination of the DNA expert, Tom confirmed that none of Wilma's DNA was found anywhere in Jack Willistone's vehicle or on Greg Zorn's property.

Powell's last witness on Wednesday was Othello Humphrey, the security guard of Zorn's subdivision, who authenticated the guardhouse video. Then Powell played the tape, which showed Wilma Newton's Mustang entering the subdivision at 10:07 p.m. on the night of May 8, 2012 and leaving at 10:38 p.m.

On Thursday morning, Powell conducted brief examinations of Happy Caldwell and Todd Shuman, the two fraternity brothers who discovered the body. Both recounted the events of their night, and their drunken tale of trying to find a spot along the shore where they could hit a golf ball over the river was some of the only testimony that elicited any laughter from the jury. Of primary importance, both kids pinpointed their location when they stumbled upon Jack Willistone's corpse in the water.

The final witness for the prosecution was Toby Dothard, the bartender from the Oasis, who testified that he saw Wilma threaten to kill Jack if he didn't pay her the money he owed her. Dothard also authenticated the video of the altercation between Jack and Wilma outside the bar, which Powell then played for the jury.

At three o'clock on Thursday afternoon, as Dothard left the witness stand, Powell stood and cleared his throat: "Your Honor, the state rests."

74

At 3:30 p.m., after the jury and attorneys had returned from a short recess, Judge Poe looked at Tom. "Is the defense ready to call its first witness?"

Tom looked at Rick, who gave the thumbs-up sign as he walked down the aisle of the courtroom. "Yes, Your Honor," Tom said. "The defense calls Ms. Robin Osborne."

Robin Osborne, Greg Zorn's paralegal and onetime lover, walked briskly down the aisle and took her place on the stand.

As she was sworn in, Tom again appraised the gallery, which had whittled down a good bit since opening statements on Tuesday. The first two rows were now barren except for Laurie Ann Newton, as Tom's son and friends had to get back to their lives and jobs, and Jackson couldn't miss a whole week of school. Tom understood, but he still felt a pang of sadness. He also couldn't help but notice that the trial was beginning to wear him out. He was strongly considering having Rick give the closing argument, because he wasn't sure he could stand in front of the jury for that long again. As he made eye contact with Laurie Ann, the teenager held up her hands, showing him that her fingers were crossed. She knew, as did Tom, that her mother's future likely rode on the outcome of the next few minutes. *This is it.*

Shaking off his anxiety and pain, Tom focused on the witness stand. "Ms. Osborne, would you please introduce yourself to the jury?"

"Robin Jeannette Osborne."

"Can you please tell the jury who you were employed by on May 7, 2012?"

Osborne turned her head and looked at the jury. "I was a paralegal for Greg Zorn."

Powell shot off his chair. "Your Honor, may we approach?"

Judge Poe ushered the attorneys forward and, once they were all gathered in front of the bench, he looked at Powell.

"Your Honor, on Tuesday morning, the defense provided the prosecution with a copy of a change of beneficiary form, allegedly signed by Jack Willistone and dated on March 18, 2012, some six weeks before the murder, where the victim purports to change the beneficiary of his three-million-dollar life insurance policy from his wife, Kathryn, to his son, Danny." Powell paused and glanced at Tom before continuing. "Your Honor, you previously ruled to exclude this form and any mention of it at the pretrial hearing last Friday. It is my assumption that Professor McMurtrie is about to go into questioning aimed at introducing this copied document to the jury, and we object."

"McMurtrie, is that your plan? Are you planning to violate my pretrial order?"

"No, Your Honor," Tom said. "I was planning to lay some foundation and then request a sidebar where I would ask you to reconsider your prior ruling." He glanced at Powell. "The prosecutor beat me to it."

"Well, we're here now and the jury is waiting. Conrad, you first."

"Judge, there is no way that Robin Osborne is qualified to testify regarding this form," Powell began, his intensity palpable. It was obvious to Tom that Powell also knew what was riding on this ruling. "All the defense has is a copy, so the Best Evidence rule applies to bar its admission. The defense has no excuse for why it can't produce the original. Further, it's the state's understanding that Ms. Osborne did not witness Mr. Willistone sign the form, nor did she see how her boss, Greg Zorn, came into possession of this form. Finally, the unauthenticated document is clearly hearsay. We would ask that the court exclude the form and any testimony by Ms. Osborne about it on these grounds."

"McMurtrie?" Poe rasped.

"Judge, Robin Osborne was a paralegal in Greg Zorn's office when Mr. Zorn brought the original of this change form back from the prison after visiting his client, Mr. Willistone. She can testify that she took the original and scanned it into the computer so that the firm would have a PDF copy. She can also testify to placing the original document in an envelope and giving it to her boss just minutes before Marcellus "Bully" Calhoun, the victim's father-in-law and also a client of Greg Zorn's, arrived at the office. Your Honor, Ms. Osborne can and will testify that the change form that we plan to introduce is a true and accurate copy of the original. And we do have an excuse for not producing the original. I have sent letters and served a subpoena on Mr. Calhoun, requesting the original, but the only response we've received is a letter from Calhoun's lawyer saying that Calhoun has never seen such a document and doesn't know what we are talking about."

Poe rubbed his chin. "What about the hearsay objection?"

"Judge, we are not offering this document to prove the truth of the matter asserted, but rather to show the state of mind of both the victim, Jack Willistone, and his father-in-law, Bully Calhoun."

"Why are the victim's and Calhoun's states of mind relevant?" Poe asked, looking down his bifocals at Tom.

Tom ground his teeth but kept his tone neutral. "As set out in our trial brief, it is the defense's theory that Mr. Calhoun had the victim murdered to hide the fact that he had prevented this change form from ever being sent to New York Life, and to make sure his daughter collected on the three million in insurance benefits. Judge, the defendant in a capital murder case is allowed to present an alternative, and any evidentiary rulings that are close should be decided in the defendant's favor."

"I agree with that, McMurtrie, but you still have to abide by the Rules of Evidence." Poe made a show of reaching under his desk to pull out a large leather-bound book. Tom knew what it was after only a second's glance. *McMurtrie's Evidence*, the fourth edition. "Is there anything in your book about ignoring the rules in favor of a capital defendant?"

"No," Tom said. "But we're not ignoring the rules. We're just saying—"

"The prosecutor's objection is sustained," the Judge said, and Tom saw a victorious gleam in Braxton Poe's eyes.

"Your Honor, I would respectfully request that you reconsider this ruling. I believe you are committing reversible error."

Poe smirked. "I've already reconsidered, and the objection is sustained. If you don't like it, then file an appeal. Now, do you still wish to ask this witness any questions?"

Tom looked at Robin Osborne, who had driven from New Orleans to be here. "Yes," he managed.

Tom only kept Osborne on the stand for five minutes. He hoped to at least establish that she had seen Bully Calhoun meeting with Zorn on May 7, 2012. But when he asked her this specific question, Osborne replied, "I can't remember." Realizing that she was unwilling to expose herself if Tom couldn't get the copy of the change form into evidence, Tom cut his losses. "No further questions, Your Honor."

75

After Osborne left the stand, Judge Poe adjourned for the day. "What are the chances you'll finish your case tomorrow, McMurtrie?" he asked once the jury had filed out of the courtroom.

"Pretty good," Tom said, knowing that unless Wilma Newton were to take the stand, he didn't have any other witnesses.

As he walked down the steps of the courthouse, Laurie Ann caught up to him. "She's screwed, isn't she?"

Tom didn't immediately answer. When they reached the sidewalk, he pulled her aside. "We've scored some points with the lack of DNA evidence and prints at Zorn's house and in Jack's car. That's something."

"It's not enough without that form, is it?"

Tom couldn't lie to her, but he didn't want to give false hope either. "I don't know."

76

After a sleepless night, Tom arrived at the courthouse Friday morning to find Happy Caldwell waiting for him at the defense table.

"Professor McMurtrie, do you have a second?"

"Not really, son," Tom said, still working through his direct examination of Wilma Newton in his mind.

"We saw something else that night," Happy said, his face pale, as if he were about to be sick. "Before we found the body, we . . . saw someone at the Cypress Inn."

Tom put his briefcase down on the table and looked at Caldwell. "Tell me."

77

"The defense calls William Henry Caldwell to the stand," Tom said, peering across the courtroom at Powell, who was talking furiously behind his chair with Wade.

After being reminded of the oath he took earlier in the week, Happy took his seat at the witness stand.

"Mr. Caldwell, did you testify earlier in this trial?"

"Yes, sir."

"And during your testimony, did you describe everything you saw and heard on the evening of May 8, 2012."

"No, I did not."

"Why not?"

"Because I was only asked about mine and Screech's discovery of the body."

"Mr. Caldwell, when you and Mr. Shuman arrived at the Cypress Inn in the wee morning hours of May 9, 2012, did you see anyone else there?"

"Not at first."

"OK," Tom said, pacing toward the back of the jury box so that Happy would have to look at the jurors when answering his questions. "Then when?"

"We were walking down the steps to the shore. Shuman was carrying the golf clubs and I had the beer. We . . . we saw a woman coming through the trees."

"Describe her."

"She was . . . kinda heavy I guess and her clothes were dirty, as if she had been walking through the woods for a while."

"Did you speak with her?"

"We probably would've just ignored her, but once we all saw each other, she came over and said something."

"What did she say?"

"Well . . . that she had four joints in her purse, and she'd sell them to us for fifty bucks."

"Did you buy them?"

"Yeah, but we talked her down to thirty-five."

"Then what happened?"

"The woman left, and we started trying to hit balls over the Black Warrior. We discovered the body about an hour later."

Tom made a show of nodding his understanding. "Mr. Caldwell, did you ever mention seeing this woman to Detective Richey during his investigation?"

Happy shook his head. "No, I was scared we'd get in trouble."

"And why are you coming forward with this information now?"

"Because I don't want an innocent woman to be put to death because I was too much of a pansy to tell the truth."

"Objection, Your Honor," Powell said. "Move to strike the witness's reference to 'innocent woman.'"

"Sustained. The jury will disregard Mr. Caldwell's characterization." He waved at Tom to continue.

"Mr. Caldwell, did you recognize the woman that sold you marijuana on the morning of May 9, 2012?"

"At the time, no."

"How about now?"

Happy nodded. "Yes, sir. I saw her in this courtroom when I testified yesterday."

"And do you see her now?"

"Yes, I do," Happy said, turning his head to the right and looking directly behind the prosecution table. "She's right there. She's the last person on the end of the front row."

Tom walked toward the woman in the gallery to whom Happy had just pointed. When he was a couple feet away, he pointed his own finger at her. "Is this the woman you saw who offered you four joints an hour before you and Mr. Shuman discovered the body of Jack Willistone?"

"Yes, sir, it is."

"Your Honor, let the record reflect that the witness has identified Barbara Willistone." Tom paused and made eye contact with as many jurors as he could. "No further questions."

78

Barbara grabbed her son's hand and tried to lead him out of the court-room, but Danny wouldn't budge. "Danny, let's go. Now." When he finally relented, she found Detective Wade Richey blocking her exit from the row.

"Just hold on now, Ms. Willistone," Wade whispered, trying not to make a scene in front of the jury but also knowing he couldn't let Barbara Willistone walk out of the courtroom after hearing the testimony of Happy Caldwell.

"Your Honor," Powell said, "the state requests a short recess."

"Very well," Judge Poe said, looking taken aback by what he'd just witnessed. "The jury is excused for ten minutes."

During the break, Barbara Willistone was taken into the custody of the Sheriff's Office. In the interim, Rick drafted up a handwritten subpoena and served it on her in the empty office operating as a makeshift holding cell.

When the jury was brought back in, Powell cross-examined Happy for five minutes about the things he did not see. He did not see Barbara Willistone shoot Jack Willistone. He did not know where Barbara had come from or what she was doing. He himself was admittedly stoned and drunk at the time.

At 10:30 a.m., Happy Caldwell was excused from the witness stand.

"Call your next witness," Judge Poe said, his voice tired. His Honor clearly wasn't enjoying the direction the case had taken.

Winking at Laurie Ann Newton, Tom cleared his throat. "The defense calls Ms. Barbara Willistone."

79

Barbara Willistone took the witness stand and glared at Tom like he might be Judas Iscariot. Before Tom could even ask a question, she spoke through clenched teeth. "I came to you for help. I gave you information, and this is how you repay me."

"Judge—"

"The witness will refrain from making statements and will only answer the questions raised by counsel. Do you understand, Ms. Willistone?"

"I understand," she said, her voice dripping with bitterness.

"Ms. Willistone, did you see your husband after his release from prison?"

"You know I did. I told you."

"And did he say anything to you about the insurance policy that he took out on his life?"

"Objection, Your Honor. Hearsay."

"Not offering for the truth, Judge. Only Ms. Willistone's state of mind."

"I'll allow it."

"Yes," Barbara said. "He told me that he had changed the beneficiary on his policy from his *wife*"—Barbara glared at Kat Willistone on the front row—"to our son, Danny."

"Did he say anything else to you?"

"No, but he showed me a copy of a change of beneficiary form that he had completed which made Danny the recipient."

"Objection, Your Honor," Powell said.

"Sustained," Poe said, glaring at Tom and motioning for the attorneys to approach. Before he could scold him, Tom offered, "Judge I didn't ask her about the form. She volunteered that information."

The judge rubbed his eyes and finally peered at the witness over his bifocals. "Ms. Willistone, do not volunteer any more information about the change form. Just answer the questions that are asked." Then he gazed at Tom with flat eyes. "Continue."

Tom resumed his place in front of the witness stand. "When did this conversation with your ex-husband take place, Ms. Willistone?"

"Tuesday, May 8, 2012. About seven o'clock."

"And when Jack Willistone left your house that night, did you believe that your son, Danny, was then the beneficiary of Jack's three-million-dollar life insurance policy?"

She nodded, and her lower lip began to tremble. "Yes."

Tom paused for a good five seconds. "Ms. Willistone, did you just hear the testimony of William Henry Caldwell?"

"Yes, I did."

"Ms. Willistone, were you on the shore below the Cypress Inn restaurant in the wee morning hours of May 9, 2012?"

Barbara Willistone closed her eyes. Tears began to fall down her cheeks. She started to speak, but Powell Conrad's loud voice overpowered her.

"Your Honor, as an officer of the court, I think it is only fair that I inform Ms. Willistone of her Fifth Amendment right not to incriminate herself."

Judge Poe sighed. "Thank you, Mr. Conrad."

"Ms. Willistone," Tom continued, "did you understand my question?"

"I did." She didn't look at Tom. Instead she gazed at her son, Danny, in the front row. "I plead the Fifth."

80

Braxton Poe had to bang his gavel for thirty seconds to get the gallery full of reporters to pipe down after Barbara Willistone pled the Fifth Amendment. When he finally had restored quiet and Barbara had been escorted out of the courtroom in police custody, he looked at Tom. "Call your next witness."

Tom whispered in Wilma's ear. "I don't think we need to explain the saliva after what just happened. Agreed, or do you want to take the stand?"

"Agreed," she whispered.

"McMurtrie?" Poe rasped.

Tom rose from his chair. As he scanned the faces of the twelve jurors, he saw the expressions that a criminal defense attorney craves: confusion, bewilderment, and curiosity.

A jury with unanswered questions won't convict, he thought.

"Your Honor, the defense rests."

81

"We're in the honey hole," Bo said as he, Tom, and Rick gathered around the conference room table and wolfed down turkey sandwiches. Bo, who had faithfully stayed away from the courthouse, had been briefed by Rick the second they arrived at the office after Judge Poe had adjourned for lunch.

"It's not over yet," Tom said. "Powell still has an opportunity for rebuttal."

"Ain't no way he can rebut what the jury just heard from Happy Caldwell and Barbara Willistone," Bo said. "The bottom line is Barbara Willistone had motive—if she kills Jack, then Danny collects the proceeds—and opportunity. Caldwell puts her at the scene of the murder." He snapped his fingers. "You could move for a continuance and demand that the prosecution take DNA samples from Barbara Willistone and compare them to the other DNA found at the scene."

Tom rubbed his chin. "I could . . . but I think that jury is about to acquit."

Bo held out his palms. "Tough call, but you gotta trust your gut."

"My gut is saying let it ride."

82

It was a somber scene inside the district attorney's office. Powell sat slumped in his chair, while Wade furiously paced around the long table. "We could recall Shuman. He might not agree with Caldwell."

Powell just looked at him. "OK, that was stupid," Wade said, shaking his head. "I can't believe those pricks didn't tell us about Barbara Willistone when we first interviewed them."

"I can," Powell said. "A druggie never reveals the identity of his dealer. That's Criminal Law 101. You're tired, Wade. I'll tell you what I can't believe. I can't believe Caldwell came clean. Kid's got brass balls."

"I can't think of anyone we can call in rebuttal who adds anything to our case or can subtract any of the damage that Barbara Willistone and Happy Caldwell just did."

Powell slapped his hands on the table. "Agreed. No rebuttal witnesses and we'll go straight to closing arguments."

"It's not over," Wade said, and Powell heard the desperation in the detective's voice. "If this were a boxing match, we're way ahead on points."

Powell smiled at his friend. "You know that's not how a capital murder case gets decided. We don't win on technical knockouts. It's got to be a true, no-questions-left knockout."

There were three loud knocks on the door.

"Come in," Powell said, rising from his chair. He opened the door and saw Samuel Moody. "You get the jury instructions done, Sam?"

The older lawyer nodded, his eyes wide. "There's someone you need to meet."

"Sam, I'm kinda in the middle of trying to decide whether to call a rebuttal witness or not. What's this about?"

When the assistant DA spoke again, his voice was nearly breathless. "There's a lady out in the waiting area that says she saw the murder."

Less than a minute later, Sam escorted a woman in her twenties into the conference room. "Gentlemen"—he looked at Powell and then Wade before gesturing to the woman—"this is Ms. Raina Farrell."

Hearing the echo of his heart racing in his chest, Powell swallowed and pointed to one of the chairs. "Please sit down, Ms. Farrell."

Once she was seated, Powell skipped the preliminaries. "Is it true? Did you see the murder of Jack Willistone?"

"Yes, sir, I did. I was at the Riverwalk and I had a clear view."

"Could you see who did it?"

Raina nodded. "Yes."

"Why now, Ms. Farrell?" Powell asked.

"I've been watching the trial all week. I thought I could sit by . . . but I can't anymore."

"Why didn't you say something beforehand?"

Raina held her hands together to keep them from shaking. "Because I didn't want to lose my golf scholarship. I'm a junior and I play number two on the team."

"I don't get it," Powell said. "How could witnessing a murder cost you your golf scholarship?"

Raina swallowed hard. "Because at the time I saw the shooting, I was having sex with astronomy professor Sean Newell on one of the benches at the Park at Manderson Landing. I was sitting in his lap, facing the river, and he was . . ." She closed her eyes. "Behind me."

"That's a distance of almost three hundred yards, ma'am. I can understand how you saw the shooting, but how could you see the shooter?"

Raina opened her eyes. Despite her anxiety, she managed a tight grin. "Because I looked through a telescope."

Powell cut a glance at Wade, whose face had quickly become wan.

"Ma'am," the detective asked, "who did you see?"

83

At 1:30 p.m., Judge Poe called the case back to order. "Mr. Conrad, will the prosecution be offering any rebuttal witnesses?"

"Yes, Your Honor. May we approach?"

When all of the attorneys were before the bench, Powell, looking at Tom, spoke. "During the break, it has come to our attention that there is an eyewitness to this murder. The witness's name is Raina Farrell, and for reasons that I will explain, she has not come forward until now."

After Powell had relayed everything that Raina had explained in the lobby of his office, Judge Poe looked to Tom. "McMurtrie, I'm inclined to allow it. What do you say?"

Tom was flabbergasted. "Judge, we invoked the rule when we started the trial, which means that no witness should have been allowed to listen to other witnesses' testimony, and Mr. Conrad wants to call someone who has sat in here the entire week, heard everything that has been said, and now wants to testify. That is extremely prejudicial to my client."

"You'll have an opportunity to cross the witness on all of that, McMurtrie. I'm going to allow it."

84

Tom walked back to the defense table in a daze and exchanged a worried look with Rick. When he sat down, Wilma was in his ear. "What's happened?"

"They have an eyewitness," Tom said, looking her directly in the eyes.

"State calls Raina Farrell," Powell said, his voice booming to the back of the courtroom. For twenty minutes, Powell took Raina through her background, her scholarship with the university golf team, her struggles in astronomy, and the affair that began with Dr. Sean Newell in April 2012. After laying all the groundwork and establishing her and Dr. Newell's presence at the Riverwalk at the Park at Manderson Landing on May 8, 2012 at approximately 10:15 p.m., he got to the nitty-gritty.

"Ms. Farrell, at the time that you and Dr. Newell were engaged in sexual intercourse on the bench by the railing, did you have a clear view across the river?"

"Yes, I did. My . . . eyes were closed at first, but then I opened them when I heard the gunshots."

"Tell the jury what you saw."

"A man was standing at the edge of a dock. Initially, he was facing me, but then he turned when a person approached him from the other end of the dock. The man was shot three times by a woman with what looked like a small handgun."

"You say a woman?" Powell asked.

"Yes."

"Did you get a good look at her?"

"It was three hundred yards across, so I could tell that she was an athletic-looking woman, but I couldn't see her that well until I looked in the viewer of the telescope."

A collective gasp rose from the jury box and the gallery, followed by murmurs. Judge Poe banged his gavel and asked for silence.

"When you looked in the viewer of the telescope, Ms. Farrell, could you see the shooter?"

"Yes, for a split second I saw her in profile."

"What do you mean in profile?"

"I had a side view of her. I could see the side of her face. She wore a white cap, pink windbreaker, khaki shorts, and white Nike tennis shoes with a red swoosh."

Powell let out a deep breath and spoke in a voice that echoed off the walls of the courtroom. "Ms. Farrell, do you see the shooter in this courtroom?"

"Yes, I do."

"Could you please point her out."

Raina Farrell stood from the witness stand and pointed directly at Wilma Newton.

Powell waited a full five seconds and then, in a slightly lower voice, he announced, "Let the record reflect that the witness has identified the defendant."

85

For the second time in three hours, the courtroom erupted in a sea of murmurs, and reporters all tried to beat each other to the exit doors to report on the latest news. Judge Poe banged his gavel on the bench and, after a full minute, finally restored order.

"Cross-examination, McMurtrie?"

Tom started to say yes, but then he felt his client pulling on his arm. "What?" Tom whispered.

"I want to plead guilty," Wilma said, her eyes wide with fear. "Right now. I want to plead guilty."

"Why?" Tom asked.

"McMurtrie, are you going to cross-examine this witness?"

"Yes, Your Honor. Just one second."

"No," Wilma said. She was now standing. "I don't want this to go any further. I want to plead guilty."

Tom looked at his client in utter bewilderment. "Why?"

Wilma's jaw stuck out and she glared at him with fire in her eyes. "Because I killed the son of a bitch."

86

At 3:00 p.m., Judge Poe entered Wilma Newton's plea of guilty on the record to all charges brought by the prosecution. He then banged his gavel and excused the jury until Monday, when the sentencing phase of the trial would begin.

For a long time, Tom and Rick sat at the defense table, alone with their thoughts. As he finally packed his briefcase to go, Tom gazed behind him at the front row and something clicked in his brain. He went over Raina Farrell's testimony again and then whispered it out loud. "I had a side view of her. I could see the side of her face. She wore a white cap, pink windbreaker, khaki shorts, and white Nike tennis shoes with a red swoosh."

Nike tennis shoes with a red swoosh.

Tom shot to his feet as if he had been fired out of a cannon. He forgot about his back and walked briskly to the exit doors.

He called her three times on the drive back to the office, but there was no answer. Then he drove to the trailer in Northport, but Tawny hadn't seen her, and Jackie wouldn't respond to his questions. He drove past Tuscaloosa High, and there was no sign of her.

Finally, he received a text.

Thanks for everything, Professor. Please tell my momma I'm sorry.

Tom replied—*Where are you?*—but his text wasn't answered.

Where the hell can she be? he asked himself over and over. He thought of everything she had told him over the past six months. How she had memorized the trial transcript. How the accident had ruined her life.

When it came to him, Tom knew he was probably already too late. He called Rick, knowing his partner was his only hope, and then he prayed.

87

Tom ignored the speed limit as he hurtled south down Highway 82. When they reached the Henshaw city limits sign, it was dusk, and Tom blinked against the coming darkness. When the light at Limestone Bottom Road came into view, he saw her. She was standing in the grass. *"There!"*

A split second later, he saw the eighteen-wheeler. It was coming in the opposite direction and hauling ass by the look of it. When the rig got within a hundred yards of the light, Laurie Ann Newton stepped into the middle of the highway.

We're too late, Tom knew, not sure whether he should speed up or slow down.

"Oh my God!" Rick screamed from the passenger seat as he saw what was about to happen.

The driver of the rig laid down his horn, but Laurie Ann stood stock still. To his right, Tom saw a figure moving across the gas station toward Laurie Ann. Just as the truck was about to plow into Wilma Newton's daughter, the figure tackled Laurie Ann to the side of the road.

88

When Keewin Brown made the save, he was able to twist his body so that he didn't land on Laurie Ann but rather his left shoulder. Though the big man had probably broken his arm, he seemed ecstatic that Laurie Ann was alive. While Rose Batson tended to him inside the Texaco and waited for the paramedics, Tom, Rick, and Laurie Ann sat on the bench outside the gas station.

"You figured it out, didn't you?" she finally asked.

Tom nodded.

"How?"

"The shoes," Tom said. "Wade did an inventory of your mother's whole apartment, and there were no white Nikes with a red swoosh. I remembered the night I drove you home when you came to the office after practice. You were wearing those shoes. The rest wasn't all that hard to decipher. You come over to your mother's house the night of May 8 and find her drunk as a skunk. She tells you that Jack Willistone propositioned her for sex, and she refused. Then she passes out. How am I doing?"

"Pretty good."

"Tell me the rest."

"I lost my grip when I saw how drunk and weak Mom was. I took the last belt off the vodka bottle and then I noticed the gun. It was lying on top of her dresser. Like maybe she had retrieved it and thought about killing him but then chickened out and was too drunk to put the gun back in its hiding place." She let out a soft sob. "I dug around the apartment for a pair of gloves, and when I found them, I took her phone and sent Jack the texts. Then I slipped on Mom's windbreaker and cap and drove her car over to Zorn's subdivision."

"Had you ever driven a car before?" Tom asked.

Laurie Ann snorted. "Are you kidding? I drive Tawny's piece of crap to the grocery store all the time, and I don't look like I'm fourteen." She licked her lips. "Anyway, when I got to the lake house, I saw the son of a bitch just standing there on the dock. I approached with caution, holding the gun behind my back. When I got within ten feet, he realized it wasn't Mom and asked me who I was. I told him and . . . he started laughing. Said he'd hoped for my momma since she was a *professional* but that popping the cherry on a virgin one more time was a gift from above." Laurie Ann stopped, and her expression turned cold. "When I pulled the gun from around my back, the grin didn't even leave his face. I don't think he ever thought I'd do it."

"But you did?"

Laurie Ann gave a swift nod. "I shot him in the chest twice. Boom. Boom. Then when he had dropped to his knees, I walked over to him and I put the gun to his head. I didn't want to shoot him again, but he lunged for me, and it was just a reaction. Blood splattered everywhere, and I dropped the pistol." She hung her head. "Then I just panicked. I looked under the dock for the gun, but it was too dark and I knew I needed to get out of there. I drove back to Mom's apartment. On the way, I stopped at a gas station and threw the gloves in a dumpster. When I got to her place, she was still passed out. I washed all my clothes and spent the rest of the night looking out her blinds and thinking it through. Since I wore gloves and left the gun under the dock, I knew the cops would eventually come." She continued to cry as she gazed out at Highway 82. "When Mom woke up, she didn't seem to remember much of anything. *I was mad at her.* I've been mad at her ever since DHR took us away. I should have said something sooner, but once she was arrested I didn't know what to do." Laurie Ann turned toward Tom. "I had read that trial transcript so many times, I knew that you'd be the one to help us. You'd be able to figure it all out. I'm sorry."

For a long minute, Tom processed everything that Laurie Ann had said. "What happens now?" she asked, her voice desperate and scared.

Tom sighed and looked up into the cloudless sky. "Well, that depends a lot on two people."

"Who?"

"Your mom . . . and the district attorney."

89

Once Wilma was seated in front of him in the consultation room, Tom got right to it. "How long have you known that your daughter killed Jack Willistone?"

Wilma sucked in a ragged breath and let it out. "Since the preliminary hearing. When the detective held up the evidence bag with my gun inside . . . I knew."

"And that's why you wouldn't talk. You were afraid that if you did I might figure it out. Or worse, that the Sheriff's Office would learn the truth."

"That's right," Wilma said.

"I could have helped you, Wilma. Powell Conrad is my friend. So is Detective Richey. These were extenuating circumstances. Laurie Ann might have been charged as a youthful offender."

"No. I would never have allowed my baby to be charged for something I should have done years ago. This is my fault and I'm going to pay for it. I've already pled guilty, and I forbid you to do anything that suggests that my daughter was the true killer. Do you understand, Professor?"

"You're willing to die or, best case, go to prison for a crime you didn't commit?"

Despite the tears that now streamed down her cheeks, Wilma Newton managed a weary smile. "Haven't you learned anything about me in the last two years, Professor McMurtrie? I'd die a thousand deaths for Laurie Ann or Jackie." She stopped and took both of his hands in her own. *"Nothing for me. Everything for them."*

90

They decided to meet at Jackie's Lounge. Tom found Powell sitting at a corner booth sipping whiskey from a glass with a half-empty fifth of Jack Daniel's Black, the top conveniently off, in the middle of the table. Tom grabbed the bottle, not bothering with the glass, and took a long pull, hoping the whiskey would ease the throbbing in his back. The opening bars of Willie Nelson's "Whiskey River" blared over the jukebox.

Before he could say a word, Powell spoke, his voice just above a whisper. "Look, before you say anything, I need to tell you something."

"OK."

"After the judge entered the plea, Wade and I interrogated Barbara Willistone."

"And?"

"And she talked. Said she went to Zorn's lake house that night about one o'clock in the morning intending to kill Jack. She didn't want to take any chances on him changing his mind on the beneficiary form that she thought he had sent in." He smacked his lips. "She parked at the Cypress Inn and walked through the woods to

Zorn's house, but when she got there, she saw Jack lying faceup on the dock with a dark-complected woman hovering over him. The woman was carrying a briefcase in her hand that looked exactly like Jack's. Barbara had seen Jack put the copy of the change of beneficiary form in his briefcase a few hours earlier. She saw the woman dig around in Jack's pants and, after taking something out—presumably his wallet, though Barbara couldn't be sure—the woman kicked his body into the river. When Jack didn't surface, Barbara knew he was dead."

"Good grief," Tom said. "Then what?"

"The woman walked toward the boathouse and a few seconds later emerged behind the wheel of a bass boat. Barbara didn't know what to do, so she ran back to the restaurant, and that's when she bumped into Shuman and Caldwell and sold them the pot."

Tom could barely believe his ears. *The river,* he thought. The truth, like he had suspected from the beginning, had always been on the river. "Whose boat?"

"Zorn's," Powell said. "When we interviewed the prick, we never asked him about how many vessels he owned. The boathouse had a pontoon party boat in it and a couple of Jet Skis, so nothing seemed out of place. We didn't know he had another one."

"There was no way you could have known that."

Powell grunted but didn't say anything.

"Did Barbara say which direction the boat was going?"

"North," Powell said. "Toward Jasper."

"Bully Calhoun."

Powell nodded. "Has to be. We know all about the Filipino hit woman who's supposed to be in Bully's employ, and Barbara's description of the woman matches the ones that Bo and Rel Jennings gave Wade."

"Have y'all had any luck tracking down the boat?"

Powell took another sip of whiskey. "We've sent out feelers, but you and I both know that we'll never see that ship again. My guess is that around May 9, 2012 it was the primary source of a nice-sized bonfire on the edge of the Sipsey Wilderness."

Tom knew the prosecutor's suspicions were probably correct. "So what are you going to do?"

Powell poured another shot of Jack Daniel's into his glass. "Right now I'm gonna get drunk and listen to this song until Weezy over there throws me out. But first thing in the morning, I'm gonna file a motion to throw out the guilty plea and dismiss all charges against Wilma Newton."

Tom felt his heart flutter. "All charges? Even murder?"

"The whole shebang," Powell said. "We have newly discovered evidence that Jack was robbed by someone who doesn't match Wilma's description, and it's a pretty easy leap to believe that this same person killed Jack before she kicked his corpse in the river."

"What about the eyewitness, Ms. Farrell?"

"I'm gonna call the university tomorrow and talk with the golf coach. Hopefully, worst case she only gets suspended for half the season. It took guts to come forward like she did."

"Great," Tom said. "But that's not what I meant. What about what Farrell says she saw?"

Powell took a sip from the glass and gazed at the brown liquid. Finally, he squinted over the rim at Tom. "Wilma Newton didn't own a pair of white Nikes, Professor."

Tom bowed his head. "You know."

"Wade and I figured it out an hour ago," Powell continued. "Freakin' tennis shoes. I can't believe it."

"Do you think Judge Poe will grant your motion and dismiss the charges?"

Powell's squint became a glare. "If he doesn't, I'm going to report him to the bar. That crotchety bastard doesn't deserve to be called Your Honor."

"What about Barbara?"

"We're going to work a deal with her. No charges for her coopera-tion in the case we're mounting against Bully Calhoun."

"You're going after him?"

Powell had fire in his eyes. "With both barrels."

"And what about Laurie Ann Newton?"

"Absent her confession, I doubt I could convince a jury to convict. Her mother was misidentified by Farrell as Jack's killer, and Barbara Willistone is an eyewitness to someone else robbing Jack just after his murder. It's too messy, and even if it wasn't, the would-be defendant is fourteen years old and been through hell in her young life." Powell met Tom's eye. "I'd like to meet her, and I want your word that she'll go to counseling. But I think it's high time the Newton family caught a break. What do you think?"

"I think you're gonna make one hell of a judge one day." He rose from his seat and Powell did the same.

They shook hands, and Powell held on when Tom tried to let go. He gazed at Tom with bloodshot eyes that had gone misty, and when he spoke his voice finally cracked from the combination of alcohol, fatigue, and emotion. "It was an honor to face you in your last trial."

"Thank you, son."

As Tom turned to go, the prosecutor's booming voice stopped him at the door. "Professor McMurtrie."

"Yeah?"

"What are you going to do now?"

Tom smiled. "I'm going to the farm."

EPILOGUE

Jasper, Alabama, December 24, 2012

It was the big team's annual tradition to have a morning match on Christmas Eve. Though the turnout was typically thin, twelve players, including Marcellus "Bully" Calhoun, teed off the first hole of the Jasper Country Club between 8:00 and 8:20 that morning. After Bully's group had completed play on the third hole, he glanced at the shade tree behind the fourth tee, feeling his stomach tighten, as it did every time he passed the familiar meeting spot. She wasn't there, and he knew he'd never see her again. Once Manny had removed the threat of Greg Zorn and Alvie Jennings, Bully had paid her off from Jack's insurance proceeds and wished her well in her future endeavors. He would need to hire another enforcer, but for now, with the district attorney of Tuscaloosa County and the FBI breathing down his neck, he'd lay low.

After Harwell and Corlew had hit their tee shots, Bully took a sip of Budweiser and put a Titleist golf ball on top of his tee. He waggled his driver once, looked down the fairway, and began his swing.

He never finished it. At the top of his backswing, his chest exploded from the force of a rifle shot. He staggered backward, and before he began to fall, a second blast caught him between the eyes.

He was dead before he hit the ground.

Santonio "Rel" Jennings clicked the safety back on the rifle and calmly lowered the bedroom window. Then he walked out the front door of the redbrick house that sat behind the fourth-tee box of the Jasper Country Club. Seconds later, he climbed back into his mail carrier vehicle and stashed the rifle under a stack of packages in the back. With his heart pounding, Rel made the remaining stops on his route, which included the single-wide trailer of a young deputy in the Walker County Sheriff's Office. After he had put the officer's mail in the latch attached to the outside of the mobile home, he jimmied the door with a coat hanger. Less than a minute later, he returned the rifle to its case and put it back under the bed, where he'd found it.

At 5:00 p.m., Rel punched the clock. He had taken the job with the postal service two weeks after his brother's murder. As a private investigator for twenty years, he had gleaned a lot of information from people who carried the mail. He knew the job would produce an opportunity, and today he seized it. He'd work another month for good measure so no one would get suspicious. Then he'd quit.

After dinner by himself at the McDonald's he used to manage, he drove over to his brother's house, which was dark. There were no cars in the lot. LaShell had taken LaByron to Birmingham to spend Christmas with her folks.

For a long time, Rel gazed at the house where his brother had tried to live the American dream. He took a pint of Jim Beam out of the glove compartment and pressed it to his lips, squinting as the liquor burned his throat. Finally, he got out of the mail unit and took the package out of the back. He had wrapped the regulation-size NBA basketball in red paper. He placed it on the front stoop and trotted back to his vehicle.

He had one more stop to make.

Even in the dark, Rel could see the ants crawling over the headstone. He swatted them away and ran his fingers over the letters, reading the words aloud.

"Alvin Lamont Jennings."

Rel raised the pint to the grave and took a sip of bourbon. "I cut the head off the snake today, Alvie." He nodded to himself, thinking about Bully's lady enforcer that was still out there. "I'll get the tail one day too. As God is my witness, I will."

Rel laid a six-pack of Yuengling on the ground below the concrete marker and tapped the top of the grave.

"Merry Christmas, little brother."

Hazel Green, Alabama, December 25, 2012

On Christmas morning, Tom rose early and was dressed before his family arrived. He watched Jackson open his present, a new baseball bat, and he talked with Jenny about all the things that Santa Claus had brought her. And he held the baby girl, born two days before Thanksgiving, just as his daughter-in-law had predicted. They had named her Julie, and Tom had a hard time keeping his voice steady when he said her name. He noticed that his son, Tommy, took a lot more video than he had during Christmases in the past, and Nancy couldn't be around him more than a few minutes without tearing up.

No one mentioned that his head was now bald, but he saw the stares and he knew that this was part of his life now.

At two o'clock in the afternoon, Bocephus Haynes and his family—Jazz, T. J., and Lila—arrived with the turkey, and they all sat around the table and gave thanks. They ate and they drank and no one said the word "cancer," but Tom knew it was all anyone could think about.

When it was time for Tommy and Nancy to make the trek to Cullman to see Nancy's family, the hugs all seemed to last a little longer. Jackson squeezed him so tight that Tom winced, but he didn't let on that he was hurting.

"I'll come see you tomorrow, Papa," he said, climbing into Tommy's minivan.

"Sounds good, Forty-Nine," Tom said, ruffling the boy's hair.

A few minutes later, Jazz, T. J, and Lila said their goodbyes, and Bo said he would catch up with them later that night. Then he and Tom, with Lee Roy clipping at their heels, walked to the northern tip of the farm.

"So what's the latest on Wilma?" Bo asked.

"My call to the General was successful, and custody of the kids was transferred to Darla Ford, whose oyster bar is thriving down in Destin, Florida. Darla was happy to take the girls on, and she gave Wilma a job waiting tables. Helen said that if Wilma can hold down employment for a year without any incidents, she'll ask the court to award full custody to her."

"What about Laurie Ann?"

"Seeing a psychiatrist on a weekly basis, as is her sister, Jackie."

"Good deal," Bo said. Then, kicking at the grass, he asked, "Did you hear about Bully Calhoun?"

"No, what happened?"

"Shot dead on the golf course in Jasper yesterday," Bo said. "Assassinated is probably the better word."

Tom let out a low whistle. "A guy in that line of work . . . I guess it was bound to happen. But Powell and Wade are going to be disappointed. They were on him like stink on horse manure. So was the FBI."

"I know," Bo said. "I guess they'll point their cannons at Kat now."

"Barbara Willistone already has," Tom said. "She filed a lawsuit against Kat for fraud related to Jack's insurance policy two weeks after Wilma's trial."

Bo smiled. "Sounds like a lot of lawyers are going to make a lot of money."

"Bingo."

"Any word on Bully's enforcer?"

Tom looked at the grass. "None."

"What about JimBone Wheeler?"

"Still locked away in a maximum-security cell on death row in Nashville."

"Think we'll ever hear from either of them again?"

Tom felt a shiver run down his arms that had nothing to do with the temperature outside. "Let's hope not."

When they reached the McMurtrie family cemetery, Tom paid his respects to his parents, Rene and Sut, his beloved Julie, and Musso, his bulldog before Lee Roy. Tom then ran his hand over a piece of dirt adjacent to Julie's grave. "I want to be buried here," he said, taking a deep breath and slowly exhaling. "I've really missed her these past few years, and when I'm gone, I want to be right beside her."

Bocephus Aurulius Haynes wiped tears from his eyes and spoke softly. "Yes, sir. But I'm betting my money with Dr. Davis. I think you'll be around for a while. You'll beat this just like you did with the bladder."

"Bo, this isn't like what I had before. I can't win this time."

Bo walked a few steps to his right and put his palm on Musso's grave. When he spoke, his voice shook with emotion. "You know, Coach Bryant said a lot of things about winning, but one of my favorite things he said was about losing. The way I remember it"—Bo's lip quivered—"is that he said it was awfully important to win with humility, but that losing was also important. He hated to lose worse than anyone, but if you never lost, you wouldn't know how to act when you won." Bo wiped his eyes and looked at Tom.

"Be humble when you win and humble when you lose," Tom whispered. "Live with dignity . . . die with dignity."

Bo nodded. "That's damn right." He looked at Tom, and the anguish was palpable in his eyes. "Professor, I know that you know this, but I, uh . . . I'm not sure that I've ever actually said the words." He paused. "I love you, sir. You're my guy, you see. When I've needed a friend . . . or a mentor . . . or a father figure in this crazy world . . . you've been my guy."

"I love you too, Bo."

They embraced, and Tom felt snowflakes beginning to fall on his neck. Looking over the headstones and across the farm to the brick home he'd built with his father six decades ago, Thomas Jackson McMurtrie breathed in the cold winter air and wondered if he'd be alive in a year.

"Merry Christmas, Bo."

AUTHOR'S NOTE

In April 2016, a few weeks after the publication of *Between Black and White*, my father, Randy Bailey, was diagnosed with lung cancer. Eight months later, on December 7, 2016, my wife, Dixie, was also diagnosed with lung cancer at forty-two years old. Dad smoked early in his life but had not touched a cigarette in four decades. Dixie had never been a smoker.

From December 2016 to March 2017, Dixie and Dad underwent treatment for lung cancer at the same time. Some days they literally received chemotherapy in adjoining chairs in the treatment wing of the Clearview Cancer Institute. I have the pictures to prove it, though I doubt they'll ever go in a photo album.

Dad fought hard, but the cancer had already spread to the bone. Curative surgery was never an option. Like Tom McMurtrie at the end of this book, Dad said right after his diagnosis that you live with dignity and you die with dignity. He never quit, but his body eventually gave out. His prognosis was six months, but he almost doubled that. He died on March 3, 2017 at the age of seventy.

Dixie's tumor had spread to the lymph nodes, but surgery was still an option. She went through a month of chemotherapy and almost forty radiation treatments. On April 3, 2017, a month after my father's death, my wife had surgery to remove the lower lobe of her right lung. During the procedure, there was a complication and the middle lobe also had to be removed. After almost two weeks in the hospital, her oncologist declared the surgery a success.

She is now cancer-free, and we celebrated her remission with a trip to Disney World. As we passed through the entrance to the happiest place on earth, Dixie and I held hands and cried as our children squealed with delight. *Time, precious time . . .*

I've heard it said that stories are oftentimes as much found as they are created. I believe this to be true. I found the building blocks for *The Last Trial* while rocking back and forth in an uncomfortable recliner in a cramped hospital room and watching my beautiful wife breathe with the assistance of a chest tube.

Cancer sucks. And sadness, as Tom McMurtrie points out early on in this story, is a part of life. But at the end of the day, hope always wins.

During one of our last conversations, when I was telling him how much I loved him and how scared I was about Dixie and that I didn't know what I was going to do, Dad motioned with his hand for me to lean close. When I did, I heard him whisper his parting advice. "Write books."

I hope you enjoyed this story. And rest assured, the Professor will be back. Just like my father, Thomas Jackson McMurtrie will beat the national average and he will return.

Stay tuned . . .

Robert Bailey
October 12, 2017

ACKNOWLEDGMENTS

My wife, Dixie, was diagnosed with lung cancer on December 7, 2016. She fought her way through chemo, radiation, and surgery and is now in remission. None of my stories would have ever found a bookstore if Dixie hadn't encouraged me to follow my dream. Thank you for fighting so hard and being my everything.

Our children—Jimmy, Bobby, and Allie—were troupers this year as their world was shaken to the core. Their resilience kept me going, and I'm so proud to be their dad.

My mother, Beth Bailey, is the strongest person I know. Her poise and grace under pressure were on full display this year as Dad and Dixie both fought lung cancer. When I think of the term "steel magnolia," I don't envision the play or the movie. I think of my mom.

My agent, Liza Fleissig, has been my wingman on this writing journey. Her belief in my stories and persistence in finding them a publisher is what every writer hopes for in an agent. She is also my friend, and I will be forever grateful for Liza's steady support during Dad and Dixie's illnesses.

Thank you to Clarence Haynes, my developmental editor, for his energy, creativity, and passion for my stories, as well as his meticulous attention to detail. Excelsior, Clarence!

Thanks also to Megha Parekh, my editor with Thomas & Mercer, who believed in this project from day one and was a constant and steady source of positive vibes.

To Kjersti Egerdahl, Sarah Shaw, and my entire editing and marketing team at Thomas & Mercer, whom I am so proud to work with and call my publisher, thank you for having my back this year and buying into my characters.

My longtime friend and law school classmate, Judge Will Powell, was a great source of information regarding criminal procedure in Alabama and was also one of my earliest readers. So many of the adventures of the characters in my books have been inspired by the good times I've had with "Powell" over the years.

My friend, Bill Fowler, has been an important sounding board for ideas and was a life raft for me during the dark times when Dad and Dixie were both going through treatment. When I was trying so hard to look after my family, Bill looked after me.

A big shout-out to my friends Rick Onkey, Mark Wittschen, Steve Shames, Dave Christopherson, Scott Tonidandel, Missy Warren, Will Elliott, and James Drake for supporting my writing and for being there for me this year when my world was on fire.

My brother, Bo Bailey, has been a rock this year as we have both dealt with our father's passing. He has also been one of my earliest readers and supporters on this writing voyage.

My father-in-law, Dr. Jim Davis, has been my go-to proofreader when it comes to firearms, and his positive outlook and infectious energy have been a blessing. This past year, he had to watch his baby girl go through cancer treatments and surgery. When the storm was raging around us, Doc was a steady hand and a calm voice.

My mother-in-law, Beverly Baca, is a warrior, and her resilience during Dixie's treatment was a source of strength and inspiration to us all.

My wonderful friends, Joe and Foncie Bullard, from Point Clear, Alabama, were two of my earliest supporters on this writing journey. I'm so grateful for their help and encouragement.

A special thanks to everyone at my law firm, Lanier Ford Shaver & Payne PC. I am eternally grateful for my colleagues' support.

My father, Randy Bailey, passed away on March 3, 2017 after a courageous battle with lung cancer. He was my hero and the best storyteller I've ever been around. I love and miss you, Dad.

ABOUT THE AUTHOR

Robert Bailey is the bestselling author of the McMurtrie & Drake legal thriller series. *The Last Trial* is the third novel in the series. The first two novels, *The Professor* and *Between Black and White*, both won the Beverly Hills Book Award for legal thriller of the year. *Between Black and White* was also a finalist for the Foreword INDIES Book of the Year. For the past eighteen years, Bailey has been a civil defense trial lawyer in his hometown of Huntsville, Alabama, where he lives with his wife and three children. For more information, please visit www.robertbaileybooks.com.